By Force of Felicity

Suzanne Campbell

Published by
Bungalowbiblia

This is a work of fiction. All of the characters, names, incidents, organizations, and dialogue in this novel are either the products of the author's imagination or are used fictitiously.

Bungalowbiblia
Woodstock, Illinois
www.bungalowbiblia. wordpress.com

ISBN: 978-0-5781-7081-7 (sc)
ISBN: 978-0-5781-7082-4 (e)

Because of the dynamic nature of the Internet, any web addresses or links contained in this book may have changed since publication and may no longer be valid. The views expressed in this work are solely those of the author and do not necessarily reflect the views of the publisher, and the publisher hereby disclaims any responsibility for them.

All quotes from *A Course in Miracles* © are from the First Edition, published in 1985, by the Foundation for Inner Peace, publisher and copyright holder, P.O. Box 598, Mill Valley, CA 94942-0598, www.acim.org and info@acim.org.

Cover image: Walter Crane, May Tree Frieze (1896)
© Victoria and Albert Museum, London

Weathervane drawing: James Campbell (2015)

Rev. date: 3/2/2016

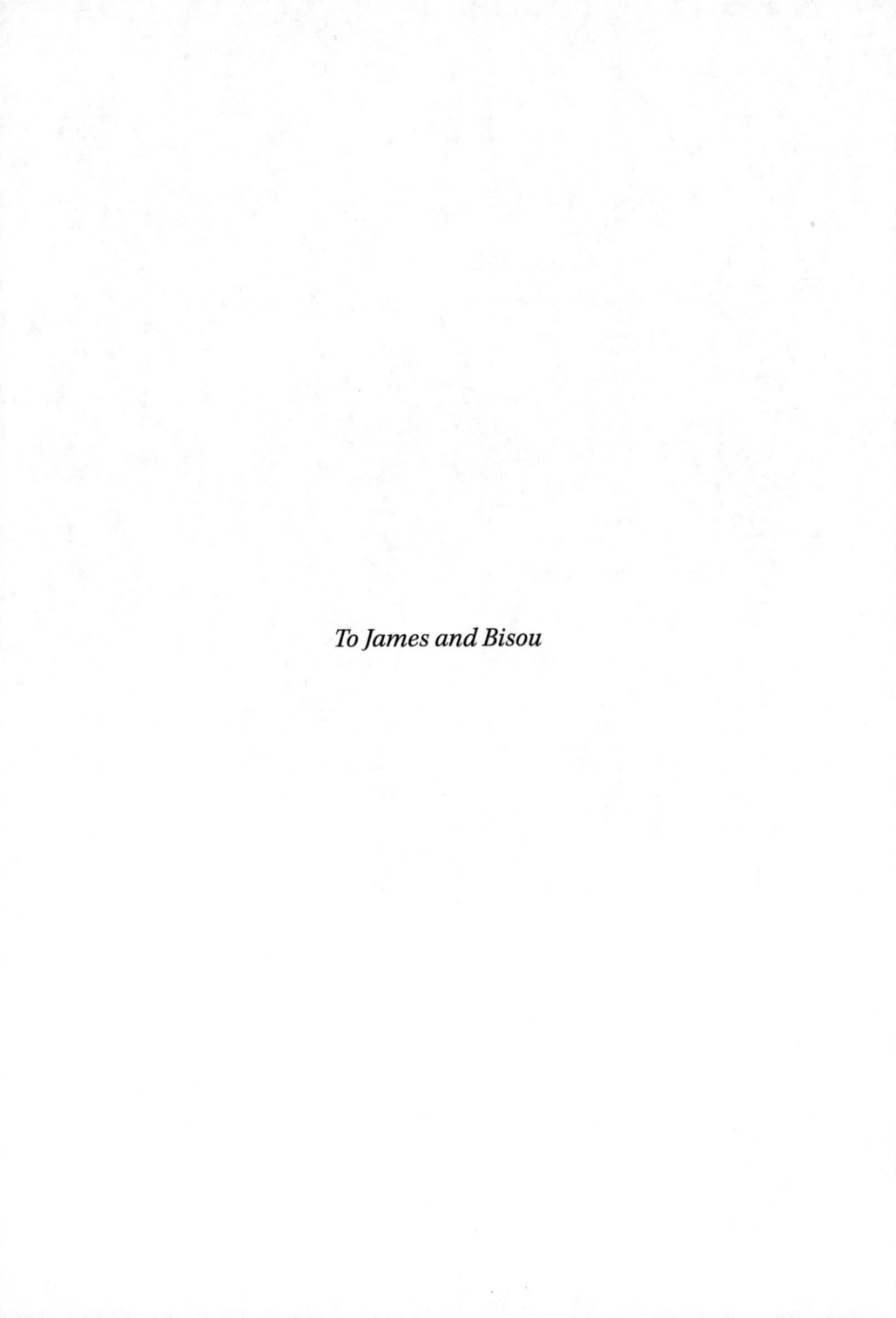

To James and Bisou

1

Mundane and Omnivorous

Althea Athnos plunged down her back steps in the dark with a mug of unsalted peanuts in one hand, a can of birdseed in the other. Nothing spilled, though her battered Wellies were about as helpful as a pair of runaway buses. One of these mornings she might fall and break every thinning bone in her body. She'd be confined to a wheelchair, baby food spooned into her sagging mouth.

A few dawdling stars welcomed her. Real stars, not planes circling O'Hare. Rooftops had crowded out the moon. Casper's wind chimes quavered in a breeze that swept hair into her mouth, where it glued into place against her lip balm.

By the unwelcome light above the Schmitts' garage she began tucking peanuts into the interstices of the backyard fence, inhaling the nutty aroma, rattling a big one. Some mornings she'd look up to see a first squirrel tilting down a neighboring roof, its beady eye fastened on her offerings.

Nobody spoiled her solitude this early; Al let her pajamas blouse over the top of her boots with swashbuckling *panache*. She poured seed onto fence posts for the cardinals, who disliked being jostled by bumptious sparrows on the ground.

Beneath the cherry tree a circle of begonias marking a cat's grave still held its own against the autumn.

"Good morning, cupcake!" she cooed, bending toward the flowers.

"MORNIN'!" barked Hal Schmitt, and opened his truck door.

Scalded, she felt herself shrivel into a potty, sexless old wreck who talked to herself. Fumbling for a viable stance, Al tried to look like she had a sense of humor.

"Morning," she said levelly. "Beautiful stars." She added a smile, wide enough to indicate wry self-acceptance but not imbecility.

"Yup." He backed down the driveway along her fence.

There'd been just sufficient pause between her acknowledgment of her poor cat Tutu's remains and her neighbor's ambush to leave merciful doubt as to whether he'd even heard her murmurs...much less mistaken them for coy amorous abandon. His skittish neighbor overwhelmed by long-suppressed ardor...

He was gone, thank heaven. Otherwise pride would have forced her to continue scattering seeds nonchalantly as he gunned the motor a few yards away. Ludicrous pajamas. PeptoBismol pink flannel, with cartoonish kitty cats. A gift; she was innocent. What was Mr. Schmitt doing up so early? She suspected him of hunting – aimlessly rather than ardently, just enough to keep up his end of masculine grunts over beer and football. She'd heard him honk his goose call for the admiring family. The dear geese, mated for life.

How long had Mrs. Bishop's bathroom light been on? Probably all the neighbors had gotten a snicker or two out of harmless dotty Mrs. Athnos in her jammies, furtively coddling the wildlife. She pumped the tin of seeds in a strident, choppy zigzag around the arbor vitae.

She was being grandiose now, as well as a poor loser, Al reflected. She hadn't earned surveillance through binoculars yet. And she'd gotten no more than she'd risked this morning. She'd just have to wriggle. Casper would be mildly amused.

Wanting something bigger, something more, she scanned the sky above the puffing chimneys and crosshatched trees hemming her in. The biggest of the remaining stars hovered in the southeast, steadfast, unassailable. She felt tears coming. Leaves fell from the ash tree so thick and fast they sounded like raindrops. She clumped back to the house.

A sign on the screen door glimmered ATTENTION: CHAT LUNATIQUE! Al struggled out of her boots in a mudroom crowded with flowerpots and carefully winnowed recycling. In the kitchen Linnet arched and purred around her stocking feet. Al inched into the dining room with the little tortoiseshell twirling about her ankles. Casper was always pointing out how much easier it would be to pick the cat up, but Linnet didn't care for heights. Besides, their waltzing was an elaborate valentine, essential to the relationship.

A coral flush stained Euclid Street's horizon. Casper might be awake for a cuddle.

"Let's go see Daddy."

Linnet labored up the stairs alongside her, hoisting and hopping, then made a detour for an urgent session with the bathroom rug. Al followed, knowing her presence provided the icing on her cat's obsessive cake. Linnet ran to her shaggy, matted bam-bam, threw herself on it and began to "nurse" feverishly at a favored spot. Al perched on the toilet to keep her company as delicate, diffident Linnet purred lustily while kneading her paws in aqua acrylic. She looked up every few seconds to make sure Al was in place. This was how Linnet succeeded in transcending her truncated babyhood. (In a rare moment of impulsivity, Casper had rescued the tiny orphan from a pet store window.) Tears threatened again; they came and went inexplicably these days. Linnet gummed away rowdily at her feet.

The dirty old rug – she dared not launder its ripeness – was an inviolable eyesore in the Athnos's carefully decorated bathroom. Al had stenciled dragonflies and a sinuous Art Nouveau tangle of reeds and waterlilies on the side of the clawfoot tub, kept cakes of almond and lavender soap dusted in the abalone shell on the fern stand, had decoupaged plump cottage roses on the milk-painted armoire. The towel that hung from the mahogany shaving mirror's rung was of fine old damask, fringed. Casper delighted in rumpling it.

Careful not to interrupt Linnet, Al twisted toward a shelf to change the page-a-day Audubon calendar. She moved yesterday's titmouse to the back of the stack. Today apparently belonged to the prosaic roadside hawk. Not a northern bird, it was "mundane in the tropics," rarely given to soaring, and omnivorous.

Not liking to abandon Linnet, she tidied around the litter box behind the door, picking up each tiny piece of errant clay separately between thumb and forefinger and tossing it back into the box.

She sneaked out of the bathroom. Casper was still but not snoring. Al tweaked the window blind next to him to peer down into the backyard.

He cleared his throat.

"Good morning."

She strode around to her side of the bed, tossed her pillow onto his chest and curled up, her arm over his heart.

"How's Althea today?" He sounded interested, stroking her hair.

"Alright. But just barely. Hal Schmitt had a treat watching me talk to Tutu in my p.j.'s. I think he was on his way to some heroic massacre. Geese, probably. Or some innocent doe. I was his first sighting of the morning."

"Well, I'm glad you got away." He patted her head.

"Can I have a hug?"

"A biggish one?" He put both arms around her and they lay there without words, comfortable. An onslaught of rasping and puncturing meant Linnet was scaling the bedclothes. She nestled into the crook of Al's knees.

"She needs a manicure."

"She'd be completely traumatized. It's a very tall bed. Maybe I could find a cute stepladder..."

"She needs her claws clipped, Althea."

She rumpled the blanket on his chest, back and forth, like a brisk erasure.

"What are we doing today? I'm going to make bread. *Pain de Provence* with olives and lavender."

"I'll have to trust your judgement on that one."

"You'll like it! Have I ever made bread you didn't like?" Her theatrical pout camouflaged the more vital question of whether bread making – whether *she* – held any real significance.

"Nope."

"So what are you doing today? I'll need you to help me stir."

"Class prep for tomorrow. Errands...banking...anything you need at the store?"

"We're almost out of Advil. That reminds me – could you do my neck?"

He rubbed his eyes.

"Sure. Get into position."

"Thanks. Let's try not to disturb Linnet."

Linnet plummeted to the floor and streaked out of the room the moment Casper started to move. Al sighed and clambered backwards to the edge of the bed.

"Which side?"

"Right."

"Yup, here it is. Big knot in the usual place."

"Ouch."

He massaged the tendon until his thumb gave out, pulled her thin shoulders back until bones popped.

"OK?"

"Thank you. I think we got it in time."

In the kitchen Al slouched on her high stool, legs tightly crossed at the knee and again at the ankles, warbling away (as she liked to imagine it) to Casper while he prepared his poached eggs and coffee.

After twenty years it still entertained her to watch him tie the white chef's apron around his thickening middle, crack the eggs precisely and flick the shells into her little earthenware bowl by the side of the stove. His hairline had receded four inches yet she still found his olive skin intriguing, the baggy, long-waisted trousers amusing, the uncharacteristically precious reading glasses a bit startling.

"I can hardly wait to finish the tapestry's sky; that'll really be progress. Could you please open that jar of olives for me when you're through? They're French, from the boutique-y place up University Avenue..."

In the early light she could see cobwebs spangling the upper corners of the sole kitchen window. It was the time of year wildlife sought shelter indoors. She tried to be fair when dusting and vacuuming, occasionally demolishing a spider's causeway or hammock when in a temper but mostly practicing benign neglect. Concern for one's domain was, after all, a universal vulnerability.

The kitchen was small, dark and exotic, an un-kitchen. A former friend had said it looked like a Tibetan bordello, which pleased Al though she hoped there was no such thing. She'd had Casper paint the walls and ceiling a dark, gleaming turquoise that closed the room in on itself and looked gratifyingly barbarous alongside the Chinese red tile floor and trim. Al stored her paring knives in a rusting Russian Caravan tea canister, lined the window ledge with pomegranates, piled kumquats in ginger jars. The dimness permitted neglect approaching squalor; flecks of spaghetti sauce, paw prints, dusty congealed grease receded obligingly until she could face them.

When Casper padded into the dining room she accepted the silence, consciously relinquishing him to the realms of Higher Thought. A conscientious teacher, he tended to ruminate over scholarly details at meals.

Al measured flour and yeast, chopped onions, drained olives while reenacting the brief but unsettling encounter with Hal Schmitt.

Memories of previous minor yet vivid embarrassments involving neighbors, public slights both imaginary and genuine, potential gossip and improbable vignettes radiated vigorously from the fresh injury. She envisioned the Schmitt kids depositing some dismembered fowl's gory feet on her front steps. (That was nonsense; they maintained mildly contemptuous but profound indifference toward the Athnoses.) Would the McDuffs and Remingtons ignore her house yet again when they ferried their trick-or-treating broods up the street? (A Jack o'lantern always flickered invitingly in the front window!) Visions of rejection and alienation multiplied, extended greedy feelers into the remote past (her mother never liked her), supplanting her portion of equanimity, strangling vitality. Casper's coffeemaker leered at her; she summoned her commitment not to caffeinate herself.

As she leveled a spoonful of salt over the sink she imagined powers-that-be plotting to take their house away from them and turn it into a dentist's office. She'd heard news stories on the radio about cities forcing little guys – especially aging little guys – out of their homes for a pittance for the "greater good"…What the university wanted, it took. Their house was modest but well-situated –

"Ready for me to stir?" Casper plunked his dishes in the sink.

"Yes, please." She felt contrite, ashamed of the clamor in her head. Why did she bruise so easily? She needed a walk.

"What are these grainy bits?"

"Lavender, remember?"

"Ah." He refrained from wondering aloud if Provençals really sprinkled lavender buds into their bread. His wife loved anyone's local color. While he subdued the doubtful ingredients into a sticky mound, she disinterred her rolling pin from amongst madeleine tins, sprouted potatoes and blackening onions in a low cupboard, then wiped down the dining room table and covered it with oilcloth.

A hoard of unopened mail fell off her chair. She had to meet the eyes of stranded polar bear cubs, starved horses and a raccoon with its paw in a trap on the envelopes as she reassembled the pyramid. *Someone* had to look. She could hardly send money anymore, much less a useful amount. A young man had phoned recently, soliciting help for kidnapped baby chimps. He told her their computers wouldn't even register a mere fifteen dollars. She couldn't bear to throw the haunting faces into the trash, as though unmoved by the multiple plights. She read just enough of them to keep abreast of the current outrages. Eventually they'd go down to the clammy basement to molder after she rescued the too-cute or bizarrely patriotic notecards for scrap paper, recycled the key chains, added the address labels to her teeming collection. Or she might throw out almost everything in a useful fit of despair. If this was neurosis, surely turning one's back wasn't health? Heartfelt witness seemed all she could give in most cases. Al wandered back into the kitchen, stubbing her toe in the doorway.

"Here you go. I'm off. Anything besides Advil?" He removed his apron.

"Linnet's tired of Seafood Bisque. Could you get a few cans of Kitty Fiesta? Thanks for stirring."

When Casper pulled out of the driveway Al assumed her post at the front door. They waved to each other vigorously. She wandered into the living room to admire her needlework project before kneading the dough.

An impressionistic seascape in shades of blue-grey and cream, mauve and wine, only half finished, it occupied a place of honor in its easel beside the wing chair. Al gloated over her fat carpetbag spewing silky coils of thread beneath the easel. The image of herself as productive, even artistic, was nearly as sustaining as the whimsical elegance of the design, the cleverness of the colors. Casper had obtained the pattern for her from a Portuguese museum on the Internet. They'd have the tapestry framed with a scrolled light above it, perfectly foiled by the rosy beige living room walls. The sweet fellow who currently read their water meter would compliment her.

After wrestling with the dough Al sat down at the floury table with a carton of yogurt. The phone rang. Sighing, she ran to the bottom of the stairs to listen to the answering machine above. Expecting a recording, Al clutched the banister as an obscurely familiar, self-assured voice sliced through the air: "Althea? Mary Lou Kishko here. Saint Vlad's is throwing a party to celebrate Father Clement's thirtieth year with us on Sunday, November blah, blah, blah..." Al resisted the impulse to put her hands over her ears. "We've missed seeing you and Casper! Hope you can make it." A phone number was repeated firmly, followed by a bright "Thanks so much!"

At least she had not been instructed to have a great day, Al reflected. They hadn't been to church since Easter. Her skin crawled at the thought of a church banquet – the racket of ricocheting voices and chairs dragged across linoleum, the self-important bustle of the anointed, the unapologetic silence of those not seated with their particular coterie. The stench of cooking meat...Her eyes glazed. The absorbed exclusivity of families, the jolly drinkers (finally in their element), the fur coats and Astrakhans. Hearty references to "our church family." Canned peas. Speeches. Al staggered back through the living room from the dark stairwell, nearly careening into the easel as her eyes readjusted to light.

What had she been doing? Her hands were terribly chilled. She saw the carton on the table, resumed spooning yogurt into her mouth as she stared, unseeing, into the backyard. Her heart raced for a moment, one of those secret tremolos she was telegraphed from time to time.

Mary Lou's smug, chirpy intrusion reverberated. She felt violated. One had hoped for an inspired day of humble beauty, glimpsing all of life in a grain of sand...Instead, one got Hal Schmitt and Mary Lou.

Realizing she was clutching the edge of her very own chair in her very own little house, she focused on a trio of mourning doves sifting through dead leaves for seed. The adrenalin that had knifed through her receded. (How *foolish*!)

On her way back into the kitchen Al noticed the Schmitts had replaced their absurd red lace dining room curtains with something opaque, snugly shut. A snub. The Athnoses dined in a fishbowl; they couldn't afford to replace the lacy blinds, so brittle and tattered she'd rolled them up so only the hems showed.

When she turned on the kitchen faucet her thumb came away smarting. She watched it turn pale grey. Savage resentment flooded her. Mary Lou's petty urgency required a response. The needs of the gregarious had to be acknowledged.

Nearly noon! Surely Casper's errands were done by now.

It occurred to Al that she'd been making bread. She yanked open the oven door, envisioning Casper slumped bloodily behind a shattered windshield, and bruised her thumb more thoroughly. A dome of dough rose eerily beneath its damp dish towel, like a tethered dirigible. She bore it to the table solemnly, a bulwark against the morning's defects.

Casper's key fumbled in the front door. He dawdled, transferring sacks of birdseed and cat litter from the porch to the interior.

"Hello-o!"

"Shut the door, will you?" She gesticulated wildly, as if the dough were a baby, or an escaped panda.

He smiled mildly, tramped through to the mudroom with the seed.

"It can't be in a draft, that's all." She shut the door on him.

When he emerged, enveloped in cold air, he pulled a bottle of Advil from his jacket pocket and put it on the counter.

"How's it coming?" He glanced at the dough.

"You're just in time for my favorite part." She floured her fist, surveyed the warm, fragrant mound and punched her hand through it to the bottom of the bowl. It gasped, puckered, deflated.

"Right in the kanibbling pin, as my dad used to say."

"It likes it. It's a game. 'In my end is my beginning'...That was Sarah Bernhardt's motto, by the way."

"Among others." He kissed her elegant cheekbone, laid his hand on the back of her neck.

"A-A-AGH! Your hand's freezing!" She giggled, disarmed, fingers smeared with oil and flour. "And what breath you've got! Onions. What've you been up to, you who never eats lunch?"

He grinned. "They were giving out samples at the A&P. Bruschetta. Chutney."

"Brilliant. How many times have I told you that's the germiest thing you can do? And at the beginning of the cold and flu season. You may as well lick their floor while you're at it. You're going to get us both killed. People without health insurance can't afford to take risks like that! Of course *you're* finally on Medicare."

He beamed, hauled the cat litter onto his shoulder and took it upstairs. She was appalled, but secretly amused. Who knew, maybe his carelessness kept them sort of inoculated.

She could tell by the small thud overhead that Linnet had jumped off their bed to hide under it. She'd procrastinated about making the bed, loathe to disturb Linnet's nap, and forgotten it. Casper had just a very few domestic standards. Beds were to be made upon rising (barring negotiations on the cat's behalf). Unable to cook anything not canned, he washed their dishes promptly. He polished his shoes daily. Apart from these, anarchy might reign. A bachelor till the age of forty-five, he remained instinctively self-sufficient. She sometimes felt superfluous.

Before disappearing completely into the computer for his class preparation Casper read her emails to her with restrained impatience. "Sierra Sanctuary needs your help to build an urgent care wing onto its clinic. Delete?...Wild Hospice asks that you phone your senators requesting them to support the mustang protection bill; I'll write the number down...Illinoisans for the Environment want our discarded cell phone. Delete..." Al pulled on her jacket. She thwacked its pockets for the crucial jangle of house keys, ferreted through her tight jeans for a tissue, located only one glove and correctly divined the other's presence on the mudroom floor.

"Althea, what's that crunching noise?"

"Oops, birdseed. It gets into my gloves. I'll vacuum as soon as I'm back." She ran into the front hall, fluffed her hair in the mirror and coiled her muffler so it hid a wattle, the latest depredation. Breathless, she blew him a kiss from the doorway.

"I'm going to Bodie Woods. Tofu Marsala for dinner. We've had it before – you like it. With bread! It's rising again in the oven, so I have to be back soon."

Casper watched her from the dining room window. They exchanged the mandatory wave, hers a merry flurry, his a pensive salute. She looked willowy, youthful and glad to escape. She'd always been able to walk twice as fast as he. He'd asked her to marry him because she was trustworthy, had intellect and distinction, and needed a mate as much as he did. But the initial spark had been her resemblance to Toulouse Lautrec's pastel of Jane Avril on her way home in the night: the tired, refined face, the taut inwardness, the vivid, angular silhouette. Casper had never mentioned it to Althea, afraid of spoiling the fantasy. He'd noticed the image in the Sunday supplement of the Chicago Tribune when the Art Institute had hosted a major exhibit. Prescient.

Al strode the ten blocks to the woods past ever more manicured yards and increasingly tasteful garages. This part of town bristled with historic plaques: "HIRAM BUGSBY HOME. 1852." The fresh air and exercise were tonic; she began to have a sense of humor about the incident with her neighbor. Mild eccentricity was prized in an academic community. Schmitt was a bit of a hick. And no need to answer Mary Lou for a couple of days.

Empty school buses chugged past; chauffeuring mothers on their way to fetch kids crowded the intersections. Self-conscious, Al hoped she looked heedless. The problem with her nature walks was the gauntlet she had to run to get to them. She felt her facial muscles freezing into the slight, insipid smile her mother had invariably assumed in public. Three teenage boys in a pick-up blaring rock music approached; she felt the same – if milder – threat to her self-esteem she'd have felt forty years ago, the same need to stare at the sidewalk till they were past. She sighed, made an effort to focus on pleasant surroundings.

One of the most glorious maples in town decked her route, a head-turner even among the preoccupied rush. Al watched herself cross the street for the pleasure of looking up at blue piercing the outrageous scarlet, orange and garnet.

It occurred to her that, prizing solitude, she was rarely truly alone. Why did she cling to the image of herself on an interior stage, as though she needed to hold someone's hand – even her own! Why was she always obsessing about other people, most of whom played such a minor role in the scheme of her life?

She walked faster. Tears were coming. Althea Athnos, the proud hermit who couldn't cross a street without her cortege of narcissistic reflections, past rejections, imaginary dialogs. She couldn't so much as peel a potato without inviting in a clamoring horde, though she loathed committees, parties, any group effort...Her toe struck an uneven bit of sidewalk, the landscape tilted, she was down on both outspread hands and a knee. Glad to see only an underdressed, unconcerned grade school kid whizzing by on a skateboard, Al continued walking, furious with herself.

The ramshackle back entrance to the woods came into view as she turned onto a side street with houses on one side, trees and gnarled blackberry canes on the other. An occasional beer can fouled the underbrush. High above her twigs fretted and cracked in the rising wind; ominous creaks issued from a maze of slanting trunks. A squirrel fled. Al hesitated by the chain link gate.

Was she hugging all this overpopulated drama to herself out of boredom, loneliness, God knows what – or did it descend on her, devouring? She gulped, and hurried up the path. She didn't own a TV, read People magazine guiltily once a year at the dentist's, avoided coffee because it was addictive. Yet she spent most of her waking minutes spellbound by a staggeringly repetitive production narrated by a sadistic bully. Most of the material was petty, negative, even paranoid. But any kind of Muzak sufficed – even whispering the grocery list to herself like a mantra.

The park's prairie meadow rose on her left, a jewelry box of russet sumac, goldenrod, towering cup plant, elderberries' dark umbels, waning purple asters. Oaks and hickories ringed the profusion against a keen blue sky. With the first frosts this dazzle would cede to a bleaker beauty.

Al headed for a secluded bench. About to sit, she found a partially-axed buckthorn sprawled full-length behind the bench, as though someone had given it a few whacks and then stood on it. Vandalism in the name of restoration. People called buckthorns junk trees despite their satiny taupe skins and blue berries. She knew perfectly well they were invasive and the problem had to be faced. Humans found it impractical to honor the common bond with all living things, their mystery and individuality. Sickened, she stroked its slender trunk above the fresh white meat of the gash.

"I'm sorry. Go with God."

Hurrying away from the bench, Al tried to outpace the surge of diatribe, half-composed letters to newspapers and imaginary confrontations with the Green League's slash-and-burn squad before it engulfed her.

Stooping in the leaves near the intersection of two paths she was able to locate the clandestine stand of Indian pipe she'd discovered in August. The waxen stalks were brown now, haggard, fleeting talismans that Al tucked back into their blanket of leaves. She felt a little better.

She strolled down to the pond to admire the noisy poplars' re-flection. Al showed up for the flash and clamor of their autumn finale every year.

Muffled traffic could be heard, and dogs in neighboring yards. But few humans ever crossed her path in Bodie, and they tended to share her reticence. She could usually count on privacy to caress a tree, to exult in the wind and the wild – however vestigial. Bodie Woods offered mute friends – constant or ephemeral – and seasonal rites, restorative medicine, the solace of resurrection. Not to mention that increasingly rare commodity, delight.

Sighing, she scrambled down the bank to retrieve a plastic bag from the water. She'd have to hold the thing away from her like a dirty diaper all the way home to the recycling box. Throwing it in a trashcan, from which it would end in a landfill, was merely a more self-congratulatory form of littering. Why were people such idiots? No one seemed able to encounter the tang at the powdery heart of a tulip, say, or the jubilation of songbirds just before dawn, comprehend, and proceed accordingly.

Al retraced her steps to the street where she threw a last look over her shoulder at the darkening treetops.

"Thank you," she whispered into her muffler.

When she got home she made herself a mug of lemongrass tea, mostly as a hand-warmer. Every day they delayed lighting the elderly furnace was money saved. Lighting it always gave her the willies. She imagined explosions, frantic entrapment, charred remains. Casper eventually saw through her pinched protestations of comfort, but not until the cold was aggressive enough that it occurred to him.

Al went out to examine her garden once the swollen dough, threat-ening to overwhelm its cookie sheet in her absence, was dispatched.

Her nasturtiums continued to hold their own in the back corner, flat green parasols punctuated by elvish orange and yellow head-dresses. She lurched through the patch, trying to step where she'd do the least damage as she plucked leaves and blossoms for a bouquet. Jackknifed with derrière at full mast, hair dangling over the nasturtiums protruding from her mouth, she groped for flowers hidden beneath their canopy.

A truck pulled into the Schmitts' driveway ten feet away.

Al feigned the absorption she no longer possessed, glad of the obvious difficulty of waving or warbling. She tried to make her posterior less evident. A masculine voice ripped through the breeze.

"Hey Howie! What's up?"

That most tenuous of pleasures, a snatch of contemplative gardening in the seclusion of her backyard, popped and frizzled. The counterpoint of sunlight and shade on foliage, the companionable robin's comments from the top of the maple, the fugitive cucumbery scent given off by rumpled nasturtiums all vanished, murdered by a cell phone.

"Heh, heh, yeah, blah blah blah…"

Al had walked around her block often enough to know that her martyrdom by Mr. Schmitt's chronic, maddeningly random megaphone-style business communications was unique. What perverse fate had planted the ubiquitous, hearty, oblivious Schmitts next to her reclusive, hypersensitive, nature-worshiping self? Dozens of homes lit by the hypnotic glower of electronic screens, with vacant, state-of-the-art lawns maintained by crews, would withstand the assault much more ably. It was almost certainly a breach – "I tell ya what, Howie…" of city regulations, as this was a residential zone. No matter how early she rose to water the garden, glimpse the sinking moon, sit on her back steps to hear birds greet the sunrise, some van with a ladder on top had driven up so Schmitt and his crew of yokels could spit, slap each other on the back and bark into phones while loading equipment. The rest of the street remained shrouded in tranquility. The Schmitts got away with it because the Athnoses didn't complain at city hall. There wasn't a blessed moment of day or night -

The Schmitts' back door slammed. He'd gone.

Al tucked her nasturtiums into a jar of water. A knot had formed at the back of her neck, and the temple on the same side ached dully. A silvery, oval bubble clung to the inner side of the jar; tiny bubbles fizzed along the stems. She felt like climbing in, safe from "the human comedy," as Casper liked to say. If only they could afford a place in the countryside.

She put the flowers on the back stairs. The garden, virtually cancelled by the intrusion, reappeared.

Clumps of asters leaned against each other for support. One last delphinium glowed cobalt above its stake. Her old-fashioned roses' late buds would certainly be nipped...In midsummer she picked Japanese beetles off them like blackberries. She dropped them into peanut butter jars with holes in the lid. Casper released them in fields along the highway, the most compassionate scheme they could devise...

With a thrill of horror Al realized she had no idea what time it was; the bread might be a singed brick by the time Casper noticed the smell – She pounded up the steps, anger with herself, potential anger with Casper already simmering, to find a modest scent of baking bread in the kitchen, Casper's mildly raised eyebrows, an accommodating clock.

"Thought I burnt the bread!"

Upstairs in the bedroom Al stripped off her jeans and sweater. As their circle of acquaintances had dwindled, so had occasions that justified a closet crammed with fragile vintage treasures, quietly glamorous dresses she'd pounced on at sales, romantic capes, kimonos, and beaded tunics in boxes because they were too heavy to hang. Casper had taken her to the Lyric Opera for her birthday that spring, knowing she'd enjoy opening night finery as much as Offenbach. By then she'd taken to dressing for dinner, a satisfyingly Edwardian ritual though tough on perishable finery. Casper had exempted himself cheerfully.

Al pulled on leggings she'd dyed apple-green, rummaged for sandals, bore the evening's intended attire into the bathroom. The parchment-colored silk robe, nearly translucent with age, fastened carelessly at the hip. Chrysanthemums, pagodas and star-shaped leaves flowed across the shoulders and down the front in shades of bittersweet, blue and acid green. Al fussed in the full-length mirror on the back of the door, delighted by her resuscitation of something old and lovely. Part of the fun was going downstairs and pirouetting for Casper.

He frowned over the top of his Trib.

"Very Bohemian. Nice knickers."

"Leggings. Do you think I'm too old for them?"

"Looks fine to me. The Chinese thing is delicate and rare, like you."

Satisfied, she covered the whole affair in one of his cast-off bathrobes, since dressing for dinner had to include making the dinner.

The Tofu Marsala succeeded. The bread, overpoweringly savory, reminded her of Thanksgiving stuffing. Casper said it was just fine.

After dinner Al kept vigil for the cardinal couple. They met under the dining room window at dusk, after the squirrels and other birds had turned in. One or the other pecked at seeds until joined by its mate. When each had finished its nightcap, they flashed simultaneously into a neighbor's yard where bed apparently awaited. Al fretted if one of them failed to keep the appointment. Tonight they adjourned in an orderly fashion as she hovered at the window, motionless.

By 7:30 Al was inclined to go upstairs. She had no more appetite for activity; reading at night gave her a headache; Linnet was becoming importunate.

"Think I'll go up now. See you in fifteen minutes or so?"

"Alrighty." Casper sat taking notes on the arm of his rocking chair, a stack of books by either foot. A paper clip teetered in his mouth.

Linnet plowed up the stairway ahead of Al and watched greedily as she opened the bed. The worn cocker spaniel from Al's preschool days, the Beanie Baby kiwi that had beckoned from a resale shop shelf and the plush otter, a gift from the Save Our Rivers Foundation, were transferred to a chair. Linnet let herself be lifted onto the bed and warmed it while Al brushed her teeth and got into her most subdued pajamas. Gladness kindled within her when she turned off the light: for privacy, for the play of leaf shadow on the closet door, for dear Linnet, for rest, release. The cool pillow was delicious, the fluttering foliage eloquent and intimate. When she heard Casper on the stairs she flipped onto her stomach and arranged her legs so that Linnet had a nook. She received an excellent back rub and fell asleep easily.

A little before midnight Al woke, tottered to the bathroom, saw Casper's usual pool of light at the bottom of the stairs. Vaguely uneasy, she plumped her pillow and lay on her back staring into the dark. Linnet curled at the bottom of the bed, seriously asleep.

Anxiety clawed her. She'd forgotten to pray for those most in need. Visions of crated Chinese dogs waiting to be skinned alive and foaming, wild-eyed horses being knifed by butchers pressed in on her. Baby whales slaughtered with their loving mothers for sushi. The young Afghan girls who burned themselves to death, or didn't quite succeed...Delicately wrought winged bodies trapped on flypaper...

"Please be with them, help them, let there be a way...keep them in the shadow of Your wing. Lord have mercy on me, a sinner..."

She writhed. Linnet jumped off the bed. She turned the hot pillow. Casper's usual rustlings and sighs over his work could be heard from below.

What would become of her without him? She knew this was a precipice she ought not approach, especially in the middle of the night. Nonetheless she imagined herself driven from the neighborhood because she couldn't keep the house painted or the sidewalks shoveled...Casper had shown her repeatedly how to fill the car with gas, but the routine always seemed to vary in some small but critical way that eluded her. Her computer illiteracy might prevent her doing

the banking (those free classes at the library had overwhelmed her)...
Who could she phone in an emergency? Her cousin, six states away?
An ambulance would bankrupt her.

A plumbless, dilating disorientation rose within her, greater than
the sum of its troubling parts. She'd become acquainted with it the
past year or two; nothing brought relief. A decade ago she could summon the face of Jesus against nighttime bouts of despair. But as her
disenchantment with church accumulated, His face had evaporated.
Moreover these newer spells included neither the familiarity of sorrow nor the physicality of panic. This quiet way madness lay.

Calling down to Casper simply exemplified the predicament. She
forced herself away from the brink: there must be a solution, but she
wouldn't find it by gasping in the vortex all night. She trudged back
to the bathroom, coaxed Linnet off her rug, settled with her and eventually fell asleep thinking about skirts to be hemmed.

When she found Casper collapsed on the kitchen floor the next
morning, she knew at once he was dead.

Communicant

Beebe Morrissey huddled by the Dank Tarn, her back to Lilybanks.
Wind shook the murky broth of dead leaves and apple-green algae in
the tiny pool, and blew back the hood of her sweatshirt. Lichen the
color of robins' eggs crept along the Tarn's concrete rim. Its frilly patterns reminded her of the marbled end papers on Bubo's set of Dante.
As a toddler she'd believed the Tarn was bottomless. Garbling family
lore, she'd thought her father had dug it for one of the winged dragons
in whose honor he made pilgrimage.

The bells of the university chapel rang four o'clock. Time to start
her homework soon. She sprawled in the grass, heedless of her bal-
looning dress, and groped in a pocket of her backpack. Beneath dog-
eared notes and a cough drop tin lay her relic of Blessed Katerina. It

wasn't a *real* relic, but a copy of the only known photo, enshrined in an Art Deco compact. Beebe meant this to resemble a tiny folding travel icon she'd seen. She opened it and peered at the disappointingly blurry figure huddled on steps. Except for the long skirt Katerina might have been a young man, with high cheekbones and ears that stuck out.

Beebe sighed, and put the compact back reverently; the lopsided pack nearly fell into the Tarn. Its bulges concealed books, toilet paper, and half a dozen of her friend Tad Bramble's cast-off Camel cigarette packs filled with petals, pebbles and other marginalia from walks.

Beebe extracted the prickly head of a teasel blossom from the collection and held it against the sky. Spiky bracts guarded its odd treasure, a sort of moth-eaten thistle with a Carmen Miranda pineapple headdress. The color of a paper bag, the specimen had toasted in the sun and wind. It was made out of the same stuff as herself, more or less, a feisty little brother. Or sister. If she had spiny bracts her bassoon instructor Mr. Browd wouldn't be able to pat her bottom before he let her go home on Thursdays. At the end of the lesson he drew a star on her chart at the back of his black binder, accompanied her to the door and gave her that friendly little pat as though it were a musical tradition. He'd complimented her on always wearing dresses. He had bad breath. It would be much easier to love Mr. Browd if he were a mourning dove, or soil. The teasel had drawn a garnet bead of blood from her finger. She put it away.

A car honked in the distance. *Attention. Be here, now.* She pulled off her shoes to feel the plush, unmowed lawn. Words receded. Leaves rustled above her; her feet felt clammy. She needed a Band-Aid. Beebe sat up, bent over to tousle the poor flattened grass and saw the ground spiral as her stomach lurched. She groped for her horehound drops, allowing herself two at once. Supper alone tonight. Bubo was stacked with back-to-back tutees on Wednesdays this semester; Lucy had a dinner date with Micah.

Lilybanks' dark shingles disappeared for a moment behind a blotchy veil that clouded her sight. She found the side effects of earnest fasting sort of endearing. Summoning inner reserves, she groped for her shoes, shouldered her pack and headed in. Early drifts of leaves met her shuffle with papery whispers. The front steps discharged the strong scent of well-watered chrysanthemums.

Beebe paused on the porch to buckle on her flats again. Aphrodite would be waiting in the hall, and there would be drool. She fished her house keys up out of her bodice and stood as close to the door latch as possible so as not to have to remove their chain from her neck. Tad had asked her to consider what might happen if anyone inside Lilybanks opened the front door just as Beebe's rather crotchety key, fastened round her neck, made contact. It seemed an exhilarating possibility.

Aphrodite blinked at her from the gloom beyond the hallway chandelier. She looked grumpy; another nap interrupted because Beebe *would* insist on leaving the premises. The elderly Newfoundland struggled to her feet and shuffled over for an embrace. Loops of saliva like matronly strings on reading glasses festooned her jowls. Her ears drooped in fond surrender.

Beebe perched on one of the dozen wooden chairs, little more than two feet high, that lined the entry beneath rows of empty coat hooks. She wiped the dog's rheumy eyes with the tatted hem of her best white apron.

"Aphrodite, your face is the Face of God." Aphrodite wagged mildly.

Everything was God's face – the quaint dark floor with its murky images of sea serpents and griffins, her own bitten fingernails, the shaft of western sun emerging from the scullery, the Tootsie Roll wrapper that had drifted under the umbrella stand...actually, she wasn't sure about the candy wrapper. She gave Aphrodite a kiss on the forehead.

Beebe pulled out her father's pocket watch – on a second chain around her neck – and snapped the lid open. The sun's descent, the thinning voices of children playing outdoors, the closing-time siren from a distant factory corroborated five o'clock. Primeval, they had heralded a "nursery tea" when she was a toddler visiting her auntie.

"Let's see what's to eat." Aphrodite followed her down the hall and through the kitchen scullery with its twin enamel sinks, white honeycomb tiles and massive dog bowls into the pantry.

Glancing at the note taped at her eye level to the wall of cream-colored cupboards and drawers (*"BEEBE – curry in pink Tupperware to heat. MILK!!!"*) she found a package of Saltines and stuffed it into her pack. Aphrodite trailed behind her into the kitchen and heaved herself down next to a radiator when she saw Beebe filling the teakettle.

It took both hands to get the dented old thing onto the stove. When she lit the burner the tip of a braid trailed through the blue flame. Alerted by the familiar smell, she chopped off the coagulated inch on the bread board and plunged the evidence deep into the waste basket.

"Pee-yew!"

The sound of her voice fluting through the vast cold kitchen wakened her. She attended to her breath, the beating of her heart, her toes tingling in the confining shoes, her cold thighs under her dress, its hem furling and unfurling against her calves as she strode through the room, displacing air that raised the down on the back of her neck. Focused on her movements, Beebe tugged open the icebox, found the things she wanted and laid them on the round worktable, keeping two eggs in each apron pocket. Sealed bowls labeled *"choc. fondant"* and *"van. pastry cream"* in her tiny script were carefully placed side by side. She knelt to pull a mixing bowl from a low cupboard, rose with eggs intact and placed them one by one in her brown Red Wing bowl. She took time to marvel at their cool, chaste forms, each bearing tiny insignia – a dimple, a stain, a shadowy vein. As Beebe cradled the bowl she welcomed its presence, sensed a kinship, felt herself honoring the body of God, of which she was a part. How happy she was here in the freezing kitchen, she told herself, and pulled up her hood. Her stomach rumbled.

The rattling kettle began to sputter. Exalted, Beebe poured a bit too much Lapsang Souchong into a chipped teapot that was allowed upstairs. Lucy seemed to have hidden the oven mitts again. Beebe concentrated on steadfast calm as the steam burnt her fingers. Two Band-Aids, maybe.

"Supper, Ditey, SUPPER!"

Yanked from a dream, Aphrodite waddled back to the scullery with her. When she'd approved the enhancement of her dismal portion of organic kibble for senior dogs with all of the curry and a generous swig of milk, Beebe tiptoed out. Aphrodite preferred to dine in strict solitude, a sentiment she shared.

A bit out of breath, Beebe went upstairs hugging the railing. Scalding dribbles of Lapsang Souchong neatly missed her ankles, falling onto the thinning runner's faded pattern of gingko leaves.

She laid the teapot down at the top of the stairs, scanning the wide upper hall. Lucy's rooms looked dark; the entire house felt Lucyless. In the dim distance a student's coat slumped over the bench outside Bubo's den. Beebe sank to the chilly floorboards and fumbled in the pack for the last horehound. With its sugar tucked beneath her tongue she resumed her burdens.

Her bedroom's glass doorknob felt cool and moist, like a whorled seashell. Inside, she backed against her door to shut it and sighed, letting the pack slide down her shoulders. She laid the teapot on a stack of books and lingered at the head of the room to sift its silence and empty space, familiar and dear. The sound of her footsteps crossing to the window had long ago become a meditative ritual. The pleasure of parting the latticework drew her, as did the crown of the crab tree just below, and the trembling needles of the taller white pine beyond.

The wind was rising with the twilight. It wasn't cold enough to see her breath yet, but the rustle of the crab's leaves had grown crisper. She thrilled at the sense of the sheer drop below her, and flicked her braids over the edge. The garden was nearly silent in the evening now, its choir of insects dispersed or daunted, and Bubo'd allowed her to remove the window screen. Come November the delicate fragrance of bruised, frostbitten crabapples would rise from the terrace. As she closed the sash against the chill a bird flew to some secret berth.

The radiator by the door hissed promisingly; she unzipped her hoody and draped it over the silver humps to toast. Snapping on the ceiling light, she faced the cheval glass. There was her pleasant face with its heart shape, moles and rosy cheeks, arched eyebrows and slightly turned-up nose. Those eyebrows and her widow's peak gave her some mystique to counter the apple dumpling effect. She was short – probably had only just squeaked past being a tall dwarf – and not only a shade plump, but top-heavy. Her head was conspicuously imposing, like a Newfoundland's. Bubo said – and Beebe had seen it herself in photographs – that she had "her father's mold, her mother's hue." Beebe knew she'd been made too drolly dollish to ever be a conventional beauty. Yet that flaw complemented her pretty, prematurely sage face strikingly. She was used to being favored and cosseted by peers as well as adults. She captivated. She made a splendid mascot.

That was alright, but irrelevant to her personal goals. Beebe planned to become a saint.

She pulled a cup and saucer from a drawer and poured tea. By now the brew was practically opaque, like the Tarn. Flipping her shoes onto the braided rug, she gave the Saltines a nest in her lap as she sat Indian-style by her pillow to warm her feet. Tomorrow she'd wear tights, like everyone else had for weeks. Delicious, the sharp squares like Civil War hardtack melting in the strong smoky tea. At lunch Tad had regretfully gulped the egg salad sandwich Lucy had made her along with his own macaroni. Grateful, Beebe had mimed pinching one of her ripe cheeks to reassure him. Her heart began to race in faint, erratic spurts.

She restored Blessed Katerina to a place of honor on the shelf in the far corner, kissing a finger and then touching the photograph, the way she'd seen the faithful in Micah's church venerate icons they couldn't reach with their lips. She rearranged its tribute: snail shells, acorns, fortune cookie oracles, a dented opal cufflink disinterred from the garden.

Beyond her door someone lugged a briefcase up the stairs, panted and headed up to the den. Beebe turned the lock in her door, and looked out the window again before drawing the curtain. A faint sliver of new moon hung in the sky, auspicious.

Bubo wanted her to read Wordsworth's "Ode: Intimations of Immortality" for the home schoolers' Martinmas hospitality night. For a surprise, Beebe was memorizing it. This would be good advertising for her aunt, on whose tutoring fees they relied so.

After an hour of mumbling and squinting furtively at her book she'd had enough. Stuffing her braids down the back of her hoodie and imagining a cloak of invisibility, she opened her door with care and stole downstairs.

Aphrodite, asleep beneath the stairs in a cushioned wicker basket the size of a bathtub, lurched into gear as Beebe shook the leash above her. They pitched out the back door, each happy to have avoided foreigners.

Once Aphrodite had safely navigated the steps in the amber glow of the porch lantern they proceeded across the terrace by starlight. Beebe made urgent little clucks, trying to prevent the dog from irrigating the cobblestones. Aphrodite's customary world-weary air tended to shred at the door into the walled garden. Hoping not to be knocked over, Beebe reached for the doorknob and pushed hard; a cluster of sea oats choked the hinges. Aphrodite strode to the first way station on her circular pilgrimage; the smell of bruised marigolds rose to Beebe's nostrils. Somewhere nearby a lone cricket caroled feebly.

As her eyes adjusted to the deeper dark, more distant stars revealed themselves tucked up in the blanket of night. Friends. She could hear Aphrodite sprinkling, snuffling, snapping brittle canes as she pushed past the windflowers. The decaying garden – its colors extinguished, the hum and buzz gone – radiated a subtle vibrancy. Great Grandma Calla's listing weathervane creaked above them as they rounded the hut. The frail crescent moon startled her between silhouetted trees. Everything was alive – the sky, the damp earth and pebbles, Lilybanks looming behind them, the rusty stork, the pennies in her pockets. She knew herself a communicant, and wondered at the dog's grave acceptance. Aphrodite's tug on the leash, her own pinched toes, her breath through a drippy nose filled her consciousness harmoniously, uncrowded by complaint or effort...Her whole body felt fizzy, exhilarated.

After the dog had gone back to bed, Beebe concentrated on producing a squadron of *religieuses* in the silent white expanse of the kitchen. She applied the detached absorption of a surgeon to her wobbly cream puff nuns, impassively tilting the unacceptably soggy first effort into the garbage. By eleven o'clock the survivors of the second batch, wimpled in gleaming mocha fondant, nestled in pleated papers. Beebe had subjected each to an examination for dog hairs with her magnifying glass, and trimmed them with white chocolate to suggest nuns' winged headgear. Victorious, she arranged them in a hatbox by a chilly window, added a piece of paper marked "FRAGILE! DO NOT DISTURB!" and dragged herself up to bed.

Her aunt, rigorously thwarted in her attempts to regulate or even witness Beebe's nocturnal rhythms for several years, had brushed her teeth and turned out her light in benignly resigned solitude. Lucy was still out.

In her room Beebe paid her respects to Blessed Katerina, careful not to yawn. Micah had bought her a history of Louis Sullivan's Orthodox church when he'd shepherded Lucy and her into Chicago to admire it. She'd felt like a field trip monitor, bashful Lucy having insisted on her coming along. But Beebe had fallen in love with the star-spangled blue interior of the dome above tiers of icons, and with the otherworldly feel of the place. Finding Katerina's photo and caption ("Parish dependent with church mouser") in the history had suggested the discovery of a kindred spirit. She prayed a moment without words and snuffed the little candle.

Unable to summon the strength to comb out her braids or brush her teeth, Beebe reflected that she was unlikely to get cavities from a thimbleful of pastry cream and a purely experimental mouthful of *choux*. She dropped her clothes on the floor, including the gooey apron she'd forgotten to remove downstairs, pulled on her nightgown and crept into bed.

Something Cozy

Even when she was frazzled Beebe liked to read something cozy before sleep. This meant one of the worn "period" children's books Bubo and she had collected for Lilybanks' library: *Rum Tum Tummy, Flower Children*, the *My Book House* set or the library's native royalty, Great Grandma Calla's *The Cats of Lilac Corner*. They possessed seven copies of the latter's first edition. It was a children's book for adults; she and Bubo liked to imagine it being passed around over mahjong or contract bridge by Calla's fashionable admirers. Bubo let her keep a stained copy by her bed, next to another indulgence: a Gaw-van Erp mica lamp, one of Calla's wedding presents. *Lilac Corner* looked especially inviting propped against its pudgy copper base. She opened the book.

The Cats of Lilac Corner

By Calla Morrissey

Author's Note: This little tale was inspired by some specially nice cats with whom she became acquainted in the Apple Hill neighborhood long ago. The district is crisscrossed by streets of cozy bungalows built in the first years of this century for their proud owners – hardworking tradesmen and families, idealistic artists and craftsmen, and teachers from the city's schools and University. The author's home, Lilybanks, is the new house "with flowers up its nose" at the top of the Ridge. Time has wrought its changes, and some of the remaining settlers of Rutledge's prospering "Bungalow District" on the hill miss the distant horizons of its more pastoral days. But the neighborhood homes still embody the original earnest, creative and nature-loving ideals. May wise, handsome and enterprising cats ever grace their hearths.

*   *   *

It was very early on a promising morning in May, and Bezique Bunting felt it was time to waken his mistress. He leapt lightly onto Mr. and Mrs. Bunting's bed and assumed his most delicious purr – deep, husky and irresistible. He sat by Mrs. Bunting's pillow for a minute to let his purr soak into her dreams. When he judged the moment ripe, Bezique gently pushed his face into Mrs. B's ear, boldly increasing the purr's volume. He pulled back to study the effect. Mrs. B. was smiling now, though her eyes were still closed. Her hand fumbled toward him. Moving in for the finale, Bezique delicately touched his moist nose to the soft furrow just above his mistress's upper lip. She laughed and grabbed him around the waist.

"Bezique-y! My little turtledove!"

Professor Bunting grunted and threw his arm over his eyes.

Bezique let himself go skillfully limp in his mistress's arms as she kissed him and poked her face in his warm, dark fur.

"You smell good, 'Zique-y. Like a baby blanket in the sun. Time to get up?"

He knew "get-up." Success. A charmingly pliable human, his mistress. She was devoted to him. He'd trained her well. She sat up and her long hair dangled over his face. He found this quite intoxicating, and purred steadily beneath his curtain. Mrs. B. thought this captivatingly ardent and silly. She kneaded the hollow between his shoulder blades until his eyes glazed with pleasure and their inner eyelids appeared.

"Come along now, we've our rounds to make."

She tucked the sheets in around the professor, jiggling and poking till she'd produced a smile. He pulled her pillow over his face. It was going to be a sunny day, Bezique observed. Energy and confidence coursed through his chest and legs to the tip of his tail.

"Snowy! Are you there?"

Mrs. B. got down on her hands and knees, peering under the bed.

"Snowy! Snowy!" She added some clucking, then crooned a few bars of "My Melancholy Baby."

Bezique observed the ritual from the bed. He disapproved of this coddling. Snowy was stubborn and temperamental. At least she knew her place at night. He reigned supreme on the bed with his mistress. Snowy claimed to prefer the lower berth. The cushions Mrs. B. had placed under the bed were caked with her feathery white fur. Most unsavory. His mistress, entirely too lenient, even kept the chamber pot in a bedside cupboard so it wouldn't dishearten Miss Fancy-Pants under the bed.

Snowy crept out onto the rug and ran the gauntlet beneath him. Once she had one paw on Mrs. B's bare foot, Snowy looked back at him from under the nightgown's flounce. Smug, she was. Not that he'd had the slightest intention of foul play – his mistress thought him a gentleman.

The three of them padded softly past the girls' room. Applesauce spent his nights in there. If roused he was apt to stand on his hind legs and wiggle the doorknob insistently, waking the children. The chubby oaf had an intellect, no doubt about it. Bezique took pride in the quality of his team, however uncooperative its members.

He paused at the top of the stairs so his mistress could sling him over her shoulder. Mrs. B. liked to watch Snowy's luxuriant bottom ups-a-daisy down the stairs ahead of her; Bezique, facing the other way, was spared this.

Bezique's meals were served under the kitchen worktable, within a fortress of table and stool legs. His mistress put him down in the kitchen and he assumed his station, telegraphing extreme interest in breakfast with his dilated stare. She ladled out a portion for each – day-old porridge, peas from the Buntings' last dinner, bread crumbs – and topped it off with milk from the icebox. Snowy ate every morsel lickety-split, then strolled into the Florida room for a bath in the sun. Bezique speared all his peas with a claw, licked them and deposited them on the floor next to his bowl before devouring everything else. Professor and Mrs. Bunting had become vegetarians in the interests of health and enlightenment; the butcher's boy delivered leavings for their cats most afternoons. In the morning they got milk or egg, and were glad to have it, for very few mice dared cross their threshold.

Delilah the collie, who spent warm nights under the back porch, pranced inside as soon as the cats were fed. As watchdog she daintily claimed her pat of butter from her mistress's fingers, then pushed the cats' bowls along the kitchen floor with her long nose in search of a morsel. From there she rattled upstairs to the Professor's bedside rug, panting and fidgeting till he sat up and tousled her fringed ears.

After pushing a tin of popover batter into the oven, Mrs. B. left Bezique in charge of the kitchen. She opened the girls' bedroom door softly and Applesauce fell out onto her feet. She opened the blinds and called, "Time to rise and shine, girls! Good morning, Marjorie, good morning Lavender, good morning, Alice." Lavender wanted braiding and buttoning, Alice to have the sandman's dust brushed from her eyes, Marjorie her lunch money and the Professor cajoled into taking a clean handkerchief, all before the popovers burnt.

Once Applesauce was safely settled before his crock of sops by the fragrant oven, Bezique strolled briskly to the Florida room. When Applesauce was unoccupied it was best to be out of reach.

He had been accepted into the Buntings' bosom before it became obvious that he was a sower of discord among cats. Bezique, who considered himself the home's steward and guardian spirit, Mrs. Bunting's true love, the number one cat and the true "guard dog," had welcomed Applesauce cordially and been rebuffed.

Applesauce had tripled in size. Fat and nimble as a sumi wrestler, he loved to lurk behind furniture and shoot across a room to collide with an indignant Bezique or outraged Snowy. No blood was ever shed, but nerves frayed, gaits tautened, haloes slipped. Thanks to Bezique's natural majesty (and support from Mrs. Bunting) the established order was not overthrown.

Poor Applesauce was not malicious, but greedy for attention and importance. Neither Mrs. B's scoldings nor banishment to a locked room ever quelled his urge to usurp thrones.

All three cats prized the sun room's bank of windows onto Donovan Street. Lace curtains and Mrs. B.'s geraniums provided privacy. The Professor's cherished Japanese chests were stacked in steps just the right size for basking or surveillance.

Bezique found Snowy lounging splendidly across her mistress's sewing table in the center of the windows. She fancied hers was the same regal pose as that of the cat on Mrs. Bunting's

"*Langues de Chats*" tin, but prettier because she was white and pink as apple blossoms instead of sly, grey and foreign. She'd placed herself so that a curtain veiled her face.

"You know, he can still see you. It just feels like he can't," Bezique offered from the floor, looking up at her plush derrière. Snowy could be a bit of a birdbrain.

Peeved, she lashed her plumy tail.

"It doesn't work for you because you're black, silly."

Bezique yawned. It was just like Snowy to miss the point. No use bickering. He leapt all the way to the very top of the tansu chests in exasperation.

"Glorious morning. She'll open the windows after the family's gone," he observed, sniffing the ruffled geranium leaves crowding around him. He pulled in his tail to accommodate Mrs. Bunting's copper watering can, whose long, artistic spout was a notable impediment.

"Here comes your inkspot," Snowy murmured, drawing herself up and peering into the narrow path hidden between the front of the Buntings' bungalow and its collar of shrubs.

Bezique plunged from his stronghold, hit the fir boards and ricocheted back up to Snowy's side, parting the curtains with his muzzle. Both were engrossed by a small black she-cat frolicking with a stray leaf in the front yard. Brimming with friskiness, she hunted and batted and worried the twirling leaf, unaware of her audience. Bezique thought guiltily of his drawerful of felt mice, crocheted gewgaws and jingle bells.

"What a hayseed!" Snowy snickered. An inch of straw stuck to the little black cat's forehead like a feeler.

Bezique, captivated, was too absorbed to disagree. His heart throbbed as she crouched in the grass, wriggling her rump, then pounced furiously on her prey. Even Snowy's eyes widened when the performance concluded with a full pirouette. The little cat moved beneath the bushes with her back to them, licking a paw as if nothing had happened.

"I grant you she has flair," said Snowy, intending a generous concession. "But she's a year old now. Perhaps a bit clownish for a full-grown she-cat." Snowy spread a paw and examined the pads – smooth as pink cameos, she mused.

Her comment hit Bezique like a spark, illuminating his own heart. Gypsy, as Mrs. B. called her, was his peer now. He'd gotten used to thinking of her as the increasingly fascinating young sprout who lived under the front of his house. She was an amusing little cricket who provided diversion when he was bored, and part of his property.

It was about a year ago that Mrs. Bunting finally heard the babyish squeaks beneath the floor boards while she stitched pantywaists for Alice. Snowy and Bezique had known about them for a couple of weeks. The sounds had made them uneasy. They pretended not to hear. Mrs. Bunting put them out of her mind, too. She didn't want to interfere, and hoped it was her imagination.

One sparkling spring noon the white-chested cat who occasionally visited the yard led a file of four bouncing kittens past the corner of the Florida room. From a bachelor's point of view they were interchangeable fuzzy-wuzzies, except for the black one straggling at the rear. Bezique was partial to black.

Throughout the summer the mother's well-disciplined parade grew increasingly ragged. Kittens popped out of hedges and from behind cabbages; kittens forayed in pairs or alone beyond the farthest Bezique and Snowy could spy from any corner of the house. One morning Bezique and his mistress saw the mother cat sitting outside the neighbors' cellar window. She stared at the Buntings' house for a long, long time. They never saw her again.

Beebe was snoring when Lucy knocked softly at her door, then opened it. Rolling her eyes, Lucy shut the book, kissed the kid on the forehead and snapped off the light.

2

Delicious

"LOOK AT THE STARS! LOOK, LOOK UP AT THE SKIES! O LOOK AT ALL THE[1] – Ditey? Aphrodite, please! It's me! Just me, Tad! Quiet, now, girl...Shhh...Oh, no."

A muffled cannonade of belched barks behind Lilybanks' venerable front door intensified. Jiminy, what an idiot he was, way too loud even alone in the dark. The old girl was going to give herself a heart attack – if Mrs. Morrissey didn't have one first. Beebe would be put out with him for sure. She liked to glide out of Lilybanks like a bat.

Tad extricated his flashlight from the mums and hurtled down the steps clutching Beebe's Penguin Hopkins. He left his backpack – the size of a small refrigerator – on the porch so they could see it was just him through the window.

The racket petered out into fitful, interrogative hiccups. Gosh, he'd never heard Aphrodite attempt more than a wheeze, except for the morning Townshend Thompkins poured his o.j. over her head from the banister.

A faint glow lit the panes at the top of the door; a deadbolt snapped open. He fumbled back up the stairs, shining the flashlight onto his face. Aphrodite forced her muzzle through the slit in the doorway, her gooey eyes expressing ardor.

Beebe managed a "Good morning" as she struggled to keep the dog from barreling over the indistinct edge of the porch.

Yup, she was definitely annoyed. That was the airline hostess voice.

"So how come you didn't look out the window before you opened the door, Beebe? It could've been anybody, some drug addict hitting you up for-"

"It's obviously just Frankenstein."

He'd forgotten to move the light from under his chin. The flickering, sepulchral shadows distorted his heavy eyebrows, inept shave and square jaw as he loomed above her. Repentant, she gently pulled the flashlight down, rescuing him from ludicrousness.

"All you need is pegs at your temples. Come inside before she hurts herself."

Tad plucked the massive backpack from the floor of the porch as though it were his purse. Aphrodite lurched backwards to make room for him, heaved a giant sigh of pure pleasure and sunk her face in his crotch. He laid the pack along three of the little chairs lining the vestibule.

"I'll be right back," Beebe whispered.

A citrusy scent wafted from the staircase's polished banisters. Beebe's little stocking feet receded across the murky linoleum towards the scullery. He watched, consumed.

The usual burnished braids hung down her back, tied together at waist height with a crooked black ribbon. That was something new. Like reins on a solid, fetching little pony, he thought. Otherwise she wore the usual uniform – one of two or three dark, moth-eaten dresses that smelled and felt a bit stale to him, like a really old, unwashed pea coat or the kind of teddy bears found in antique shops. Their long sleeves were puffed or tight or puckered in unexpected places. A row of fussy little buttons marched all the way down the front or back. If she were in a good mood – or a really bad, defiant mood – she'd add one of her pretty white aprons, fragile old ones trimmed with intricate stuff probably crocheted a hundred years ago for a trousseau or shroud. He loved the way Beebe never held back, went right ahead and climbed the tree or ate the watermelon in these things – pinafores, she'd explained; aprons were another thing, for her precious *beignets* and all that. But he didn't like to see the snowy white things torn and stained. They always smelled of lavender, like Beebe.

Tad realized Ditey was making a big stain on his front. He sat down on the cold floor and pulled off a shoe, revealing a sweaty sock for the dog's delectation...Beebe also always wore the heart-shaped locket he'd given her, a huge concession. When Beebe got withdrawn and stayed that way for such a long time it felt like...like she was lost in exaltation inside a crypt in Uzbekistan, or when she got so reckless it made him cry – when those lonely times happened that locket dangling from under her collar kept him glued together.

Beebe reappeared, skating across the floor in thick black tights, which Tad approved of but knew better than to say so. For a nature girl, Beebe could be oddly oblivious to the weather. Beyond the chandelier's glow her heart-shaped face floated toward him above the lunar disc of a huge white hatbox.

"Let's go."

"Let me carry it." He gave Aphrodite's forehead a sympathetic knead, tucked Hopkins into one of his vintage pack's innumerable pockets and shouldered its frame. Beebe's eyebrows contorted with angst as she surrendered the box with its satin bow to Tad's outstretched hands, twice the size of her own. He insisted on performing this service, promising he'd guard her treasures with all the strength of his prematurely adult bulk at the first screech of brakes, the first growl of an unleashed dog.

She pulled a substantial dog biscuit from under her arm and lured Aphrodite to her basket. Undeceived but resigned, Aphrodite watched Tad steal out the front door on tiptoe before she collapsed onto her cushion under the stairs.

Stifling an admonitory cluck, Tad made himself look away as

Beebe scrunched over Lilybanks' front door handle, groping to fit the key around her neck into its lock. Sometimes the key stuck and she'd yank it out hard enough to be catapulted backwards into his arms if he had the foresight to put the hatbox aside.

"Where's the flashlight?"

"Right side, on top."

"Bend down more, can you?"

He could smell the deodorant he'd gotten her as she poked around in the pack. It was lavender, too. His ancient thermos careened tinnily back and forth against the flashlight. A silken plait grazed his ear. He tried to think of schoolwork.

"Got it. What were you doing to make deaf old Ditey hear you, anyway? You're holding it with both hands, of course?"

"Yup. Sorry. I was practicing the Hopkins poem."

"So let's hear it."

She lit their way along Lilybanks' crumbling sidewalk and gnarled trumpet vine arbor into Corrie Street. Maintaining a critical ear, Beebe watched Tad's breath issue in cloudy puffs, the first of the season, as he recited.

"Fire-folk, not fairy-folk. He sees the stars burning like little lanterns...Shall I carry them for awhile?"

"It's fine, Beebe. 'Wind-beat whitebeam! Airy abeles set on a –'"

"Airy abeles! That sounds like beagles, or hairy seals. Listen, Tad: 'Airy abeles set on a flare –' DA duh, DA duh, dadadaDA! Doesn't that sound nicer? It's about the way poplars look when the wind turns the silvery sides of their leaves up. 'Airy abeles.' Like 'merry maples.'" She looked up at him, soft and patient.

Something inside him turned deliciously wet and silver and slithered through him like hot fudge on painfully cold ice cream. Her grey eyes held glints of kindness for him; her breath grazed his hands glued to the sides of the hatbox.

"Okay, airy abeles. Like merry maples...Or hairy navels."

She snorted in horrified delight, executed a sort of prance. Again he thought of a costly, high-strung pony. A filly, with powerful hindquarters.

Beebe snuggled her hand in his jacket pocket, familiar with the broken bits of pencil and sticky, lint-covered coins. A cab slowed alongside them and she waved, exchanging smiles with the Ethiopian driver with whom they sometimes chatted for blocks. The stars were growing fainter through Corrie Street's half mile of big old maples and horse chestnuts.

"Look out, Tad. The sidewalk's uneven here." Wresting her watch up out of her collar, she checked the time. Gloria liked to have the pastries by five, when she arranged the showcases – and before anyone was there to witness their transaction.

Traffic lights and glimpses of neon ahead of them signaled the edge of the Brinkle Street shopping district. Here "historic homes" had mostly been partitioned into student housing. Bicycles, foreign flags and the skeletal remains of potted sunflowers replaced trophy grills and topiary on second-floor balconies.

Only the occasional city bus halted at intersections they crossed. To the less sleepy passengers they might have looked like father and child on some arcane immigrant errand – perhaps a family wedding breakfast in the back of a rug merchant's shop.

They strode up the Euclid Street pedestrian mall with its darkened ice cream and bicycle shops, shuttered cafes and tiny attic theaters, negotiated a long alley full of dumpsters and NO PARKING signs, then turned into another.

Before dwindling into moped parking and ramshackle garages, Maven Alley's cerebral bookstores, avant-garde hair salons, pottery workshop and rickety, legendary bakery attracted connoisseurs in the neighborhood and beyond.

Ochre frills of Art Nouveau script on a dark blue placard running the length of its storefront and window boxes proclaimed "The Maven

Alley Bakery, Est. 1997, Purveyor of the Rare, Rich and Rococo." A saggy, longhaired cat balked, then resumed her place in front of a saucer of kibble when Tad's oversized shoes hit the doormat near her. Beebe jangled the bell cord by the screen door. The cat ignored it.

Beebe poked Tad in the ribs until he relinquished the hatbox. A string of multicolored Christmas lights framing the door lit up.

"C'mon in quick! Don't let the heat out!" Gloria's flat, bloodless face and henna'd hair appeared. She was in her brisk, prep-and-assembly mode, all business.

"*Religieuses?*"

Beebe nodded and laid the box on a glass countertop to untie the bow, then brought it back down to inspect the contents. She shot a smile at Tad, handed the box to Gloria.

"Ooh." Gloria removed a tray of hazelnut baklava from the most important showcase to make way for Beebe's voluptuous nuns. Tad beamed from a polite distance. Gloria unlocked the cash register and took out a pair of twenties for Beebe.

"Coffee'll be ready in a minute."

Thanks, Gloria!...What would you think of herbal chocolate truffles? I've got some preserved angelica I put up this summer. And geranium?"

Despite the deference Gloria sensed Beebe's increasing confidence in her own ability to realize ambitious plans. She suppressed a twinge of envy.

"Make 'em right, I'll take all you can give me. It's got to be top-of-the-line chocolate. That's expensive. And Beebe? Botulism can't even be a possibility, much less a concern. No sealing stewed rosehips in 'sterilized' Mason jars, right?"

"Right!" she grinned, aware it was unfair to feel impatient when Gloria issued one of her caveats. She knew that out of entrepreneurial flair and friendship for Lucy, Gloria had stretched and snapped the Health Department's rules like so much scorched toffee. But sometimes she felt like she was working under the table for a back-alley abortion clinic, not a patisserie.

Remembering herself, she stopped creating a problem and focused on her breath, the careful threading of her way through tables and chairs, her cold fingers. The alley's shapes and planes appeared abstract and softly radiant through the lace curtains ahead of her.

Tad parked his knapsack on the far end of a polka-dotted pew bench and sat down gingerly at the most recessed of four round, glass-topped tables with chairs that looked made of pipe cleaners. He excavated his knitting from the pack.

"Want me to look at your math?"

"Yes please. I forgot it till I was too tired, so I got up at three."

Tad pondered the dark circles under her eyes, refrained from comment. He helped himself to the textbook in her backpack as she laid the empty hatbox on the pew. The part down the middle of her forehead was perfect.

"I'll get the coffee."

She returned with two mugs. His coffee had a bit of cream in it; hers was a celebratory beige pudding with three surreptitious, heaping tablespoons of sugar. Tad was absorbed in checking her homework; he loomed over the dainty table, squinting at the figures as a muffler full of gaps and lumps coiled from jumbo-sized needles over his heavy thighs. For a moment as the caffeine and sugar struck, Beebe glimpsed Tad's utter subjugation, felt the weight of responsibility and the little thrill of excitement snaking through her middle. Acknowledged and dismissed, they receded.

"I can't hang out this afternoon. Bubo's interviewing another candidate for the sisterhood, and she wants me around. Lucy hasn't set a date yet, but she acts more gaga about Micah than ever. Even if she keeps helping with daycare after she's married it wouldn't be the same. Not that it's easy to find the right person for Lilybanks…" She drained her mug. "Lucy's so contented with Micah it's hard to begrudge her."

Tad looked down at the math. Lucy's prenuptial bliss was a two-edged sword; when he'd initially remarked upon it wistfully Beebe's obvious scorn for such arrangements affected him like toothache.

"Number three's not quite right. Check your decimal point. Can you look at my French, Beebe? How much time do we have?"

She ferreted out the chain, popped open the heirloom watch's lid. He noticed her fingernails were bitten down again.

"Twenty minutes till opening." It was best that they and the hat-box be gone before then. "I'm going to teach myself Russian. Bubo's ordering me a book."

He shoved his book review of *The Three Musketeers* over to her a bit forcefully. Mrs. Morrissey operated Lilybanks in a well-read, well-intentioned coma.

"You don't have to move to Russia to be a Holy Fool, Beebe." It came out more fiercely than intended; he didn't care for the way coffee affected him, but it was a cozy thing to do with Beebe at the bakery.

Electrified, she looked for Gloria, who seemed to be safely preoccupied with peeling apricot Danish off papered trays. Tad's preposterously deep voice booming through libraries, lunches and buses created a perpetual series of social disasters narrowly averted. Sparks danced along her veins; something made her want to crumple his French paper and jam it down into the remains of his coffee. The extravagance of the image roused her; she came to, and the stampeding thoughts evaporated. So Tad had a deep voice. She stared at his essay for a minute, waiting for the adrenaline to recede.

"*Palais* isn't feminine...That's exactly what I said. It's just sort of a tribute. Learning someone's language is a very intimate thing, you know, like getting under their skin, wearing their clothes." She was quoting Lucy shamelessly. "Russian will pull me closer to my inspiration, that's all."

"Okay."

It took half an hour to walk to the turreted painted lady where

Mrs. Mueller deciphered high school-level math for her convalescent son and a few homeschoolers before going to work. After they were out of Gloria's sight and off the bus route, Beebe let Tad hold her hand. The hatbox thumped against her leg. Mourning doves cooed from gables. They watched a Boston terrier fetch a morning paper more than half his size and applauded. His human waved to them. Beebe's hand felt like a warm little bird in Tad's.

"You could practice your Hopkins."

"It'll be alright. 'Airy abeles.' Like buried cables."

"And sherry labels." She smiled her huge, twinkling smile and pulled her hand back into her pocket.

Sisterhood

Althea alighted from the bus onto Corrie Street's sunny, sloping sidewalk with a presentiment of good. She felt confident her appearance hit the nail on the head: folkloric black skirt with bright, whimsical ribbons, embroidered handbag, little black jacket that pulled it all together. "Waldorf-inspired daycare," the index card on the university extension bulletin board had said. That could mean jeans, but the woman on the phone had definitely not sounded like jeans. Moreover, she was probably due for some luck – luck, which she no longer heeded.

She pushed up her sleeve to check Casper's watch for the second time in three minutes, yet its worn leather band on her thin forearm startled her. Nameless dread struck without warning, so physical that she felt herself reel and grabbed the steep embankment's metal handrail. She pulled the bag off her shoulder and pretended to search it – if someone had noticed her peculiar gesture she'd say she'd thought she'd lost something important. Al made an effort to pull herself together, focus on the bright blue sky, the hilly lawns with terraces or serpentine paths up to quaint homes on lush, secluded lots...This was her favorite neighborhood...She was probably dehydrated again. Anyway, what could you expect? Alarmed by this sloppy state of mind, Al reminded herself of Linnet, whose potential homelessness provided the astringent correction.

Blue and white porcelain tile numerals embedded in the steps of the next lawn's sidewalk suggested the bus had dropped her disconcertingly close to her destination. Seven o seven Corrie Street was apparently a near neighbor of Lilybanks, whose annual house tour she seldom missed.

Her appointment with the rather formal woman whose name she'd failed to ask was for one o'clock; she had four minutes.

Lilybanks' wide, chalet-style front gable came into view at the top of the hill; Al petitioned its familiar brown shingles for a blessing as she passed. She'd been enthusiastic about the Corrie Street address after the phone conversation, but now the neighborhood suggested the puniness of her station in life. Endearing as they were, these fairy-tale bungalows and big, homey foursquares were highly desirable real estate, as far beyond her means as castles.

If Casper was watching he was annoyed; she pulled her shoulders back. After all, how formidable could a household that ran a daycare center be?

She realized she'd wandered past the address and turned back in a rush, annoyed with herself.

Eventually it appeared that either seven o seven was Lilybanks or she'd written down the wrong number. Giving in, she navigated the buckling sidewalk beneath a canopy of tangled vines that threatened to overwhelm their aged pergola. Beyond caring whether she'd bungled yet another appointment, Al let herself fall under the spell of the house.

Its low eaves and latticed windows were painted a subdued blue-green that enhanced the dark shingles and blended harmoniously with the long-needled pines that framed its upper corners. High above the recessed entryway with its Japanese lantern a window box trailed nasturtium vines. Some years she'd seen red geraniums.

She allowed herself a nervous laugh as brass numerals below the dangling tendrils came into focus: 707. Just for a moment, as she took in the open doorway and figures milling within, Al thought she was arriving for the tour.

Children's voices and footsteps issued from the interior. Self-conscious, Al mounted the wide concrete steps. Pinky-gold mums, her favorite variety, filled the terra cotta urns. A good sign. She rubbed a leaf between her fingers and inhaled the pungent fragrance. The wooden landing had been painted to match the steps. It was peeling in places.

"Take your sister's hand, Townshend. We're going to be late." A bored-looking woman with metallic hair and a suede jacket appeared in the entryway. Her huge leather handbag yawned open as she eyed Althea vacantly. The latter took her in unhappily, noting the large, brassy earrings like shields, the jangled car keys dangling sleek electronic gadgets, the careless indifference. As the woman didn't cede the doorway, Al stood aside and watched skinny blond Townshend dart over to the handbag, seize some type of over-endowed cell phone from its depths and attack it ardently. His sister was propelled out the door and he followed in a trance, not holding her hand. Althea would not have guessed him old enough to turn on a television without supervision. They whisked past her.

Al crossed the threshold onto the curious, figured tiles. The cock-eyed rows of little wooden chairs that lined the entrance hall struck her as foreboding, though had they ever been present on a tour she'd have thought them sweet. A sodden jelly sandwich, cut in the shape of a heart, lay bleeding on a seat. She imagined it was Townshend's.

A mousy kid in a pink cardigan and purple pants, whom she wanted to like, emerged from somewhere in the back of the house. She stared at Althea, appalled, and reached for her mother's hand.

Feeling more equal to this encounter, Al approached, trying to be perky.

"Could you please point me in the direction of whoever's in charge?"

"Sorry, what?" faltered the woman, as if interrupted from weighty deliberations.

"I was just wondering if you could tell me where to find the person in charge here?"

Pink-and-purple shrank behind her mother, who seemed uncertain whether or not the person might be outside in the back. They nearly tiptoed out the front door. Al felt aggrieved at her inability to arouse any interest, particularly in this special place with which she'd fatuously imagined a bond over the years. Out of nowhere the memory of the backhoe lurking in the distance at Casper's funeral appeared; the image had attached itself to her, leering at unpredictable intervals.

Distant conversation rose and fell from the back of the house; Al considered the unaffordable self-indulgence of simply leaving. She sighed and walked toward the voices, leaving behind the fabled Arts and Crafts staircase and foregoing a peek into the inglenook library. She paused to venerate the grandfather clock in the hall, a rare Hyacinth McCall. Its warped case bore an inscription from Plato she'd memorized: *Wherefore the Creator resolved to have a moving image of Eternity, and this image we call Time.*

A small body plowed into her knees. This proved to be a wobbly boy sporting a runnel of mucus and, judging by his capacious and apparently damp bottom, diapers. To her immense relief, he smiled at her.

"Oh! Thank heavens you slowed him down. Last week we found him in the scullery with fistfuls of dog food. Have you come to talk with Marian? I'm Lucy. Just let me dispatch our friend here and I'll be right back – Can you wave, Harry?"

No, but Harry could burble, and launched a sequence of drooly trills as he pondered Al before waddling off in a courtly manner with his hand in his attendant's.

Marian. Lucy. And, thank God, Harry. Al caught a glimpse of a handsome man in a business suit claiming the child. She had a moment to clear her throat, loosen the damp hair from the back of her neck, unfurl. The back door opened; an inviting wedge of sunlight appeared on the floor ahead of her, wavered and disappeared. Al remembered the Lilybanks garden.

She heard Lucy returning and pretended to be casually admiring the ceiling's carved molding. A crack in the plaster above her crept jaggedly toward the chandelier. She'd not noticed it on tours.

"I try to think of it as wabi-sabi," Lucy said, following Al's gaze. "I'm sorry there was no one to meet you at the door. The children leave at one; it's kind of a mad dash. Lucy Murgatroyd." She extended a hand robustly. Al was surprised by its fragility. She was immediately taken by the pretty young woman's soft voice, bouncing cap of dark brown hair with bangs, and red rubber boots up to the knees of her jeans. An artist, she thought.

"I'm Althea Athnos." She usually said "Althea, Althea Athnos" to let the three syllables sink in, but Lucy Murgatroyd seemed capable of more. "It must've been Marian I spoke with on the phone? About the ad. She said to come at one."

"Well, I've still got stragglers to attend to down here, so I'll send you up on your own..." Lucy put her arm around Al in a way Al hoped was comradely rather than sympathetic, and steered her back up the hall.

"Turn right at the top. Then it's a way to the first door on the left. You'll see a bench. Good luck! Don't let her scare you. If Lilybanks is a good fit for you, she'll catch on." The encouragement sounded genuine. Al gave her a brave smile and patted her forearm in silent thanks. She proceeded up the familiar staircase regally, not deigning to use the banister.

How could Lilybanks not be a good fit for her?

Every door on the second floor was shut, creating an unexpectedly dour effect but for the bank of windows ahead of her at the far end of the hall, beyond which shone buoyant blue sky.

"You'll be Althea. Welcome. I'm Marian."

The door had opened so suddenly, and the woman was so obscured by the light behind her that Althea received a sense of immateriality, not entirely agreeable.

"Nice to meet you," she said, regretting the limpness of the phrase yet impatient with the awkward moment, not of her own making.

"Do come in." A fuzzy arm extended, and Al preceded it into the spacious, book-lined den she'd periodically savored. A parchment brown version of William Morris's "Marigold" papered what little of the walls weren't covered by bookshelves. (Al had happily overspent to acquire a set of sheets and pillowcases in the green pattern.) Somewhat disarmed by the heavy breathing and mutters behind her ("That's right!...Here we are..."), Al got as far as the sprawling library table and turned around.

The apparent mistress of her fate was mildly goggle-eyed, thickset and lumpy, with patches of red on her skin and the kind of haphazard short grey hair Al could only endure in jail. The eyes that met hers were pale blue-grey behind oval silver frames, the smile benign. Althea anticipated brilliance.

"Let's sit by the window. The table's for my undergrads. Helps keep them awake." Beyond the table a pair of rockers faced each other across a window seat, on which lay china and a tasseled tea-cozy, somewhat askew. Through the diamond panes of the dormer windows Al spotted the storybook weathervane and the faded garden. She waited politely.

"Either chair, help yourself." Al seized on the one with the limp old poppy-embroidered cushion, though it looked different than she'd recalled. If the choked gurgles coming from the radiator behind the door indicated the heat was on, it had yet to contend with the draft from the windows.

Marian bent over the tea. Her shapeless, lead-colored dress was badly creased in back as though she'd been sitting all day; a white hanky peeked out from a sleeve of the sweater.

"Rosehip. Will you have sugar? I've stopped bringing up honey. Treacherous stuff for books and papers." Her breath was labored but the hand that lifted the saucer was steady. She poured her own cup, settled in. Al discovered her tea was room-temperature.

"You've just lost your husband. I'm so sorry. I lost my own five years ago. December 21, 2006. Massive heart attack, no warning."

"Mine had a brain aneurism, they said. I found him on the kitchen floor. Gone."

"Oh, my dear. It's so disorienting, isn't it? Besides the grief and the shock, I mean. One's small world suddenly unrecognizable."

One's small world. If only she could keep her beloved little world. But here was a glimpse of rapport, at least in theory.

"Perhaps it's just as well that I have to sell the house." (Every time she said it she thought of the cotton wadding her dentist used, insulating her from the effect of the words "have to sell...husband died...") "Since everything's going to be new anyway." (Of course it wasn't just as well, but she couldn't expect to make a favorable impression by revealing the depth of her reluctance.)

"Have you family nearby?"

Though Marian looked solicitous, Al bridled.

"Only a cousin, in Connecticut. I won't be penniless after the house is sold. Just unable to afford more than a modest apartment." Discarding strategy she found herself adding, "By the way, I have a cat. From whom I won't be parted. Would that be a problem?" She was at the dentist's again, rubber-lipped.

"A cat. I suppose it has its claws?"

"Yes, but she's trained to use scratching posts. She's very good about it, actually...I wouldn't want her here myself if I thought she'd damage things."

"Well, we have a rabbit, two box turtles and a deaf old dog. No doubt a courteous cat could be accommodated. I think the question will be, rather, can you put up with us, Althea? As the ad says, our "housemate" will need to be quite adaptable. Are you prepared to take on a hostile, homesick three-year-old at six in the morning? Some of our clients have to drop off their children well before school starts. There is the rare diaper to be negotiated." (Althea thought she saw a suppressed shudder.) "Can you share a bathroom with two other women? Lucy forgets to knock or lock the door; my niece practices piping cupcakes with the toothpaste; a turtle occasionally requires detention in the tub. The house has been in my family's possession since it was built, but it's also part of Rutledge's public heritage. We are visited by Arts and Crafts enthusiasts and scholars from all over the country – even from Great Britain (and a fellow from Finland!) – during our annual house tour. The murals, for instance, are unique. None of us wants the life to go out of Lilybanks. It is above all a home. But there are inevitably moments when one feels the responsibility. In addition, there are the inconveniences encountered in any old house that hasn't been modernized much. Drafts, antiquated plumbing, sticky windows... And we live rather simply here. No television, no dishwasher. Minimal air conditioning; I was forced to make that concession the summer before last. I was afraid we'd lose Aphrodite. (And the girls worried about me.) I was also persuaded to allow the necessary arrangements for Lucy's computer – alas, no bungalow is an island, Mrs. Athnos. Althea. I do feel strongly that someone addicted to the bells and whistles of modern technology would not be a compatible Lilybanker."

Althea, who had been squirming with earnestness to reveal her exceptional suitability (even beyond what she'd foreseen) stood up – ostensibly to return her cup and saucer to the window seat – to seize her chance before the monologue passed her by.

"Marian! My husband used to call me a natural-born Luddite. We never had a microwave. I find dishwashers alarming." (She wanted to say, "I can barely drive," but refrained.) "I've enjoyed the Lilybanks tour at least five times. My own house was built in 1905. Casper re-wired it but we didn't add so much as a doorbell. I've been a vegetarian for nearly twenty years, as was my husband. I answered your ad because it sounded like a strikingly good fit." Calculating that the crest of the wave was the best point at which to mention a qualm, she sat back down, crossing a leg in what she meant to be a relaxed, confident manner while holding Marian's gaze.

"I'm quite fond of children but I'd like to know more about the responsibilities of the aide you need. I take it the new housemate would be Lucy's helper rather than unassisted?" (Stuck with a dozen or more anarchical brats – throwing oneself between them and the glazed dadoes, prying their sticky fingers off fistfuls of vintage lace curtain while their parents fortified their stock portfolios.)

Marian listened intently, taking Al in as though attending to her was the only concern of the day. One would have thought, from her relaxed, interested countenance, that Marian harbored no bias about who she wanted the housemate to be, beyond the situation's require-ments. Al found this disconcerting. Used to being overlooked, she expected a personal expression of delight from Marian, an overture of friendship, in response to her special traits (appropriate, for once).

"Lucy will join us shortly. You met downstairs? She's most in-volved with the children. I am the titular head of the daycare pro-gram, responsible for the paperwork, the maintenance of its 'prestige,' if you will," (Marian smiled with amusement) "in the community. Lucy is a marvel with the children – of whom we enjoy nine at the moment. She is a trained Waldorf teacher and gives afternoon classes in dance and art at Stubblefield Waldorf School. Lucy has given our little program much of its charm. The Waldorf emphasis on spiritu-ality, art and nature is a perfect match for Lilybanks." (Al nodded, warbled, mimed her emphatic agreement.) "We call ourselves 'Kinder on Corrie' because the German word for children's so suitable for Waldorf – founded in Germany, you know – but every business imaginable was already Kindersomething. Nothing left but Kinderturds, as Lucy says. So we hit on our play of words. After all, we do try to be kinder!" Bewildered, Al felt her smile deflating.

"I am of course always on hand, though Lucy copes wonderfully. My niece helps when available, but her commitment must be to her own studies. Our new assistant will not be expected to work solo, Althea. However, someone needs to be on duty at six a.m. when the earliest of our clients arrives. A matter of babysitting, really, until we officially begin our morning at Lilybanks. Are you able to keep early hours?"

"I'm always up by five," Al deadpanned, unwilling to wag her tail and pant again.

"Really. We have found our little hive quite invigorating. As a cooperative effort I must say it is a success. However, we must all be willing to step into the breach at any moment. The daycare program provides our daily bread." Marian sounded just a little sober.

It occurred to Al for the first time that Lilybanks might need rescuing as badly as she did. She'd missed cookies with tea.

"How old are you, Althea?"

"Fifty-seven." She regretted her grade-school promptness.

"I'm seventy. Marian looked out into the garden. "To have at least one foot on the path to old age...to have suddenly lost a great part of one's world...it's a gift, Althea." She looked back towards Al and smiled. "Possess it. Untie the fearsome ribbons; encounter your secret calling."

Al felt her smile stiffen. Perhaps Marian was a lesbian. Or – yes, here it comes, she thought: the spiritual stuff. They'd want her to spend her afternoons in saffron robes, chanting on street corners to the accompaniment of finger cymbals. But that was *passé*. Perhaps they'd ask her to contribute her life savings toward some real estate scheme, a sacrifice at the altar of prosperity consciousness and Positive Thinking. Her purse leaned safely against her chair. It contained seven dollars.

"Are you familiar with Eckhart Tolle?"

Althea recalled a photo of a neatly bearded man with a benignly elvish face. One of those New Age gurus, probably a charlatan. A borrowed name, no doubt.

"Only very vaguely. Something to do with New Age spirituality, I think?" It could be far worse. A nudist ashram. Scientology.

"One might call it that." Marian looked merry, which became her. *"The Power of Now*, mentioned in our want ad, is the title of a book Eckhart wrote."[2]

Annoyed by her apparent negligence, Al reflected that she might have dashed to the library to cram, had they only underlined the title properly. ("Must share cooking, etc. and The Power of Now." She'd thought it a mere vagary.)

"Ah. I wondered what that referred to..."

Marian giggled. The red patches got darker. Al began to feel mirthful, too. She allowed herself a friendly crinkle. If she laughed she'd probably cry.

"Is the book easy to find?"

"I'll lend you a copy." Marian trudged across the room and pulled a dog-eared paperback off a stack on a shelf. Al received the odd impression that there was nothing in the world Marian would rather do than fetch the book, yet there was no personal eagerness, no messy egotism involved. Marian looked peaceful.

"The teaching in this book has become the essence of our lives here at Lilybanks. We think of ourselves as a sisterhood, members of a contemplative order. It's our great hope that any new housemate would be open to the study and practice of its truths. You look apprehensive, my dear! Perhaps it sounds disingenuous, but the teachings are very old, and not incompatible with one's religion – at least, what's worth keeping of one's religion."

Al liked Marian's twinkling gravity, but suddenly felt very tired. Tired of daylight, tired of memories, tired of trying not to look "apprehensive." She summoned a worldly smile.

"Oh, don't worry. I'm not narrow and rabid. I joined my husband's church when we married. Eastern Orthodox. Very beautiful, though some of it never really 'took.'" Al made quotation marks with her fingers in the air. "We certainly didn't attend every Sunday..." She felt she was in elementary school again. "I guess I'd say I'm a wobbly Christian. I like some of the Buddhist ideas." (How fatuous.) A line from the Orthodox prayer before communion drifted by: "I will not speak of Thy mysteries to Thine enemies." Unwilling to betray whatever had kept her going for the past three weeks, she blurted, "I do believe in God. God's love." She sat up straighter, dared to look Marian in the eyes at length.

"I know you do, my friend. Tolle's book is just a compelling, contemporary version of the Perennial Philosophy, Althea. Christian mystics, Buddha, some of our greatest writers have shared these same insights through the ages."

"*The Perennial Philosophy* by Aldous Huxley! One of my favorite books in college. I think I still have a copy somewhere..."

Marian handed her the paperback. Al took it respectfully, not really minding the sensation of being a clever dog receiving a biscuit.

"I'll be interested in your impressions. So you enjoy old houses, Althea. Five tours put you on nearly an intimate footing with Lilybanks! Calla Morrissey was my grandmother. Such a -"

Someone knocked on the door; Lucy's shining cap of hair tilted around the door.

"Come in, Lucy."

She bounced in, miming circumspection and clasping three mugs to the stained front of her white sweatshirt. Baggies of pretzels and something that looked like chunky Lucite jewelry hung from her belt loops. Al saw Lucy's attraction for preschoolers; she needed only a hardhat to resemble a sort of Lego telephone line repairman.

"I think I forgot to have breakfast." Lucy hoisted a chair from the library table and settled between them, not quite dropping any of the mugs.

"Pretzels, or gummy bears, or both? I promise they're fresh from the pantry. Not retrieved from under tiny chairs, not sneezed on, not groped."

"Oh, both, please," answered Al, feeling reckless. Lucy handed her a brimming mug with alternating layers of bears and pretzels like a parfait.

"Actually, they taste good eaten together. Have you ever tried salting a piece of orange?"

"Althea has been on *five* tours of Lilybanks, Lucy. No thank you."

"That's great! You can retrieve me when I get lost." Her hands shook a bit as she composed a bear and pretzel twist sandwich. Al wondered what anyone so sweetly pretty could have to be nervous about.

"Lucy, don't budge. I'll go see if Beebe's available."

Lucy waited for the footsteps to fade, then smiled at her.

"That means you're a viable candidate. The unsuitables don't get as far as Beebe. Have you read Eckhart?" She nodded at the book in Al's lap.

"Not at all. But I will, immediately." (If I make it past "Beebe," she reflected.) "So the daycare program's doing well?"

"Well, we're trendy, at least among the more relaxed parents who didn't sign their children up for a fast-track college prep preschool as soon as they got pregnant. A lot of our parents are professors or grad students, or artistic types. Some of the kids will go on to Stubblefield. And some are 'special needs' kids. Refugees from more standard daycare programs."

Al decided she was too recently widowed to feign insouciance about problem children.

"It's not grim, Althea. I promise. You could do it. I don't know if we're right for you, but don't let the daycare work scare you off if everything else seems attractive. Could you pass the teapot?"

Someone pulled open a second door from an adjoining room. Unnerved, Al realized she'd actually felt comfortable for the last twenty seconds or so.

"Go ahead." Lucy took Al's mug and nodded toward the next room.

Al proceeded, to find the tallest and most beautiful of the Munchkins smiling up at her benevolently and extending a gracious hand.

"Please come in. I'm Beebe Morrissey. A pleasure to meet you."

"Althea Athnos." She felt herself on the verge of hysterics. The laughing kind, this time.

The enchanted expanse of the famous Millefleurs Mural Room waited in abeyance as the radiant, elfin person searched her face. Al was too captivated to feel foolish. She remembered a pale, intense child with painfully tight braids brooding discomfitingly in a bedroom corner on a tour or two. But this seemed to be a young woman, in spite of the prim, old-fashioned dress.

The quaint creature turned and walked toward the nearest of the Mural Room's latticed windows, where a decaying, disagreeably theatrical old harp presided, taller than herself. She bent, collected a package and returned to Al, who was only momentarily disconcerted to find she was being handed a turtle. She grasped the hinged casket long enough to admire the mottled amber carapace, then returned it to the floor.

"'All the king's horses and all the king's men,' you know."

Although Al could feel Marian waiting across the room, they both crouched to watch the turtle. Eventually glowing red eyes peeked out from its cowl. It took a few hesitant steps on the polished marquetry before Beebe plucked it up to deposit tenderly in a basket in an empty fireplace.

"Clumber lives in Lucy's room. He'll be alright here for the time being," she said, reading the doubt on Al's face.

Lucy had followed with the remains of their preschool feast. She waved to Al from an oasis of dark settles and Morris chairs across the marquetry desert on which Calla Morrissey had capered for guests. For a moment Al was at the Lindstadt Family Funeral Home, crossing an acre of beige carpeting to reach the plush settee and chairs from which her dutiful cousin signaled. But no, she was walking through familiar woods, embraced by dark trees and verdant banks of wildflowers. The undergrowth concealed a dreamlike miscellany of creatures who welcomed her trustfully or continued their gambols through the patterned tangles. And here was – what was her name? – Marian, eyeing her with her cousin's expectation that she'd get lost on her way across a room.

"Please feel free to explore the murals at length after we finish chatting, Althea. Impossible to take it all in on a tour." Marian patted the place on the settle next to her, which Al assumed docilely.

Beebe Morrissey now peered at her from the sloping depths of a chair with armrests like planks, her Mary Janes protruding stiffly ahead of her. Al felt an unexpected flicker of antipathy. It would be indelicate to ask the girl's age; perhaps she suffered from a hormonal imbalance.

"Althea has only just now encountered Eckhart Tolle, Beebe. I've lent her *The Power of Now*. Althea *is* familiar with Huxley's book on the Perennial Philosophy. Perhaps you'd share with us a little about your spiritual path, Althea? Please don't feel you're being tested. Living with the perception of divine truth is a matter of grace, and then of willingness, surely, rather than memberships or erudition?" Al nodded. "As for myself, I used to be Episcopalian, with quite a bit of mysticism tucked in around the edges," Marian smiled gaily. "My late husband was an Englishman – Church of England – whom I met at Oxford. Eventually we were both tenured here at Rutledge, teaching English literature with emphasis on the mystical thread – the Metaphysical poets, Wordsworth, Traherne, (oh, *dear* Traherne), Hopkins; we parleyed with the philosophy and religion departments to create marvelous seminars; a select handful of students did doctoral work with us. Why, our summer field trips..." The self-satisfied, glazed animation was throttled; Marian unapologetically returned to the matter at hand. "Mr. Tolle's teachings are consonant with the ancient truths of the world's religions, Althea. Your Christianity may seem clarified. Buddhism is particularly harmonious with – ah, but I'll let you speak, my dear."

"Well...I don't know if we should refer to 'my Christianity'; my affiliation is fraught with ambivalence..." She heard herself mimicking Marian. "I've been interested in mysticism in the broad, 'Perennial Philosophy' sense since my college days, but I never seem able to go anywhere with it...As for Buddhism, I attended a ten-day crash course in meditation at a rural retreat center a couple of years ago, more out of curiosity than commitment. No talking allowed, no medications, no sugar, and no leaving!" Marian's eyebrows rose; Lucy stopped munching; Beebe leaned forward, giving the impression of watching Al through her shoes.

"Once I got through the worst of the paranoia brought on by low blood sugar and 'trapped' feelings I began to make small progress. By day five or so I'd actually experienced a period of alert presence free of all my idiotic thoughts. It lasted maybe five minutes? Less? Such a relief, and pleasure. Wild geese flew over the building and I met their calls as though we were on equal terms...except there was no 'I.' That's how it felt.

"Well, that was the best of it. A few days later gunshots broke out during meditation. I figured it had to be hunting. I HATE hunting. And in the middle of a meditation center? It went through me like a knife – to have that open, reverent silence and space violated.

"And then to realize that no one else was interrupted. No one budged! It could have been some nut on a rampage. I had to ask myself if that kind of passivity was what I sought, and the answer was no. I went outside. A couple of men with rifles were shooting into a corn-field beyond the retreat center's fence. I broke silence and was told the men belonged to a gun club and were just shooting into the field to get the rabbits moving." Al began to feel she'd been carried away from her subject and was too tired to care.

"I was told no one had ever complained before. To this day I won-der if the situation was being downplayed so their headquarters out east didn't get word of an ongoing problem. Probably the staff mem-ber was just telling the truth. I think a number of the people were there to increase their productivity at work."

"My dear. How interesting that you were met with such a con-summate challenge, custom-made, as it were. Most auspicious. Most expeditious."

That seemed complimentary, if opaque. She was ready to go home, tired. Perhaps they'd let her look at the murals when she returned the book...

Beebe scrambled over and clutched her shoulder, too tightly.

"Althea, could you get me the address or phone number for that place?"

Startled, and fraying, Al was on the verge of an unfortunate ges-ture when she realized Beebe was all tender earnestness.

"A lot of my papers are boxed up right now. But I'll get it for you, Beebe."

Lucy and Marian looked at each other.

"Althea, this has been lovely. I look forward to chatting with you again. Very generous of you to share your time with us in the midst of your upheaval...We hope to bring these interviews to a close within the week; I'm sure everyone involved would like the question settled soon."

Al found herself being strolled across the marquetry between

Marian and Lucy. She caught a glimpse of Beebe's back as the girl crouched by the fireplace.

In a moment she was at the bus stop, blinking in the sun and trying not to eat the last of the gummy bears Lucy'd thrust upon her for fear of smearing *The Power of Now*.

The bus was nearly empty, and unseasonably air-conditioned. Althea shriveled into her corner, drained. She envisioned spaghetti, her favorite supper since childhood, in bed with Linnet draped over her knees.

On her walk up Euclid Street she saw the realtor's Velveeta-colored Hummer parked in front of the house. A man in a long-sleeved white shirt occupied her yard, looking up at the second story with his hands on his hips. Her front door opened. A woman emerged, calling down from the steps to the white shirt. Althea imagined Linnet immobilized in the deepest corner of an upstairs closet, from which not even Althea could pry her for at least an hour after the prospective buyers' departure.

She retreated to the public library around the corner, reflecting that her presence was of no use anyway. She couldn't answer the most basic questions – how much did the heating cost? – how old was the roofing? This would be noted, along with her tense unfriendliness. There'd be a rush to erase traces of her.

She felt insubstantial walking down the sidewalk, a husk full of loud, distracting thoughts and feelings. Shame, hostility, envy, sardonic judgements crashed and boomed importantly. For one dizzy moment in the library reading room she sensed the sheer terror of annihilation they disguised.

Priorities

"'Hence in a season of calm weather though inland far – ' OW! Sorry." Her fault for not seeing the little rock in time. She forgave her foot, accepting its limitations. Some day her feet would be as meek and leathery as Blessed Katerina's who wore sandals in January when she slept in streetcars with a squirming nest of abandoned, frostbitten kittens inside her bodice, tickling her armpits.

"'...though inland far we be, our souls have sight of that immortal sea which brought us hither...'"[3] Between and beneath Wordsworth's lines she listened to the silence, the crunchy padding of her feet, the swoosh of the air running past her ears as she parted it like water. Hearing a distant growl, she turned to find one of Moraine Woods' dusty green pick-ups approaching.

"Howdy, Beebe!" Roger Smeltzer's boxy shoulders and Santa Claus beard came into view. She moved onto the stubbly, fresh-mown shoulder and waited for him to stop.

"Hi, Mr. Smeltzer! I've been hoping to see you! The day before yesterday I was rounding a curve up on that ridge where all the honeysuckle grows, and a dark brown animal like a ferret only not so skinny darted across the path. Was it a mink, do you think?"

"You're right, Beebe, I'm sure that's just what it was. We've got plenty of 'em, but they're stealthy. Rare to see one." He looked at her approvingly.

"I think the wooly bears have started cruising, Mr. Smeltzer. I've seen two of them on the road in the past five minutes." She hoped he would take the hint, wincing at the vision of the damage his tires might inflict on his way back to headquarters. They'd had several debates about the effect of traffic on tiny native pilgrimages already.

"Well, it's that time of year. About the end of the barefoot season, too, wouldn't you think?" he parried. Beebe grinned; he took his foot off the brake and gave her a comradely wave. There was a name for all that; he'd looked it up. Jainism. What could you expect, growing up in a haunted house with no parents. "Home schooled." Of course, it was in her genes; her great-grandma's meddlesome will was the reason he had to run around with a dart gun, shooting up does with contraceptives. All the same, he didn't like to see 'em starve.

Feeling professional, Beebe left the road for the increasingly mushy terrain bordering a fen, beyond which glittered the extravagant midnight blue waters of Lake Defiance. A blackbird abandoned its outpost among the straw-colored reeds and fat, sausage-y cattails leaking their stuffing. "You're right, Beebe." She loved the way Mr. Smeltzer's thick, sunburnt forearm crooked over his open window when he stopped to talk.

She dabbled her hands in the cold, marshy soup to clear her mind; as she crouched she felt the bottom of her dress grow heavier. A world of striated satiny canes, jointed weeds bearing faded pennants, seedy tassels, crazed, bent networks of spent stems above rotting submerged disintegration met her gaze. Each tiny element was substantial in its own sphere, each brittle fracture, airborne release or descent into shadow an event of consequence. It all shone with importance and an unpredictable, unsanctioned grace and rightness – a sort of perfection – when she paid attention. She liked to tune into that fuzzy but increasingly coherent channel whereby the dance inside all this stuff pulsed in her and all around her...Beebe realized her toes were growing numb in the squelching, fibrous sediment and lurched back through the harsh canes and scum to the higher ground by the roadside.

She threw her backpack down among the first trees that framed a glimpse of the lake's dark brilliance and screened her from the trail. Ignoring her sodden skirt, Beebe curled up against an oak and pulled her aged Tupperware out from under the shoes in her pack. She had the last two mealy potatoes from the daycare garden project and a fistful of lanky, bolted arugula with pale flowers, overlooked that summer. The potatoes had a musty, mushroomy taste; the bitter deckled greens, she reflected, might as well be elm leaves. A really excellent meal. Sometimes Beebe devoured a whole carton of spinach, or thick rubber-banded sheaves of collards or chard. She imagined green and molten silver running along her veins. The raw, peppery cud that stung her gums and tongue made her gag. Always she thanked the plants and asked their pardon. When she died the toilers underground might mistake her for a rhododendron.

*   *   *

That evening Beebe continued *The Cats of Lilac Corner*, pulling the bedclothes up to her chin to compensate for the temperamental radiator:

"Blacky! Cinnamon!" Mrs. Bunting knelt under the mock oranges with a pitcher full of sops. Every day at noon she appeared along the side of the house with lunch for "the girls."

They'd been born underneath her Florida room, after all. If she'd been bolder and harder of heart she'd have taken the four kittens from their mother when they were still young enough to tame. She could have found them real homes. Instead, by the time she'd made up her mind to it they were all confirmed savages, just so many little windborne tumbleweeds frisking in and out of the Buntings' picket fence and vanishing at the first Bunting footfall or rasp of the screen door's hinge.

By mid-October's chill two of the youngsters seemed to have struck out for new territory. But the impish black one with round yellow eyes like buttons sewn on just a tad unevenly and her shy tortoiseshell sister (Mrs. B. was sure they were girls) claimed their wandering mother's nest. She'd had Mr. Bunting stuff a couple of crates with clean straw and shove them through a hatch into the dark earth-floored chamber beneath the front of the house where he stored bits of lumber.

The wild cats had taken it over, squeezing through a couple of shallow holes along the foundation. All winter Mrs. B. brought them bowls of warm water at first light. During the February blizzard she'd had to shovel them out. How sweet to watch them sunbathing in the side yard among the snowdrops!

And now with summer nearly here Cinnamon had gone missing.

Oh, she'd seen them prowling all over the neighborhood, both headed in the same direction. Blacky and Cinnamon came and went, eluding the collie and the children; Mrs. B. hadn't time to dillydally by the window all day. But they most always showed up for their lunch, lurking in the shrubbery when the sun was highest until she came out.

Here was Blacky, without her sister for the fourth day in a row.

"Where's your sister, Miss?" The little she-cat barely glanced at her, wolfing down the crusts and milk that spattered her tiny triangular chin. But Mrs. Bunting had seen her keeping vigil in the side yard's bluebells, facing southwest, the two young cats' favorite route. She imagined watchdogs, motorcars, slingshots. She thought of her cat Benny, mistaken for a raccoon four years ago this autumn.

On her way back indoors she forgot to beckon chummily to Bezique, who supervised from a dining room window. He winced, hoping his charming outdoor acquaintance hadn't noticed. When Mrs. B. had begun serving the two young ladies luncheon a few months ago, Bezique had watched possessively from the window, beheading potted primroses with his lashing tail. When his mistress returned he sniffed the hem of her skirt jealously, outraged at the unauthorized loan of her tender ministrations.

Whenever the blossoming kittens appeared in the side yard Bezique interrupted Mrs. B. for a ride in her arms, meowing plaintively at her feet and attempting irresistible little hops until she pulled him onto her shoulder, floury hands or no. As she danced him around the dining room he made sure to lavish her with particular attentions beside the window, frantically running his cheeks along hers, labeling her with his choicest signature musk and looking back over his shoulder to make sure the upstarts were impressed. Mrs. B., always easily trained, soon learned to oblige him, bearing him to and fro in front of windows as he perched regally on her arm. The kittens ignored them.

It had been surprisingly difficult to attract the dashing cricket's attention once Bezique decided she was worthy of his. He fancied the sunlight's reflections on the windowpanes dazzled her eyes, or perhaps his dark form was camouflaged in the dim room. He began to feel lonely. She was usually absorbed in some game of her own – romping through the tulips, scaling a tree – or sparring with her more decorous sister. As a last resort today Bezique ventured a soft but urgent salute through the window screen.

The young she-cat took one last, unhurried lick at a black glove and turned her head towards the window. Once he had her attention Bezique didn't know what more to do with it. Considering that any mark of interest from him should inspire an enthusiastic response, he waited. She merely stared up at the window. A breeze ruffled the fur on her chest most flatteringly.

The longer she looked at him, self-assured, mildly curious, the less privileged his lofty seat behind the window screen seemed to Bezique. When she finally rose and walked closer, cordial but hardly deferential, his regret at not being able to move closer himself was sharper than any bird or mocking squirrel had ever wrung from him.

Freeborn little minx! The notion of his superior status rankled; he cast it off. She'd come so near he could see light glancing off the dainty feelers above her eyes.

"Come play?" Her voice was tangy and wild like the frilly salad greens the girls tried to fob off on Delilah under the table. He abandoned all but a few shreds of dignity.

"Not now. Soon, though." Bezique paced back and forth between the window ledge and Mrs. B.'s terra cotta pots, thrashing his tail, rubbing his chin furiously against the window frame in a turbulent attempt to cast his scent on the breeze.

He regretted his abandon when he looked down again, for she seemed a bit unnerved. Her fur had plumped up as though she were chilled, making her round amber eyes smaller and more drolly intense than ever; she looked as though she might wheel away any moment. Contrite, Bezique reflected on what a youngster she was, after all. He groped for some impersonal, levelheaded remark.

"Lovely day." He thought he heard Snowy snort somewhere to his rear.

"My sister is lost." She stopped herself in the middle of a forlorn, involuntary mew, then gazed into the distance in the direction of those expeditions he'd watched her troop off on through neighboring yards and fields with the secretive tortoiseshell.

"Perhaps she'll return soon," he said in his kindest tones, and blinked reassurance when she turned to search his face. She took a few flustered licks at a shoulder.

"You'll be alright. My human will see to it. A safe place. Food. Always."

She watched him, unmoved.

"I'll help you search."

She boxed at a fluttering ivy leaf on the wall beneath him; he couldn't see her face. When she resumed her seat Bezique thought he detected a mirthful glint. His ears flattened just a trifle; he examined a paw.

"You'd get lost," she piped up to him in a matter-of-fact tone.

He threw himself into a thorough manicure. Hard-boiled brat. All that pathetic self-sufficiency had sucked the sweetness right out of her. He nibbled the tender skin between each claw, ignoring her. Lost? He had a superb inner compass, by day or darkest night. The idea. He started in on the other paw. He'd grown up here, surveyed the territory from every possible window – yards, sheds, gardens, fields, roads, woods...He flexed the unsheathed claws, keen, clean, perfect. Well of course he'd get lost.

He glanced down at her as he maneuvered his tail, intending to groom it exhaustively. She had a pretty way of sitting, with her trim, soldierly boots snugly together, especially appealing when one knew she might prance away or frolic at any moment. Bother his tail. He drew himself up elegantly.

"Very well then, I'd get lost. And when I was done being lost I'd take command of the situation. I think you'd find there are advantages to being with someone who knows his way around the humans. Do you think I couldn't get outside if I chose? Think again. It's a matter of priorities, of loyalty. Of...love. They rely on me. And another thing: you think we're pampered in here? Lax? Why, I'd put my money on a well-fed, self-disciplined, cosmopolitan house cat over some flea-bitten one-eyed exhausted Tom any day. I happen to be in superb physical –" She rolled over and over in the grass, stretched, trotted back and stood on her hind legs, braced against the house below him. She gazed at him with delight.

"Come soon."

"Yes. What's your name?"

"My mother called me 'Gypsy.'"

"My name is Bezique. A word from across the ocean, I believe."

She looked baffled, but intrigued.

"I'll go now, Bah-seek. Come very soon. You'll see why the matter is urgent." She searched his face a moment and slipped between the pickets.

'Bah-seek.' Had a sort of tribal grandeur to it. "Gypsy"? He might have guessed. Quite charming. He soared through the primroses onto the dining room rug, landing nose-to-nose with a formidably puffed-up Snowy lashing her tail like a scythe.

"Priorities! Loyalty! That sly-boots bats her eyes at you and you're ready to abandon your post to wrestle with a pack of ragamuffins in the dandelions! You'll break our mistress's heart. Wait till Applesauce hears about this! He'll take your place on

Mrs. B.'s bed. And I'll be left to fend off the big, trampling clod all by myself. You're a cad, Bezique Bunting."

He licked her forehead. Operatic temperaments required management.

"Now Snowy, she needs our help. Her sister's disappeared. Imagine. Who will she snuggle with on winter nights? How will she face down Toms all by herself? It's serious, Snowy. She's been putting a brave face on it but I think the little thing's going to pieces. It's no joke, being on your own out there. She needs counsel. Her sister's got to be found. Why, she might be just a few back yards away, accidentally locked in someone's tool shed, too scared to meow. Mrs. B. is already upset about it. You heard her sniffling. Even Delilah knows what's wrong...Those outdoor cats think we're mollycoddled, Snowy. I'll show them. But I need your help."

She wheeled away petulantly.

"If you think I'm going to wander around in circles picking up burrs and fleas until I get treed by some drooling hound dog –"

Bezique followed her, assuming a conspiratorial tone.

"I need someone I can trust to keep an eye on things while I'm out on missions, Snowy. Applesauce will be too busy eating and sleeping. Delilah's an open book – couldn't keep a secret to save a soup bone. You'll have to monitor all the windows (well, all the ones you can reach), receive and transmit important messages, assist my getaways, and rally demoralized spirits."

"Flattery will get you nowhere with *me*!" Snowy assumed a pose under Mrs. B.'s favorite fern, wrapping her plumy tail around her paws. Its tip twitched as she considered the proposal.

"Please, Snowy? I think we have to help."

"Just promise me one thing."

"What's that?"

"Promise you'll come back, Bezique."

*   *   *

"Promise you'll come back, Beebe!"

Mr. Smeltzer, Gloria and Tad, elbowing each other in the doorway of the Maven Street bakery, waved to her with toothy grins. Who'd have thought Mr. Smeltzer would want to run a patisserie? Tad hopped up and down, brandishing a long-handled wooden spoon, his towering white headgear tilting like an airport windsock. They'd kindly packed a briefcase full of croissants for her hike to Tibet.

When the book smacked the floor Beebe woke up long enough to rescue it, tug at the lamp chain and snuggle back under the covers. The croissants seemed to be tuna fish sandwiches, but she could give them to Bezique...

3

Artistically Inclined
[1911]

"Glory be."

Golden light winked through tiers of flouncing foliage, dappling the woodland floor with quivering constellations. Spring's greens, tender, keen, and gaudy, unfurled around them. Shuddering leaves and bird trill barely plumbed the depths of still silence. A fragrance like that shed by some passing goddess's trailing robes flirted on the breeze. Hebe.

"Didn't know you went in for nature, Fred." Apparently even plotting anarchists responded to the ancient spell of the Garden.

"No need to be arch. Two thousand acres of this, you say. For a couple of your parasites."

"My parasites keep us in the style to which you've become accustomed. Wheels likely to get mired if we go up any further. You may as well go into town, loiter around the university. Study up on your Greek or something."

The elegantly older man balanced an oversized portfolio on the roof of the Peerless, bent and pulled a chauffeur's cap from the front seat. He thrust it at Fred with a dry, not unaffectionate laugh and tucked his papers back under an arm.

"Come back in, say, two hours."

Jamming the cap down over his red curls with a mirthless smile,

Fred lavished three seconds of observation upon his employer's departure. Stooped, powerful shoulders beneath the affectedly wide-brimmed hat. Beak already red in the sharp air. The customary narrow coat (merino in winter, linen for the seaside,) its deep pleat wrung from his tailor in style or not to accommodate the long stride.

The engine ignited more savagely than necessary behind him, but Crumrind gazed tranquilly up the wooded hill. He approved the raw footpath; the Morrisseys had honored his insistence on taking charge of the approach to the house, the driveway, the walks. He hoped to make this property something of a showcase. These clients were providentially young and malleable.

Not that the wife hadn't displayed some mettle during their meetings in the city. The echoing, "intimate" conference room in her husband's bank provided a pompous gilt frame for the pretty Californian's soliloquies on simplicity, honesty and the arts' communion with nature. After several too many of her charmingly interruptive little lectures to him over the preliminary blueprints, he'd wanted to roll her up *au naturel* in a Navajo blanket with a hand-plaited basket over her head and ship her back to San Francisco's smoky, bourgeoning ruins by a slow boat.

Crumrind's formula for diverting artistically inclined wives sacrificed some insignificant room on the second story to their frenzied ministrations. He and his assistant Merrick Field had worked a few of these shrines into blueprints in the wake of firmly warbled predilections for flocked wallpaper or statuary in niches. Mrs. Morrissey would have to be dealt with more skillfully. He intended her home to be a diadem of harmony and restraint crowning Hebe's rustic brow, this wooded hill set above a counterpane of fields, orchard, fen, oak groves and a steely jewel of a little lake...Lake Defiance, the locals called it. His tribute to fecund four-season Eden in Illinois, the property would reign chastely over the university below and a populace of growing families and prospering academics eager for tasteful homes.

Mrs. Morrissey's leanings were not antipathetic to his own. It might suffice to get her interested in weaving. He imagined her expending some of that earnest energy on the intricacies of a mammoth hand-loom purchased with some of First Trust and Savings' profits. Perhaps a titanic tapestry requiring years of labor – he'd mention Burne-Jones...

By now the haunting floral fragrance assaulted him on every side; he felt a sinus in his temple twinge. Liles-of-the-valley at their zenith lay on both sides of the path and carpeted the incline right up to the roots of the oaks and their understory of viburnum and sylphlike redbuds. Exquisite; he congratulated himself on self-control when Merrick revealed the machinations undertaken to honor Mrs. Morrissey's plea that the little flowers not be violated during construction. Now he wished he'd kept Fred up here to hunt for a pink lily-of-the-valley sport for the Pratts' conservatory.

Crum's heart jumped at the first glimpse of his house's dark hull. Intermittent snatches of blue-green flickered through the dense foliage; a narrow chimney's pied bricks appeared above the trees' canopy.

The path's incline leveled off; the woods thinned dramatically, and in the clearing a stunned John Crumrind waylaid the object of his hopes and dreams. Clad in a diaphanous green cloak and bare to the shoulders, as yet innocent of experience, unself-conscious but strikingly distinctive, she thrilled him.

Elated, foolish, shy, Crumrind circled discreetly and entered the house's rude backyard. A silly, backward approach no doubt, but he loitered contentedly, lovesick, overcome and even fearful of this longed-for perfection. The dark shingles' sullen romanticism, the provocative rapport between the lower windows' stern modernity and the quaintly lozenged ones above, the barest hint of the Orient about the lantern's throat and the door's latch and fittings – it had all come true. He'd have the front landscaped, walks put in, press for creation of a real street immediately. Must arrange for rooms in

Rutledge before going back into the city tonight. Plenty remained to do; he'd require complete control. By the –

Hammer strokes rang out from the far side of the house with a terrible clarity. Merrick, his assistant, was on his way to Buffalo. No one else had authority to touch his...my God, the Morrisseys.

Imagining some grave injury – monogrammed shutters? – Crumrind shot across the clods of upturned soil in search of the culprit. He needed only to turn the far corner – taking in its admirable copper gutter pipe – to find his knee-brace bracketed side balcony under assault by some misguided laborer.

Not generally given to violence, Crumrind overcame the urge to jiggle the ladder with the full force of his expensively maintained biceps.

"STOP there. STOP AT ONCE. How dare you meddle! What are you about, man? Speak!"

Merely in his teens, the lad gazed down at him coolly enough though reddening. He dandled the hefty, new-looking hammer playfully just above Crum's saucer-brimmed hat.

"Mrs. Morrissey wants her window boxes installed, sir. Mr. Field explained what's wanted."

Already aware of a crick in his neck and the inferior position, Crumrind ignored him. He stalked several yards further from the house to see better and force the fellow to twist to address him.

A resonant feminine voice pelted him between the shoulder blades. He swung to see a woman in a nightgown – presumably Mrs. Morrissey? He couldn't place the face – leaning over the balcony looking intolerably amused.

"I'm sure you can't disapprove, Mr. Crumrind. Merrick had the planters made to your specifications. Ross and I received counsel on what kind of nails must be used. We've been terribly obedient. Though I believe I'll be putting in nasturtiums. I'm told you favor geraniums. Mr. Crumrind, this is our neighbor Ross Nicol. His father has the orchard across the way. Ross, John Crumrind. The genius who gave me my house."

Instantly restored, Crumrind removed his hat, bowed. The nightgown must belong to the species of Hellenic peignoirs favored by socialites given to prancing about barefoot at charity teas.

"An honor. You suit it," he called up, carefully leaning his portfolio and hat against the house to shake the boy's hand. She really looked very satisfactory hanging off the balcony. Much primmer at the bank, all the tendrils tucked in. Wasted on "Merrick," that paragon.

"Your first viewing!" She started to add "We've been expecting you," but thought better of it. Merrick Field had explained he had an assignment in New York, and promised Crumrind's prompt arrival on the heels of his departure. (Apparently Mrs. Pratt had finally wrung the last corbel and crannied wall from the architect for her Chicago estate.) She had breathlessly cancelled all her engagements so as not to miss a moment with the Meisterbilder. Extraordinary hat. He'd need protecting here.

"My heart's been here for months."

In spite of his earlier compliment, which had hit home, her architect's eyes roved over his low eaves and unpainted cedar with absorption. Recognizing the kindled, proprietary gaze of passion, she felt jealousy stir: his house, but *her* hearth.

He moved with alacrity, even boyishness; the silver at the temples, the dry self-confidence she recalled during their meetings in Chicago had suggested a maturity that belied his (perhaps mostly mythical?) reputation for moody eccentricity. A temper, certainly, finally exposed.

"The overhang's just right, to the inch. Shingles are first-rate; our fellow deserves a medal. Harmonious surroundings – don't let anyone touch that copper beech, Mrs. Morrissey..."

"Calla."

Panting, giggling, he staggered around the corner to confront the façade. She trotted along above him as far as the balcony permitted for a glimpse of that first encounter. Thank God the paint on the front steps and landing had dried; they'd tinkered with it right up to the eve of Merrick's departure to achieve Crumrind's prescribed hue, "unglazed earthenware."

The front lawn remained an unnegotiable jumble of blackberry thickets, raw stumps, stacked flagstones and wheelbarrows. Her dear Lilybanks stood utterly naked before its maker; he'd insisted that not so much as a hydrangea be planted along the foundation until he could personally supervise the landscaping. *Professor* Crumrind the botanist. Thrilling. Annoying.

He'd tripped over something, not watching where he was going in the effort to gain some foreground and steal a peek at the same time. Mindless of the exquisite coat, he plopped down into the dirt, hugging his gawky knees to his chest, then leaning back on his elbows, taking the house in.

He seemed to be frowning? She wanted to slap him, nearly showed herself from behind the roofline. Now he was smiling, wiping his eyes. Calla moved away.

"Just carry on, Ross. It's fine."

She gave him a wink and disappeared through the bank of French doors along the balcony.

Heavens. Really just an ample bungalow with its hat set rakishly low and a youthful glint in its eyes. How silly he was...they both of them were. Sweeping through the studio, she turned to see the room through his eyes before closing the door again.

A hodgepodge waiting to be unpacked, and Swedenborg, whom her father'd sent to "watch over" her. His bust looked expectant on its pedestal in the spring sunshine.

Might as well keep the door open, she realized. Crumrind must understand her. This was no guest.

Calla tore down the hallway, ransacked the library table and window seats for notes she'd been scribbling since they'd moved in last week. Martin had had to be propelled all the way, not grasping the urgency. Essential to occupy the property, to preside, when the Master arrived. A foppish, rather giddy master, but Master nonetheless. She was no stranger to artistic temperaments. (Martin thought she possessed one herself – how little he realized his good fortune!)

Lifting her hem to rush downstairs, Calla felt damp coils of hair sticking to her jaw and thought better of it. She sank onto the top step, pulled the gown's neckline open to blow on moist skin, swept at her hair with summoned assurance and descended, mistress of the house.

The front door opened wide when she'd gotten halfway down. Calla recognized the hat and reedy height in spite of the blinding nimbus of sunshine behind Crumrind.

He hadn't even knocked; rage threatened to betray her humiliation. Speechless, she gripped the banister.

After a prolonged silence he shut the door.

"We've done it, Mrs. Morrissey."

She waited.

"You, me, Mother Nature, Mr. Morrissey's bank and the eternal Tao. Your house is very fine."

She came near enough to see dirty tear-streaked smudges below both eyes. He looked painfully vulnerable – and weirdly reminiscent of the aging actress Hermione Laurel, unconcernedly removing sludgy black eye makeup with mineral oil while welcoming Calla and Martin in her dressing room after performing *Phedre* at Berkeley's Greek Theater.

Calla found herself laughing a little deliriously, took Crumrind's arm with relief and steered him over the raw fir planks. Unresisting, he let himself be drawn across the vestibule, down the hall – glimpsing the garden wall he'd previously ignored through the back door's glass – and into the tiled kitchen.

"Trade me."

She pried his hat from long fingers glued to the portfolio under his arm and thrust her wad of notes at him. He pocketed them. She placed the precious hat on top of a breadbox, patting it reassuringly.

"I'd offer you tea but I've not managed to find it. We'll only have a cook here – well, and a fellow for the heavy work – and ours refused to leave the city. Martin survives on a massive lunch at Berghoff's – comical, we're vegetarian; they regale him with leeks and cheeses and hothouse grapes while he reads the financial papers amidst their stuffed pheasants and antler racks...Let's at least get you a spoonful of tonic before we get to work. Euphoria can be as much a strain as grief." She'd observed the dripping nose.

He watched her rifling the pantry cupboards, slamming one, standing on a crate to paw through another, managing the voluminous loose gown, everything white and ivory. Bemused, he imagined a ministering, slightly daft angel who would heed his tenets. A jar crammed with parrot feathers appeared momentarily on one shelf, a hefty corked jug on another. A basket of pods or nuts tipped over, raining its contents on her shoulders. Unperturbed, she held a bottle up triumphantly.

"What's that?"

"Elderberry liqueur, with a few helpful plants...California poppy –"

"No, the landslide."

"Eucalyptus buttons. Something from home."

"*This* is your home." Crumrind sounded hurt, peremptory. He crossed his arms.

"Don't be stern. I'll add some mullein powder..." She was on the floor, rummaging through boxes in a sea of billowing white. Every movement was consciously graceful, as though on a stage. He remembered she gave performances.

"Here we are...can you stir it with a finger? No, never mind, here's a brand new pencil." Convulsed by his obvious distaste she watched him stir her potion in one of Martin's shot glasses, hand the pencil back gingerly and raise his arm for a toast.

"To…Lilybanks, is it?"

She nodded, finally serious.

"My home till death do us part. Or perhaps longer."

He swallowed her offering, in spite of botanical qualms.

"Come see our ballroom." And she was off, through the hygienic, glittering scullery, up the hall again. The uncreated garden behind its wall tugged at his back, but it would wait. They paused at the dim foot of the stairs, simultaneously poking at the push button in the wallpaper. She took in the sere, merely neutral chuckle as he dropped his hand in concession, unengaged by her accidental touch. Annoyed by her own responsiveness – she wanted no conquests – Calla groped for some inanity to chirp.

"What made you insist on the gingko pattern for the stairs, Professor?"

He seemed to have forgotten her, gaping in his exigent manner at the lit chandelier's tubular corollas.

"I was dreading your liliaceous sparkler here, but it's beautifully restrained and comparatively accurate, botanically speaking. Hungarians. Like to see more of their work. John. Sacred tree for a temple." He continued examining the lights' effect from different angles, absorbed, then turned to her with a searching smile. The unruly hairs in his eyebrows came to an impish point in the middle.

"Are all your instincts this good?"

Calla assumed the first stair, reaching his eye level.

"How did you intend to proceed if you didn't like my lily-lights? Quite mercilessly, no doubt. Don't answer. We're to be allies." She took his arm, determined to avoid a race.

She'd kept the ballroom doors closed, looking forward to a dramatic unveiling of their creative collaboration. Making the slowest, most dignified lunge possible for the doorknob, Calla realized Crumrind observed this with some amusement. Again, another man might have made other use of the opportunity.

Yards of polished wood lay before them, ablaze in the light from the bank of diamond panes to their left. A slight odor of lacquer remained; the marquetry had been finished only recently. Innocent of furniture, the pristine floor inlaid with ropes of wildflowers invited music and footfall. Calla ran noiselessly to unfasten the lattices; Crumrind finally noticed she was barefoot.

Something dark stirred in the nearer fireplace; a black cat unfurled, stretched and shimmied crazily, its legs rigid, back humped. Crumrind grimaced.

It padded deliberately across the floor toward its mistress, keeping its eyes on Calla as though mesmerizing her from behind. She turned immediately, scooped up the eerie beast and whirled out onto the dance floor with it, twirling slowly at first, then faster and wider in some initiation rite that Crumrind felt included him. Rapt, he watched the white dress balloon as the cat clung to her shoulder. He wanted to snicker, imagining the cat sucked out into orbit and crashing through a window, but recognized surrender in his soul.

Not at all breathless, merely brighter, she slowed down and crouched in a prayerful gesture. The cat disembarked to go groom itself in a corner, aloof now.

Utterly unselfconscious, Mrs. Morrissey smiled dazzlingly, pushing her hair off her face.

"Come admire the garden! Visible only to the noetic mind yet, of course." Crumrind took a moment to digest this. She spread the windows wide and leaned out, patting the sill next to her. He obliged.

"I sailed right past the wall when I arrived. Feel a bit sheepish about that," he chuckled, searching her face now instead of arranging his own expression.

"Lovesick," she observed. He looked younger, more appealing when less aware of himself.

He nodded, studying the garden's high wall.

"The door looks well. Very well. Even without my oriental

ironwork." He sounded rueful but his grey eyes kindled. "Your purple glass door knob adds a homely touch."

"Exactly. The garden's an extension of the enchanted home."

"Sounds like a ladies' magazine. Or am I being too noetic?" He looked down at her, his height an unfair advantage.

"My father's a professor of classics at the University of California. It tended to rub off on his family. I'll try to restrain myself."

"Please don't." Laughter as well as the elements seemed to redden his nose. "I've thought what your little ritual with the cat reminded me of: the Sufis. Mrs. Morrissey, the whirling dervish. I wonder...I have an acquaintance in the city, an antiquarian bookbinder from India. He's playing host to a few traveling compatriots. Sufis. I've been invited to a performance for just a very few of Mr. Khan's intimates and family. An honor, he surprised me. Would you like to come along if I can arrange it?"

Flattered more than she liked to show, Calla suspected that her susceptible hothead architect needed to keep an iron grip on his *amour propre.*

"Really more of a prayer than a performance, isn't it?" His eyebrows spoke volumes; there they went again. "Papa's hobby is world religions. He gives weekend lectures to an avid coterie in Mr. Maybeck's Unity Hall these days. I guess that's rubbed off, too. Something of a gamble for you; won't they think you turned the event into an exotic field trip with which to blandish a wealthy client?"

He looked thunderstruck, then peeved. "I haven't got time for gambling."

"I'm being an idiot – while trying to show you I'm not. Shall we strike a bargain? You grant me an intellect, and I'll admit I'd walk all the way to Chicago to encounter a dance with divinity."

Mollified, almost bashful, he offered his hand with an eagerness that belied the long thin fingers' careful, tepid clasp. She glimpsed a boy masquerading as a worldly middle-aged dignitary, however eccentric.

Drawn again to the view below, Crumrind tapped his fingers on the window sash. "I'd advise a few of the smaller, really quite exquisite Japanese maples in the garden. I've already managed to finagle a generous shipment of them for the grounds – along with a wet nurse of a garden boy to ensure they arrive alive." One eyebrow went up. She imagined explaining the wet nurse bill to Martin.

"How wonderful. You read my mind. Papa negotiated with the tea garden's caretaker in Golden Gate park for me. He's sent eight of my favorites with leaves like crabbed little crimson stars by Union Pacific. They'll arrive any day. Might you recover them for us once we get the telegram?"

Crumrind sighed, enjoying his defeat.

"Oh, lord. There's a heron down there making a luncheon of Martin's latest hobby. Should've gotten netting over the tub – I'm spread so thin without help yet..."

Crum strode after her, amused, as she galloped out to the hall and plummeted down the staircase, clutching her dress in both hands. Perhaps Mr. Morrissey had taken to rearing lobsters for his rural table.

He flagged in the downstairs hall, craning for a glimpse of the dining room, lollygagging in the living room doorway till her muffled shrieks and a queer clattering impelled him into the courtyard.

Calla knelt in the upturned soil, having stretched her ample hem over the top of a gleaming hip bath with both hands. Thus entrenched she gazed into the eyes of a tall, toy-like bird that held its ground not more than a yard from her. Something black, bulbous and lacy disappeared between its jaws with a jerk of its head.

"One of the Moors," she groaned. "Martin's favorite goldfish, with great goggle-eyes like Mrs. Pratt's Pekinese."

The weird, leathery head on a long fuzzy neck continued to regard her.

Crumrind doubted Mrs. Pratt would let that massive cutlass of a beak anywhere near her.

"Seems like it's waiting for the next course." He studied the bird, reluctant to shoo it away.

"The poor darling. It's deformed. Or sick; its feathers are falling out. Funny little dinosaur on stilts."

"Looks pretty unearthly, doesn't it." Crumrind circled the bath and crouched, investigating the creature as it waited stolidly. Mostly ashy white with a wide black edge to its wings and tail, it had the face of a scissor-billed, wizened troll. Satisfied, Crumrind stood up.

"Lilybanks has its first foreign emissary. This is a stork. I believe it's a wood stork from the Florida Keys. How it got up here – and why it's tolerating our presence -- I can't imagine."

Her bankers' wives had mentioned cunning stucco cottages in Florida among the architect's successes, Calla recalled.

"So the old dear's been blown off course by a hurricane? Could we take him back down there by train when he's well?" She'd already begun to see it was quite handsome, in a wizardly way, and male.

Crum snorted, then regretted it. Papa and Martin must spoil her. He could understand that.

"In diapers and a muzzle? More hazardous than the storm. Besides, it's not acting like a wild bird, is it? Perhaps it's a runaway from the Zoo. I'll make some inquiries tomorrow." He smiled more kindly. "Making my back hurt to look at you. I take it these are goldfish? Not likely to last long in a hip bath. I noticed some chicken wire somewhere in front. That, and a few bricks and a board..."

"Marvelous, yes, thank you. Something of a debacle. We're expecting a shipment of instruments to aerate the tank, the latest gadgets from a German inventor Martin's subsidizing. Somehow the fish arrived first..."

The shimmering, muffled crash of a gong resounded from the interior of the house.

"Martin! He must've left early to join us. Never mind about the bricks and all, he or Ross can manage. Open the door and call, will you? But don't scare our friend."

Annoyed, he let himself back in and sauntered down the hall.

"Who's there?" A boyish head appeared over the banister above him; nauseating waves of sound continued to roil from the gong. "Crumrind?"

The fellow bounced down the stairs as energetically as his wife; this was the first time Crum had bothered to observe his person below the waist. No doubt they had nothing in common but a haberdasher. Where'd he left his portfolio?

"Morrissey. A pleasure. Afraid I'm just leaving, have to arrange a room in town before a round of consultations in the city." He overran the fellow's compliments. "Starting tomorrow I'll be here nearly round the clock for as long as it takes. Mrs. Morrissey's just out back. A bit embroiled. Please give her my regrets; no idea what time it was." He glanced pointedly in the direction of the hallway clock. "I'll just collect my things and let myself out." He came perilously close to propelling Martin out the back door.

Refugees

"I wonder what I'll think about next."

Al held her breath and stared out the dining room window. Tufts of white pine needles bobbed in a breeze, each long shaft scintillating in the sunlight...It was doing pretty well for an ex-Christmas tree that never really got enough light. She'd twisted Casper's arm to try a live tree they could plant in their yard after the holidays. He'd been a dear about it after he got used to –

There she went again. For a few moments the pine tree twinkled with life, unaccountably magnetic, and then she caught herself engrossed in storytelling. As though the tree's aliveness was an unexpurgated text from which she had to be diverted, and any stale, thrice-told tale served the purpose.

She fingered the book Marian had lent her last week, trying to concentrate on its sharp corner beneath her fingertips, the smooth, cool paper cover in the lap of her skirt. How mild and peaceful were the few seconds of attention to the Here and Now she could wrest from the glob of revolving once-and-future theatrics her brain seemed to have become. What a relief, if unimpressive, those moments of respite while examining the kitchen sponge's pores, inhaling an orange rind before she tossed it in the garbage, listening to the rising and falling swoosh of a car passing in the night, its lights traveling across the top of her bedroom wall. Those few seconds provided a refuge from the collapsing debris of her life, like coming up for air before being submerged again.

Eckhart Tolle said that she wasn't Althea Athnos at all, which she was quite glad to hear. According to Eckhart she was really, well, Consciousness, sort of timeless, immortal and, if she had it right, made of formless God-stuff. Most people didn't have a clue about who they really were, but if you wanted a glimpse you could try the "what'll I think next?" exercise. In the little gap between the query and the answer a spaciousness arose. It was like turning off a radio and actively appreciating the ensuing silence. That consciousness aware of itself without the usual racket was who she really was. The racket was just her clamoring ego.

Oh, she'd heard it all before. Lovely stuff, but somehow unavailable when filling out futile job applications in a windowless room full of people half one's age, or fending off the bald stare of a more gifted mortal as one failed to negotiate the gas pump, the scanner, the left-hand turn. The gap between lofty, mystical generalizations and personal emergencies (imploding self-hatred, financial realities) yawned frustratingly wide. Over the years she'd given up trying to bring heaven to earth in her life, grateful at least to witness their fusion in nature.

All the same, this funny little fellow who'd apparently had some kind of nervous breakdown (she couldn't help thinking of Harvey the Rabbit and Elwood P. Dowd) seemed to have included practical nuts-and-bolts tips in his book that otherwise had the uncompromising ring of holy scripture.

She'd been trying some of them out. Eckhart claimed that the way to enlightenment was through the body, not beyond it. One was supposed to become aware of the energy inside oneself, and stay in touch with it at all times. Eckhart made it sound like a sort of golden ginger ale, fizzy and buoyant. Al couldn't locate hers. She wasn't surprised. Sometimes she felt a bit of action in her fingertips. And one morning she'd taken the time to run her consciousness all over her body systematically, refusing, say, to try feeling her inner eyebrows before she'd managed to get in contact with at least some of her scalp. Eckhart claimed her body adored the attention, right down to its cells. She noticed she did feel refreshed afterwards, though she couldn't visualize twinkly metallic stuff flowing along her veins. And as to staying in touch with her inner body! She had enough trouble staying in contact with the outer one. In the shower she couldn't remember what she'd lathered or rinsed. She had to sleep with her shoes on to remind herself that the bedroom and hall were a treacherous maze of half-packed boxes. Last week she'd sprawled full-length after tripping on a stack in the dark on her way to the bathroom. Her right shin remained battleship grey.

Al turned to find Linnet staring at her from the far end of the kitchen counter, seated among her finicky accumulation of food and water bowls.

"Ah! So how long have you been boring a hole in the side of my head?"

Gratified, Linnet stood up and leaned over the edge of the counter, maneuvering her sumptuous tail up and away from the clotted remnants of an early breakfast. Their noses met.

Al had assigned Linnet a countertop table setting years ago, with Casper's reluctant acquiescence, when their tubby older cat Tutu displayed an ungovernable urge to raid the little newcomer's bowls. Once Linnet had become an only child Casper'd wanted to reclaim the counter space, but Linnet continued to leap to her place as though eating on the indifferently cleaned floor were as unthinkable to her as to humans.

"Here you go, sweetie. Just a pair of refugees, aren't we?" She spooned out some shredded tuna. Dismayed by the transformation of her kingdom into a generic, angular terrain of cardboard boxes, the cat alternated between peevish inertia and clingy, querulous reproaches. Al fantasized about acquiring tranquilizers for Linnet and herself and then retiring to a dim corner with a few boxes of kibble, graham crackers and the fusty bambam until the house sold.

She'd forced herself through a few more apartment viewings (orange shag carpeting with a view mostly of the next-door neighbors' crooked, gaping blinds, a dark swampy "garden" unit, reasonably priced due to a history of minor flooding, the entire second floor of an elderly lady with a seriously yappy Pomeranian, the tenant clearly expected to help her remain "independent" lest her well-intentioned, concerned son and daughter-in-law sell the house out from under both of them...These were the leftovers after the university students' onslaught. At least she had time to pick and choose among the rejects, if Lilybanks fell through. According to her practical cousin she was really supposed to be finding "a modest condo." She imagined finding one she could afford in some place like Fargo. It would have a spacious view of oil derricks and snowmobilers. Time for that later.

After licking all the gravy off her rubbery tuna Linnet hurtled off the counter and leapt to the top of the dining room piano to groom, as usual. A dormant remnant of Al's childhood, the piano was due to be picked up any day now, donated to a church basement preschool. Poor Linnet.

The phone rang. Al barely flinched.

"Althea?" She couldn't place the voice.

"Marian Morrissey here."

"Oh, Marian! I didn't recognize your voice! How *are* you?" Al recognized the desperation under her friendliness. She found herself clinging eagerly to comments about the weather from her dry cleaner, a kindly bank teller's ministrations, anonymous jocularity at a bus stop.

"Fine, dear. We're all fine here. We so much enjoyed your visit, Althea, and we'd very much like to have you back soon. You could have a more leisurely encounter with Calla's mural, perhaps stay for lunch. How are you finding Eckhart Tolle"?

Al groped for a few phrases she'd prepared for just such a question.

"Authentic is the word that comes to mind first, Marian. Certainly doesn't mince his words. Uncompromising – almost *scriptural*. And systematic – it all seems to hang together. I'm grateful to you. It's like a key to the gates to Paradise. I'm only halfway through...So much to think about!" Among other things.

"Good, good. Keep at it. You'll be richly repaid, Althea. I should tell you that we've decided on a housemate. A German girl, Waldorf-schooled! She's taking a break from the University of Heidelberg to visit family in the U.S. Only nineteen. So lively with the children! You'll meet Ursula when you come to lunch. Oh, we were reluctant to pass up your uncanny suitability for Lilybanks, but we're glad to think we'll see you here often anyway...May I call you next week to set a luncheon date? Ursula's very involved with the children this week, learning the ropes – Oh! And we have to arrange for her 'green card.' Never a dull moment!"

"Ursula sounds perfect. I would have loved being your housemate, but I can understand your choice. I'll look forward to meeting her. Talk to you next week, then." She hoped she sounded breezy, but wouldn't be able to keep it up much longer.

"Yes, till then. Bye bye, Althea."

"Bye bye!"

She hung up the treacherous phone, which had glowed with potentiality all week. It reassumed its usual alien menace.

"Oh, Linnet."

Numb, she hurried out to the living room armchair, as though to reach a resting place before the fracture shattered.

She seemed alright. But that was how she usually felt after a stunning blow. One flattered oneself that the setback was being negotiated surprisingly well, and then the first signs of internal bleeding began to show up, then months or years of seething and festering and tender areas to be avoided...Marian's book was a slab of silver in the sunlight flooding the dining room window. Too bad. It had seemed revelatory, something she'd given up hoping for, that had perhaps found her when she most needed it. Now she'd associate it with her artful rejection by the elite Lilybankers. She hadn't been energetic enough or scholarly enough or interesting enough. They'd accurately seen her for what she was – a sentimental phony mediocrity in dire straits.

The pain had begun. But the inner voice sounded, if only for a moment, not really her own. The tiniest bit tinny. Willing herself not to think, she got back up and fetched the book, blinking in the glare from the window.

Star-struck

Micah Fennel allowed his eyes to wander as the young lady at the podium gesticulated between two towering corn shocks, delivering her translation into German of a poem by Ralph Waldo Emerson.

The Unitarian church's basement auditorium sported a ceiling

spangled with the zodiac. A soothing rainbow of pale pastels progressed along the walls; Lucy said the impressionistic technique was
a Waldorf trade secret. (The Unitarians received a fat rent for the
takeover of their space by the Waldorfers, he understood. No doubt
they'd be equally receptive to a Hindu contingent.) Tiers of homemade lanterns – more Waldorf arcana, he guessed – lined the stage,
above which a suspended felt banner that spelled out "MARTINMAS
BLESSINGS" in tipsy capitals swayed in the floodlights' heat.

The speaker wore a lopsided knitted get-up – plainly handmade –
in dubious colors that Lucy would no doubt term puce and aubergine,
or some such, if he elbowed her. It jutted over jeans that seemed to
have been painted on and disappeared into expensive-looking riding
boots. The tassel on the ski cap she inexplicably wore quivered spas-
tically in time with the impressively guttural syllables. Micah had
studied ancient Greek, Hebrew and enough French to satisfy himself,
but hadn't found time for German.

The audience, a mix of parents amid shoals of unruly but toler-
able children and older students (mostly festive, with a fashionably
sullen minority) punctuated by earnest organizers – Lucy's full-time
colleagues, he assumed – broke into ripples of applause.

"Next comes Tad!" Lucy whispered. Her breath smelled like an
apple orchard in spring. She sat up straighter. Lucy was so protective
of those she loved! He expanded with pride but decided against patting her thigh reassuringly, for fear of interrupting her concentration.

As the stage remained vacant the silence floating above a buzzing
undertow grew more profound. A snigger erupted from the (comparatively vapid until then) pair of teenagers sitting on his left. From a
loud whisper that skillfully included him – the nearest, safely unfamiliar adult – Micah thought he deciphered something to the effect
of "busy letting Morrissey measure his strudel." Students in the front
rows began clapping in unison: "TAD! TAD! TAD! TAD!" Lucy shot
him a flushed, wobbly smile, apparently uncertain whether this was

endearing or catastrophic. The lights dimmed. Someone whistled; the pandemonium faded.

A spectral candlelit lantern emerged from the wings and floated along the stage. As Micah's eyes adjusted to the semi-darkness he saw that it was attached to a stout branch wielded by Tad, who looked more enormous than usual in a hooded monk's robe.

The lantern hovered before the mike, then inched beyond it. For one piteous moment Tad looked desperately out into the audience, then licked his lips and began, in splendid isolation, to address the ceiling:

"Look at the stars! look, look up at the skies!
O look at all the fire-folk sitting in the air!..."

Captivated by the fairylike opening, Tad's audience hung on through Gerard Manley Hopkins' increasingly cryptic, reverent poem.

"...Christ and his mother and all his hallows."[4]

Childish, pagan and shockingly religious by turns, the poem's exaltation and Tad's dazed but unfaltering delivery seemed to have hit just the right note among the Waldorfers. Initially careful, churchlike applause followed by a few adult enthusiasts standing up authoritatively became an ovation. Arty-looking teenagers climbed onto the stage and engulfed the hooded hermit before pushing him forward to acknowledge his success. Someone had tied a bent red carnation to his lantern's staff. The lights turned up. Tad looked utterly baffled but pleased.

Lucy squeezed his hand. She had tears in her eyes.

"I'm so proud of them all. All of us. Isn't that silly?" Micah put his arm around her; she was vibrating in that alarming way he was getting used to. The leather-clad pair to his left had departed for the stage. Definitely a flakey, highbrow crew. Compassionate and discerning if a bit too stylishly earnest, he considered. The Waldorf crowd was beginning to grow on him, though he still felt the impulse to rescue Lucy from Rudolf Steiner's clutches.

As Tad and his apparently unexpected throng of well-wishers (Micah had understood he was as haplessly incompatible with his peers as Beebe, if less captivating) funneled off the stage, Lucy squeezed his arm and pointed to the opposite wing. A stately old lady with an elegant silver French twist, reading glasses on a chain and dark skirt with French-cuffed white blouse marched to the podium.

"First cello," Micah whispered.

"Actually, Mrs. Hassenpfeffer. Head of the school."

Somehow the totemic corn shocks looked more suitable when she arrived between them. A comparative hush descended at once; Micah's neighbors to the left slid back into their seats. Mrs. Hassenpfeffer cleared her throat, casting a mild smile across her flock.

"Dear members and guests of our Stubblefield Waldorf community – such a pleasure and privilege once more to gather round the hearth of friendship for yet another Martinmas night! Special thanks are due our gifted older students, who have been practicing for tonight's poetry bee since Michaelmas, or even harvest time." Raising her arms, she pantomimed applause to no one in particular, and the audience obliged.

"Thank you so much, senior students. We'll be lighting our lanterns for the neighborhood procession shortly, after which we hope you'll all return to the upper hall for refreshments generously provided by our students and families. But first, a poetic 'grande finale' – one of the youngest of our senior home school's students has prepared a bountiful offering for us. Beebe Morrissey will recite the "Ode: Intimations of Immortality" by William Wordsworth. Ms. Lucy Murgatroyd has assembled a slide show of landscapes from our art library to accompany the verses. Beebe?"

The lights dimmed again as Beebe bustled across the stage. A minor ripple of kindly laughter met her adjustment of a movable set of steps behind the podium. She looked animated and self-possessed; her precociously arched eyebrows and heart-shaped face reminded Micah of Elizabeth Taylor. She'd be a knockout some day.

In the meantime Lucy had patted his knee and bumbled over shoes and knees to the center aisle. Straining over his shoulder, Micah made out the apparatus for an old-fashioned slide presentation stationed in the aisle.

Beebe, ever pert and composed, with the kind of relaxed but perfect posture that evoked invisible stacks of books on her head, watched Lucy for her cue. Never in this century had two long braids and a ruffled pinafore seemed more unstudied. Beebe looked neither prim nor "gamine"; she exuded authenticity. Micah discerned natural authority. He found himself uncomfortably riveted, almost starstruck. This was the pudgy-cheeked orphan Lucy fretted over and doted on? He'd only seen her through Lucy's eyes; hadn't, apparently, paid attention. If Beebe were really the tangle of neurosis and naiveté Lucy treasured, perhaps she belonged onstage.

Beebe nodded and smiled, glanced behind her at the Constable moor suddenly hovering on the screen, and closed her eyes. Somewhere a preschooler shrieked. The lanky kid next to Micah muttered, "Shut up!" and sat up straighter.

"There was a time when meadow, grove and stream,
The earth, and every common sight,
To me did seem
Appareled in celestial light..."[5]

Hay wains and Turner mists followed Beatrix Potter stiles and hedgehogs, verdant Lake District photography, sensitive drawings of squirrels with fuzzy peaked Old World ears. Initially rapt, the audience grew consciously devoted. One might have been at the Lyric. (Later, at home, Micah thought of clandestine *samizdat* poetry readings during the Stalin era, so committed had the audience around him felt. Had he been in the United States? Maybe not.)

"...too deep for tears."[6]

When she'd finished Beebe stood stock-still, eyes closed again. She nursed the reverent hush for just a fitting moment before expertly acknowledging the strident applause without exploiting it. She gave a reasonable little wave to everyone, bent to light the two nearest lanterns waiting at the stage edge, and hoisted them overhead. Micah was reminded, however extravagantly, of Isadora Duncan in Moscow. In response to her invitation people surged toward the stage.

Mrs. Hassenpfeffer commanded the mike again.

"Please approach the stage from the two side aisles! We'll hand out lanterns from either end of the stage! Families and students who have brought their own lanterns may adjourn toward the front doors, where staff will light your lanterns as you exit. As always, PLEASE OBSERVE THE FIRE CODE! Only staff may light lanterns, only at the front doors! We'll process up Green Street, turning right on Van Ness and continuing around our block! (Here you go, dear,...You'll need to share, girls...) We'll see you back here for hot chocolate, cider and dessert! (Mr. Frankfurter, I think it's unwise to give the punched tin lanterns to our youngest friends...)"

Lucy had disappeared; no dark shiny cap of hair floated amongst the confusion around Micah. She was probably one of the lamplighters in the front vestibule. Beebe, Tad and other senior students were supervising lantern allotments, accepting congratulatory hugs and thumps, unwinding behind the footlights. No one had turned the lights back up. Feeling a bit out of it all, Micah strolled along toward the front of the church (temple? space? What did Unitarians say?)

and waited patiently behind the bottleneck of students and families waiting to join the lantern-lit procession. A solemn little kid in glasses and a red corduroy jacket contemplated his dark lantern as it bobbled on its slender, arching pole. An earmuffed teenager buttoned up her boyfriend's coat as he blew frosty puffs of air over her bent head. They had a flashlight instead of a lantern. Micah stuck his hands in his pockets. The draft from the open doors crept down the stairs and around his ankles.

He spotted Lucy up ahead, lighting a match for a fellow with a yawning piggyback passenger. Lucy wore only one of her red mittens. He imagined finding its slightly trampled mate for her once the crowd had thinned out. Lucy's hair fell forward in wings as she bent to admire some toddler's flashlight with that fragile, nearly imperceptible wobbliness that wrung his heart. Saint Martin was the protector of outcasts.

Somewhere behind him a female shrieked, muffled commotion broke out, then died down right away. People behind him in line stopped talking, searched each other's faces, mutually concluded nothing momentous was going on. Teenagers.

It took a certain amount of maneuvering to press to the right so he'd end up on Lucy's side of the doorway. When he reached her, the round, ruddy-cheeked older woman in a baggy jumper next to her twinkled at him.

"Go along, Lucy, I'll manage fine. Go on!" she called, inundated by a cluster of girls wearing what looked like glow-in-the-dark hula hoops around their necks in addition to their lanterns. Quaintness was apparently optional.

Lucy leaned into his arm around her shoulder, stole a glance up at him and tolerated his kiss in front of students well as they headed down the sidewalk. They had to yank the candle out of her lantern to get a light from giggling kids behind them, one of whom inscrutably wore a paper crown taped to his ski cap. Once they moved beyond the light from the church's gigantic faux-Gothic sconces he couldn't see anything but the family just ahead of them and an undulating file of floating flames that extended the length of the long block ahead. Lucy's lantern was of patterned, pierced tin that sprinkled faces and cars and concrete with tiny, swaying stars.

Lucy let him wrap her head in his striped university scarf though she was perfectly warm enough. They took turns holding the nodding lantern's arching rod away from hedges and a dignified German shepherd on a leash. Micah, who would have been glad to ferry Lucy through any number of puerile parades, found himself enchanted with this group's ability to let the inherent poetry of the event speak for itself. No alien cell phone monologues, no loud, self-conscious adolescent profanity, no oblivious gossips catching up on the latest, no advertising. Just a murmuring, appreciative, orderly throng out to make something beautiful. They bolstered his faith in Lucy's inner compass. She seemed to have a nose for true north, in spite of, well, a lot of gyrations.

Word passed down the line that folks had seen a shooting star. Lucy smiled at him, wide-eyed with delight. He held her striped head in both hands and kissed her as hard as he could. A few people behind them clapped.

When they'd doused their candle and stowed Lucy's lantern behind some church shrubbery (his idea – she'd have put it down any old where in the church hall) Micah secured two frilly glass punch cups of hot cider.

"To the art of life, and to my favorite artist."

They clinked carefully. He liked the way his scarf still encircled her neck in a careless tangle. His little dove in a nest.

"Who *is* your favorite artist, Micah?" Her eyes expressed innocent interest. She continued to look uncertain when he answered, "You, my love," with tender annoyance.

A few metal folding tables away from them Mr. Frankfurter, the woodcraft and German instructor, waved a knife and spatula over his head while he boomed for attention.

"Alright, everyone, get yourselves over here with a plate – we're about to slice up this eight-foot-long *apfelstrudel*! I'm told there's a nice fat prune hiding in there somewhere. If it turns up in your slice, you win the tie-dyed comforter on the bench over there, a fundraiser art project our senior students dreamed up. Our pastry chef Beebe Morrissey put this monster together, but she tells me she doesn't have any idea where that prune is. She'll cut the honorary first slice, and then Marcy and Ham here will start in from either end. Beebe?"

Micah hung back from the surge toward the strudel queues and watched Lucy beaming on tiptoe along the fringe of the huddle. She considered Beebe her waifish protégée, but Micah wondered which one needed more looking after. Beebe seemed pretty robust to Micah. Something about her annoyed him. Tad's devotion made him wince. His own aberrant, stage-struck response to her this evening embarrassed him now. Oh well.

He approached Tad, who was dawdling about as though making sure Beebe's guests were served properly.

"Hi, Micah!" (At last. He'd had to be urged several times not to refer to him as "Mr. Fennel." Micah had heard Tad's father was in the military.)

"I really enjoyed that Hopkins poem, Tad. Very nice delivery."

"Beebe coached me. But thank you. Did you see what happened?"

"No, what's that?" Tad's beetle-brows were often knit.

"Beebe's braid caught on fire. Onstage. Leaned over one of those lanterns she lit. Don't tell anyone – besides Lucy – Micah, but, ah, Beebe wasn't supposed to do that. Mrs. H. let her get away with it. Beebe just got carried away. Mrs. H. wants to take the blame. I heard her say we could lose our lease with the church. Never saw Mrs. H. look so ruffled. She *never* ruffles...Now half her hair's three inches shorter than the other side."

While Micah tried to comprehend Mrs. Hassenpfeffer's traumatic asymmetrical hair loss, Tad pulled something from his shirt pocket. He held out his hand, palm up, and Micah made out a blackened, coagulated, hairy pod with a barely recognizable remnant of ribbon. It reeked.

"Good grief. Beebe's lucky she's unhurt. That's right, isn't it?"

Tad nodded. He looked unguardedly tired for a moment.

"So throw it out, Tad. Looks like something a cat threw up. There's a garbage can right there." Tad obeyed, looking not quite as sheepish as he ought. Micah thought of mummified relics he'd seen in churches in Greece.

Nearby, two grave teenage girls in identical sherpa caps and nose rings fed each other halves of flakey strudel from a single plate.

"...hungry for attention, actually."

"Hmm. Well, she got a bellyful tonight, didn't she? The little cutie." Micah examined their faces as he pretended to move past them purposefully. They looked self-important but not unkind.

Lucy seemed embroiled with some doting family. He took himself off to the men's room down a corridor that ended in a fire exit, glad for a break from the social buzz. The hall was empty and dim, but someone had propped open the exit with a folding chair. It seemed a little odd, and as he strode past the washroom to investigate he discovered snowflakes – the first – falling in the narrow walkway between the church and the neighboring building's bricks. He stuck his head out around the corner and was startled to find Beebe Morrissey two feet away, looking startled also, then contrite.

"Micah! It's you! It's snowing!" Her braids had disappeared and her long hair rippled in crinkled waves. He decided not to indulge her by asking about the mishap, while she professed remorse for pushing up the church's heating bill so she could steal a few moments of solitude. He noticed the faint sprinkling of freckles under her eyes, and the dark, pliant curve of her bottom lip. She smelled a little fusty, almost like a wet dog. He restrained himself from telling her how silly the white pinafore thing looked, and couldn't think of anything else to say. She banged the chair together and the door slowly swooshed shut.

"Tad's probably wondering where you've gotten to," he flung back over his shoulder as he bolted to the men's room.

Iridescent Tourmaline Sunangel

The daily calendar page featured a hummingbird called an iridescent tourmaline sunangel. A portent of extravagant loveliness? Mere functional, stable mediocrity sounded desirable at this point. Al forced herself to blend a streak of undereye concealer into the bruise-colored stains below each vacant eye. Now they glowed pale lavender – only arguably an improvement. Her face had gone orange, perhaps from the lavish daily allotment of coffee she now required. It must have drenched every cell in her body. She thought of caffeine as her medication, and the trembling hands, twisted speech and careless, over-extroverted remarks to strangers as unavoidable side effects.

She had a 10:30 appointment to view an affordable studio sublet with an unbelievable location on the plusher edge of a student neighborhood. Some type of breakdown or overdose, she'd gathered from the landlord; parents just wanted to get it off their hands. The landlord had stressed how small the place was, but it sounded clean, new and neutral, and he'd allow Linnet. Unless the corridors smelled of urine or she detected fleas (unlikely, but there always seemed to be something,) she'd pounce on it no matter how tiny. Location, location, location, she reminded herself, feeling reassuringly urbane above the overcaffeinated turmoil. Casper would approve.

She opened the mirrored cabinet above the sink for toothpaste, wondering as she now habitually did if the new owners, the Augsbergers, would tear everything out of the bathroom and start anew. After all, she and Casper had, keeping only the trophy clawfoot tub. Maybe they'd replace the tub with a Jacuzzi; they were emp-ty-nester attorneys.

The downstairs phone rang dimly. Of course her mouth was full of toothpaste. She rushed into the hallway and grabbed the mute vintage phone's clunky receiver before the answering machine kicked in; Casper had it set for just three rings and, now that she had to navigate rolled up rugs and packing boxes, she had no idea how to adjust the thing.

"Hewwo?" A splotch of pale blue foam hit the dial.

"Althea! So glad I caught you. Awfully early; did I waken you?"

"No no, thaz fine…" (The realtor's receptionist?) Her caustic pud-dle of Crest threatened to overflow. Al shuddered and nearly gagged; she searched her jeans for a tissue. Linnet arrived and sat on the notepad.

"Althea, I'm afraid we've committed quite a blunder…"

Someone had snapped up the sublet overnight. She sagged onto the floor, resenting the overly friendly use of her first name. A faint gurgle escaped her.

"What's that? Oh, dear. Ursula proved quite unreliable. Yesterday – no, the day before – the neighbors phoned to say our poor old Volvo was sitting in the middle of Banks Street with its doors open and the engine running. Ursula had attempted some sort of foray, a lark, I suppose, in spite of our clearest understanding to the contrary – no valid license! – and just abandoned ship! Even Lucy was unable to unravel the whole story – panic attack? Congenital carelessness? Simply bored and spoiled? We've had to pack her off to her relatives, as delicately as possible – just imagine the doubt cast on our judgement should our parents hear the story! Mercifully, the Goldsberries are most discreet, some of our oldest neighbors. We've found half a dozen empty cough syrup bottles in Ursula's closet, and Lucy's missing a new bottle of St. John's wort pills – "

Al held her breath, forcing herself just to listen and not jump ahead. She watched Linnet sniff her toothbrush daintily, then recoil.

"Oh dear. Forgive me. Might there be any chance you'd still be interested in moving to Lilybanks, Althea? All three of us feel we were led astray by her Waldorf credentials. Oh dear, I listened to the wrong side of my brain, in spite of your having turned up so felicitously and seeming so intuitively right. Such a forceful reminder of the perils of over-thinking when –"

"Stay in the Now, Marian," Al was astonished to hear herself say, swallowing her toothpaste recklessly. "I was just on my way out the door to finalize a lease on a brand new studio in University Heights." (Almost University Heights.) "But Lilybanks still tugs at my heart. Why don't I come over to discuss it with you this morning before I do anything irreversible. Or no, you're probably all tied up with the children at the mo –"

"Do come right over, dear. We'll welcome you with open arms. Oh, *mea culpa*! But you're so right; what's passed is in the past. Beebe's here; we'll manage. How providential that I took the liberty of phoning so early – just as soon as we got that unfortunate person off our hands – and managed a night's sleep feeling safe in our own beds once again… Should we be so fortunate as to acquire you as a comrade in arms here, Althea, I must tell you I feel it only fair to remunerate you in some way for any inconvenience we've created…Perhaps we might subsidize your kitty's meal allowance? But we'll see you presently. Watch your step in the front vestibule – some tiles had to be re-grouted – children do take their toll! – and our man for all seasons Mr. Watkins could only fit us in during school hours. Thank you, thank you, Althea."

"A pleasure, Marian. See you shortly."

Al replaced the receiver. She imagined ricocheting off the wall like a kitten.

"Thank you dear God." She could feel Casper's presence, his pulling of strings for her.

How glib she'd been! What had come over her? The moment she'd realized she held the winning hand her hurt feelings had emerged, however coyly. But she *had* acknowledged her keenness, had ultimately been genuine. Perversely the irrelevant studio, potentially luminous, snug and spotless lingered in her imagination, intensified by a newborn foreboding of constraint, intrusiveness and mildew. The tiny rent the Lilybankers were asking suddenly seemed all too appropriate for live-in help.

My God, could she never embrace life? Just "surrender," as her new housemates' guru suggested?

She scooped Linnet up and plunked her down on the bathroom bambam.

"This must be what's right for us, sugarplum. We have to make the very best of it."

Welcome

"Remember the time the tornado sirens went off and we'd mislaid Carpenter? You're careening around the yard under a swirling dark green sky, bellowing, while I'm down in the cellar with Melodie who's practically hyperventilating because of the spider webs, and Bubo's wrestling Aphrodite down the cellar steps..." Beebe smacked another generous helping of popcorn into her mouth and turned towards Al.

"They found him in the hydrangeas. 'Playing hide and seek.' By then it was pelting hail, and Bubo had trampled her glasses. They might never have found him if his battery-lit sneakers hadn't given him away...Or how about the time Townshend confiscated Jailbait Jimmy's phone and virtuously threw it into the Tarn?"

Lucy shot Beebe a rueful smile, though her eyes were dancing.

"She's going to have you thinking daycare's all Chinese fire drills and juvenile delinquency, Althea. Most of the time we're pretty orderly, really. I love it when the children are rapt with some craft project in the inglenook. It can be so hushed I can make out the ticking of the clock in the hall."

Beebe erupted in joyous, strangled snickers.

"Yeah, there was a really big hush when the Musgrove twins discovered Carpenter had glued their mittens to their chairs. That happened during story time, didn't we figure? Carpenter works best in a quiet environment. Bubo had some explaining to do about those hand-knit mittens."

"Bubo? Is that Marian?"

Beebe nodded, grabbing Al's half-full bowl of popcorn and shoveling it through her enormous one so that it brimmed again.

"Latin. The great European eagle-owl. Even a four-year-old could see she was magisterial, reticent, bookish, so that was my name for her. Probably picked it up from my dad. He was a wildlife biologist."

Beebe looked barely out of elementary school to Althea. Such a precocious vocabulary. One felt Beebe mightn't suffer fools gladly, in spite of the dimples.

"A wildlife biologist," Al repeated, as though it were her favorite flavor of ice cream.

Beebe regarded her impassively until Lucy provided a detour, piping, "Must be where Beebe gets her green soul. She'd rather commune with a tree than – " Beebe cut her off.

"My parents were killed in an avalanche in Switzerland. Skiing. She was 28. He was 55. Would you like to see their pictures?" Expressionless, she was already scrambling to her feet.

"I would," Al replied to a vanishing pair of bare feet below a nightgown.

She'd decided at the interview that fantasy was Beebe's native element. This sounded like a film scenario. Aware that her social discernment had shredded under the weight of exhaustion, suppressed distress and wary self-consciousness, she looked to Lucy.

"Marian's tried very hard to provide a good home and education." This sounded too dutiful. "She and her husband were happily childless academics, both tenured at the University." Lucy lowered her voice.

"There was no one else to take Beebe. It all fell to her Aunt Marian; her husband was oblivious: an otherworldly sage wrapped up in his grad students." She brightened. "Inspired marriage, though. They fell in love in England, his home. She was his student. Pretty romantic for – well, someone like Marian. She brought him back here to Lilybanks. Her grandma Calla passed away while Marian was overseas, and left the place to her. Perfect timing. I came on board to help start the daycare when she was newly widowed. You'd think two pensions would suffice, but she wants to send Beebe to Oxford and Lilybanks is a constant drain – any repair has to be authentic. You can't just call the roofers, you need to hunt down impeccably duplicate shingles..."

Althea nodded sympathetically but didn't feel so. "You can't just call the roofers." She knew all about that. She and Casper had gone without birthdays or Christmas, and taken a calculator through the grocery store for a year when their roof needed work. Casper made careful additions each time she added a loaf or can to the cart. How touching, even carefree, (even desirable!), their economies and worries seemed now. She forced herself to pick up the thread of Lucy's words –

"...to have worked out. For instance she's very independent. A good thing, don't you think? She's already nearly a professional baker – *patissière*, that's what she likes to be called. And so imaginative; the cocoa is par for the course around here." Lucy bent forward. "She wanted you to have something special tonight!"

"It was perfect," Al answered, genuinely fervent. After Marian had wished her a cordial good night Lucy had brought up the homemade popcorn and Beebe produced three mugs of hot white chocolate, like lavish cupcakes with thick, fluted whipped cream caps improbably flecked with candied violets. Althea had been reassured by this portent of affinity. Conscious once more of Lilybanks as her merciful, express fate, her spirits veered upward.

Beebe strode in, flopping onto the mattress with an easy familiarity for which Althea was grateful.

"My mother's high school graduation photo. My dad in Indonesia." She held up a small frame in each hand, not letting go but keeping them steady for Al to examine. She studied them herself, upside down.

The mother was sweetly beautiful, with Beebe's dark hair, ripeness and composure. A strong likeness. Beebe's father hunched toward the camera, beaming squintily through oversized glasses. Binoculars hung from his neck; he clutched a pith helmet. He seemed confident, even radiant, though his ears stuck out badly and he reminded Al more of a chimp than a suitable mate for the princess in the sweater set. A smallish Komodo dragon made its way out of the frame safely to his rear.

"She's lovely, Beebe. So like you. And your father!…I thought those lizards are ferocious."

Absorbed, Beebe shrugged.

"They are. I think it's a young one."

Al considered Beebe's plump, perfect feet and pulled her own beneath her. Lately the gnarled, blue-grey veins on top had become quite pronounced.

Lucy, who wore tailored pajamas and a pair of fleecy clip-clops with bunny ears, squiggled up to the other end of the mattress and began gently undoing Beebe's braids.

"I love your animals, Althea. The dog looks like an old friend?" Lucy had a way of pruning conversations; Al couldn't decide if it was deliberate or part of her sweet but scary out-to-lunchedness.

"We're inseparable," Al said, brazen. Early in the day's unpacking and arranging she'd decided, tired and defiant, to re-install her threadbare cocker spaniel and his sidekicks on her bed pillows rather than abandon them to a shelf like amusing kitsch.

"His name's Cookie. I can't remember a time before him. He's getting a little shabby, but age will do that." (She'd intended to add "but so am I," and thought better of it.)

"Is this an otter?...And a kiwi!" Beebe clutched her tiny parents to her chest; the enormity of the girl's loss struck Al. Her eyes filled.

"I could make him a little jacket to protect that seam up his back from more wear and tear. Shall I? A jaunty red one to match his nose?"

"She loves to sew. She made Skippy a little sleeping bag!"

Al, who'd just lost her heart to Lucy, feigned confusion to conceal her response.

"Skippy?"

"My rabbit. I'll introduce you tomorrow, Althea. He's gone to bed. I didn't bring him in for fear of distressing the kitty, but he loves to party. Skippy's very open-minded; I hope they'll be buddies."

This struck Al as sanguine in the extreme, but she smiled gamely. Linnet had retreated to the depths of Al's awkward new closet under the eaves; a pair of phosphorescent orbs occasionally hovered above the bags of shoes.

"He's a Dutch rabbit – white with black jacket and accessories. The electrical wires in Lucy's room have special padding so he can't bite into them." Lucy was finger-combing Beebe's loose hair now in big-sister fashion, though Al thought their respective ages tenuous.

"Lucy's room is the nursery. You must've seen it on tours. Bubo let her paint the closet door, and a border all round the room."

"I *do* remember. I *love* your room, Lucy! Storks, and zoo animals in party caps – the funniest little monkey!...on a sort of parchment color. And the door – delphiniums and snapdragons – I remember a snail down in one corner. And a marble? I thought it was original to the house."

"I copied old toys and wallpaper. I'm glad you like it." Lucy had long dark eyelashes and a shy smile, wide but closed.

With a twinge Althea thought how she'd have loved showing her home off to Lucy. The Augsbergers might be moving in as they spoke, giggling at Al's gaudy, determined decoration – the stenciled dining room ceiling she'd fallen off the stepladder for, the decoupaged potting table in the mudroom that proved too massive to move...Or maybe they ignored all the outlandish departures from their own vision of a home, focusing on where to install the immense TV screen, the hot tub...Oh, her beloved garden...

Beebe dragged the oversized popcorn bowl back into the lap of her nightgown and raised an eyebrow at Al's untouched bowl.

"Come on, Althea. We can't finish this by ourselves. And Aphrodite doesn't like popcorn. Lucy lived in Paris for two years."

Al felt a pang of envy, subsumed by blossoming devotion.

"Really! My husband and I were there on our honeymoon. What were you up to?" She and Beebe both gazed admiringly at Lucy, who rolled her eyes. When she shook her head her angled hair shimmered.

"Just being there. I was an illegal au pair, a dog-walker, apartment cleaner, a go-fer for a Swiss countess – that was fun...strictly under-the-table stuff. It was exhilarating some of the time, and my French improved...but eventually it seemed time to come home." The tremor was back; Al had noticed it in the afternoon and attributed it to fatigue. Lucy's hands fluttered disconcertingly from Beebe's thick tresses to a quivering glass of water. Althea couldn't help but stare. Their eyes met; Al attempted an encouraging smile but Lucy's glance had already caromed away. She fanned the air in front of her face, as though she'd swallowed some torrid spice.

"I met a person in Paris...whom I ended up living with in San Francisco." Lucy looked bewildered now, and Beebe looked apprehensive.

"It didn't work out. So I moved here, eventually. By then I'd completed my Waldorf training in the Bay area." She shrugged as though discussing some baffling third party.

"You know, Lucy – I think Cookie would love a dapper little jacket."

"Maybe a hoody!" crowed Beebe. "Lucy's getting married to Micah Fennel. Wait till you meet *him*. He's a librarian at the humanities library, an eternal student who's actually responsible and mature, he's good-looking, and he's a man of God!"

Slightly taken aback by Beebe's last pious exclamation, Al didn't know what to say. She caught Lucy blushing, which she found sweet but vaguely alarming.

"We haven't actually set a date. I met him at the Lakeside craft show in May. He attends the Russian Orthodox church on Scribner Street, which has captured Beebe's imagination."

"My husband grew up in the Orthodox church. Our wedding was on Scribner Street." And she'd joined but never quite gotten the hang of it, a chronic goat in sheepskin, in spite of the somber, numinous interior of the historic building. (Had she told them this?) She felt that Beebe was sizing her up, maybe pigeonholing her as wishy-washy, terminally tepid, in the black-and-white manner she'd favored in her own youth.

"Actually, I'm becoming very interested in Eckhart Tolle's teachings."

Lucy rested her chin on her knees and pulled at her rabbit ears.

"They saved me," she said softly, in a rather thrilling and embarrassing way.

"In what sense? I mean, I'm sure it's very personal, Lucy, but can you give me a general idea without going into your details?" She'd tried not to sound as urgent as she felt, and ended by sounding clinical.

"Sure." Lucy sat up straight; she looked different, seemed to have sharper edges, as though she were more willing to be delineated.

"I was being devoured by my own thoughts. You've read about what Eckhart calls the 'pain-body'?"

"A bit. Sort of a cesspool of all the negative emotions you've ever felt, that likes to leak into the present moment."

"Well, my pain-body was in charge nearly all the time. I'm still not sure how I got through the teacher training. Craft skills and self-control in public. My last set of roommates told me I had to find a new place when my sublet expired. They were afraid I was headed for the psych ward or going to kill myself. One of their boyfriends – oh, he was so sweet, and handsome – I'm sure he was really gay – gave me a copy of *The Power of Now*. I couldn't put it down, slept with it in my arms, and he – Paul, his name was – arranged for me to have three weeks at a monastery on the Russian River. I quit my job at a café and just studied the book all alone for three weeks; didn't have to interact with anyone. I emerged with the tools I needed so I didn't have to live at the mercy of my self-hatred anymore. I'd been insane – but only a slightly more intense version of most people's "sanity": I identified with my thoughts. And now I don't! I don't repress them. I just…gently detach and they evaporate, I guess you could say. I'm kind of muzzy sometimes, and I'd be the first to admit I'm not "present" all the time. But I am pretty often, which is a miracle, believe me, Althea."

Encouraged but reluctant to reveal her own inner turmoil, touched by Lucy's openness but a little dismayed by her oddness (psych ward?), Althea settled for grabbing one of Lucy's hands and patting it.

"Thank you so much. I haven't been able to go at the book very methodically yet but I look forward to doing that."

"Please, Althea, anything but that!" Beebe practically shrieked, and then began choking on her popcorn theatrically till Lucy had to pound her on the back, if only to get her to settle down.

"PLEASE don't look forward to doing it!" Beebe got into a prayerful attitude on her knees facing the utterly disconcerted Al.

"She means just do it," smiled Lucy in the mild, prim manner Althea had begun to rely on. Beebe fell on her and shoved a handful of popcorn down the back of her pajama top.

"Althea doesn't want popcorn all over her floor, you ninny…" They were tickling each other, nearly wrestling; Al reflected wearily that she could never hope to be anything but a third wheel alongside these two. Of course there was Booboo (surely not? How exhausted she was)…Beeboo?

"You can watch Eckhart lecture and answer questions online, Althea. I've got a computer lurking in my bedroom -- you can come listen anytime."

"I'd like to see what he's like in person. Could we do it fairly soon?" Though even if the computer revealed someone pretty off-putting, it was a bit late to jump ship now.

"Well, sure we could! How does tomorrow sound?"

Al nodded, feeling like one of Lucy's preschoolers.

"I suppose you know Lilybanks hasn't entered the electronic age yet?" Beebe spoke over a shoulder while gathering squashed popcorn. "No computers, except for the one Micah gave Lucy and talked Bubo into, no TV, no cell phones. Lilybanks is meant to be a serene sanctuary from all that. Did Bubo confiscate your phone at the door?"

"Good heavens, no. It's packed away somewhere here. My husband had it most of the time. I haven't used it since – he's been gone. Never really deciphered it, except for calling out. And I gave our computer to my cousin's kid." In spite of her relief not to be the low-tech lame duck, Al felt a little uneasy at joining a whole flock of lame ducks. Was it in her best interests to be entering some reactionary sect?

But there was something so endearing about Lucy, so reassuringly weighty about Marian, so beguiling about Lilybanks. No doubt she was just feeling characteristically reluctant to belong to any club that would have her as a member. Contrite and grateful, Al sought to offer up some intimate disclosure as a gesture of solidarity.

"It's so lovely to be here. I imagined I'd have to move to some uninspired apartment. There wasn't money left for a condominium – as my cousin out east advised – after back taxes. Casper and I sort of had to eat our home up over these past years, leaving just a hollow shell." She paused to control the tremor in her voice. "We looked alright, but we couldn't keep up with the property taxes. I hadn't realized how thoroughly we'd used up our only asset. Anyway. Here I am at Lilybanks.

It's a tremendous blessing." No need to go into the penurious salary of untenured, adjunct teachers, or her own ostrich-like failure to acquire the most basic computer skills needed for a job.

As Lucy murmured sympathetically, Beebe blurted, "You didn't have children?"

"No. I was 37 when we married. Casper didn't have much interest in kids, and I was content. It was always, well...an older marriage. I do enjoy children, of course," she said, remembering the upcoming daycare duties.

To her surprise, Beebe nodded vigorously.

"I'm not having kids either. Too demanding, too distracting!"

"Some people seem more destined for parenthood than others. Your friend Tad seems like he'd make a great dad some day." Shameless fishing. Did Beebe think of him as a boyfriend? "And what nice manners; he called me ma'am. I haven't heard that for decades, except from policemen and telemarketers."

"That's the Lakehurst Academy effect. Private military school his dad packed him off to after his mother died. His dad's an army engineer. The manners sort of suit Tad. But the snobby repressive atmosphere didn't." Beebe sighed. "You're right; he wants at least five kids. He's the type who'll be married by 21." She rolled her eyes.

"Tad's a simple, soulful guy. When he became friends with us and liked the feel of Beebe's Waldorf home-schooling, he refused to go back to Lakehurst this fall. His father has to travel a lot, and worried about the lack of supervision."

Beebe's cynical laugh interrupted Lucy.

"What was his dad thinking? Tad's famously responsible, conscientious, irreproachable." She looked as though she found this regrettable.

"Anyway," Lucy continued, "Marian told Captain Bramble we'd sort of keep him under Lilybanks' wing. You can imagine how handy it is to have him around. The little boys worship him. They were intractable, as Marian would say, last month – all they wanted to do was have Tad fling them into leaf piles."

"You're leaving a lot out, Lucy. Tad and his father had a huge showdown. Can you imagine what it's like when Tad finally, FINALLY gets really mad? And he's half a foot taller than his dad. Captain Bramble threatened to have Stubblefield's home school program for older students shut down by pulling a few strings. Tad threatened to disappear." Much as she liked Tad, the thought of the gravely masculine, five o'clock-shadowed, nominal minor running away from home struck Al as hilarious.

"Bubo and Lucy had Captain Bramble here for tea and negotiations, and talked him 'round. He could hardly stand to *look* at me. But I'm growing on him! He likes my sticky buns."

"Beebe is a superb, self-taught baker, Al. *Une patisssière,*" Lucy repeated.

"They sell my work at the Maven Alley Bakery."

"That's one of my favorite places! My goodness, Beebe, how old are you? Not out of high school yet and already in business!" Al felt a new respect, though she wondered if it were a case of a family friend letting the kid decorate cookies.

"I plan to support myself as a *patissière*. Once you get highly skilled you can bake yourself around the world." She displayed a steely complacency and hadn't even bothered with her age, as though Al could save questions like that for daycare. A new envy for those whose life lay ahead of them instead of behind curdled Althea's vision of tarts and marzipan.

"I'm going to make Lucy and Micah's wedding cake." Beebe laid her head on Lucy's shoulder. Lucy patted her cheek and felt her forehead, as though Beebe required habitual maternal monitoring. The older girl (as Althea realized she thought of her, though Lucy might be thirty), somehow insubstantial in spite of her unflappable good cheer, made a pleasing foil for the fierce younger one. She could guess how well they got along; Lucy disarming, Beebe engaging. In an irrational flash Al realized she disliked Micah Fennel sight unseen.

"Althea, you must be drooping. We didn't even let you unpack your jammies! I'm going to bed; the bathroom's all yours. What about you, Beebe?" Lucy threw them each a kiss and left. Her punctilious outburst and Al's increasingly faded silence sent Beebe scrabbling off the mattress.

"I'm off downstairs to check on my *pots de crème*. Don't worry about me, Althea, I won't be in the bathroom either. Oh, but may I say goodnight to your Linnet?"

Embarrassed by her rustiness, Al had to maneuver herself onto hands and knees before she dared attempt standing. Her lower back twinged; she covered the wince with a phony yawn. Usually her aging body mildly exasperated Al; just now she felt sadness, a kind of exile, at the others' heedless elasticity. She plodded over to the closet to forestall Beebe; Linnet might spend the whole night pressed furrily against the hems of Al's clothes if Beebe spooked her.

"Do you think Linnet would like some warm milk, Althea? Blessed Katerina used to heat milk she'd begged and leave saucers on church steps for starving cats. Once a little boy (who grew up to be a deacon) saw a vision of a winged cat, an angel, in the flames of Katerina's outdoor bonfire for homeless folk and creatures." Her eyes lit up. "And we could try the *pots de crème*. You want to?"

"How marvelous! You're sure you're not too tired?" But Beebe was already in the hallway. At least Linnet was unperturbed.

Casper's watch, which she'd been surreptitiously checking since the impromptu pajama party had blossomed, read 11:40. It hadn't seemed politic to nip Beebe's overtures in the bud, and she never *had* had the discipline to turn down an offer of dessert, much less one for Linnet. Blessed Katerina? She must have missed something.

Althea plunked back down onto the mattress. This was nearly the first time she'd been alone since she'd rung the doorbell. She had to force herself to leave the door ajar for Beebe.

An odd sensation, seeing her belongings floating (or thunking) up Lilybanks' staircase. They'd taken a pizza break amidst stacks of boxes and roped, padded furniture, her door wide open in spite of startled students arriving for tutorials. Beebe and Lucy had admired and advised as Tad maneuvered the largest pieces of Al's furniture. Poor dazed Linnet had been mercifully sequestered in Marian's bathroom with her bambam. Eventually Tad and Beebe had gone out, and Marian supplied a sort of orientation in her study. There'd been tea with "gingernuts" (this was much more like it). Lucy'd lingered, which helped.

Marian had typed up a rough daily schedule. It seemed they all met regularly to discuss household wrinkles, personal challenges, and the weekly reading – some passage from Tolle or another source, which they took turns choosing. She'd received a sheaf of stapled notes on kitchen duty and chores, peppered with edicts: "Only vegetarian fare passes through our portals: carnivorous guests will not be coddled." "Please don't pollute Lilybanks with insecticides, cigarette smoke or NEGATIVITY." "KEEP TURTLES AWAY FROM STAIRS." "Salt-free peanuts ONLY for students wishing to feed squirrels: taste if unsure." "Please make sure you're *present* before handling Calla's Roycroft dinner service!"

Al considered pinching herself. At last, a niche she fit. How tenderly God and Casper had provided for her.

The kindness! She stole a shy glance at the exquisite vintage shawl draped over the folding screen next to the mattress. Bundled in tissue paper bound with velvet ribbon, its card read "To our sister Lilybanker with love and confidence." Marian had insisted she open it first thing after the moving van drove off. They'd left Tad upstairs to unfurl a carpet and convened in the sitting room, one of Althea's favorites. They'd perched her in a window seat like a new queen and stared contentedly. The green silk embroidered with ivory lilies ravished Althea and provided a charm against dark moments all day.

There'd also been a bag of cat toys that provoked tears she didn't try to hide. And later she'd found Eckhart's *The Power of Now* and *A New Earth*, stacked and beribboned (who'd finessed that?) on her newly installed desk that looked down on Corrie Street.

When Al had half-jokingly asked Beebe if she had to take some kind of vow to join the sisterhood, Beebe had looked at her appraisingly and replied, "Well, if you like. I think a vow to serve flora, fauna and felicity would suit you." After Marian bellowed for Tad from the bottom of the stairs Lucy had produced champagne glasses – the old-fashioned, shallow kind Althea loved – and they'd all toasted her with charmingly improbable, bubbly elderflower water from England: "To our conscious unity."

She'd expected nothing like this. Al had to gnaw on her hand to keep the sense of the past weeks' desolation at bay. On a crate near her pillow her new house keys lay beside Casper's watch. Lucy and Beebe had made her a key ring of old buttons and beads from the Lilybanks attic. (*That* wasn't included on the tour!) How could she be worthy of this generous belief in her ability to belong? Tears brimmed again. She was too tired.

Funny that after her excited, middle-of-the-night floor plans the focal point of her new space should be a venerable *über*-philodendron, worthy of a jungle, which had proven impossible to evict without formidable surgery. It presided from its own oak tambour, a botanical deity whose many arms twisted up toward the ample light from three banks of windows.

This had been Calla Morrissey's studio, running along the more secluded side of the house, with a single window peeking out onto Corrie from behind Lilybanks' chalet front. Odds and ends Althea remembered from tours – a plaster bust, ancient squashed tubes of paint, a croquet set – had been sent to the attic till Tour Day. Al had kept Calla's dressmaking mannequin, and an old trunk.

The long wall across from the door presented a series of French doors opening onto window boxes it would be Al's job to water come spring. She had no fear of the ultra-prudent Linnet plummeting over the edge. The balcony room might prove too sunny for her migraines, though. Al reminded herself to ask Lucy where she'd bought her adorable tomato-red sunglasses.

Marian had admitted this was one of the harder rooms to heat, and offered to supply as many mobile heaters as Al wanted. After all, Marian's only other expense so far had been to replace the flyblown matchstick blinds – authentic but scarcely functional – with Roman shades of unbleached linen. Lucy had offered to help stencil their hems once Al was established.

She gingerly reviewed the survivors of a brutal triage: the "meadow cabinet," as she and Casper had named the bookcase whose glass doors bore leaded greenery; the stacked pair of 1890's tansu chests they'd bought, intoxicated, with her small inheritance from a great-aunt; the tall black lacquer "butterfly cupboard" from China with its fanciful winged latch, the best of the oriental carpets, two Arts and Crafts rockers, a drop-leaf desk with heart-shaped cut-outs, a stained glass lamp, Casper's antique chest of drawers from Prague, two folding screens.

The realtor's savvy sister was selling what was too special for estate-sale scavengers on e-bay for a tidy but not ruthless fee. The MacDuffs up the street, who'd kept a canny eye on Al's proceedings, offered to take the cat-scratched double bed for a guest room, to Al's relief. (Impossible to sleep in now, impossible to junk.) The whimsical dining room set and bathroom armoire she'd decoupaged with such earnest passion years ago might be huddling under the stars in her driveway this very minute; the estate sale impresario had briskly assured her that items unsold on Saturday would be "safe" till Sunday's half-price finale. None of that bore thinking on, of course...

She began to wonder how much longer cataloguing could keep homesickness at bay.

"Althea?" The breathy voice and glimpse of white gown struck Al as unnervingly spectral. Beebe, still startlingly short, held spoons and a pair of custard cups. She perched on the steamer trunk, and Al sat next to her so they could keep their voices low. She was too tired and wound up to have a sense of the other bedrooms' distance.

They clinked, and tucked in.

"Ambrosia. Thank you again for your help all day, Beebe, and Tad's. Everyone's been so kind. Lucy must have been exhausted, with her daycare responsibilities in addition to all my upheaval. She seemed very...fatigued, at times, just now."

"Lucy's old boyfriend was a drunk who beat the tar out of her, Althea. That's why she seems kind of vacant sometimes. She doesn't mind my telling you. Micah's her first relationship since the abuser."

Al felt a trapdoor in her gut give way, not entirely unexpectedly.

"How terrible. Is she on medication?" (In charge of all those children!)

"No. She's fine. Just threadbare in places – memory, nerves. Micah's okay with it. She's still a treasure."

"Yes, a treasure."

"I'm sorry your husband died, Althea. And everything. It must feel pretty strange, being here. I hope you can just embrace us all, as we are. Like we're embracing you."

Reflecting on the subtle ambivalence of Beebe's last remark, Al exchanged hugs with her as she rose to leave.

"Oops, I forgot Linnet's milk!"

"That's okay. Her digestion gets tricky when she's rattled. Good night!" She waited till Beebe's footsteps receded before turning the skeleton key in its lock.

Numb with overexertion of all kinds, Al coaxed Linnet from the closet by commandeering the bambam, installed both on her mattress, and slept.

Reading in Bed

Beebe huddled against her bed, turning *Lilac Corner*'s yellowed pages. She planned to sleep on the floor tonight, having promised Tad not to sleep in the garden again till March. He'd campaigned for April, but she simply couldn't miss those ferocious March winds.

How patient one needed to be. Althea Athnos was so fragile and complicated. You could tell there were interesting stories in there, of course. But Althea took the stories very seriously, as though they were a flock of baby birds that needed regular attention and feeding and outings. Beebe had difficulty imagining Althea just "being," at least around other people. Safer to retreat into layer after habitual layer of reticence and wounds and subterfuge.

Her judgments began to echo tinnily. She dropped them like white-hot knives. Just as easy to say Althea was appreciative and gentle. And the real Althea was beyond labels. Here was her page...

A pale blue envelope marked *"par avion"* tumbled out of the book onto the floor. Beebe retrieved it and, as if taking a hint, considered its familiar contents. She'd culled the letter from a shoebox Bubo had turned over to her on her seventh birthday, the age of reason. Over the years she'd realized her aunt had never read a line of Beebe's father's love letters to her mother.

> *...hope you know me better than to worry about "scientific" caution OR family legends about sideshow spectacles. Neither you nor I, Bernie, cares a plugged nickel about such concerns, so we need never discuss it again but just live our life together with love and charity. Our children will be beautiful in every way.*
>
> *Speaking of family secrets, the Morrisseys have one that leaves quite a bit of pie on our mugs, and your*

intended awkwardly finds himself its sole living heir. Since you're on the verge of joining the family, my darling, let me pass you the hot potato before it's too late to escape. Seems our celebrated Grandma Calla didn't actually write that 1920's flash-in-the-pan book about kitties and storks and doggies she somewhat famously illustrated. It's been out of print for years, a perfectly commonplace anecdote not particularly written for children that masqueraded as a clever must-have for the nursery set due to Cal's quirky drawings and her minor local repute as princess of all things avant-garde, or what passed for such on the prairie.

Old Fez isn't on the family coat of arms yet, but the book's irretrievably part of the Lilybanks mystique (however modest). Some day when I've retired from the field (ha!) to help raise our nestlings, getting landmark status for the family castle will be on my list of domestic chores. We'll tell the truth insofar as we know it – after all, Grandma did the illustrations for sure – and provide the public with an amusing little mystery. In the meantime I'm reluctant to spill the beans, hurting my sister's feelings being not the least of reasons.

I was Mother's favorite – maybe Marian was too much like her for comfort – and she asked me to keep the riddle of the author to myself. She was getting older and just wanted to unburden herself. Seems Calla thought Mother wrote it and Mother let her think so in order to avoid some unpleasantness of a murky nature regarding who Mother guessed the author was. Of course Calla wanted her daughter's name emblazoned on the cover and made enthusiastic plans for the illustrations. Mother quashed this. (She was an inexorable

*quasher, honed by years of Grandma's attempts to make
her what she was not.) So Calla got the thing published
under her own name, upgrading a final flattering scene
by adding an automobile and her favorite French scarf
to make it more* au courant.

*Mother'd only tell me she thought it was written
for her by one of the more unsettling oddballs in Calla's
entourage. She used to make obscure references to domestic irregularities during her childhood – more intuition than knowledge, it seemed. (Marian claims not to
remember this. Her determined opacity about people's
private lives makes her the perfect keeper of the family
flame, devoted to quarter-sawn Lily-lore and superbly
indifferent to dirty vintage underwear!)*

*So no more angst about Great-uncle Tom Thumb,
Bern, no one's family tree's without its share of curious
customers.*

Twenty-three days and counting,
Your Arthur

Beebe's heart lifted with love for her father, and for Bubo. She
resumed the story, recognizing an enigmatic little passage she loved:

A ripe moon, fresh and cool and soothing, hovered through the
jagged doorway. Its bright veil surrounded her. It seemed there
was no further need for effort. The pull of action had receded;
she barely sensed its faint foolish pulse at a growing distance.
Somehow she was well looked after now. The moon shared its
peace lavishly. How simple, how peaceful to take refuge against
its loving heart...Far, far away kittens romped. They were safe.
And so was she, Willow, though it had taken so long to remember in this crooked silvery nest in the sky.

* * *

Giddy, guilty and gleeful, Bezique streaked across his front yard, half way up the young hickory on the far side of the picket fence, back down again and into the thicket of lilacs and ferns before he collected himself. Must've been the thrill of the wind in his fur. Of course he'd wanted to outrun the butcher's boy, who might have imagined a fat tip from Mrs. B. for his pains. As it was, neither had noticed a thing.

That Snowy! Bezique wriggled his rump and rolled in the ferns, applauding her performance. While Mrs. B. chatted over the chitterlings at the front door, Snowy jumped onto the parlor table where her mistress had laid out some needlework. When he'd signaled, she'd stuck a claw in the tablecloth and dived overboard in a rip-roaring, tangled blur of spilling scissors and pincushions and growling somersault. He'd bolted between the boy's knickerbockers.

Only now did it occur to him that he'd lost his head; the plan was to run along the front of the house and dive into the hole under the porch. Gypsy! He sagged. Amid all the careful, clandestine plans for his getaway he'd never thought to alert Gypsy. She might be twelve houses and two fields away at the moment. He needed to be back inside well before dark; he had responsibilities.

Imagining Snowy's scorn should his mission fizzle, he decided to search the property at once before Mrs. B. realized he'd gotten outside.

In fifteen minutes he'd left pungent calling cards at the cellar door, under the arbor, behind Delilah's doghouse (wouldn't *she* be surprised), along the woodshed, among the foxgloves, between the forget-me-nots. He'd mewed softly under the mock oranges, noisily sharpened his claws near the porch, rubbed his cheeks along the pickets till they smarted, conducted inspections of neighboring grounds from the tall outhouse elm. No Gypsy. At least she'd find that Bah-seek kept his word.

He decided to take the liberty of investigating her place under the porch. Perhaps she was at home, sound asleep, though he doubted it. Not the type to let moss grow beneath her paws, that one. Bezique retraced his steps under mock oranges, turned at the front corner of the house and crept along the cat-sized alley between its boards and the shrubs.

He caught traces of her mild, delectable scent. The shallow tunnel below the Florida room smelled irresistibly of his darl – of the little black imp. Hesitating on the threshold a moment, Bezique tweaked his whiskers. Bezique the Bold. He crouched and thrust his head into the darkness.

Pairs of eery little eyeballs glistened at him in silence.

He shot backwards, glimpsed more eyes beside him and skyrocketed into Mrs. B.'s window box, nearly losing his balance as he came face to face with a dumbfounded Applesauce through the window. Mrs.'s B.'s geraniums snapped juicily beneath him.

"Bah-seek!"

He peered down into the shadows beneath the shrubs.

"Gypsy?"

"What are you doing, Bah-seek?"

He teetered along the window box's narrow rim, summoning considerable reserves of dignity.

"As you see. Patrolling. I think there's a family of young possums in your shelter, Gypsy. They must have snuck in while you were out. I recommend that we –"

"Bah-seek, come down at once. It's alright, they're not possums."

When he leapt down she purred softly and batted at the scarlet petal between his ears.

"Whaa?"

"Silly. 'Keep offstage.' That was our mother's rule about

patrolling…Oh, Bah-seek, you've come!" He felt her warm breath on his face as Gypsy's velvety purr rose and fell. Suddenly bashful, his eyes crossed with delight.

"Come, I'll show you."

Dubious, he flattened himself into the hole behind her, prepared to defend her to his last breath.

A chorus of peeping mews greeted Gypsy, punctuated by tiny hisses in his direction. Enlightened but still confused, Bezique telegraphed his question through the dark.

"My sister's kittens. So young to be weaned…Oh, we must find her very soon Bah-seek. It's alright, children. This is the powerful friend who will help us." She turned toward him. "You're the hero of their bedtime stories. Don't be afraid, children."

A pair of absurdly small paws stumbled over his.

"I can help, Bah-seek," someone squeaked up at him. "Take me with you. I want to find our Mama."

"That's Scout, the first-born. Her mother's helpmate." Bezique heard the pride in Gypsy's voice. This was clearly not the moment to waffle about like some aloof bachelor who couldn't tell a teething twig from a tail.

In a tone that he hoped sounded like distant thunder, he replied, "Listen well, Lionheart. I want you to stay here and guard your brothers. Your mother would want that also. Show me that I can rely on you."

Bezique's eyes had adjusted to the dark enough to see the kitten's dim outline retreating into the furry huddle with tail raised high like a proud pennant. So far, so good.

"How many are there?"

"Four. Scout, Pippin, Twinkle and Scholar."

"Scholar?"

"He likes to think things over. My sister is small and unassuming, but she lavished attention on her kittens. She pored over their names, finding just the right one for each. We discussed the choices at length." Gypsy's gaze grew distant. "Oh Bah-seek, she would never abandon us. Sometimes I...fear the worst."

He touched her nose lightly with his own. "I should be back inside by sundown. Let's make the most of our time, Gypsy. Teach me the lay of the land beyond my windows. We can discuss possibilities as we patrol." He raised his voice. "I am confident the kittens have a vigilant guard in their sister Scout." Squeaks and murmurs rose from behind a short stack of Mr. Bunting's bricks.

Suddenly acutely aware that he'd missed out on the butcher boy's delivery, he realized how smugly oblivious he and the others were indoors.

"What are they eating?"

"I bring them what I can from the bowl, and sometimes a nice soft vole. Their tummies and tongues are too tender for crunching yet. I sneak them out to your kind lady's saucer for water when I can, but it's not easy. Your lady is watchful."

"You're mistaken, Gypsy. She would help. No need to hide them!"

Gypsy drew herself up.

"Never. It's against our code. We are different from you and your friends inside."

*　　*　　*

Beebe sighed, unfurling another blanket. She knew the feeling.

4

School Days

Thank God for long underwear. Althea huddled over her bowl of oatmeal and stewed prunes, keeping vigil for headlights through vintage lace. She almost fancied she could see her breath, and played suspicious little games with it. Her spoon thumped a cinnamon stick. It had been Beebe's turn to make breakfast in the wee hours before being chaperoned across the slick sidewalks to Maven Alley by Tad. Althea had seen her toiling over marzipan holly for their popular cinnamon rolls.

Bored and a bit apprehensive – this was her solo debut on the early-bird shift, Lucy having hovered to introduce and reassure both parents and kids for several days – Al tucked the bowl under a plant stand and hugged her sweater closer. With prescience she'd saved it from high school days; pumpkin-colored Italian mohair (with mohair buttons!), 1960's Sears. On the first day it had become abundantly clear that the bottom half of Al's daycare uniform would be jeans and sensible shoes. But protective plumage kept her spirits up; one wanted to look like an amused, cultivated mentor rather than any old –

How fatuous! Benighted! Was this all she could summon to encounter the day? "Having one's head up one's butt," was the phrase that came to mind. Groping for one of Eckhart's antidotes, Al breathed in deeply and exhaled, managing to pay attention only to that. She began to be able to feel sensation in her lips, as well as nostrils, and then a tingling in her fingers. Relief. Shutting her eyes, she concentrated on listening while keeping in touch with face and hands and the rise and fall of her breath. Intermittent whispery gushes from the radiator...Aphrodite snoring in her basket under the stairs. (Only too clear that the dog found Althea utterly uninteresting.)

STOP. There she was, defiling the chaste predawn stillness with her knee-jerk negativity. How small, how *impacted*. Wait – Eckhart said not to judge the junk popping up in one's mind. Self-criticism (especially in her signature sardonic mode) just prolonged the mistake with more of the same negativity. Better to drop the entire monologue like a hot potato, and start over with the breathing.

Al shut her eyes and inhaled deeply. A hint of headlights glided over her eyelids. She stiffened and scurried into the hall. Mercifully, she was not expected to skate down to the street to extricate children from car seats (as she'd doggedly attempted on her first morning, while two carpoolers shivered and groaned). Al suppressed the urge to check herself in the hallway mirror again, fortified by the novelty – still heady – of tugging open Lilybanks' front door from the inside.

Embrace the Now! (Let it be Melodie...) A pink nylon gnome trudged towards her up the powdered lawn, skirting the slick Lilybanks sidewalk. Mrs. Osterman, supervising from below, tossed Al a wave. Plump pink mittens hung from Melodie's cuffs and flapped against her pastel lunchbox; synthetic rustling accompanied her every move.

"Just look at you! What a beautiful snowsuit!" (And poignantly excessive.) She'd forgotten how sweet little children could be. Melodie seemed to be in a trance. Al tried again, smiling theatrically for the distant Mrs. O.

"Is it new?"

Melodie nodded demurely.

"I'm so happy to see you, Melodie. Let's wave to your mother." She noticed the small smile waver as Melodie whirled to stare at the car.

"Melodie, let's take some snow in to the doggy! I bet she'd love to see some snow! Shall we put your mittens on, and you can scoop some up?"

Melodie looked dubious but permitted the procedure, perhaps picking up the desperation in Al's voice. Mrs. Osterman drove off unheeded.

Al still marveled at the children's nonchalant crossing of the Lilybanks threshold. She hoped the place would enchant their dreams many years from now, though they seemed to miss their parents' microwaves and laptops. Melodie was very uneasy with the first-floor bathroom, whose dim corners and assortment of chubby, crazed porcelain handles clearly felt alien.

"Sit down on your chair, dear, and we'll get your boots off so we don't get the hallway floor all wet."

Al coaxed the stiffly tiptoeing Melodie over to the dog's basket, and had to resort to clapping to waken Aphrodite. Seeming to realize what was required, Ditey greeted Melodie with a long-suffering wag and then snorted, obliterating what was left of the snow.

Melodie giggled, to Al's relief, and scampered into the "kindernook," Lilybanks' library and inglenook during daycare hours. For a moment Al could sense her own leaden, resistant stance, her tension. She'd been steeled against some great potential blow, possibly delivered by a three-year-old. Absurd. Perhaps one could lighten up? Glimpsing some more pliant alternative – luminous, effervescent – Al took a deep breath. She felt a bit fizzy.

Someone hammered on the door. Carpenter's alarming, self-assured father, no doubt. The Blaines' hectic, variable schedule had been explained to her. She fluttered forward, determined to muster a little more inner bounce.

"Morning! Carpenter has a bit of a cold. Needs another dose of this at lunchtime. Okay, buddy, see you tonight!" He patted his son's shoulder and handed Al a brown bag, gratifying her with a genuine smile and amused salute before skidding ornamentally down the walk. Those blue eyes! As she helped Carpenter struggle out of his rather premature ski gear, Al congratulated herself. At Lilybanks her slender social requirements could be met without venturing out of the house. A thimbleful of attention, a glimpse of fashion, and the simple, mammalian pleasures and exertions the children provided were sufficient to ward off the tongue-thickening feral inclinations that had threatened to envelop her when the last of the funeral chores had been performed.

She followed the boy into the kindernook, feeling that, much as she liked Lucy and depended on Marian, it was lovely to hold sway unsupervised. Regulations prevented them from treating the children to the spell of crackling flames in the nook's fireplace. Any other mischief Carpenter might concoct before Marian trudged downstairs at eight o'clock paled in comparison to arson.

He'd sprawled across a low table in the adjoining library, where Melodie tolerated his upside down inspection of the new insect book.

A carton at the top of built-in bookcases held high-tech gadgets forfeited by young smugglers; the rule at Kinder on Corrie was that music was to be live, objects "natural," and information imparted by spoken word, page, or art only, so that young souls might not be fast-forwarded or overwhelmed. Carpenter was one of those shocking preschoolers who required weaning from glowing screens. Both children were gratifyingly engrossed in an oversized photo of a garden spider.

A childhood epiphany came to mind: turning a corner on an elementary school hike to find a spangled web hung across milkweed, in the heart of which a glittering spider presided at heart-stopping eye level. The unsettling magnificence of that foreign kingdom had survived the accretions of fifty years. Her heart leapt at the promise of daycare expeditions to the park at their back door. And her bike! Casper and she had loved riding on Moraine Woods' paths. She pretended to look out the window as tears came. She'd been so sure she'd never look forward to anything again.

So sustaining, these random memories, fleeting vapors that seeped into the present with haunting sweetness. What would Eckhart say to Proust? Perhaps he'd advise neither resisting nor cultivating these will-o'-the-wisps, like any other thought that –

"A-A-AHHGH!"

She spun to find that a rather flatteringly worried Carpenter had apparently tattooed the pristine toe of Melodie's lavender ballet slipper.

"It's alright, dear – we can wash that marker right off." Hopefully. "Carpenter, where did that marker come from? Please ask for permission before opening the Art Chest. Why did you write on Melodie's slipper?"

"She said I could." Melodie howled anew at this blasphemy.

"Perhaps there was a misunderstanding. You can help wash it off." (Fresh groans from Melodie.) "Let's all go to the kitchen sink. We'll get a wet paper towel and – and maybe find some animal crackers." (Bribery! What would Marian think of her moony incompetence?)

The three of them trudged toward the kitchen, holding hands. Aphrodite followed, marveling at this promising lapse in the early morning's routine.

What if she couldn't restore the shoe, and the pleasantly bland Mrs. Osterman became enraged? Melodie was quite attached to her pearly lavender slip-ons. Each child was required to keep a pair of soft-soled slippers at Lilybanks for indoor wear. Althea thought she'd detected some rivalry among the embroidered Chinese flats, glittery "jellies" and fluffy critters tucked beneath the miniature chairs in the front vestibule. Al realized she'd wrung out a sponge for Carpenter so fiercely that two of her fingers were turning mauve.

She held him by his elasticized waist as he daubed at the slipper from a kitchen stool. Below them Melodie cautiously inserted a succession of Fruit Loops organized by colors into Aphrodite's dribbly maw. Patterns of light trembled across the floor. Al took a conscious breath. She could see the windowsill's sprig of winterberries reflected in the soaking oatmeal pan. She could actually feel her lips, her heartbeat, her clenched stomach which she was able to let sag. The orange constellation on Melodie's slipper seemed to be fading in spite of Carpenter's hit-or-miss method. Althea reviewed the house of cards she'd been bent on constructing: "What if her threadbare attention span was the first stage of Alzheimer's?" "What if Marian and Lucy kindly, pityingly had to ask her to move out?" "What if she was headed for the county rest home: enforced bingo and pablum and unsupervised, underpaid spitefulness?" The self-pity and anguish she'd been courting would have been no more real than the thoughts that provoked them. She imagined peeling it all, a thin, friable tissue, from her mind. Simply not real!

"Please don't splash me, honey. Keep at it; you're doing fine."

"OW!" Carpenter had toppled off the stool onto her foot. Irritation and resentment raced along her veins. Eckhart said one's progress could be measured by one's reactions to life's little reversals. She'd just flunked. She took a couple of breaths and handed Melodie her soggy slipper.

*　　*　　*

At "recess," as Stubblefield's seniors called the half-hour between Earth Science and Handicrafts, Tad Bramble and Beebe Morrissey disappeared into the snarl of tall, rimy grass, sumac, and scrub pines on the rise behind the building. No one followed, as covert missions had yielded nothing more memorable than snatches of dull conversation and the rare chigger bite.

Tad lit a second filterless Camel off the glowing butt of the first, before grinding the butt out on his boulder.

"Careful of the lichens, Tad! I mean, they're alive, aren't they?"

His usual gravely earnest expression had seemed flat all morning. And she knew he hadn't touched a cigarette in eight days. He exhaled fiercely and refused to look at her.

Only mildly interested, Beebe continued sketching below him, wearing scarlet gloves whose right-hand fingers had been cut off. The Intermediate Art pet portraits were due today, "no exceptions."

"Looks more like Beethoven than Aphrodite."

"Well, that could be a good thing..." she replied absentmindedly. A bulb of mucus pulsed at her nostrils.

He waited till she'd started stuffing things back into her pencil case.

"Beebe."

"Uh huh?"

"Beebe I really can't stand it. Something terrible's going to happen if you can't develop more self-scrutiny."

She loved Tad's vocabulary. Any other guy would have said "watch what you're doing." They'd been over this ground before. She smiled up at him encouragingly, trying to give him her full attention. Beneath the heavy dark eyebrows his plain little eyes smoldered. The excitement that neither wanted to acknowledge began to uncoil within her; she consciously withdrew her attention from it.

"Those jerks on Seventh Street would have been serious trouble if I hadn't been there. They thought you were damaged. People like that wander around sniffing for blood, and when they find it, they salivate."

(Classic Tad! "Salivate!") She was glad to see he'd perked up.

"You know I don't enjoy going over this with you, Beebe. I love you. But for all your 'Here and Now' stuff, you have a way of not paying attention to – to the way you act, the effect you have on..." She was looking up at him with that compassionate, nonjudgmental gaze that could be so off-putting. Maybe she needed slapping, though he'd never be the one to do it.

"For Pete's sake. Really try to understand the importance of what I'm telling you, Beebe." He sacrificed half the cigarette, tucking it under his shoe.

"You know you've got this sort of attraction for people. They notice you, sometimes they're a little fascinated. A variety of people – not just the desirable ones. Just because you tune it out doesn't mean you aren't...don't tend to be...kind of high profile. So when you're unintentionally...rude, or ah, uncouth...it gets noticed. More than usual." He sighed. "Those guys this morning thought you were special in a negative sense." He leaned further forward. "You can't FART, Beebe. You can't. And you forget! You can't ever forget in public. It's like the deodorant – You can't just remember *most* of the time!" She looked deeply sympathetic. He felt close to tears, though some little part of him wanted to laugh.

"Do you want Lucy or Bubo or me to have to identify your body in the trunk of some car?"

To his horror she actually gasped. Next thing he knew she was hugging his knees, crying onto his pants, and he was bent over her, crying too. Success? Beebe almost never cried. He hated making her cry.

She was so little, and he loved her so much, and the things he loved most were the most painful. He should have been able to shake off the retinue of three dropout types they'd collected on the way between Maven Alley and class. The skinny one in the raveling neon orange ski cap, with high cheekbones sharp as a mummy's, had asked her if she was taking him home for milk and cookies. Beebe turned her head and shot them one of those big, disinterested, disarming smiles of hers. Only it looked like she was missing several teeth, thanks to some chocolate contraption Gloria had asked her to sample. Other girls checked in the mirror, didn't they? She'd had a fleck of cappuccino foam the size of a Buick dried onto her tilted little nose. His fault; he'd been enjoying the thought of licking it off, which she wouldn't have permitted. Though it was the chocolate teeth that tipped the scale. He could always tell. But she looked great in chocolate teeth! He felt sobs rising, and tried to steady his breath, grateful that he could rely on himself for that…He'd hurried her up the empty block pretty ably, and then Beebe had broken wind into the menacing silence behind them, a resonant cannonade ending in an elaborate putt-putt-putt. Oblivious. Probably admiring some icy puddle, or tuned into the orchestration of wind, distant traffic and footfall. Oh, he knew her.

The sleazy bunch behind them had started swearing at her, ferociously scandalized, like rabid wolves whose tea party had been disgraced. Even degenerates couldn't abide Beebe's *faux pas*. They made people nuts, like the Mistral or something. Uninterested in proving anything, he'd pulled her into the middle of the street and lunged at the first empty cab. (So much for his lunch money.) He pulled a sticky strand of hair out of her eyes, and managed a sort of smile.

"Does she really look like Beethoven?" While he scrutinized her sketch with fussy politeness she calculated how to borrow some change to feed him.

"Actually, more like a musk ox. No, really, it's good. As usual." She produced a delighted little laugh, bending over the drawing so he couldn't see her face.

Tad lurched back down toward the school, hurrying so she wouldn't be late. Beebe kept up somehow, disembodied and incandescent, so scalding was the intuition of her burdensomeness.

The Cygnet's Nest

Judging by the pine garlands' thumps against the garage as they sashayed in the north wind, the snowy forecast was reliable.

Althea's spirits danced as she climbed the plank stairway up the side of Lilybanks' two-story garage. Friday. She felt festive and cozy, like a schoolgirl. (Absurd, but why question shreds of irrational happiness?)

Last night at her Stubblefield recital Lucy had cancelled today's final eurhythmy class before winter break. So she'd be around to help Althea ply customers with hot peppermint possets and cut velvet cloaks.

Scarcely more than a year ago Lilybanks had begun trafficking in exquisite, seriously vintage (1880-1965 their specialty) clothing. Althea had eventually read about The Cygnet's Nest and nervously planned what might prove an intimidating foray; death had dismantled her silly little projects. Now she helped run the business two afternoons a week or "by appointment," as their discreet card tacked up in desirable antique shops suggested. Lucy and Beebe's idea for a boutique had received Marian's fond if incurious support. The Nest helped plug the hole in Lilybanks' maintenance fund. It showcased Lucy's nearly *couterière*-level skills while Beebe's seductive tea cart entertained shoppers who couldn't squeeze into the clothes.

This had been Marian's husband's bailiwick. Professor Crabbe – Marian had kept her own surname, ostensibly to avoid confusion within the English Department – blithely referred to the former billiard room in the loft as his Temple of Learning. He'd borrowed the idea, Marian had informed Al, from his Yankee hero Bronson Alcott, the Concord transcendentalist. They'd had a minimal kitchen installed so the professor could serve his disciples tea, and keep body and soul together without slogging down to Lilybanks in messy weather or after dark. It sounded to Althea like he'd been wedged up there rather firmly, perhaps assuring marital harmony.

At the top of the stairs the sign – featuring a stenciled nest and one elegant baby swan jauntily crowned with eggshell – read "OPEN." The door was unlocked.

"Yoo-hoo! It's me! Thanks for opening! I have your thread. Primrose yellow, the last spool...whoa!"

Lucy had appeared from behind the screen that hid the kitchenette, resplendent in a Santa Claus cap, futilely bosomy emerald taffeta slip, and red Wellies.

"What do you think? I'm hoping to dumbfound Mrs. Throckmorton. She keeps pressing me to stencil her niece's nursery with rubber duckies in sailor suits. We artsy-craftsies have our standards. I thought to fend her off with a glimpse of my fundamental depravity. Don't we have a bottle of the Professor's cognac up here somewhere? I thought a whiff of that –"

"You're full of beans, and you're going to catch a cold." Althea handed Lucy a Bakelite cigarette holder, gesturing toward the full-length mirror. (How long had it been since her own shoulders were so firm and well upholstered?)

"It adds something, doesn't it...Just unwinding. No Stubblefield for three weeks, and Micah's asked me to fly back to Williamsburg to meet his mother."

Al felt her stomach lurch, but didn't falter.

"Christmas in Williamsburg! How perfect! Oh, Lucy...they'll have candlelit caroling and swags of pineapples and pomegranates over the doors and..." She took care to seem carried away.

"Oh, heavens, we won't leave till Boxing Day. I want to be here at Lilybanks with you all for Christmas. Mrs. Fennel and her sister are staunch agnostics who spend the day at some museum gala, so it's not as if we'll be missed. Aren't you going to take off your coat? I'd hide it."

"You're probably right!" Al gushed, turning to conceal her fingers trembling over the huge embroidered buttons. She only wore her flying monkey coat, as Lucy'd named it, when she felt secure enough to carry it off. Casper had spotted it spilling out of a neglected trunk in a flea market tent. Remarkable passementerie reminiscent of a vainglorious turn-of-the century band uniform flowed down its back and across its wide cuffs.

"Eckhart might say my coat draws attention to myself – unhelpful egoic baggage. Think so?"

"If it feels like a big impediment to you I'll be happy to borrow it!" Lucy smiled. "Do you think dressing less creatively will diminish the ego's need to be important? Play around with it, Althea. But the answer's inside you, never outside." She took the coat and hung it in the broom closet. "Now you won't be tempted by someone offering you a ransom for that treasure."

Replete, Al bustled past the folding screen and crouched to hunt through a pygmy fridge.

"Let's fill the place with peppermint fumes. Mrs. Throckmorton's due at 2:30. I'll heat the milk and all." Beebe had devised the Nest's holiday drink, an implausible but addictive blend of peppermint, maple syrup and secret ingredients.

"Okay, but don't put the punch bowl on the card table. You don't want to know what happened last year. Several casualties," Lucy winced. "Hot mulled cider may as well be battery acid when it splashes on rayon teddies."

"Sit down and finish her hem, Lucy. I'll put the nubbly raspberry dress on the mannequin, don't you think? Mrs. Throckmorton's very firm about her colors, but if we get a little holiday rush this afternoon someone's going to snap it up before her eyes. I think she likes to monopolize the Jackie items, "her color" or not. Of course they *all* look wonderful on you, Lucy. You're really sure you don't want it?... Snowflakes!"

The camel bell on a string outside their door tinkled.

"I'll get it!" Althea strode across the boutique's worn oriental rug in a glazed, happy dither, reflecting dimly that she wasn't "present."

A baggy, twinkly woman she couldn't quite place filled the doorway. Someone else stamped and puffed behind her.

"Hi, Evvie," Lucy called helpfully from across the room.

"Althea, isn't it? We met at Lucy's dance-a-thon." Al had heard that such irreverence was unusual at Stubblefield.

"Yes, nice to see you again!" One of the older members of the Waldorf staff, and Lucy's trustworthy confidante. Al relaxed in spite of the perfunctory smile Evvie's elaborately made up, aloof young companion produced in her direction. Snap judgments ("silly old lady") were *so* egoic; no need to reciprocate with one of her own.

"My granddaughter Kirstin."

Lucy tossed Mrs. Throckmorton's skirt onto the lawn flamingo in a bow tie beside her divan and pounced.

"Hey, it's great to see you! How's DePaul? How long's your break?" Kirstin, whose jeans appeared to have been decoupaged onto her flesh, thawed out by fits and starts under this barrage, eventually admitting to the dean's list and to curiosity about Lucy's rumored fiancé. As Althea stooped to rescue the Santa cap she glimpsed a pair of unmistakably Throckmortonesque pumps gracing the doormat.

"Good afternoon, nice to see you! You're a tiny bit earlier than we expected, but Lucy will have your primrose set ready in just a few minutes. May I take your coat?" Mrs. T. proffered a patient smile, fluttered an expensive hand in Lucy's direction and applied herself to gingerly poking at a rack of kimonos. Althea wondered if Mrs. T. were so accustomed to being waited on that she was helpless, but couldn't summon the self-assurance to rescue her. She settled for pinching Lucy in the ribs and gesturing.

"Skirt almost ready?...Evvie, do you like Hawaiian shirts? We have one in back I think might look sensational on you – just got a little job in the kitchen, and then I'll show you...I'll put some tissue in a box, Lucy." Someone else could have the Jacky-ish raspberry *bouclé*; she couldn't be everywhere at once...

By the time the steps up to The Cygnet's Nest had accumulated a fluffy inch of snow a delightful minty aroma hovered in the boutique, Mrs. Throckmorton had painstakingly descended with five hundred dollars worth of pristine 60's dresses in sherbet colors with complementary cloches (envisioning shoes dyed to match) and Althea had accepted Evvie Bruchner's invitation to a Twelfth Night party which she now planned to host in her new Hawaiian shirt.

These early birds having been merrily dispatched (Mrs. T. smugly elated and privately determined never to breathe a word of the little Nest's existence to rivals), fresh customers sampled Beebe's rum balls. (Where *was* Beebe?) Lucy buttoned a beaded cardigan for a chatty neighbor with sticky fingers as Al gift-wrapped the dragon-embroidered robe that Mr. Kreworuka's wife had asked he be steered toward.

"Mission accomplished! Thank you, ladies. May I?" Mr. Kreworuka popped another rum ball in his mouth – "For the road! Going to get slippery..." and saluted Lucy as he left. Althea fussed over her tape and ribbon, suddenly acutely aware there'd be no much-anticipated gift, prearranged or not, from Casper on Christmas morning. Perhaps he'd want her to choose something for herself – something he might have picked out, with his "fool's luck," as they joked, and she'd be able to sense his presence as she –

Completely absorbed, Al knocked the scissors off the table. The entire needy drama shriveled and dissolved. She took a couple of conscious breaths – two in a row was a feat in public – and congratulated herself. Frequently now she was able to observe thoughts – entire little worlds, really, it seemed – come and go, arise and depart, like bubbles. Of course if she'd been alone she'd have gotten a lump in her throat and been stuck in the emotion –

In the full-length mirror across the room Al could see Beebe clutching the doorknob for balance as she pulled off her sodden Mary Janes. Excellent. The court jester had arrived and Al could recede into the background while little Miss Applecheeks fascinated the customers. It was growing dark, and Al's perkiness had become a stale imitation. Her lips didn't feel capable of enunciating an offer of peppermint posset one more time.

Lucy intercepted Beebe as she tiptoed toward the kitchen.

"Hi! I was starting to worry. I suppose you had Tad making angels in the snow on the library lawn or something..."

Beebe flinched.

"You okay?"

"I'm standing in a puddle. We should pass out tour booties up here in winter. Can you pass me the broom? The stairs are goopy."

Althea, who'd overheard Lucy's comment, twittered to herself at the thought of Thunder-thighs, supine in the snow, obligingly fanning away under Beebe's supervision.

Once Beebe had lurched back outside in saturated shoes she'd barely jammed back on, Lucy sidled over to Al past a cluster of students cooing over Edwardian petticoats.

"I'm going to send her back to the house. It's only another hour; you and I can manage on our own. Do you mind? She looks a little grey around the gills to me."

Al, perfectly aware that she competed with Beebe for Lucy's attention, summoned a flicker of animation.

"Hot water bottle, that's what she needs. Bet we sell every one of those lace curtain shawls before we close...I'll prep a couple more boxes."

Lucy propelled a flustered first-timer toward their makeshift dressing room, a tent-like affair involving India prints and bamboo which Marian's crotchety retainer Mr. Watkins had been persuaded to assemble against his better judgement. Chagrined, Althea retreated to the kitchenette. Shuffling about in a creaky drawer for more tissue paper, she paused to listen to muffled laughter, eager blurts, a seriously acquisitive hush. The fridge hiccupped. One of her molars with a slight crack stung. Could she feel her lips, her scalp? Could she feel herself breathing? That was something. But why, oh why, was she so nasty? So selfish? For the hundredth time she concluded it was futile to become embroiled in such questions. Ego. A quagmire. Eckhart said you can never win a battle with the ego. Even her cleverest insights into its machinations had little effect. Just be present. Be still, be the awareness behind the Althea-centered babble.

She savored the deep drawer's familiar, obliging rasp as she shoved it closed with a knee, and the heft of the crisp beige tissue buckling against her forearm. Top of the line, chemical-free paper for museum-quality – STOP. Stop the voice. Reminding herself fuzzily (she didn't want to *think* about it) to experiment with embracing life, Althea headed back into the shop with a measure of tranquility.

Christmas Eve

Marian Morrissey hunched over a steaming cup of Twining's English Breakfast on the third step from the top of Lilybanks' staircase. She'd persuaded Beebe, who'd been ill with a spectacular mixture of flu, bronchitis and pleurisy ever since vacation began, to drink hers in bed.

Automatically swiping at her own nose with one of several crumbling Kleenex tucked up a misshapen cardigan sleeve, Marian sagged just a bit. Beebe had expressed merely mild, polite interest in decorating the tree – which Tad was delivering on Christmas Eve morning so that she could participate. Form was indeed unstable! Thoughts, emotions, marriages, bungalows – all impermanent. No sooner had one grown to rely on the endearing, invasive exigencies of childhood than it dissolved, leaving one behind, rather childishly forsaken oneself, to dismantle an obsolete framework one had forgotten was temporary. Over the past year her headstrong, affectionate little Beebe had revealed an adamantine independence, become so perfectly self-contained one might accuse her of sneakiness were the reticence not so consummate, and confined her formerly lavish, very physical expressions of love to brief verbal formulae. Her husband's death had seemed less final a departure. Most salutary, really. Suffering was damned instructive. One survived one's own adolescence; one might reasonably hope to survive Beebe's.

Eckhart loved to quote from *A Course in Miracles*: "Nothing real can be threatened. Nothing unreal exists."[7] Marian peered down at the dog-eared carton of tinsel and garlands shoved into a corner of the hall and sighed. Phantasms, all of it. And her current mood? Scrooge's "bit of beef gristle."

She took another sip. Where *was* the boy? Nearly infallibly punctual. Father'd have to drive, though. Next year she'd need to tackle the carpeting on these stairs, no if's, and's or but's. Couldn't things be rewoven? Or she'd have to commission a copy. Tad was so implausibly right for the girl. Curious they'd found each other so early. Of course Beebe reached unfathomable depths – in spite of hormones and perplexing fixations. One did wonder if she realized what a pearl she'd trolled. Geoffrey and she had had the advantage of greater maturity. Or Geoffrey had, anyway. Like Lucy and Micah. O, dear. One would have to soldier on bravely when Lucy inevitably moved out. She'd probably continue with daycare, at least for awhile, but it wouldn't be the same...

Something about that last phrase caught her attention, and she recognized the old voice. Good heavens. She swigged back the rest of the tea, took a few deep breaths, coughed, breathed more calmly and attentively. The familiar glow pulsed along her veins; a sort of interior halo drew her attention from the disintegrating script. Wavy patterns of light through old glass shimmered on the tiles below her. Delightful to stand and stretch. Micah would be an asset to Lilybanks. And how lucky she was to have Lucy in her life! Lucky to have this moment. This deep, peaceful moment...

Someone hammered at the door. Marian lurched downstairs, keeping her cup snug in its saucer and her awareness firmly in the present moment. Aphrodite materialized fussily, recognizing the blur beyond the door.

"Out of the way, Ditey, for mercy's sake. Ow, you're standing on my foot."

"Sorry we're late, Mrs. Morrissey! Clogged up with Salvation Army bell ringers and last-minute shoppers and live Nativity scenes just about the whole way here. My dad's parking. Give us three minutes. Bring 'er in right through here?"

Tad swayed from one duck boot to the other, launching lavish gusts of steamy breath onto the frigid air.

"Yes, thank you, dear. We've got the stand set up. Tell your father there's a martini waiting for him in the kitchen." (Outrageously un-Lilybanksian, but almost certainly a brilliant stroke, she'd decided.)

Tad, who normally wore a deadpan expression worthy of the Secret Service, glittered for just a second before re-crossing the porch.

Aphrodite, ignored and implacable, charged.

"Tad?!"

"I've got her, Mrs. Morrissey. Why don't you throw me her leash? She won't be any trouble." Marian grabbed the worn strap nailed most unhistorically to the vestibule woodwork and tossed it. She'd just have time to throw things together for cocoa.

Upstairs, Beebe had listened for the Brambles' arrival and scooted into Lucy's bedroom. Skippy examined her from the depths of his favorite drawer as she peered through the diamond panes at the street. It took the rabbit a moment to identify Beebe inside the earmuffs, hoody, sweatpants, sweaters and bulging chenille bathrobe decreed by Marian.

Captain Bramble advanced smartly up the snowy walk with the trunk of a Douglas fir under one arm, leaving Tad to wrestle with the boughs. Aphrodite struggled to keep up.

"She'll sleep right through Christmas," Beebe thought.

Tad startled her, a stranger. She saw that he was really attractive – maybe a little husky – if you didn't know he was at least five disconcerting years younger than he looked. (Maybe ten.) At Stubblefield they called him Studpuppy behind his back. Not to his face; he was too nice. And too big. Right now he wore that look she never tired of, though she sometimes dreaded it – grave, innocent, expectant. Hadn't anyone ever taught him to protect himself? Of course she didn't put much effort into protecting herself, either, but that was deliberate, an educated habit of being. She had all kinds of reliable resources to fall back on right away when things seemed to fall apart. Tad had only a nice disposition and her.

Skippy scrabbled to get her attention. Beebe gave him a cuddle and retreated from the room, feeling woozy. Lucy paid extra on the heating bill to keep her rooms toasty in the winter. Otherwise the tortoises hibernated.

She could hear Captain Bramble conducting the mooring of the Christmas tree with curt directives to Tad, and some milling about. Beebe lowered herself to the floor behind the upstairs railing. She heard her aunt tell the Captain in a no-nonsense tone to come into the kitchen for a drink.

"You'll have some cocoa, Tad?"

"Thanks, Mrs. M. I'll clean up a little, first."

The adults filed out of earshot. Tad ordered the worshipful Ditey out of the pine needles and into her basket, grabbed a broom and worked his way to the bottom of the stairs.

Startled by Tad's soft, two-note whistling between his teeth – goodness, how hot she was – Beebe wondered why a joyful little zigzag raced through her insides. Usually his whistle annoyed her, though she never showed it. She stood to wave at him over the railing.

He looked up at her with concern, which also always exasperated her, though this time she could feel exultation close behind. Any other boy would look amused, or sorry for himself.

"She let me take the mittens off to have my tea."

Now he smiled. "You wearing that to dinner?"

Beebe wavered, uncertain if he could tell she felt shy.

"Nope. I'll be back in uniform for dinner. I'm not contagious anymore, you know. I can breathe all over everyone at the table. I'm just supposed to take it easy until my pills are all used up...Bubo gave me your phone messages." It was awkward, as though they'd spent months apart, not eight days.

"Well, you can breathe all over *me* tonight." It sounded just a little too solemn.

To their mutual confusion, Tad's father materialized, handing his son a mug.

"Hope you still like marshmallows. I said you probably do. Merry Christmas, young lady," he added seamlessly, subjecting Beebe to his usual impassive scrutiny, as though trying to crack a code.

Summoning all her attention, she gave him a genuine, welcoming smile.

"Merry Christmas, Captain Bramble! It was kind of you to take the time to drive our tree over."

He shrugged, a slightly more elegant edition of Tad's deprecating response to gratitude. They didn't look much alike, Tad getting most everything but his size from the serene, dark-eyed mother she'd examined in a photo album. For the first time it occurred to Beebe how much that might mean to his widowed father.

"And thanks for lending us Tad tonight." She wanted to add, "We'll take good care of him!" but thought it might not be welcome...or even true.

He nodded, still scrutinizing.

"Well...I guess I'm supposed to be resting. Good to see you both!" (It actually *was* good to see the captain...his inner essence, anyway.) She shuffled back to her room, the Abominable Snowgirl in chenille, she supposed. But no matter.

Tad watched her out of sight, then leaned the broom against the banister's incised pattern of square-petaled prairie flowers. He tried his cocoa.

Disarmed but ever truthful, Captain Bramble groped for a positive comment.

"Nice earmuffs."

His son looked surprised, then grinned. Tad was probably

unaware of the whipped cream on his upper lip, and might have been four years old again, it seemed.

*   *   *

Althea sat in a pleasant daze, nodding at Professor Bakeoven from time to time and taking care not to trail the sumptuous fringe on her Lilybanks shawl through the cranberry relish. She'd had just enough champagne, wild rice and mushrooms *en croûte* to insulate her nerves, and had made what she considered sufficient conversational sallies into the respective territories of the strangers on all sides whom Marian (with flattering if misplaced confidence) had seen fit to seat her among. Professor Bakeoven was given to generous anecdote (perhaps Marian had been rather acute, after all) and Althea felt justified in wandering out to pasture, as it were, for a bit.

Tad, the only familiar face nearby, seemed similarly inclined to ruminate; his shirt buttons looked seriously strained by his attempts to do the feast justice, and he stared vacantly in the direction of his more garrulous neighbors. Judging by ongoing waves of hilarity, emphatic exchange and learned monologue emanating from Marian's end of the table, Lilybanks' apparent guest of honor was well looked after. An underfed Anglican choirboy from Toronto (people in their twenties looked like children to Al now; when had that happened?), Marian's "tooty" seemed accommodating but monomaniacal. Al noted his reverent maneuverings: "Had Dr. Crabbe taken into account those unpublished fragments blah blah blah"; "Thanks to *Marian's* kind supervision..." (Ought Marian allow such familiarity?)

On her right the mastermind of the Maven Alley Bakery fidgeted with her parsley and poured herself another glass of wine from the napkin-wrapped bottle she'd commandeered. Beebe having been exiled from the kitchen, Gloria had taken on the most substantial elements of the Christmas Eve meal herself, arriving early with an elaborate two-foot slab of mushrooms encased in frilly pastry with fluted airholes. Althea felt Gloria had earned the right to sit there blurting emphatic, ill-timed comments at random between thoughtful sips. Marian's efforts had been confined to the purchase of a Crosse & Blackwell Christmas pudding.

Althea herself had contributed the centerpiece, having decanted her pampered cyclamens from the chilly street-side corner of her room into one of Lilybanks' choicest majolica basins. Their scarlet wings drooped over heart-shaped leaves, the sole holiday decoration on the white tablecloth or anywhere else in the room.

Al gloried in her surroundings. Above the built-in sideboard and cabinets, above the French doors, above the drafty bank of windows onto Corrie Street a vivid frieze of hawthorns blossomed against a parakeet blue sky. The drifts of ivory petals, the furrowed cloud bank, the green meadow still ravished her. The Crabbe-Morrisseys had a portion of it repainted after a recalcitrant upstairs toilet had wreaked havoc, blighting a corner. The restoration had rejoiced Althea on her second tour; she'd feared -

That pressure on her toe was apparently being deliberately applied, judging by its syncopation.

"I said, I hear you're fond of animals. Would that be correct?"

Too amused by the eccentric, abrasive neighbor across from her -- Libby Somebody or Other – to feel abused, Althea replied superbly, "Yes, it certainly would be." She paused. "Why do you ask?" (Daringly curt; champagne was a wonderful thing.)

"I've got a new schedule that requires my absence from home every other Thursday evening, and I need someone to walk my dogs."

Althea wondered how Libby Whomever successfully concluded any negotiation with such a pugilistic manner.

"What kind of dogs?" she hedged, still amused.

"Several. I'd leave the pit bull and the dobie in their run. You don't look like you'd be up to them." Her eyes traveled over the fussy shawl and the thin frame beneath it. (She was compact and thickset, with unkempt curls she was forever pushing out of her face.)

"You're right. The muscular guard dog types with megaphone barks aren't my favorites." She stared meaningfully, but Libby merely smiled and continued.

"Won't need you for a couple of weeks; wouldn't that give you time to meet them? I'll call you....Or not."

Althea must have looked as reluctant as she felt. Wasn't she supposed to be embracing life?

"I'd enjoy meeting them, actually. And then we'll see."

Libby looked pleased for a moment. Althea reflected that she'd managed to be nonresistant, if not nonjudgmental.

Lucy was removing Professor Bakeoven's dinner plate. Tad had staggered to his feet. Althea bundled her shawl onto her chair and shoved it safely under the table, then grabbed Gloria's and her own plates in a rush to establish both her appreciation and her identity as a Lilybanker. In her eagerness to follow Tad to the kitchen Aphrodite nearly crushed Al in the doorway. She lost her balance briefly but managed to send only a few forks clattering into the hallway.

"Allow me." Professor Bakeoven, returning from the first floor washroom (purged of diminutive stools and frog and bunny soaps), restored the sterling nimbly for someone who might be in his seventies. He gave Althea a kindly smile and rather searching look, compared to the bland oratorical gaze proffered those within earshot at the table. She gave him a lively, "nothing to worry about here!" smile back. Perhaps old people were better at spotting potential loneliness; Althea didn't care to be seen through on that score, however sensitively. She bustled into the pantry. If he were closer to her age she'd wonder if he were attracted to her. However limply. Such beautiful eyes and hands; the white mustache. A widower, perhaps. Al caught herself thinking he was probably comfortably well-off.

She narrowly avoided being mown down by Tad and Lucy returning for more dirty dishes.

"Open that bottle of brandy, will you Al?" Lucy looked pink and radiant, Tad dogged. "We've got two puddings now, thank heavens. Bakeoven brought another."

Eventually Al had to bear in one of the holly-wreathed salvers behind Lucy, who'd turned the lights down to play up the eerie blue flames flitting over the desserts. While the professor – "Bakeoven," he seemed to be called by everyone – recited Christopher Smart's Christmas poem, apparently a tradition, Libby briskly served herself a triple helping of hard sauce. Next to the perspiring Tad, Beebe thumped the tablecloth with her runcible spoon in time with the cadences. Micah, who'd pushed his chair back a bit from the table, studied her as though the childish performance displeased him.

Althea felt the oddness of fate, of being there. Unable to keep up with the verse, whose exalted lines flowed past her mostly undigested (oh, but it concerned the Christ child, for whom she was abruptly homesick) she anchored herself to Presence. Breathe in, breathe out; feel the tingling in her hands, the press of the chair seat; truly observe the cyclamen's moist velvet (must remember to rush them back to their bower tonight...)

"...God all-bounteous, all-creative,
Whom no ills from good dissuade,
Is incarnate, and a native
Of the very world he made."[8]

Insomnia

Exhausted but relieved finally to be alone again, Beebe listened to Marian's slippers shuffle down the hall. She fumbled for the flashlight beneath her pillows and found her bookmark.

* * *

Gypsy had led Bezique through half a dozen backyards beyond his own, acquainting him with feline nooks and crannies, as well as detours around hazards.

Pausing beneath floppy bluebell leaves in the woodlot behind an outhouse, she gazed at the tiny cottage in the next yard.

"The home of a good cat who will help. His human provided him with a little door just right for a cat. He comes and goes as he pleases. He watches for Willow."

"Willow?" Bezique found it difficult to concentrate; blue and pink petals danced against Gypsy's shoulders most beguilingly.

"My sister. Our mother called her Willow because she's slender and supple. Pliant. You have seen her, Bah-seek? Not like me."

"And how are you?" He hoped to draw her out.

"Square and sturdy. Stubborn." Her tail wrapped around her shapely young haunches a bit tighter. "You're sure you'll recognize her?"

He pulled himself together. "Oh yes. Trim little thing. White front, white feet, flanks like stippled beech leaves in autumn. My mistress calls her 'Cinnamon.' A fragrant red-brown spice."

"She chose well. My sister is lovely. Oh, Bah-seek, her white breast and paws are so bright, so difficult to conceal, a disadvantage...look, here he comes."

A white cat with black ears and a lopsided black patch on his head emerged from a flapped opening by the cottage's back door. Bezique, feeling competitive, had expected a cat with his own private door to be formidable. But this fellow looked rather whimsical, blinking in the sunshine and allowing a sparrow to alight nearby without offering the slightest challenge.

"Come, Bah-seek." She led him down a slight incline to the edge of a vegetable garden – mostly freshly turned soil and some stakes with ragged ribbons – on the near side of the cottage yard. They sat in the shade of a wheelbarrow and looked away politely, letting their host choose a greeting.

The cottage cat flung himself on his back among the dandelions and rolled from side to side. Finally he ambled over, taking time to savor the scent of fresh manure in the garden.

"Eh-eh-eh-eh-eh? Meeeooow."

Gypsy emerged from the shadow, uttering a soft cry, and presented her forehead for a ceremonial sniff. When he'd reciprocated they turned to Bezique.

"Beanie, this is Bah-seek, of the house above my den. He's come out to help find Willow."

Beanie extended his forehead encouragingly. Bezique obliged him with an elegant sniff and allowed Beanie a whiff of his own choice musk. The fellow seemed amiable enough. Perhaps a bit of a yokel. Beanie had a swollen pink underlip that looked a trifle silly, and he sashayed as though the first strong-minded squirrel that crossed his path might knock him over. A lover, not a fighter, Bezique decided, and more of an absent-minded bachelor than a lover. Gypsy had met him with mere comradely trust. This said much for Beanie's reliability, if not for his initiative, and Bezique found himself well disposed toward the unpretentious fellow.

"Our young friend here speaks very highly of you, Bah-seek, and of your mistress. I know the house; we call it the Lilac Corner. An inoffensive collie, and little girls who make birds' nests from the grass cuttings." Bezique looked a bit alarmed, so Beanie added that his handsome picket fence must relieve Bezique of constant window patrols. Beanie himself, he was careful to mention, strolled by very rarely, "just to keep up-to-date, you know."

"Willow and I always travel through Beanie's yard, Bah-seek. I'm certain my sister's path lies in this direction. Our wander-ground reaches from our den through the yards between it and the orchard, into the meadows and up to the fen." (Orchard? Fen? Bezique preserved a noncommittal silence.) Gypsy's eyes grew wider. "I'm told mink sometimes raid the outskirts of the fen."

Beanie and Bezique looked at each other over her head.

"Easy pickings there for a moonlighting mink. Plenty of muskrats and ducks and marsh hens – no need to make a fool of himself over a fleet-footed young cat."

Though reluctant to admit he had no clear idea of what a mink was, Bezique hadn't liked the look of Beanie's covert warning.

"Come along, Gypsy. Let's take Bah-seek up to the orchard. If Willow's managed to get herself good and lost, the orchard hill might be a landmark. You should become acquainted with it, Bah-seek."

Gypsy stretched her back legs, shook herself all over and bounded across the yard, eager to do something purposeful. Bezique decided not to ask Beanie's opinion of Willow's chances, feeling it would be disloyal to Gypsy. Besides, he was curious about something else.

"You come and go as you please through your door, Beanie? Your humans make no fuss?" He felt just the slightest bit disloyal to Mrs. B.

"Just one human. Delightful fellow. That's his name: Oliver Goodfellow. Carpenter. And he gives music lessons. Plays the fiddle and a funny little flute. Popular, my human. Lots of friends, and they make music together. You should come round some evening, Bah-seek...someone often brings me a scrap of cheese or fish; you'd be welcomed. Of course it's a bit loud if you're not used to -"

"This business of getting outdoors isn't quite as easy as Gypsy may think, Beanie. We're three cats at my house, and all three stay inside. Quite happily, of course, excellent accommodations, apple of the family's eye and all. I understand that as a child my mistress saw a beloved kitten lost beneath a wagon wheel when the horse shied. She fears for our safety. She's so fond of me, you know, I don't like to insist on going out too much...actually, had to create a diversion to slip out today..." He certainly wasn't ready to admit this was the first time he'd ever felt grass underfoot.

"Mighty good of you," Beanie broke in. "If you're able to manage it for Gypsy's sake from time to time without too much of a ruckus on the home front, head over here. It's a peaceful yard – no mastiffs or sheds full of rats and rusty scythes, just me and the vegetables. Oliver wouldn't hurt a flea, so it's a good thing we haven't got any. What marvelous ears you have, Bah-seek. Must come in very handy. Little Gypsy's thrilled to have your assistance. Plucky girl...the outdoor cats have to grow up very fast."

Gypsy, who'd scampered halfway up a grassy knoll, had turned to watch them. She held her tail straight up like a flag; its tip flicked impatiently.

"Coming! Anyway, she's accepted my offer of the yard as base camp for the search, and you're always welcome." Beanie had begun to trot; Bezique had the feeling that was his top speed except in emergencies, when any cat can lay claim to startling swiftness. Pleasantly chatty for such a mild-mannered fellow. Courteous, and discreetly sensitive. Just the opposite of Applesauce...Bezique strode up the hill toward Gypsy as forcefully as he could without leaving Beanie behind.

"By the way," he said over his shoulder while they were still alone, "'Bah-seek' seems to be her special name for me. Mrs. Bunting named me Bezique. French word. You know how the ladies can be." (No need to mention it was the word for Mr. Bunting's favorite card game.)

Beanie looked nonplussed, knowing neither French nor ladies. From then on he referred to Bezique as Zeke, which mystified Gypsy and amused his new friend.

"Come, Bah-seek! See the white clouds on the hill! It's the orchard kingdom. Come see how high it is, and lovely. The clouds smell like the flowers in your mistress's garden. You've come at the best time! Beanie says the fragrance comes only in the spring. Hurry!"

She sounded as if she thought the spring might end at any moment. He and Beanie clambered up the hillside behind her. Bezique wondered if this might be where Marjorie flew her kite and reflected that she must be home from school by now, and looking for him. He promised himself he'd place his wet nose against her eyelids and purr heavily once she was done scolding him.

Exhilarating as the great open world of sky and grass on the hillside was, Bezique felt more at ease upon reaching the orchard at its crest, with its low, flowering roof and hiding places where light and shadow frolicked with each other. Perhaps this was the kind of place the humans meant when they spoke of "heaven." Pinky-white flowers filled the arms of the gnarled old grandfather trees and spangled the grass; they smelled like the scent in Mrs. B.'s stoppered glass bottle on the dresser, only fresher and even more intoxicating. Bees clung and buzzed about the sprays of blossoms; the puffy white clouds he'd raced up the hill snagged on the highest branches, hovering in a patchwork of blue like the enamel on the Buntings' milk pitcher.

Bezique and Gypsy chased each other among the tree trunks like giddy kittens. When they returned to Beanie's side Gypsy groomed her rumpled fur to conceal her confusion.

"Tell him about the apples, Beanie."

Feeling a bit unstrung, Bezique stretched out at Beanie's feet and examined his claws.

"They're called Prairie Spies. They come, small and green, after the flowers leave the trees. They grow all summer and ripen to red at harvest time. In the autumn Mr. Nicol and his boys bring bushel baskets, ladders and barrels and a wagon team. Oliver and others come to help pick the apples. They make cider from the windfalls. Possums and raccoons like to eat the windfalls, too. The Nicols have a cider party with a bonfire in the stable yard. Oliver brings his fiddle. Rorie and his father play the bagpipes. A fierce, grand noise like giant geese flying in thunder and lightning. The skirling, cawing music makes the humans dance. And in the winter the children come to the top of the orchard with their sleds." Bezique began to suspect Beanie guessed the extent of his inexperience.

"Wouldn't you like to see these things, Bah-seek? When Willow returns we can bring the kittens to romp here..." She drew herself up. "We should return now, Bah-seek. Little Scout is too young to be in charge for long. Let's search the stable on the way, can't we, Beanie?"

The air had grown cooler. Bezique felt that their exuberant, fur-raising descent was hastened by unspoken disquiet. Near the bottom of the slope Gypsy swerved; he and Beanie followed her to a red barn and stable yard behind a big frame house with hens pecking in the path to the back door.

"Last homestead on Donovan Street. Open ground till the fen from here," Beanie observed. "Gypsy, you search that side of the stable; Bezique and I will take this side. Watch out for hooves. Meet at the front of the stable, or in my yard if there's a problem."

Gypsy plunged into the hay-scented semi-darkness.

"Pay attention to dark corners and deep straw, Zeke. If Willow's injured she may not be able to call to us. The horses are good sorts. Just take care not to startle them."

Fifteen minutes later all three emerged unscathed, in spite of some threatening swoops from a nesting swallow, but had seen no sign of Willow. Bezique thought Gypsy sagged just a bit.

"Tomorrow I'll check along the fen again. First thing in the morning," Beanie said, flicking his tail comfortingly over her shoulders. "I keep an ear and eye out for her at night, you know. Never was a sound sleeper."

They filed back to Beanie's place, Gypsy in the middle and very quiet, and parted at Beanie's little door. Bezique began to yearn for his home when he saw light through the cottage windows. He sniffed a hint of roast potatoes and gravy.

Gypsy took the lead as the two of them continued in the chilly twilight. Bezique watched her sturdy little hindquarters with a pang; she was hurrying home to share a one-cat handout with four bawling kittens in a clammy underground hole. No sound sleep for her tonight. And what good had he been so far, the mighty Bah-seek? Just an infatuated mollycoddle along for the tour.

Instead of crossing the split-rail fence she'd just scooted under, Bezique stopped and watched Gypsy continue unawares past the next yard's clothesline and dripping pump. He felt the need to watch her make her way in the world, forlorn, brave, solitary. Without him.

Two and a half back yards away the little black nubbin stopped.

He flew.

"What happened, Bah-seek?"

"I love you, Gypsy. I'll always love you. Once we get these problems cleared up I want you to be my mate. We'll figure out a way. Will you have me, do you think?"

Gypsy blinked at him and bounded away, heading straight for Lilac Corner. Just before vaulting the picket fence she looped the loop.

*   *   *

Marian lay limp in Calla Morrissey's bed beneath the mural room's eaves. A bit snug during her marriage, it was commodious now – if drafty. Designed to fold away, its mechanisms weren't as spry as they'd been when her father first dryly demonstrated them to her new husband. At least she made the bed every morning, though it only vanished into the wall for Tour Day and the rare festivity. Lucy had already diffidently accepted her proposal of a reception at Lilybanks. (How charming she'd be, descending the staircase in her wedding gown – or jeans and Wellies, one never knew – but no, Micah would never countenance that. They'd have the knot tied in his church.) Goodness, when would Lucy appreciate the man's resolution? She'd be evasive and hesitant till the day after the ceremony…

That sounded like sleet being flung on the windowpanes. Probably turning the decorative inch or two of snow into a skating rink. Saint Nick would get a bracing workout tonight…Beebe had listened reverently year after year to her reading of "The Night Before Christmas" at bedtime. Last year she'd felt the tiniest bit patronized – droll, really; to each thing its season – and tonight Beebe's genuine fatigue (her first socializing in two weeks) had gracefully obscured the fact that she'd forgotten all about "the moon on the breast of the new-fallen snow."[9]

She felt a hard lump rise in her throat. Gracious. One had intended to concentrate on a few breaths, and the next thing one knew one was casting a mental movie, a tear-jerker this time. She gave the woeful lump her full attention, careful not to use words. It slowly melted away, leaving her in a cold but fundamentally comfortable room, at peace with Beebe and the marginally helpful hot water bottle and the dim, angular patterns of light emanating from the Corrie Street lamp.

*   *   *

Somehow *Lilac Corner* wasn't working. Beebe's evening remained indigestible.

"Come on out to the fireplace with me. I've got something for you," Tad had mimed to her after the Christmas crackers had been opened. She'd gotten the swan charm. He'd gotten the goose. She'd cut them each a cluster of sugar-frosted green grapes from the platter in the middle of the table and followed him leadenly out to the inglenook. (Tad refused to use the word "inglenook." Lucy said Micah did, too. "It's not possible," he'd told her.) Bakeoven had winked at her from afar, popping a grape into his mouth. "Young love," he was probably thinking. To give him credit, she'd thought he looked sympathetic. Tad was so...inexorable. No wonder Ditey wanted to pair off with him. Kindred spirits.

Usually Tad looked like an eager puppy while she opened his present. This time he'd seemed bravely resigned. He'd sat on the chimney corner, as though the cozy old settle in front of the fire were unsuitable for the coming ordeal.

She'd made it clear that he wasn't to give her anything wildly inappropriate, any absurd symbol. She wore his locket, but had tucked it inside her eyelet ruffle for dinner. She'd felt he was trying to count the chains around her neck. But that was unfair. Tad wasn't fussy or petty.

By the time he'd thudded into the vestibule to pull a box from a coat pocket, Aphrodite had hunted them down and parked carefully in front of the settle. The fire screen, bearing an upside down heart of hammered brass, had fallen over on her once. Beebe concentrated on the dog's tiny reflection on the metal as the fire snapped.

Tad strode back in. The annual glass of champagne didn't seem to have soothed his jitters. They could count on only a few minutes before some stray guest might wander in.

"Well, Merry Christmas, Beebe!" He'd handed her a white box – the standard jewelry store variety, bound with a simple ribbon.

When peril loomed, she gave the moment all her attention. She could smell Ditey's holiday shampoo from the day before, and Tad's scratchy wool dress slacks. By firelight she could no longer make out the white tee (so boyish, innocent!) under his shirt. She'd felt her posture becoming impeccable.

"This too shall pass." She'd made herself look up at him before she untied the knot. That Adam's apple. She'd wondered which of them looked uneasier, and stifled a smile of compassion that might be misinterpreted.

The ribbon dropped to her lap; she pulled off the lid recklessly, lifted the predictable square of gauze.

A ticket. Thank God, just a ticket.

Two tickets. Airline tickets. Chicago to...Moscow. July.

Part of her wanted to run shrieking to Lucy: "Tad and I are going to Russia this summer!" Part of her wanted to throw the tickets in his face and pound that know-it-all Teddy bear belly as hard as she could. Safest to keep looking down at the tickets.

"You know you want to go, Beebe. This would give you a fore-taste..." He'd determined on that word ahead of time. "So when you *really* go you'll, like, have a better idea of how to go about it...Beebe?"

She had to look at him now, and fought for what she could only hope was a neutral expression.

"The other ticket's not for me. Anybody you want, Beebe, but you need to go with somebody the first time, honey. Oops." (He knew she hated his endearments. They made her feel like they were playing house.) "It's round trip. You know Bubo will let you pay for the other expenses out of your trust fund. She'll be excited for you. Like me." He looked stoic, not excited.

"How did you pay for these, Tad? They must have cost a fortune." He'd still be paying his father back after she'd faded guiltily from his life.

"Odd jobs. I've been saving. They're all paid up. No borrowing. I wanted to do it for you. No strings attached, Beebe."

He'd gotten up.

"I've gotta get back. Dad expects me to show up at his party. I'll go say bye." He bolted without looking at her or patting Ditey. Usually he'd linger, give her a kiss – at least on the forehead, whether wanted or not – and ask what time he should come over tomorrow.

The recollection made her face burn in the dark of her room now, hurt her throat.

Sorely tempted to steal into the woods, she'd instead retreated to her bedroom doorway while he left. She'd heard the front door open and close with a sort of anguished pleasure. She remembered with satisfaction how nonchalantly she'd gone back down to mingle with the company. No one thought to ask if he'd given her a gift. Lucy had studied her, but left to spend the night at Micah's (after all the guests went home – sweetly Victorian!) without their having a bedtime chat.

And she was wide awake on Christmas Eve because she'd realized that Tad – in his gentle, responsible way – was dumping her. She'd been bent on embracing her sacrifice, had finally realized how much distress she caused him, and always would. He could surrender his unintentional, remorseful possessiveness; she could surrender... what? She hadn't really even *wanted* a "boyfriend." He was mostly an unlooked-for ally. The minute he'd ferreted Mr. Browd's fondles out of her the bassoon instructor was scotched. They'd heard he'd be moving.

Tad was a good, decent, dear person. And he didn't find her fascinating and peculiar the way so many people did...because he loved her.

Whereas she'd just appreciated having a friend.

Be honest. This distress wasn't about losing a friend. She had Lucy, and Bubo. Even Mr. Smeltzer. And Blessed Katerina. And she was fine on her own. Most importantly, life was her friend.

She felt tears welling up. She was probably still sick. And all the holiday fuss, and Lucy more and more caught up in Micah (though of course she was glad for her)...

What she'd do was, she'd lighten up on this Tad business. It would all take care of itself. No need to try to control the future. They'd just carry on, and everything would happen for the best without her tying herself in futile knots. She'd always known she was just a phase Tad needed to go through.

The ache returned. It made her a stranger to herself.

No wonder! Thinking about the future when she could be Here and Now, her dear homeland.

A small plunk of a noise carried through the wall from Althea's room. Probably Linnet, who seemed to have a rather active nightlife.

This was Althea's first Christmas without her husband. Perhaps she'd felt quite forlorn during the festivities. She was sure Althea felt the need to keep her end up, to earn her place at Lilybanks or lose it. How dreadful.

It would never occur to Al that Beebe was all alone too. Bubo, too. And Lucy, really. Everyone, for that matter. When you turned off the mental noise, unplugged the ego-bound emotions, you were all alone in the space and stillness. Quite stark. Yet at the same time more connected, more "belonging," than ever. Paradise wasn't for sissies.

Beebe got out of bed, attending to the cold wooden boards against the soles of her feet, the folds of nightgown caught between her knees, the radiator's silence. She blew out the candle in front of Katerina's photograph, snuffed it with a wet finger and crossed herself confusedly, unable to remember which shoulder came first.

*   *   *

Althea woke suddenly, pleased to understand at once where she was. Progress. It took longer to remember that this was the night before Christmas. Burdens accumulated: she should participate cheerfully but discreetly; she should ward off a potential emotional landslide; the day should present her with sensitive insights and new coping skills. Ugh. And yet around the edges of all that was a mild excitement.

The dinner came slowly into focus. Of course. The wine explained her abrupt wakefulness. She began poking about gingerly through the recollected episodes for pain. No particular *faux pas* or internal meltdowns came to mind...her brief fantasies concerning frail old Bakeoven came back to her, silly, vain, but private. She'd been condescending toward Libby, for which she felt only an intellectual sort of self-reproach, and the slightest bit envious of Lucy's skittish happiness – probably pardonable.

Congratulating herself on having emerged fairly unscathed, she turned over without checking the clock, not wanting to know if it was Christmas yet. She groped for Linnet, nestled in a tight, unresponsive ball at the foot of the mattress. A faint wisp of melancholy wound upward from the floor of her stomach. She ignored it.

Something like sleet hit the windows. She wondered if the squirrels she used to feed at home – no, "on Euclid Street," she'd trained herself to say – were managing to stay aloft in their preposterous leafy nests. Nearly every winter on her walks around the neighborhood she'd find one frozen at the foot of its tree. She'd rush home for a bag and have Casper dig a shallow grave in their yard so no dog or callous boy would worry the poor thing.

Casper had indulged her. How could he have let this happen? She and Linnet on a drafty mattress at the mercy of strangers on Christmas Eve. Christmas was probably as dead as he was now, as far as she was concerned, in spite of play-acting.

Al heard herself laugh, as she often did now when noting her useless, crazy thoughts. How pleasant to feel the familiar old taffeta comforter beneath her fingers. What a pleasant, gritty noise the snow made as the wind hurled it against the house. Who cared what the weather did; it wasn't as if she had to go out anywhere tomorrow. In fact, when she turned her thoughts off for a moment, or even just paid attention to what was going on underneath and around the thoughts, everything was okay. "Do you have a problem right now? Right this instant?" Eckhart would ask.

The worst had happened and she was okay right now. She had Linnet, they had a roof over their heads and plenty to eat. In fact, in some respects living at Lilybanks thrilled her. She had not become paralyzed or unhinged. (So far.) She could enjoy the trace of scent that lingered in the crook of her arm. And she was able to stop tormenting herself just now and realize she was fine – fine enough for right now – because she was discovering a new way of being in the world, discovering the "power of presence."

Perhaps Casper knew more about presence than she did, now. She felt he was not completely lost to her. "Nothing real can be threatened."[10]

There she was thinking again. Whenever she was able to stop for awhile, she felt as she had when learning to ice skate as a little girl: "Enough! Time to hobble back to safety." What was one supposed to *do* with all that space, especially here in the dark with no landscape to savor, no eloquent play of light?

She'd come to understand that she invited useless thinking – lazy conjecture, intricate analysis, drama – out of habit (addiction!) of course, but at bottom out of an unwillingness to experience the radical, companionable stillness.

She smiled – a small smile – in the dark.

Design
[*1911*]

"The Empress," Calla murmured, tossing the first card onto the bed. Venus, really. "Influenced by the six of cups." Obscure. "Childhood bonds and memories create new pleasures?" She laid a third card across the others.

"The obstacle: more cups, seven. Harmless enough as obstacles go, I suppose. Reminds me of that overpowering millinery shop on Wabash – too many choices, even without the feathered offerings, which I always ignore, Fez." She licked a finger, rifling through a small book without a cover; some pages had fallen out and been jammed in upside down or back to front.

"'Illusion. Susceptibility. Vice. But also intuition and powerful spells.'"

A breathy rasp – more like the rustle of dead leaves after a hard frost than a voice – issued from the far corner. Having contributed a remark, the bird resumed its inspection of the riveting individual in the cheval glass.

John Crumrind had dissolved into slightly disapproving merriment at the stork's bewildered devotion to its twin in the mirror. She'd never heard him laugh before – real laughter, not the dry skeptical cough that passed for it.

Her kimono slipped down a shoulder as she placed a card above the others on the soiled sheet. Beneath a rainbow a fond couple embraced as children romped around them. She frowned, fell into a reverie, flushed. Suppressing a moment of shock and sorrow over her betrayal of Martin and their future family, Calla knew she'd deliberately leaped heedless and headlong into her situation.

Pulling the wrinkled kimono closed, she slapped down seven more Tarot cards in haste, turning over the last more deliberately.

"Four of wands. Felicity!"

With relief she fell back against the pillows, exhausted, sticky, in need of a bath. Poor Fez wouldn't be able to get out through the open window; it had proved far too narrow to allow those Valkyrie wings a purchase on the breeze. If he shat on Martin's Persian rug she'd get the thing cleaned somehow before he got back from Cleveland. (Surely it was Cleveland?)

Conscious of her wistful masquerade of slatternliness, Calla hugged her elation all the closer. These three weeks since John – no, Crum, so much dearer – had been in Rutledge had aged her, something she'd nearly despaired of achieving. He took her seriously now, was even, she suspected, a little afraid of her.

They'd worked as though demented since that first morning. He'd shown up at dawn, pounding the Japanese temple bell her father'd sent for a housewarming gift as though Lilybanks were on fire. She and Martin nearly fell out of bed, appalled, till realizing their architect had chosen to announce himself with the bonshō mallet.

"Seems to be enjoying himself. I'll go down," Martin had grinned, dawdling to kiss her. Later he told her Crumrind had shaken his hand and asked if bare feet were a rule of the house. (Calla had wondered if their Meisterbilder had deafened himself for the sake of dramatic effect; now she knew Crum carried earplugs at all times as insurance against insomnia, saws and automobile horns.)

Dressed, she'd descended to find three immense, fawn-colored dogs with heads like the Art Institute's guardian lions in her hall. For one eerie moment all three rose to stare at her; the tallest could have bitten her heart out. No tail wagged. She'd perceived their melting eyes betrayed compassionate restraint, the finest sort of delicate manners. They might have been a trio of Quakers, hats in hand, come to distribute or request alms as her station might indicate. They met her open-armed coos by gently knocking her flat with offerings of giant webbed paws. A few careful licks on the face sealed the accord. They let her pull herself up on them like redwood stumps. The four of them had proceeded out the open back door with conscious pomp.

Last night she'd watched their plumy breeches sashay in the moonlight as she and Crum descended into town behind them. Realizing he wasn't a hand-holder she'd made do with an unproffered arm's camaraderie. Blitzen, the most acute of his entourage, had stopped several times to sniff both of them dolefully like a foiled duenna.

He'd left his elegant cigarettes behind. She dove to pick them up off the rug, lit one of the nasty things eagerly.

"Only one person at a time could lean out the window onto the garden," she recounted to herself, yesterday's tableau having assumed the allure of a cryptic fairytale.

Inhaling the smoke hungrily – it no longer made her choke – Calla doted on the transformation beyond her garden wall. The two of them had toiled till they stumbled, ruined prized "work clothes," (they were both of them peacocks) and dined speechless, blistered and limp while Martin indulged them with good-humored monologues for ten evenings. An unrelenting greed for beauty had driven them harder than his limited time, harder than pride, competition and cautious infatuation.

Harmonious in their mutual transport, they wanted no help, kept Ross about as a sort of unwitting chaperone. Crum had infuriated his mocking, pinch-faced chauffeur by sending him back and forth to far-flung nurseries in search of oakleaf hydrangeas on a stormy day. Usually Crum let him hang about the university; it seemed his real interest was some sort of clandestine socialist agenda.

She and Crum had plundered glades of Mayapples and yellow celandines, leaving enough behind to continue their dynasties while stuffing dozens of uprooted plants into bushel baskets. The dogs packed them back to Lilybanks pannier-style, eager to oblige.

All laid out and tilled, the garden bristled with baby shrubs, stakes and string. Runic concoctions of stones and planks marked future pergolas, pools, outbuildings and statuary. The lush black soil promised pleasure and peace.

A volatile element, peace. She'd left Mr. Khan's brownstone court-yard laden with it last week. His reticent Sufi guests, whose fickle English only communicated good will, had turned into spiraling chalices of pure spirit, pure Knowing while she and Crum huddled on back porch steps in the sharp spring dusk. Muffled traffic, a newsboy's bray,

Crum's jade signet ring winking in the gloom as he tapped his knee to the music, a lingering scent of damask rose that had enveloped their host's rooms, intermittent vertigo and exaltation all funneled toward paradise and swept her up too.

Humbled into profound silence, the two of them had groped for expressions of gratitude and headed toward Union Depot, pausing to loiter under the stars. She'd pulled him into shadow under the roaring el tracks to give a heedless car a wide berth. He'd kissed her hand in that courtly, naïve manner of his that made her want to laugh but hit its mark anyway. Crum looked tremendously wistful. Calla let him hold the hand to his cheek tenderly; she suspected a confirmed bachelor's little charade. She'd taken a hotel room for the night, and suffered him only to bundle her into a cab she flagged at once in a parody of primness. Surprisingly desolate, she waved him goodnight with sisterly affection. He seemed content with that.

By the time she'd dismissed the hotel ladies' maid Calla's legs were trembling; the remnants of an excellent curry threatened to rise in her mouth. She'd been turned inside out and emptied for a sweet hour with the Sufis, then restored all lopsided beneath the screeching train tracks.

Consumed and resentful, she'd recognized Martin's departure on business two days later as an element in an unheeded design she'd been spinning diligently since Crum's hat hit the breadbox.

Yesterday she'd suggested they let the view from the back bedroom inspire their choice of a tree below it. He'd rolled up his sleeves to lean out the lattice; she'd stood nearby, admiring his arms. Was this how incest felt? Hansel and Gretel in a house made of sweets?

Never quite pompous but certainly fond of the lectern, Crum waxed eloquent on the virtues of larches. She'd responded with a light caress where misinterpretation was impossible. Startled, he laughed – yelped, really – with what seemed equal parts distress and delight.

When nothing more seemed forthcoming except his embarrassed retreat she'd taken charge with a willfulness that exempted him from transgression in both their minds. Counting on the profound reluctance to wound that she knew lay beneath his fragile self-conceit, Calla was willing to accept a surrender out of mere courtesy. His passivity – even ineptness – became irrelevant. Kindred spirits could make do with one body, mightn't they? Hers fascinated him, at least.

The bond was the thing, acknowledged tangibly now. However tepid and confused, the misfired consummation had occurred. She recalled a muddle of bashful laughter, awe, pity, concealed disappointment, resignation, a sort of polite mutual famine until she let him revert to custom, a one-sided affair of feverish suckling culminating in calibrated artifice. Afterwards she'd felt like a court eunuch carefully wiping the dowager empress's bottom; he'd passed her his monogrammed hanky. They'd possessed each other as best possible; the thing had been done, if not strictly so in a technical sense. In the eyes of the world they were lovers.

Realizing that even her shrewd husband would never suspect a thing, Calla luxuriated in the situation's potential. The dervishes were Mohammedans; didn't they take more than one wife? Darling Martin, her refuge – and she, his. Demanding, elusive Crum – her muse – and she his. Dizzy, she turned to smooth the bed. Her fingers still picked at the sheets' furrows as she dozed off in a dream of Turk's cap lilies and bitter chauffeurs.

Once the smoke had cleared the stork pattered to the bedside, tentatively opening its wings slightly and hugging them close again. Alternately baffled and inspired by its newest habitat it examined Calla eagerly, enduring the rise and fall of her breath on its breast. When she woke open-eyed the horny bill struck at its glittering prey with instinctive force.

5

Unison

Tad got dressed by flashlight, the teensy bulb in the desk lamp having proven unequal to his sleepless night.

He'd never really noticed how loud the zippers on his pack were. And jagged creaks erupted unpredictably from the floor boards no matter how he tried to outwit them by crawling over the bed or inching past a previous offender. He hoped Lucy was a sound sleeper.

The flashlight got him down the hall to the stairs, boots in hand. He'd washed up the night before, charmed by Lucy's compact and lip gloss perched on the ledge of the sink, strands of Beebe's long hair in the tub, a translucent bar of soap whose scent – honeysuckle, he thought – haunted even the toilet paper he'd dabbed on a shaving nick. He'd decided it was impossible to park his toothbrush in a medicine cabinet that contained Kotex.

The chink of light he'd seen under Beebe's door on his way to bed was missing now. He crept down the stairs, reflecting that if Beebe weren't up soon he'd have to knock on her door. The thought filled him with dread. The first day back to classes was bleak enough under his current cockeyed circumstances without annoying Beebe.

Tad stowed his pack by the front door and switched on the chandelier to avoid a collision with Aphrodite. In spite of Beebe's perpetual joke that the whole house shook when Tad walked, peaceful snores issued from the armpit of the bathrobe he'd donated last night to distract the dog from keeping vigil at the bottom of the stairs. His moving into Lilybanks had made one sentient being happier, at least.

He glided past her into the scullery and stopped to tug on his boots. A ghostly glow emanated from the depths of the kitchen. A nightlight? Distant metallic clatter disturbed the silence.

Tad switched off his flashlight and tightened his grip on it just in case. But it was most likely a Lilybanker – threatening enough. He suspected his fear of surprising one of them in the midst of some enterprise a male shouldn't see would be chronic. Deciding that his chances of discovering a burglar his first morning were remote, Tad cleared his throat loudly before turning the corner past the pantry.

"Hello?"

Beebe, so tightly braided or underslept that her eyes had an oriental cast, studied him severely. In the glow of the titanic old refrigerator's open door her pale face looked Halloweenish; he would have laughed if he'd dared.

The worktable she used for kneading bread had been spread with a tablecloth. Two cereal bowls between napkins and spoons faced each other across the tabletop.

Obviously an interloper, Tad groped for words.

"Mind if I grab some cornflakes before you guys eat?" His father had made sure Tad contributed a starter bag of groceries to the kitchen. His dad could be pretty sharp. He had a fleeting vision of the carpeted breakfast nook at home.

Beebe took in his confusion, the goofy dropped jaw that made him look dumb, the tummy, the warm brown eyes. Her irritation at being startled on her personal turf (where had all this ego come from all of a sudden?) vanished.

"'You guys' is us, Tad."

He still looked hesitant.

"It's for you and me. I made oatmeal, and there's maple syrup or brown sugar." She patted the further chair. "You can sit here. How's

Beowulf going?" Beebe turned her back tactfully, lingering over a milk bottle. Creaky chair legs and the familiar clunk and sigh of Tad's dumped backpack filled the noticeable silence. It would be indelicate to giggle, stingy not to chat. She couldn't think of a thing to say. Maybe he hadn't even opened Beowulf without her. She glanced up in spite of herself.

Tad looked happy for the first time in weeks. Normally that entailed the eager, expectant gaze of a beloved child about to blow out his birthday candles. It drove her nuts, for some reason.

Now he looked happy in a careful, older way that wrung her heart, kindling a depth of compassion for him from which she'd always been sealed off, though she took its presence for granted.

There was no safe thing to do, through no fault of theirs.

Unsmiling, extremely alert, still, she dished up their oatmeal. One of her braids nearly swerved into the pot. He tucked it behind her shoulder automatically. She placed her bowl at the end of the table, moved her chair so it was no longer across from his but next to it, and sat down.

He watched Beebe put her hand into his where it rested on his thigh.

"Good thing I can eat left-handed," she observed.

They breakfasted in a musical, jubilant silence.

Tad and Beebe left the house mitten to mitten. It wasn't a delivery morning and they were much too early, neither having any idea why the other had risen so prematurely. The glistening constellations and bitter air seemed to share Beebe's exaltation. Outwitted, undone, upstaged by cosmic creativity, she was charmed by the simplicity of the path before her where she'd seen only a frustrating tangled mess an hour ago.

Baffled but profoundly aware of a sea change, Tad preserved his grateful silence. Smiles sufficed. An unprecedented unison prevailed at last in spite of his hamstrung, flailing ineptitude.

Neither wanted a bus, neither cared where they went or what time they got there. Replete, surrendered, nearly calm, Beebe treasured every perception. The dirty slush that framed their footprints, the street lamps' hum, a gelled newspaper with ruffling pages on a bus stop bench, the usually unbearable tingle of sugar on her unbrushed teeth all conspired in a joyous, anarchical truce. When thoughts – mostly delicious plans – appeared she let them sink under their own weight, preferring her boundless refuge in the present.

When they ended up under the eaves at the bakery's front door, Beebe quietly shed her backpack, hopped onto the milkman's delivery crate and kissed Tad before he had time to see it coming. It was a sweet, almost chaste kiss; she knew her man. When he stood back to look at her the stubby little icicles lining the eave cracked off noisily into his fallen hood; water dripped down his neck. All he noticed was the exquisite plummy pink staining her cheeks and the sprinkling of tiny freckles across the bridge of her nose.

She swatted at the dribbles down the front of his parka, clucking. "You."

Beebe yanked the bell cord before he'd recovered. Gloria, who could make out quite a bit through the lacy curtains, concealed her glee as Tad walked in a little unsteadily.

"You look like you could use an espresso, Tad. First day back and all." She managed to sound offhanded, but couldn't resist adding that Beebe looked like she'd gotten her health back.

Lucy had confided in her about Captain Bramble's announcement to Tad the day after Christmas that they'd be moving to Washington, D.C. He'd been reassigned. Tad had categorically refused, but as a minor had no feasible alternative. Marian, who doted on Tad (unhelpfully, as far as Beebe was concerned, Gloria suspected) wanted to offer him a roof. She sought Lucy's opinion. Lucy asked for Gloria's advice. The result had been a request for the Captain's consent, ostensibly so Tad could complete the school year without disruption. Apparently the Captain never inquired about the sleeping arrangements: just a pair of curtained doors that didn't lock between Tad's "nursery" and Lucy's inner sanctum.

She studied them from behind the espresso machine while they thawed out. Tad seemed especially attractive in spite of a red nose; when he managed to get animated and lost the lugubrious look he was a knockout. Completely oblivious, of course. Once he'd lost fifteen pounds, let his daddy send him through the Ivy League and gotten roughed up a little by life, the oafish, jumbo cherub would be a self-assured heartthrob. Probably always a bit stuffy, though. A banker. Trustworthy but sternly realistic. Why couldn't her ex have been like that? She could be running a prestigious, upscale place in Florida, instead of doomed to terminal bohemianism in Rutledge's colorful, seedy student quarter. Her knee twinged. It didn't like winter either.

Tad was so addled he'd neglected to veto the espresso. She'd make his cocoa anyway; a caffeinated, kissed Tad might leave puncture marks in the sidewalk.

Beebe approached, still in earmuffs.

"I like the '*Bonne Fête*' sign by the galettes. Did you sell a lot in advance?" She scrutinized the shelves with a proprietary eye that Gloria appreciated. Beebe had become part of her support system. Her doctoral candidate baguette baker and the cute dishwasher from Guam had other plans than marketing confections.

"Yup. After all, who wants to have a Twelfth Night party on a Thursday?"

"Evvie Bruchner."

"Well, I can't go. Two weddings this week. You working hard on those nests?"

"Thirty marzipan lovebirds in puff pastry nests with *glacé* rose petals tucked in here and there. I'll do the nests Wednesday and assemble them Thursday night. The birds look good. Buxom, as you requested."

"Great." Gloria leaned over the counter confidentially. "Nice scarf," she smiled.

Beebe fumbled at the loopy, navy blue gnarl at her neck, having forgotten she was wearing Tad's scarf.

"Oh. Thank you!" she beamed, and joined him in the tiny eating area.

Gloria poked through a dented canister full of Twelfth Night charms and notes to herself, searching for the register key. She'd told Lucy that Tad had a tiger by the tail, that they were temperamentally unsuited and it would all fizzle out, so why not let them be? That way none of the adults would have to put up with their resentful mooning over a truncated romance. Secretly Gloria thought Beebe simply tolerated Tad but would know what to do with such an opportunity right in her lap, so to speak. It looked like she was already running with the ball.

Beebe warmed her hands under her armpits. "The drinks will take a minute."

"Not a problem." He pulled her chair closer, tugged her down and put his arm around her.

His face seemed quite different two inches away; she'd be getting used to that. He looked like he wanted to laugh.

"That scarf is impossible."

The Guild
[1911]

Taken aback, Crumrind lost his footing. A pleasurable, unctuous cool saturated his sock as his right shoe plunged into a velvety soup of pond bilge. The turn in the path had brought him face to face with his own binoculars. Stationed at the end of a low pier fringed with cattails, Calla resembled a pale dragonfly, the ends of her filmy scarf tugged by the breeze and the monstrous lenses aimed right at him.

The impression of metallic, invertebrate scrutiny by a woman struck him as a profoundly modern image. Alarmed, Crum made haste to dismantle it.

"You're missing the towhee in the tulip tree. Usually see them on the ground," he called.

The binoculars remained trained on him a moment longer. Calla pivoted in the direction he pointed toward, pleased to show she knew which tree that was.

"Where? I can't -"

"It just flew off, Cal." Out of breath, he disarmed her with a flip of the leather strap. Reunited after five minutes apart, each searched the other's face. Binoculars restored to his neck, Crum took her hand and faintly kissed the inside tenderly, part of an entire repertoire of gauche, musty chivalry Calla dreaded and couldn't do without.

He'd quickly taught himself not to flinch at her scar. The celebrated surgeon he'd insisted on providing in an excess of remorse (and deaf to Calla's prudence) insisted the wound would fade to the faintest of ephemeral, shimmering streaks in "a year or two." Scaling and puckered, the rosy little crescent framed her eye parenthetically. He marveled at her indifference and mimicked it.

"Maybe we should be getting back; the dogs look like they're feeling the heat." She had his poor sodden shoe in mind. The discretion was acquired; his consciousness of being twice her age, or some other caustic pride, flared between them unpredictably.

He took her arm and they turned toward Lilybanks, each enjoying cozy ambiguity as to who was coddling whom. Their lumbering escort surrounded them.

"What's in your hatband?"

"Ah." He pulled off the citified hat for inspection. Such childish pleasures bound them. (Or did his students earn a similar intimacy?)

Calla twirled the succulent stem, still moist, between her fingers.

"How elegant. Like an arrowhead." The ribbed leaf's exaggerated contours suggested a spidery Art Nouveau border, or perhaps a more primitive geometric effect reminiscent of the giant urns and friezes Mr. Frank Lloyd Wright favored. (Another subject requiring discretion...)

"That's what it's called. Get it into your press as soon as we're back. It's what I was looking for in among the reeds."

She savored the last mile during which her hip might brush rhythmically, lusciously, against him and she could inhale the sere, chaste, intimate smell of him. Her imagination scurried through Lilybanks in search of arrowhead habitat. Her Meisterbilder had decreed all things oaken and druidical for the ballroom; they'd agreed on idyllic spring in the dining room...Unless Crum insisted on yet another native plant on some lintel frieze, she'd poach his arrowheads for the dainty little clawfoot tub in her dressing room. Resolving never to remind him of the plant, Calla dropped it into her reticule.

"You've got the gleam of an otter fattened on caviar."

Mistaking the comparison's intent, she caught her breath.

"It's an illusion. I hold water when the moon grows full."

"No, you're radiating a sort of...rightness. Deep-rooted unity. Singleness of effect, like a fruiting orchard."

"Yes, I feel so." She made him meet her eyes. "And yourself?"

He held her face in his hands, drew his forehead down to touch hers, said nothing.

A dim suggestion of chimney and gable appeared across the field, above a copse of hawthorns. Calla moved apart, watched for the grave quickening she sensed when he entered the house's sphere, even more vital than their own reunions.

"Stupid to have forgotten my sketchbook. I'll bring it tomorrow. To draw the linden." She looked away, smiling, coloring, nearly Mrs. Morrissey again.

Glancing up, she met the predictable response. He thought his arch smile concealed the puppyish pride. Her sketchbook and pencils had fallen under the icebox in the wake of Crum's consciously piquant insistence they linger in the scullery upon her return from Martin's early train. His twinkle depended on a fatuous conceit of eccentric adequacy that she nurtured. No one, least of all Crum, was to understand her emperor had no clothes.

Her morning's real treasure had to be their contentment leaning against each other beneath a handsome linden in full, fragrant bloom. They'd taken turns reading aloud passages in a book by Lafcadio Hearne from which Crum had been inseparable all week. When they resumed their stroll to search for specimens, Calla already nostalgic for the linden knoll, he'd commented that the green slope would make a lovely little cemetery.

Swollen with consciousness of mutual devotion and the impossibility of acknowledging it to others, they approached Lilybanks increasingly slowly. The pace grew laggard, perhaps vividly so, and Calla forced herself awake.

"Sam will be here by now."

"Mmm. Look how well the hop vine's taking over your little Buddha's shrine."

"You were right. It likes the shade."

He stopped to remove his shoes and socks, giving the impression of having walked barefoot all the way home as he followed her up the back steps. Now he always let her enter first unless they were alone, but never asked if the dogs were welcome. They fell in behind, rattling the new hazel bush's young branches pushing through the railing.

"I want some of your Berkeley sandals, Cal," Crum roared unintentionally over the clatter of three Leonbergers on flagstone.

"I'll ask my brother." Her mother would not appreciate the situation.

Crum turned into the sitting room and sank full-length onto the settle; the dogs hesitated, their warm eyes studying Calla.

"It's alright. Stay here with Papa...I'll just see how Sam's getting on."

Bruno hovered at the French doors, curious about something. Calla peeped into the dining room.

"Miss Mapes! Ruth. Didn't realize. Sketching looks wonderful, very exciting. We're so lucky to have you here. Do you have everything you need? A black coffee?...bourbon?" she smiled up, afraid to offend with anything not extreme. Only two or three years younger than herself, the rigidly iconoclastic Miss Mapes was saddled with a wealthy local family who doted on their baffling only child. Plain as porridge and fiercely ascetic in spite of her adopted bohemianism, the art student had immediately made Calla her confidante when singled out for an introduction by the prescient dean of arts.

Perched midway up a ladder, Ruth twisted away from her penciled meadow, flicking her yard-long braid back with a ruler.

"It can't look like much till I start in with my oils...No thanks, I'm fasting."

Crum, who glimpsed Ruth's hem and bare feet, tousled the nearest dog to disguise a giggle. Miss Mapes might prove difficult to locate should her ironing-board physique be much reduced by fasting. Though the astonishing diamond that pierced her right nostril might serve as a beacon. Sighing, he pulled himself together and stood. Blitzen and Monk rose at once; Bruno cocked an ear from the tarp-covered dining room.

"You evoke Florence, Miss Mapes," he called in a nasal, disarming tenor that seemed to belong to a younger man. He drew close to Calla, doubling his impact. The stern Miss Mapes' shy reverence made her easy to dodge. "The Morrisseys are fortunate to have you in Lilybanks' little guild." Calla and Ruth exchanged a furtive glance at this before Crumrind all but herded his employer back out, tripping on a wad of billowing tarp.

"Your Ruffey's more likely to appreciate that bourbon. We'd best go see if he wants fortifying."

Sam Ruffey could carve acres of nuts and furtive squirrels with no more sustenance than the joy he took in his craft. An old friend of Calla's from the California School of Arts and Crafts, he'd quickly grasped what Calla wanted, and what Crumrind didn't. He and Crum understood each other. The ballroom's dark columnar facades harbored bluejays and titmice, sprouted sprays of oak and acorns without clutter or sentimentality. Ruffey's squirrels might scurry down to nip a guest. Leaves looked ready to flutter if Calla breezed past. Each image counted; the principle of simplicity had been cheerfully tweaked but not violated. Crum exalted in the ballroom's restrained enchantment; it would reign throughout Lilybanks if he could govern Calla's prodigal imagination...

Ever the hostess, she took the stairs two at a time ahead of him. Women's ankles were appearing in public now; at home Calla's impressive calves advanced and receded from under beaded pagan smocks and artful Grecian affairs she must sew in the middle of the night.

Privately longing to get into her studio, Calla raced up the sunlit hall, so wide Crum's missing chauffeur might have driven the Peerless along it. Crum found her in Sam's pudgy arms as he steadied her on a stepladder; her tiptoed enthusiasm for a new pair of delicately lobed leaves emerging from a shaft had threatened to defy gravity.

"Ruffey! Sorry to interrupt, we're taking orders for tea. (Miss Mapes has declined.)"

Calla swiveled to watch her friend's sturdy hand clench the Meister's. Sam's wholehearted acceptance of Crumrind as an admirable comrade had sealed her confidence. How well Crum would fit among Berkeley's easygoing community of intellectuals and artists; she longed to make Lilybanks such a hive.

"Mind the shavings!" Sam swung her off the step and parked her beyond his debris like a doting elephant. "I'll take you up on the tea. Nothing more, thanks. Too much wine last night. So none of your lettuce tonics or purslane pudding, madame. Unless you've still got some of your neighbor lady's excellent shortbread in the pantry? Her menfolk plan to make a piper of me. I've the force and the fingers, they say. By the way, that fellow you've hired to make a fence plays the pennywhistle like a genie. Let's all of us go 'round his place some evening. We're invited. A couple of fiddlers, too. Tell your Ruthie," he winked.

Calla watched Crum arrange a façade of vague interest, then crouch to examine Sam's collection of chisels.

"Martin will be in his element. We'll dance reels. He grew up with all that...I'm away for the tea." She plucked her reticule from the floor and padded off in the wrong direction. Sam would take sugar, Crum would not. Difficult to imagine the university drama department's set designer finding time to stencil the ballroom ceiling once classes were in session; Sam had been firm about seeing his woodcraft completed and securely shrouded before Mrs. Erikson began painting. Yet an inspired momentum seemed to reign throughout Lilybanks. Calla felt she'd have her ballroom ready by the first snow.

She turned toward her dressing room. Through its doorway Gompy the black cat watched her from his stack of hat boxes, square and snug as a baker's loaf, paws folded from sight. A new red collar and tag emphasized his position as a cat of consequence.

"I see you've been expecting me."

The cat's dilated stare became a dewy, cross-eyed squint; his nose moistened. She stroked his head, thinking with guilty amusement of her successful failure to hire a live-in cook.

"*Courage*, this can't go on forever. You're all being very patient. If handy Ross Nicol didn't net you those unlucky minnows you'd be eating scrambled eggs, my love."

Humming "The Dashing White Sergeant," Calla dropped to the adjacent bathroom's honeycombed tiles.

"White, white, white. You'd think color carried germs." She pulled the wilting arrowhead leaf out and dangled it against the side of the tub – a mere tureen – she'd had Crum wedge into the gleaming cubbyhole. She'd requested that everything here be too petite and prettily inconvenient to serve Martin. This delighted her husband. He found the close, scented little room arousing when he fumbled through it from the hall on nights he'd caught the last train home. Darling Martin.

"A row of these, and pickerel frogs with golden eyes..."

She rose and aimed a particular little cluck at the cat, who'd followed her onto the tiles. He crouched and jumped into her arms, nibbling the arrowhead's gummy stem as they sailed down the hall.

"We'll press it under Mama's cookbook for the time being."

As they passed the vacant nursery she remembered Martin's request over breakfast. She was to ask that the locks and keyholes on its interior French doors be removed. They struck him as inadvisable.

Replete, she swung the cat onto her shoulder and descended.

Sam and Crum both stayed for a sprightly supper with the Morrisseys, taking the measure of each other and sharing their visions for their hosts' house with animation far into the evening.

When Crum finally entered his room on Moss Street he walked to his bed in darkness. His fickle, unpredictable chauffeur had waited. The relief of an effortless response dwindled into a sense of tremendous weariness that sleep was unlikely to cure.

Lilyminded Monkeybanker

"Gotta run! Big meeting!" Sally Osterman shouted through her cupped gloves and waved, then hustled around to the driver's side of the car and tooled off.

Melodie shoved past Althea, shed boots and snowsuit at her little chair with new expertise and sprinted to the creepy bathroom while sharing a stream-of-consciousness narrative about her cousins. Sally had told Al about their holiday plans at her brother's ranch in Montana. The reluctant Melodie had clearly been aged by the experience. Althea heard herself commenting amusedly on this to Melodie's mother; Sally had suggested they go out for coffee sometime...

There she went again, lost in vivid imaginings. They weren't *real*; just tissue-y mental debris, usually easy enough to dismiss when she finally caught herself.

She listened to Melodie thumping about behind the partially closed door, and practiced feeling her inner body. The usually faint fizz was more twinkly today. At the breakfast table she'd imagined what levitating must be like, she'd felt so light and porous. Progress. Of course it was partly the coffee.

She'd forgotten how much fun caffeine was, associating it with the aftermath of Casper's death, till Evvie urged some on her when Al ran into her at the bakery. She had begun squandering money at the nearest Starbucks. Certainly stimulants weren't ideal, but heightened alertness seemed to help her tune into Presence. And she was a new widow who could use all the little pleasures she could find. Coffee made her more outgoing. Her conversation seemed less rusty. Emails, too. Lucy had urged Al to borrow her computer and taught her how to send messages and check for replies. She'd made it simpler than Casper had ever managed.

"Okay, Mrs. Affdus!"

Like the little cymbals Eckhart used, Melodie's summons woke Al up out of the dream again. How many times had she participated in this coffee monologue recently? She envisioned her crummy childhood record player in its cardboard case, impassively delivering the same chords over and over again when some scratchy 45 tripped it up. Her mind seemed to prefer twice-warmed leftovers to almost any here and now.

Melodie had navigated the stool and leaned over the sink on her elbows, soberly examining the new piggy soap she clutched.

"Misty an' Hayden have glitter soap. In a bottle."

Al cooed appreciatively, enjoying the warm, salty smell of Melodie's head.

"Let's roll up your sleeves a little. Is that a new sweater for Christmas, Melodie?"

"Our dogs come home today."

"Ah. They had to stay at the vet's while you were gone?"

Melodie trampled Althea's foot getting off the stool. It didn't matter. Very little really mattered. Lovely. Parentheses of reflected light glowed on the toilet seat.

*   *   *

As soon as all their charges had been packaged and dispatched the sisterhood headed upstairs for a session.

"We'll be in Millefleurs," Marian huffed over her shoulder as she tackled the stairs.

"I have to make a ziggurat. Papier-mâché, do you think, or dough?" Beebe asked Lucy in Marian's wake. She'd just returned from her new mythology class. Al thought she could smell mothballs from Beebe's faded Edwardian cape. First day back to school after an illness and Beebe was wearing a flimsy museum piece against the January elements. "Bubo's" supervision seemed sporadic.

They filed down the dark hallway behind Marian, Beebe in the rear after filching Lucy's rabbit slippers from the bathroom to disguise her wet feet.

A wan, wintry glow at the lattice windows barely brightened Millefleurs. Al hurried to claim the chair closest to her favorite breach in the mural's luxuriant hedgerow, from which an otter bearing a gaudy sprig of hawthorn berries peeked. The otter's warm eye communicated a preference for children and other discreet, patient dawdlers, Al thought.

Was the mural's intricacy to some purpose beyond delight? A magpie sipping from a starlit puddle kept one eye cocked on its trophy, a lady's filigree ear-bob dangling from a twig. Not far off a mourning cloak warmed its wings in a shaft of sunlight among autumn leaves; a covey of quail chicks looked on from beneath their mother's wings. Grape hyacinths' spires of tiny cobalt chalices embroidered the long grass bending under a newt's progress. The enchanted labyrinth foiled charting. Occasionally Althea thought some shady hollow had shifted or an entire scene momentarily overran its single dimension.

"Althea, you've fallen under Millefleurs' spell, methinks. Can you join us? A few conscious breaths, perhaps." From the depths of the other Morris Marian looked remote.

Lucy winked at Al from the settle. Beebe sat next to her in a half lotus, the fleecy ears on her feet ludicrously erect.

After a lengthy silence Marian cleared her throat, a sort of minimalist ritual. Althea concentrated on staying in touch with her lips and toes to discourage her kudzu-like thoughts. Caffeine didn't seem to help with monkey-mind.

Lucy finally deciphered a memo penned across her palm.

"Ah. A daycare budget issue. Half our tofu hot dogs are disappearing into Aphrodite. We're all guilty, and the kids are the worst. Julia Montini discovered three rotting Smart Dogs in Lincoln's pencil case last night; he said he'd meant to give them to Ditey before the holiday break but forgot when Carpenter wet his pants. Just as an example. Three weeks in a row someone's had to make an extra run for lunch supplies."

Althea, who'd just covertly indulged in the extra carry-out espresso that now augmented her morning Starbucks visit, surprised herself.

"I'd be happy to write a perky memo to parents about the danger to the dog's shapely figure."

"Splendid. Much obliged, Althea...Mr. Watkins informs me that the bird feeder's post was replaced with materials he rummaged from the garden hut, so your piggybank need not be disturbed." (Marian, Micah, Professor Bakeoven and even Captain Bramble had convinced Al not to give up Casper's car. She had backed it into one of Lilybanks' countless bird feeders when requested to make room for the chimney sweep's van a few weeks back, yet no one seemed to harbor misgivings.) Al nodded sheepishly, desperate to hang on to lips and toes.

"Any other nuts and bolts items?" Beebe shook her head; Althea decided against bringing up her wildly unpredictable radiator in the wake of the bird feeder incident.

Marian pulled Professor Crabbe's bulky, pilling cardigan tighter around her sagging midriff, a rare acknowledgement of Lilybanks' rigorous climate beyond the necessarily snug kindernook. Althea felt sure Marian's Anglophilia had convinced her the drafts were "bracing."

"In that case, I think we should move along to a frank discussion of our new circumstances. I am acutely aware of my sole responsibility for offering Tad sanctuary, though no one dissented. His presence has both tangible and intangible effects. I feel it paramount for the general good that we all feel free to openly acknowledge these effects and initiate change where change must be. Please don't suffer in silence should -"

An extravagant, playful snort interrupted Marian's cryptic scruples.

"This *is* Tad Bramble we're talking about? Quiet, conscientious, nonjudgmental, tirelessly helpful Tad? We appreciate your concern, Marian, but lighten up! My only concern is that the poor boy's so busy being useful to Lilybankers that he hasn't time for his homework. This is a Godsend! You can get the attic cleared out, for instance – all the chores left undone because it would be so unamusing to get crotchety Watkins involved."

The others suspected the motive behind Lucy's animation: for

Beebe's sake she hoped to minimize the real thrust of Marian's concerns. Althea found herself guiltily savoring the undercurrent: would Marian still wander around in her shabby bathrobe and daubs of eczema cream after 8 pm? Would Tad stumble upon the perpetually forgetful Lucy in the bath? Would (the most unmentionable "tangible effect") Beebe and Tad end up sleeping together? Eager to be numbered among those who still possessed a sexual identity (however marginal), Althea volunteered that "it will be lovely to have a man around." She and Lucy both tried not to look at Beebe; Al had overheard enough snippets of dissension between Marian and Beebe in the past week to know that Beebe had some volatile mixed feelings about an onsite Tad.

"Tad's very happy," Beebe offered, with the suave little smile she seemed to adopt when getting her way.

How obliging of him, Al thought, now perversely focused on the probable loss of the pajama party aura that often reigned upstairs, and on being forced to witness young love.

"I'm very glad. Let's keep the lines of communication open, everyone." Marian sounded hearty but looked skeptical. "I assume this means Tad's first night in the nursery was uneventful for you and your roommates, Lucy."

Typically, Al thought, the only concern her "sisters" ignored was what the neighbors would think. The only reputations anyone here seemed to care about were for academic excellence and historical accuracy. Beebe could spend 24 hours a day with a hormonally precocious boy who knitted, as long as all Lilybanks' closets sported "correct" faux vintage light bulbs dangling from homely faux vintage cords.

"Althea contributed our reading, a prayer from the Orthodox church...Althea?"

Dismayed by the depths she'd just been industriously mucking about in, Al recited with her eyes closed, hoping to contain her utter lack of presence. (Though probably the Lilybankers could smell it on her.)

"O Heavenly King, the Comforter, the Spirit of Truth Who art everywhere and fillest all things. Treasury of Blessings and Giver of Life: Come and abide in us, and cleanse us from every impurity, and save our souls, O Good One."[11]

Al groped for threads of the brief commentary she'd prepared: "It's a prayer to the Holy Spirit, one of the most common prayers in Orthodox usage. It's all about presence, isn't it? Orthodox Christians would be horrified by some of Eckhart's ideas about Jesus, but I think this prayer is exactly what he teaches. And the impurity referred to would be ego. 'Everywhere and fillest *all things*' – that would be the holiness and aliveness everywhere, in animals, plants, rocks..."

Beebe looked involved in the conversation for the first time. "And the 'come and abide in us' is, well, our responsibility to choose consciousness, to grow in presence! Sort of an invitation to the wisdom and power of the universe to abide in us. It implies we're willing to make room for that."

Al found her eyes filling with tears, an embarrassment and a relief.

"I'm having a lot of trouble with that. Being rilling to make woom – willing to make room instead of succumbing to mental habits."

"My dear, my dear. We all know what you mean. Take comfort in the fact that the moment you realize you've missed the mark, 'identified with form,' as Eckhart says, whether it be materialism or thought-forms or transient emotion, you're back on track."

Althea blinked back her tears, attempted a dutiful smile.

"I wish you'd come with Lucy and me to Micah's church for Theophany, Althea. It might do you more good than a Twelfth Night party."

Touched that Beebe genuinely wanted to include her, Al hesitated for the sake of the invitation – albeit to her own church – rather than the destination.

"I'd like to, but I told Evvie I'd be there. I mean, she'll understand why Lucy and Micah arrive at the tail end, but I never mentioned church to her..." she faltered.

"'Everywhere present,' as the prayer says," Marian coached. "You can be just as aware of who you really are beyond ego at the party as the church. At least, if you stay away from the punch bowl," Marian smiled, and Al resolved upon an evening without alcohol, in order to have a chance at some presence – her highest priority, after all.

After five minutes of silent stillness they dispersed. Althea got a hug from Lucy, who then chased Beebe down the hallway to make sure she put Lucy's damp slippers on a radiator. While they were in the bathroom Althea slipped into her room and shut the door noiselessly. She added a sweatshirt to her long underwear and two sweaters, grabbed Casper's watch and pilfered a couple of PayDay bars from the spa-stickered trunk. The cache served as a hedge against what she felt was the impossibility of groping her way downstairs and past Aphrodite in the middle of the night.

Reflecting as she stole downstairs that what she was doing felt like her shy student days in a dormitory, Al sighed. Not the first time she'd noticed there was something infantilizing about her life at Lilybanks. Real adults didn't have to sneak a cup of coffee like an addict. What deficiency, what backwardness had caused her to forego a snug little apartment in favor of a kind of boarding school? She tugged her jacket off a hook above the preschoolers' chairs; a new sign by the door caught her eye.

"Please do NOT let cat outside under any circumstances."

Lucy, Marian and Beebe had all helped post the hand-lettered placards at every conceivable exit, including the tiny pantry window that had no screen. It had been decided at a November meeting that as a Lilybanker Linnet deserved the run of the house after parents, grandparents and au pairs had claimed their charges.

Al hung her coat back up. Where else could she and Linnet have encountered such doting kindness?

She found Linnet basking in the sitting room window seat where she could keep one sleepy eye on the bleached, fluttering weeds that teased so exasperatingly against the other side of the wavy glass.

"Prowt?" Linnet jumped down and trotted over to Al, tail held stiffly vertical with satisfaction. She had finally put on a little weight; she looked like she'd been zipped into a tight pair of footed p.j.'s. They communed until Aphrodite shuffled into the doorway. Linnet returned to her cushion, unable to account for the presence of a gigantic, smelly dog in her new realm.

Al blew her a kiss. "Back soon, sweetie." She lingered a moment to make sure Aphrodite retreated to her basket. Linnet was still unwilling to let any of the new humans approach her unless Al hovered nearby, but she'd been more than willing to tangle with Aphrodite. Unfortunately the dog found Linnet's hisses and half-feigned cuffs on the nose comical; only Tad could produce as much tail-wagging. When Ditey lumbered off Al was tempted to reward her with the usual hot dog, but caught herself.

Embracing the Now

Out on Corrie Street two plumped-up mourning doves roosted in the neighbors' naked maple. Most likely they were the same pair that huddled over Beebe's or Althea's broadcast birdseed at dawn.

Slogging through plowed snowbanks to avoid the slick sidewalk, Althea wondered if the frigid sanctuary of the Lilybanks garden weren't preferable to breaking her neck on Rutledge's only hills. Beebe and Tad usually kept snowdrifts from jamming the garden door, but they'd let it slip this week...Someone honked long and hard; Al had walked out into an intersection imagining a stop sign where none was. She fluttered a hand in the driver's direction. So much for presence. Here she was trapped in her head when she could be laying one foot down and then the other, again and again, recognizing the here and now.

That exercise proved impossible to accomplish with the Zen-like purity she envisioned, but she was able to reach Bodie Woods' main entrance mostly in touch and peaceful, in spite of snow inside her boots.

Al started up her favorite path, taking in the stillness. Shriveled scarlet berries encased in ice drooped from a twig; a sapling's clutch of curled ochre leaves had become little purses stuffed with fluffy snow. A dog barked in the distance. She stopped at the first bench, wiped it off and sat heavily.

It seemed essential to decamp occasionally, to disentangle Althea Athnos from Lilybanks. Eckhart Tolle advised simply not worrying about who one was, which shocked and elated her. Permission to forego the interminable renovation and buttressing of her persona struck Al not only as a tremendous relief but a gleeful, rebellious anarchy.

On the other hand one had to function in the outer world, if only to keep body and soul together. Some consistent public identity was helpful to negotiate other realms than that of the sympathetic but rather contingent Lilybanks...

Footsteps and a flash of vermilion in the middle distance shattered her musings. Braced, Althea tried to pay attention to her breath and the feel of the bench beneath her rather than being knocked utterly "unconscious" by the encounter.

A tall, regal dog came swerving past its human. It spotted her and wagged, bouncing a buffoonish mop of curls. No longer feeling trapped, Althea realized the Muppety lion's human seemed to recognize her. When his disagreeably refined little mustache came into focus she recognized Professor Bakeoven, looking uncharacteristically robust in a puffy quilted jacket. He seemed pleased to see her. She hoped it wasn't because the dreary new "sister" was getting some hygienic fresh air. The dog appeared to have the better of him.

"Mrs. Athnos! A lucky find! Quite rare to happen upon one of the prized but elusive members of the species Lilybanksia outside of their eponymous habitat. Rumba, stop that! Please excuse us – we haven't quite got the choreography down yet – he's an unsought but probably permanent acquisition from my delightful, capricious niece. Sunny disposition, won't bite you – STOP, Rumba! – but over-eager if you don't care for dogs..." He fiddled ineffectively with the leash, one of those retractable contraptions, while Rumba licked Al's face.

"Good heavens. I apologize. We should go home. Driving without a license." Though Mrs. Athnos seemed equal to the situation.

"What a charmer! What sort of dog is he, do you know?" She assumed it was a male without peeking. The professor, who seemed out of his depth but game, might not be able to tell a poodle from a Pyrenees.

"Stella – my niece – claims he's a Golden Doodle. Sounds more like a variety of chicken soup than a dog breed. She was pretty humorless about his pedigree; paid a terrific sum for him. But her hypersensitive boyfriend thinks he's barbaric and the downstairs tenants complained vigorously about thuds and clatter. Uncle Bakeoven was cajoled, and here we are. Now Stella's getting a Scottish Fold, whatever that is." He looked on dotingly as Rumba kicked up snow in a gregarious frenzy.

"How kind of you to take him on," she said, alarmed both for the dog and the professor.

"And kind of you to tolerate our invasion of your wintry glade." He searched her face, smiling and frowning at the same time, which she found inoffensive, having seen him study Beebe and Libby and Captain Bramble similarly on Christmas Eve.

"Will I see you at Evvie's tonight?" Al ventured. "Lucy mentioned your name among the guests she thought I'd know. Such a social neighborhood, the Hill District. Euclid Street – where I used to live – has a lot of historic homes too, but most were more, oh, self-contained. People stuck to their families and an adjacent neighbor or two.

Much more festive and friendly around Lilybanks." She suspected the reason was that the inhabitants of the Hills had more time and money with which to show off. It wouldn't do to say that; the Professor probably lived a simple, scholarly life in a crumbling childhood home on a highly desirable lot – a goose that would lay him a golden egg whenever that seemed timely. Many of the people she'd met in Rutledge had modest lifestyles quietly underpinned by family connections or inherited comfort. Only she and Casper seemed unmoored and isolated, dependent on faltering paychecks for temporary security.

"Sometimes regrettably so, for those of us who are hermits by nature." He frowned and smiled at her. She found icy, pale eyes disconcerting. Did he include himself as a hermit? Surely career teachers lacked the necessary insularity. Certainly he included Althea. Easy enough to pose as a connoisseur of personalities from the Olympian heights of a distinguished retirement. Embarrassed, she conceded only a thin smile.

"I sent Evvie my regrets, pleading weary old bones and the new roommate here. My chess night was the first time we've been separated, and the folks on the other side of the hall had to put up with inconsolable howling. I'm the landlord, but one aims for harmony. And to tell the truth I'll gladly forego another bout of inebriated decrees from Ubu Roi or Reine, not to mention the chance to break a tooth on the lucky charm."

Flattered that he'd trusted her with a literary reference in spite of her lowly estate as a daycare aide, Al flashed him a real smile this time. Bakeoven looked surprised, almost abashed, at having scored. He considered a moment, then ventured, quite humbly,

"Would you care to have dinner with us before your party? Just Rumba and me, at home. I'm capable of turning out an edible vegetarian meal, and I've got a bottle of really august sherry, a New Year's gift from an old friend, to soothe us while I fuss around the kitchen. Only a moderate sort of fussing. Then we'll drop you off at Evvie's, fortified for the ordeal...Will you?"

Too disarmed to dodge, Al was surprised to hear herself accept.

"That sounds lovely. How kind. Can I bring something?"

"Excellent! You see we hold the advantage, tempting you with a warm meal while you huddle on a park bench..." She began to see how students might remember him affectionately.

"Now let's see, I believe the Twelfth Night affair begins at..."

"Oh, no, I just remembered! I'm due at Libby Merchant's at five for a last-minute review of procedures before my debut as her dog-sitter. What a shame. But duty calls." The dinner was beginning to alarm her; at least she'd spontaneously "embraced the Now" before remembering her appointment. So she was safe on all fronts, if oddly disappointed.

Bakeoven squared his puffy polyester shoulders, inspired by the genuine groan.

"Five o'clock? How long of a review – surely not more than half an hour. Libby needs managing, that's all. I'm sure the oven can spare me for ten minutes while I dash over there to pick you up; we'll be serenely ensconced before our sherry by 5:45; I'll have you on Evvie's doorstep as the clock chimes seven."

"That's perfect, in theory. But Libby seems to become quite expansive on the subject of her animal companions, and I find she's not easily deflected from her course."

He gave her another genial frown.

"You two are a match made in heaven. She'll have you washing their plates between courses. I'll be there at 5:30."

"Fine!" she flared. If he thought her such a weakling, his own interest in her was highly suspect. Nettled with Libby as well as Bakeoven and herself, she patted Rumba and strode back down to the entrance, not turning to wave.

At Libby's

Althea set out for Libby's at a quarter to five, hugging a noisy brown bag containing her suede boots. The early darkness mercifully obscured the clunky shoe-boots destroying the effect of her most flattering coat. She clutched at guard railings and shrubs, resorting to snow higher than her shoes when necessary to avoid a slalom over the treacherous, partially shoveled sidewalks. She refused to drive after dark in winter, but this brittle, groveling descent in party attire from Lilybanks' heights now seemed equally foolhardy. Al was so accustomed to being a passenger that Bakeoven's insistence on picking her up at Libby's – with its assumption she'd not be driving herself – hadn't snagged her attention till just now. Oh, he thought she was a little old scaredy-cat, for sure.

And so she was, perhaps, yet this evening's social triple-header required every atom of pluck she could muster, and she had chosen it. A brief appearance at Evvie's party would have been hard to avoid without looking like an intractable recluse to her housemates, but Al could have eluded Bakeoven and snuffed Libby's overbearing arrangements. Why was quiet, low-profile courage never recognized? Why was everything so hard? If she slipped and snapped one of her thinning bones tonight the Lilybankers might learn she had no insurance. The prosperously artsy guests at Evvie's undoubtedly all had health insurance, not to mention stock portfolios and 401(k)s (whatever those were).

Ah. The familiar voice, creating problems where there was only scrunching beneath a fuzzy moon in a gauzy, star-studded sky.

Al heard herself snort, a new habit. She managed for a short while to concentrate on the knobby, pocked terrain and her labored breath, then settled for an intentionally charitable contemplation of her previous encounter with Libby's realm.

That had fortunately been a daytime visit, since the tiny house at the back of a narrow, sunken corner lot bore no address. She'd rung several neighbors' doorbells in a futile effort to avoid facing down the unsmiling German shepherd outside its door. Eventually a mail truck had pulled up; its driver knew the dog's name (Clipper? Clobber?) as well as Ms. Merchant's and reassured Al only marginally by saying the "difficult" dogs were never left alone in the yard. The shepherd proved to be mild-mannered and discerning, administering a few tail thunks against Althea's hip before receding.

Al had pressed the doorbell, activating a chorus of barking, clatter and parrot-like shrieks, while contemplating the house's faux stone siding. A dented aluminum storm door protected a front door with three diamond-shaped fifties-style windows. No one in the neighborhood had windows like that, even on a tool shed. Though she'd expected something more commanding, somehow Al wasn't too surprised.

"Be right with you, Alice. You're early," Libby's voice had boomed distantly through an intercom, all of which alienated her visitor. Casper's trustworthy watch indicated she was four minutes late, due to the missing house number.

Considerably later Libby had appeared – in an overpoweringly pink pullover that made her round, freckled face look feverish – after wrestling with several chains and bolts. This had struck Al as comic, but her palms were beginning to sweat at the thought of crossing Libby's threshold into a dim void that smelt of cat pee.

"Meant to have some tea on for you. I was upstairs giving the kitties some cuddling and fell asleep." Libby's bushy brown curls did seem a little flattened in back as she turned to let Al follow. She wore crocheted slip-ons over thin white socks; Al decided against voluntarily removing her shoes, imagining puddles and snarling muzzles.

Libby had flipped on a light.

Four or five mongrels wagged and panted at her quite civilly without surrendering their seats around an old-fashioned stove (vintage but neither stylish nor especially safe, Al judged). Its crooked pipe disappeared into the wall at ceiling height through what looked like a paper plate. Lots of folks had heaters like that in Al's early childhood, though not, she thought, front and center behind the front door.

Libby moved around briskly shutting curtains, snapping on lamps. With each illumination another ecosphere of slightly startled creatures, jungly houseplants and various odd arrangements appeared.

"Good grief, Libby, you rescue plants as well as animals? I hope you're not out of town often; you'd need a whole battalion of people in here to keep everything going!" Her words were left to hang in silence and she realized she'd emphasized the slightly scary excess, when in fact the goofy prodigality delighted her.

"Onto the library steps!" Libby bellowed. "Up!" She strong-armed Althea by a coat sleeve toward a dark, boxy mass that Al eventually mounted after bruising a shin. A massive calico hurtled toward her, hissing like a cobra. Libby held her by the wrist.

"KNOCK IT OFF, Tiffany! She'll probably calm down in a minute, but just in case..." Libby handed her a banana-shaped water pistol. "Just let her examine you from a distance. You're safe; she doesn't like stairs." Firmly clamped by Libby, surrounded by unblinking stares, Al felt she was being auctioned off, displayed for a tyrant's consideration. Had it been wise to wear her best jeans? She hugged her bag tighter. The ancient stove hiccuped somewhere to her left; judged by Libby's irregular living arrangements it might well explode at any moment.

When she realized that the windowsill driftwood next to a Campbell's soup can full of Wandering Jew was really an unrestrained, biggish iguana, Althea pulled herself together. She needed to leave. Or surrender? A few conscious breaths. Lips. Belly button. Toes.

Several bright little beaks caroled from a cage suspended from the ceiling among the green antlers of a massive fern.

Clearing her throat, she extricated herself from Libby.

"I've found my balance. Will you put this bag out of harm's way? While I'm treed here perhaps we could have some introductions. Who's the leathery individual in the window, for starters?"

Fluffy Tiffany's gimlet glare, enhanced with periodic growls, remained fastened on her while Libby made room for the boot bag on top of a grimy refrigerator as dated as the heater. Generous wads of flesh ("love handles," Al's mother had called them) appeared between the bubblegum-colored sweater and the snug denim mounds of Libby's jeans as she reached up. When she returned without a word and examined Althea's face as though searching for telltale symptoms of the plague, Al mustered an innocent smile and waited. Behind her one of the dogs' tails thumped.

Libby shoved her fingertips – all that would fit – into her jeans pockets.

"Lizard's name is Mustapha. I liberated him from a neglectful kid last year. He's made himself right at home. The dogs think he's hilarious; the cats give him a wide berth."

"Cats? Tiffany has friends?" The troublemaker eyed her coolly while bathing a paw.

"Seven more, on the second floor. They're all rescues with issues to work through. They manage to sort things out among themselves as long as I keep the tyrannosaurus here out of the mix. I had to install a door at the bottom of the stairway. Some of them come down once in a while, strictly on a *sauve qui peut* basis." Libby giggled in what Al couldn't rule out as a slightly unhinged manner. "You have a cat?"

"An undersized Maine Coon my husband saved from a drafty pet store window. They'd obviously taken her from her mother too soon. Her name's Linnet...I don't know what I'd do without her," Al found herself informing a hole in Libby's nearest bootie.

A not uncompanionable silence had followed. Tiffany seemed to be growing bored.

"Marian said you got a degree here at the university, Libby. Did you grow up in Rutledge?"

"Yup. Degree's in Romance Languages. I wanted to get another in math but I couldn't test out of trigonometry and calculus and it got too involved, expensive, disjointed. You can come on down. She's in her litter box. I think you're a free woman. But if you've got some tall rubber boots I'd recommend wearing 'em when you're over here. Tiffany's not a jumper; she goes for the ankles."

Al sank into a dumpy orange lounger that had a Salvation Army look to it. Bliss. Tiffany marched out of the room emitting a faint, businesslike hiss like a steam iron.

Of the five mild-mannered dogs in front of her, one looked old and weary, another wary, the rest too lazily comfy to investigate her closely. Each had a bed of sorts. She saw an old handmade quilt with yarn knots at the corner of each dingy square under a chipper-looking black and white spaniel.

"Who's this pretty girl on the quilt?"

"That's Socks. My partner. I found her wandering up and down a beach three autumns ago, thin as a slat. We shared my French fries and we've been buddies ever since. Nothing not to like about Socks. She cuddles kittens, brings in the paper, reassures the meter readers and door-to-door Mormons, makes sure I answer the doorbell and pay my bills." Socks cocked her ears but made no effort to join them.

"How come they're not tripping over each other to sniff me?" Al wondered if Libby had them all on tranquilizers in order to cope. Or maybe they were all mildly sedated by carbon monoxide fumes? She sat up straighter and pinched herself.

Libby had pulled up one of the folding chairs from the tiny kitchen's table.

"Good manners for survival's sake" – that's our motto around here.

First thing we learn after they trust me is civics. Gotta make the fat curly lady look good. I don't care if they gnaw on the chair legs or shed all over, but they can't be an out of control pack of hoodlums. I've had a few run-ins with the police thanks to a hostile neighbor or two. We have to be on our best behavior, and I am not going to be shut down because some barky Bozo ruins this for everybody." Libby sounded like the hard-bitten manager of a bootleg distillery. Althea knew better than to smile.

"They know they'll get a chance to interact with you if you're important." (Al had immediately wanted to be so.) "Frankly, several of them have little reason to be friendly with humans. They're self-contained because they know they're finally safe, in a pack around the fire, not because they get scolded for licking faces." She stretched and yawned. "Also, they all had an hour in Moraine Woods after lunch, floundering around in the snow. Pinky over there on the pillow kept up beautifully and then passed out in the car; he hardly opened an eye when I carried him into the house. Let's have that tea."

Pinky seemed to be the misshapen miniature poodle with leaky eyes, a fairly wretched representative of the breed. When Al caught his eye it glowed an eerie red above his heart-shaped mound of greasy-looking satin.

"He's not from a puppy mill, is he?" Althea avoided using the dog's name. He looked a little nervous.

"Yeah. Several of his sibs had to be put down; epilepsy. But I think he's okay. Very affectionate, but still insecure and moody. He wreaks havoc on walks, getting the leashes tangled, growling at invisible threats, but he'll yearn and whine himself into a lather if you don't include him on the promenade."

"*The* promenade? You don't want me to take five dogs out at once, do you? I've walked two at a time for neighbors and nearly got pulled under a van. I have zero upper arm strength, Libby. They'd definitely be taking me for a walk. I'm happy to do three or four shorter walks if need be. I can't just let them out into the yard for a run?"

Libby surveyed her. "Yeah, you're pretty sylphlike. I guess in winter you could do the yard thing if you like, since it's only twice a month...Hopefully by spring you'll all be on more intimate terms and you'll see how manageable the routine is."

"Maybe." Althea imagined herself in the middle of an intersection, macraméd into immobility by a quintet of canine personalities at cross purposes. "I might jeopardize your low profile."

"Marigold or peony?" Apparently unperturbed by Al's faintheartedness, Libby was opening jars and fussing with tea strainers.

Charmed by the unlikely choices, Al wondered if she might also have lilac or bachelor button tea.

"Peony, please."

"Before you leave we'll go visit Spike and Violet."

"Neighbors?"

"The dobie and the pit bull. I believe I mentioned them. They're in the run along the side of the house. My neighbor has a sturdy chain link fence. She teaches creative writing at the university. No tenure. I let her know I'd spotted several flourishing marijuana plants on her terrace; we've agreed to live and let live. And Spike and Vi aren't chronic barkers. They're just not safe around humans yet."

"How do I feed them? Fling pork chops over the barbed wire?"

"Not a bad idea. I guess you can if you want to. But you don't have to feed them or mess with them in any way. It's more a matter of checking out any odd noises. I don't want anyone teasing them."

"What in heaven's name do you plan on doing with them? You're not a professional dog trainer, are you? They sound like difficult customers, Libby." "Vicious" was the word that really came to mind. Was Libby some kind of animal hoarder, pulling off dramatic rescues and then letting impossible situations vegetate, unwilling to face hard decisions? Having to be the whistle-blower on a soft-hearted eccentric was a hard decision Althea wished to avoid. She wondered how much Marian and Lucy really knew about what went on over here...

"Relax. They're not wallowing in feces and chewing holes in the chain links, Alice. One of the local veterinarians specializes in Dobermans. She put me in touch with a guy who trains security dogs. He's the best, and he's happy to take Spike on. We're moving up his waiting list, and in the meantime Spike's learning how reliable and gentle a human – me – can be. And Violet's already enrolled in an obedience class specially for pit bulls."

"Actually, my name's Althea, not Alice." Al imagined Libby would have learned the name at once if she were a cocker spaniel.

"Sorry."

"That's alright. And how do you get Violet to her class? Armored car?"

Libby handed her a chipped souvenir mug ("Welcome Waggin': 20th Anniversary") filled with a steaming taupe liquid evidently decocted from withered peony stalks rather than petals.

"She sits in the back seat of my Mercedes with her toys and favorite flannel pillowcase. She's devoted to me. The problem is men and small mammals...Althea."

Libby had begun to look a trifle more conscious of Al as something other than a tool in the service of more deserving species. "How's your tea?"

"Tastes like hot water with a faint overtone of mulch," Althea had ventured. Libby struck her as so well defended that Al could experiment with honest abrasiveness without it really counting, like tossing suction-cup darts at a rhinoceros. She –

"WHERE YA GOING?"

Libby's bellicose remonstrance shriveled the entire recollection, skewering a mortified, disoriented Althea. She groped for some plausible excuse for walking right past her destination, and had only a vague idea of how she'd gotten there.

She let the memories of her previous visit evaporate. Inhale, exhale, inhale. Lips, scalp, thighs. Fingers waving. Forgive it all and be present.

Libby met her at the gate, packed into the same outdated pantsuit she'd worn on Christmas Eve.

"Sorry. Wandering down Memory Lane on automatic pilot, I guess," Al smiled, mild and enigmatic.

"Lucky I happened to look up and see you sleepwalking out here. You're all dressed up. Evvie's annual masquerade brawl? Stay away from the punchbowl unless you handle vodka better than I'd guess."

"And where are you off to?" Pale hairs of various persuasions stippled Libby's dark jacket so densely that Al could see them by her jam jar lantern's glow.

"A briefing on how to run the snack bar at Alley Katz. I didn't tell you? That's the new, extremely part-time job that'll bring you here every other Thursday. Owner's wife wants more time with the new grandchild. My little monthly paycheck should help keep everybody's shots current. The Katzes get my personable dispensing of Coke and Fritos plus some swabbing of the deck, I get up-to-date rabies tags, you get...we haven't discussed that, have we?"

As she followed Libby inside Al digested the news that she'd be taking on seven dogs, eight cats, an iguana, three peach-faced lovebirds and a teeming population of zebra finches so this rather off-putting woman she barely knew could mop the floor at a bowling alley. If she got bitten Libby probably couldn't spare her a Band-Aid. Recognizing the shrill, helpless inner monologue, Al dropped it. She felt a weight on her foot, breathy inquiries around the hem of her coat and warm, wet noses thrust into her gloves.

"See, you're becoming more popular already. They can tell I'm leaving. Katz just phoned to ask if I'd come over. I tried to call you. You have to have your phone while you're here." (Typical of Libby not to soften any remark that could be turned into a blunt instrument, Althea noted.)

"Luckily, I had time to jot down some notes this week." She thrust a typed manuscript at Althea, who saw it was at least a quarter of an inch thick. "I have no idea what time I'll be back."

"Libby, you'd said half an hour. I'm going out to dinner. My ride will be here at 5:30." She heard herself mimicking Libby.

"Fiddle. Well, it's not as if they're never left alone. Stay as long as you can. Go upstairs if you like. I've locked Tiffany in her Kitty Cottage." She pulled a key out from under a sour cream carton jammed with pink blossoms. (Al's African violet produced a feeble flower or two once a season.) "This can be yours. Don't worry about all the gizmos on the door. Captain's on duty. He's got his snow gear on."

Not quite ready to be the sole biped in the crowd, Al trailed out of the house after Libby, ostensibly to ingratiate herself with Captain. They stood together at the gate, watching Libby get into the bulky old grey car parked along the curb. Captain, who looked fully capable of eating Goldilocks' grandmother, whined very faintly. As she patted his quilted vest Al noticed a vaguely familiar doohickey on the car's hood.

Libby plunged across the seat to roll down her curbside window.

"We still haven't talked about how I pay you back. Make friends!" The car pulled slowly away like a barge leaving its dock. This time Al recognized the three-pointed star on the rear. Libby hadn't been joking.

Twelfth Night

Having resolved to recycle any foreign object in her slice of galette into Evvie's hallway bowl of potpourri, Althea quietly rejoiced when her cautious progress through the colorless ooze yielded no surprises. She'd been informed by a chatty habituée that tonight's recipient of the Twelfth Night charm would be crowned and sceptered while seated on the back of the antique merry-go-round ostrich, a neighborhood landmark, that graced the Bruchners' bay window.

For the rest of the evening (and wee hours of the morning?) the guests were at the mercy of their monarch. Judging by the cheery anecdotes, the imagination and clemency of those wielding the festive scepter varied alarmingly. One year a taciturn neighbor on the verge of retiring to Phoenix proved quite a dark horse. He'd overindulged at the punchbowl with the shortsighted equanimity of one possessing neither charisma nor luck. His startled coronation launched a blitz-krieg of naughty edicts smoldering with repressed genius. Rumors still abounded, apparently – whose frayed underpants travelled up and down the dumbwaiter? Had the dean of Women's Studies actu-ally swallowed a spoonful of Ken-L-Ration Beefy Nuggets rather than reveal the immigration status of her au pair? Finally Evvie's husband surreptitiously turned their furnace off so she was "forced" to send everyone home. The Bruchners took a holiday cruise the following year. Last Twelfth Night Stubblefield's sweet young intern had dis-covered the charm on her plate (sabotage suspected), and everyone had politely endured a night of communal singing, hugs and support for New Year's resolutions.

A single glimpse of herself sliding down the Bruchner ostrich's sloping back in a decorous sidesaddle bid to preserve the seams of her 1920's tunic dress decided Al on abdication at all costs if necessary. How amused Bakeoven would be at her resolve. He'd admired her dress; it reminded him of Nijinsky and the Russian Ballet. Perhaps he was gay? The slender bones, the soft white complexion...

"You look dispirited, Althea. Have a canapé." Evvie's Hawaiian palms and orchids came into focus.

"Oh, no. Just lost in thought." (For shame! But such fun!)

"I hope your housemates show up. You know, Lucy's girls at Stubblefield are enthralled with her romance, in spite of her reti-cence – or maybe because of it! They're under the impression they'll all be invited to the wedding, and she hasn't had the heart to hint anything to the contrary. I think she'd just as soon they not know anything about it, but the minute Micah started showing up at events with her the cat was out of the bag. He cuts a handsome figure, doesn't he?...These are stuffed with ratatouille, Althea, no meat...How is Marian doing? She seems not to be making the rounds lately. Give her my love, will you?"

A somewhat studied squeal pierced the babble around the refreshment table. Althea recognized the vivid chalice of a "sherbet Jackie's" sleeve thrust triumphantly overhead as Mrs. Throckmorton displayed the royal indigestible between color-coordinated fingertips.

"Thank God," Evvie muttered before excusing herself. Presumably Mrs. T. could be relied upon to steer her ship of state into sunny waters.

From the edge of the throng Al watched their queen adjust a tipsy paper tiara. Her raspberry bouclé did The Cygnet's Nest credit, creeping prettily above La Throckmorton's stylishly gaunt knees as two men hoisted her sideways onto the ostrich's gilt saddle. Perhaps next year she'd watch with Bakeoven at her elbow, an acknowledged couple of sorts, the subject of polite curiosity themselves. To her surprise he'd worn an agreeable, rather worldly scent that evening, not the sort of outdated aftershave an old dodderer would dose himself with as a worn-out gesture. A gift from the niece? Stella might be a valuable ally if one became interested in staving off Bakeoven's decline. He'd offered a blanket to tuck around her legs on the ride to Evvie's. Unnecessary; the wine and very respectable eggplant Parmesan still warmed even her habitually frigid hands.

She felt an arm around her waist.

"Duck. Our queen's sizing up her subjects," Lucy giggled.

"How was church?"

"Churchy. Micah kept us up on what was going on. 'The Great Blessing of the Waters.' The place always feels a little spooky to me, but I know it means a lot to Micah. Beebe's first liturgy: she's in a trance." Lucy nodded toward the abandoned buffet, where Beebe clutched a lemonade as Micah gesticulated solemnly with a sprig of grapes.

"Hopefully we're out of harm's way, since Mrs. T. looks like a satisfied customer. Have you seen the Bruchners' library? She's got a fabulous collection of fairytales from around the world..." They fled, leaving Micah and Beebe to fend for themselves.

From the smelly depths of a pair of hobnailed leather armchairs they admired a few brittle picture books before the conversation grew subjective. Althea thought she'd better mention dinner at Bakeoven's; the sisterhood was bound to hear about it, and secretiveness would encourage embarrassing interpretations. Besides, Bakeoven could be unavailable in any number of ways, in spite of a sensitive smile and a sharp intellect. Might they shed some light on the family friend?

Catching the stark, metallic ring of her thoughts, Al saw they were as predatory and glacial as she feared this man who'd shown a slight interest in her might be. *She* was the defective one – "zero at the bone," like Emily Dickinson's snake. Then recognizing the familiar flailing that served only to inflate ego, she dropped the whole game: "Hot potato!" just like her preschoolers.

"...the entire school just to fill the pews! Of course they don't have pews, do they..."

Lucy hadn't noticed the gap in Al's attention. She felt a rush of warmth for Lucy, Bakeoven, second chances.

"No, you're encouraged to stand. By the way, guess where I had dinner tonight? Bakeoven's place! His new dog, a giant Golden Noodle, something like that, nearly ran me over in Bodie Woods..."

Lucy's face displayed pleasant interest but no curiosity or encouragement as Althea delivered an increasingly nonchalant rendition of the visit. She felt her spirits plummet; Lucy's bland reaction must mean Bakeoven pottered about with all the Lilybankers as part of his retired bachelor's social fitness regime. The invitation signified nothing. He'd kindly pored over the photos of her home on Euclid (carried around in her purse as though they were her children's). How foolish she felt! Of course she hadn't really been misled, had indulged in conjecture – but oh, the silly excitement. Quite dashed now – a frail hour or two of delusion, demolished as easily as a cobweb. A particularly loud wave of laughter drifted in from the party; the thought of having to perform like a trained poodle for Mrs. Throckmorton seemed increasingly dismaying..."Marian's shriveled au pair, *en costume*"...Lucy's skin was so smooth and firm; how lovely to have a handsome fiancé in the next room...Oh to be Lucy, or Micah, or Beebe, even La Throckmorton, anyone but her flimsy, helplessly vulnerable, mean little self.

For once she knew what to do.

"Lucy, I know it's inconvenient, but I – I'm having an attack of self-hatred, really awful. Hit me over the head, won't you, or quote me some Eckhart – I know it's not real but it feels unbearable. Just – just remind me of what's real, can't you?"

"Of course. Don't fight it, Althea. Come back into your body. Breathe, sweetie. Come back here, and now. Remember who you are beyond the mental noise. Can you feel your inner body?" Lucy's voice was confident and sunny. She hung over the arm of her chair, but kept a distance.

"Sort of. Fizzy arms, at least. And lips."

Well, light it all up and then tell me if you have a problem *now*?" Lucy waited in silence.

Dimly aware that she felt a little self-conscious, and that it was of no consequence, Al eventually shook her head. "No problem here. No problem now."

"Keep making the choice, Althea. Make no more problems. Just accept whatever was getting to you until you can do something about it."

Al giggled. "I think it dissolved, Lucy."

"Funny about that. C'mon, let's go embrace our circumstances. Hiding in here was a bad idea. I need the powder room, and something to eat. Find us a seat, will you?"

They emerged into buzzing hives of conversation, laughter, a muffled Piaf recording. In a far corner a balding, blindfolded man was being ordered about; they caught a glimpse of raspberry pink. Althea squeezed through the throng, unable to find a perch; even the drafty window seats were swamped with overheated, overfed partiers. Giving up, she circled back to wait for Lucy by the buffet at the thin edge of the melee. Wine stains and crumbs blotted the white damask; broccoli and baby carrots whose dip had run out languished beneath the globed chandelier; the fishbowl full of handmade fortune cookies now contained only a wadded-up tissue and a couple of Perrier caps. Near a ravished platter of deviled eggs Micah Fennel orated into thin air with his back to Al, swishing a glass full of ice cubes with a repetitive circular motion worthy of a mesmerist. Curious, she leaned across to rescue the least congealed egg for Lucy and realized that Beebe was the recipient of Micah's erudition. Neither noticed her; he bestowed implicitly flattering terms – "epistemology," "liturgics" – upon her neatly parted head while Beebe, dressed in her usual whimsically funereal daguerrotype-ready attire, hung edifyingly on every philological cartwheel.

Althea withdrew circumspectly after registering the voltage of Beebe's exuberant, rosy prettiness intensified by her dignified, curiously disproportionate bearing. Micah's forearms were appealingly muscular. The hair on them glinted red-gold under the chandelier.

She retreated to neglected remnants of squashed baked Brie and a thawing, unidentifiable ice sculpture at the furthest corner of the table. Lucy, sleek and perky in a pale yellow shift, breezed toward her from a hallway.

"Give me that!" She relieved Al of her paper plate, gulped down the egg and attacked the overwrought Brie. "Let's go learn something." Lucy nodded in Beebe and Micah's direction; a smear of blueberry preserves shimmered in one corner of her smile.

Al trailed behind as Lucy quietly joined their friends, nestling against Micah's tailored shoulder as she licked her thumb. Al saw Beebe grin at Lucy; she couldn't tell how Micah had acknowledged his fiancée's arrival. The ice continued to orbit, hugged to his chest.

How wonderful, the haven of a trustworthy bond – its unspoken depths. She could remember standing silent, apparently unattached, next to Casper at a church coffee or theater intermission, uninvolved in someone's harangue, confident of her place at his side... Astronomically unlikely ever to have that again, pessimist or not.

She leaned against the table, trying to breathe naturally in spite of her tense diaphragm, trying to stay in touch with the subtle fizz behind her face, in the crook of her arm. The awareness would doubtless evaporate if someone accosted her with so much as an "excuse me" on the way to the bathroom: automatic adrenal armament.

On the other hand, here she was at a party, experiencing – if only in flickers – consciousness beyond the mind.

*　　*　　*

Too full of lemonade and liturgics, Beebe cuddled her storybook sleepily:

Bezique pined when his humans proved unrelentingly shrewd about preventing a second "accidental" outing. When Gypsy began mewing up to him beneath windows at any hour of the day or night, Mrs. Bunting quickly grasped the situation. Efforts to lure the little she-cat inside were fruitless.

One morning after the children left for school Mrs. Bunting gave Bezique a squeeze and watched him streak out the open back door. Once down the steps he recollected himself and gazed at her with a moist, concentrated twinkle.

"Mind the automobiles, Bezique. Come back soon."

Determined to wash every floor in the house to ease her trial, Mrs. B. first shoved a brick against the screen door to keep it open six inches.

Applesauce, who'd just rounded the corner into the kitchen,

found himself unceremoniously herded through the parlor by Mrs. B.'s broom.

"You'll have to spend the day upstairs, I'm afraid, unless you're tired of your home too, Applesauce?" He looked up at her with guileless eyes, a pudgy portrait of domesticity.

"That's a good fellow." She shut the parlor door on his nose, rolling up her sleeves while imagining bird nests in her teacups, squirrels playing trapeze among her hanging ferns. No telling who might help themselves to that open back door. She felt reckless, and began to hum.

Upstairs in the girls' room Applesauce stropped his claws noisily on the worn old crib quilt Alice still liked to clutch in the dark.

Torn from her dreams of pedigreed suitors, Snowy growled at him from the forbidden folds of Marjorie's second-best pinafore, accidentally left on the bed.

"You'll be even more peevish when you hear the news. We're stuck up here till the cows come home because Blackbottom's finally gotten his way."

Snowy, who'd begun her toilette, froze with her tongue hanging out and one leg over her head.

"Nice try. You almost had me fooled. Next you'll be telling me you can fly. Applesauce the dirigible." At the thought of his ample form wafting serenely over rooftops Snowy broke into a purry snicker.

Applesauce heaved himself up onto Lavender's bed. He looked unusually earnest.

"I'm finding it hard to believe myself, but what would *you* make of this – I'm headed toward the kitchen and I hear Ma's voice. 'Come back soon,' I swear that's what I heard, and she's propping the back door open. Naturally the minute she lays eyes on me she's skating toward me with her broom like I'm a hockey puck, sweeping me upstairs, and says that's it for the day, *'unless I'm tired of my home, too!'* And where's His Majesty? He's not up here. Not even in Ma's glove box."

They gazed at each other, then raced into Mr. and Mrs. Bunting's bedroom. Trying to reach the back window first, Applesauce hurled himself onto the Professor's bedside table so heedlessly that he banged his nose against the glass. Snowy hopped up beside him and surveyed the back yard while Applesauce bathed his muzzle, cross-eyed. She was just in time to see two little black splotches fade out of sight beyond a split-rail fence.

Their cozy home felt terribly quiet and cavernous. Snowy jumped down and slunk out of the room.

"Hey! Didja see him? Didja?" Snowy's drooping tail answered as it disappeared around the bedroom door.

Inspired, Applesauce hunkered down on the Professor's bedtime reading, staring out the window and lashing his tail. Bezique was more than welcome to the confusing, coldhearted world beyond the Buntings' doors. Applesauce had gotten a taste of it as an orphan. Assured that the landscape was quite free of black cats, he rolled onto his back, knocking several books onto the floor. He succumbed to a delicious nap after annexing the greater part of Bezique's treasures in his imagination – Mrs. B.'s lap, the sun-drenched tansu, the glove box...the Buntings' prestigious, lofty bed...first dibs at inspecting the girls' hands and hems and satchels, the first to be hugged, kissed and carried about on Mrs. B.'s shoulder when she came home from shopping. (Well, maybe not on her shoulder.)

In the meantime the black splotches quarreled companionably beneath a canopy of Mayapples in a woodlot.

"Mrs. Bunting's come more than halfway now, Gypsy. She's behaved most handsomely. Nothing would please her more than your letting her pet you a little. I'd be right there beside you. And the little girls! They adore cats." A velvety, lovestruck purr laced his persuasion.

Gypsy twitched the tip of her tail.

"Bah-seek, surely they can pet Icy and Applesauce. Much more to pet, all those jowls and pouches and swollen flanks."

"Snowy. You'd like her once you got to know her. She's got too much starch in her tucker sometimes but she makes a loyal friend."

To change the subject Gypsy gave him a saucy "Meowt?" and zipped up the nearest sapling. Curving under her weight, the young birch arched over Bezique and she batted at him playfully, springing up and down.

"I have a notion we might introduce Beanie to your Snow-toes, Bah-seek. I think he needs a lady-friend." Gypsy skittered back down and cut a caper, chasing her tail before collapsing dizzily at his side.

Bezique buried his nose in her neck, inhaling the clean, tangy scent of catkins, spring gales and humus.

"Let him be, busy-boots. He's a contented bachelor. Snowy would overpower him with her whims and moods and decrees. You'd throw your lamb to a lioness?"

"Ah, but she'd be a gaudy amateur fresh from the cage, dependent on her modest lord's competence."

Bezique rolled onto his back and stretched, amused by the idea, until he sifted her words.

"That isn't how you imagine our life together, Gypsy? I'm still getting the knack of things out here. There's only so much you can puzzle out from a windowsill, darling. Even little Scholar knows more about raindrops than I. You'll have to put up with your backward greenhorn for a while longer, Gypsy, but I'll soon have the outdoors mastered."

She gazed at him, savoring her sweetheart's fine, chiseled face with its extravagant ears, dilated nostrils and notably visible fangs.

"Oh Bah-seek, we will never master the world – the outside door, you call it? We can only be grateful for its gifts, until we can no longer endure them and we return to our Great Mother's belly. Were you not taught this as a kitten, Bah-seek?"

He considered.

"My brothers and I were taken from our mother as soon as we were old enough to be given humans. There was no time for philosophy. But I do possess something in her purrs and lullabies...an impression...that we have a home inside us that can't be taken away, regardless of bad dreams..."

"Yes, the same home, for all the Great One's creatures. We are never to be parted. So we must yield graciously when the – the 'outside door' demands it." Gypsy puffed out her soft little chest.

"My wise cricket." Bezique's eyes crossed with tenderness. "We will live on both sides of the door. You needn't fear being trapped; we'll have our liberty. My mistress read my heart. Think of Beanie – he has the best of both worlds. You will have this too, now that we're together."

In the distance what looked like a white hen and some rock doves, apparently flown from the coop, skittered across Beanie's back yard. As they approached Bezique made out a tail and a cockeyed black cap.

Stalks rustled behind him, and Gypsy was at his shoulder.

Just as Bezique realized two kittens trailed behind Beanie, Gypsy plunged out of the wildflowers. He managed to keep up with her as she dashed across the yards; the kittens – one yellow, one grey – began to trot when they saw her.

Everyone meowed at once. Gypsy pummeled the youngsters willy-nilly, checking for injuries, scolding, comforting. Bezique recognized the puny, trembling Scholar. The sooty kitten with a white blaze down its face answered to Twinkle, and tried to tell Gypsy some tale in garbled squeaks. Beanie tried to explain amidst the commotion.

"SILENCE!" A thick hush descended at once. (Why didn't this work at home?) "Speak, Beanie."

"Scholar tells me his sister and brothers wanted to help search for their mother. He followed, not choosing to be left alone in the dark." (Scholar blinked miserably up at Bezique; his tiny pink nose looked scuffed. Twinkle hid his face in Gypsy's fur.) "They crossed your street and the one beyond it, out of our customary territory –" Gypsy cuffed Twinkle's tail.

"How could you do that? Your mother and I told you all dozens of --"

"We think Mother must have gone out of the derrydorry," Twinkle piped. He sought Bezique's eyes. "Even Scholar thinks so, though he didn't want to disobey. Our paws led us across those streets...Oh, Aunt Gypsy, he got Scout and Pippin!"

Beanie winced. "Leo has them, Gypsy. I spotted these two stumbling home and got the story. The four of 'em got surrounded by a pack of dogs in the brickyard. They say a wicked-looking Tom distracted the curs and these two were able to flee. They watched the Tom hold the pack off Scout and Pippin till one of the bricklayers chased the dogs with a stick."

"A spitting, whiskered old soldier-cat, Auntie!" Twinkle exclaimed, as Scholar's ears flattened at the memory.

"A crooked face! Big wads of fur in his ears! Dirty, snarling! He – he told us to go home to our hole in the ground, fit for chipmunks," Scholar shuddered.

"He told Scout and Pip to stay with him or he'd make sure none of us got home again!"

"I'm sure it was Leo, Gypsy. They say he was grey with a lot of fringe on his face and shoulders –"

"Like a hawk, Bah-seek!" Twinkle blurted.

"Who's Leo?" Bezique demanded.

"Ugly codger, jealous of my mother's preference for Father," Gypsy replied.

"But brave and seasoned, Gypsy. A survival artist. A loner who sneers at humans. He won't hurt the kittens; they're safe with him...(But we'll have the devil of a time getting 'em back)," Beanie muttered to Bezique.

"His breath smells like dung," Twinkle mewed excitedly.

"He saved your lives, you ninnies," Beanie snapped, startling even Bezique.

"I'm not afraid of Leo. He likes me," Gypsy said. "We came upon each other along the fen, where I was searching for Willow. He knew who she was. He called me 'Plucky,' and said I was free to go, like a warrior. A bitter face, but his eyes are thoughtful." Scholar and Twinkle stared at each other.

"I must find Leo, and beg for the kittens. Beanie, will you accompany me? Bah-seek, will you guard these two? Leo will dislike you, I feel certain, but Beanie is transparent and yielding like water..."

Beanie saw Bezique's ears flattening, and nosed him aside.

"She's right, you know. This needs a diplomat, not a lover. Show her you're not just another proud, thick-headed Tom. If Leo gets a whiff of doilies and dumplings off you, he won't rest till you're humiliated. The bargaining would fall apart. Leave it to old wishy-washy here."

Making a supreme effort, and unable to meet Gypsy's eye, Bezique shook himself and strode off towards home.

"Come along, you two," he growled, not looking over his shoulder.

Twinkle scampered after him at once. Scholar looked into his aunt's solemn face, saw her nod, and followed at a headlong, zigzag stumble.

"Let's see them safely home, Beanie. I'll never forgive myself if anything happens to the two with Leo." Gypsy headed toward Lilac Corner herself, drooping.

"This could turn out well. We can ask Leo what he knows of Willow. And the kittens will never disobey again! Very discerning of Zeke not to insist on accompanying you, though he clearly had his heart set on it. But he's just the sort of handsome, clever, human-friendly chap Leo would like to chew up and spit out in front of as many spectators as possible..." Beanie and Gypsy began to trot; he noticed the little bounce return to her carriage.

Once Bezique had his two charges assembled in the side yard they waited for the others to catch up. He'd seen Mrs. B. observe their arrival, then duck back inside. She knew better than to frighten off kittens.

Gypsy and Beanie slithered through the fence pickets, touched noses with Bezique and counseled the kittens to stay in the den till their return.

"I'll just make sure everything's as usual," Gypsy called as she sniffed around the back of the house. The kittens raced around the front corner, eager to see if their brother and sister might have returned.

Bezique pursued them, just in time to catch Scholar's yellow tail vanish into the hollow under the house front. Before he had time to slink down into the darkness himself (greased lightning, these kittens!) Gypsy came hurtling toward him from the opposite side of the house.

"Don't let anyone into the den, Bah-Seek! There's a human in there! The little door at the far end is open – someone's searching!"

Muffled squeaks, hissing and thuds burst from the darkness. Stricken, Bezique looked into Gypsy's horrified eyes and dove into the hole.

6

Prelude

Inhaling the fruity grape hyacinths at his feet, Micah Fennel experienced intimations of paradise, if not immortality. Here he was gathering dew-drenched blossoms with a pair of nymphs at dawn; life's potential seemed limitless. He snipped another half dozen stalks and plunged them into icy water. Leave it to Lucy to hand him a sandbox pail; no doubt she owned several, with matching shovels.

He watched his sprightly beloved dispatching a crowd of tulips and daffodils, her red boots weaving through a maze of buckets fluffy with flowers. The dark wings chopped into her hair swung back and forth as she hopped about, delicate and sporty in her leggy jeans, his gamine Eve. He could still taste her lemony lip balm.

She was waving to him now, pointing at Beebe, whom he saw squatting in a semicircle of pansies in the sort of meditative coma he'd come to recognize as inherently Lilybanksian. Lucy wriggled a "tell-her-to-get-going" signal that he extinguished with a placid wave.

Micah put down his tools and walked over to the inveterately weird kid, whom he increasingly found irritating for no particular reason. As usual she wore one of those somber dresses, stiff with the unhealthy accretions of a century, pulled on as though it were a pair of overalls. Just the thing for muddy gardening. No one appreciated Lilybanks' rich, many-layered aesthetic better than he, but sometimes one just wanted to rescue Lucy.

He cleared his throat.

"Are you in conference?"

Beebe shone him a gracious, self-possessed smile: the cordial dwarf. Her hair was falling out of yesterday's slept-in braids, her dress front half unbuttoned. Not that it mattered; she was too young for cleavage. Was she too stunted to ever develop?

"You can join us."

Her feet were bare in spite of (or because of?) the nip in the breeze and dew. Feeling like an anthropologist, he crouched, facing her across the pansy border, in an effort to win some cooperation.

"It seems a shame to cut any. But it's for a good cause, and only once a year. Smell."

Beebe held a flower up for his inspection.

"These dark ones are more secretive than the pansies with faces," she scowled, fingering a velvet edge. The movement released a complex medley of unidentifiable, weedy, not quite fetid odors he found himself savoring furtively. Unsought images of monastery closets, skunk cabbage and harem unguents materialized...Opium peddler. Lilith.

She smiled up at him again, candid and foreign. A fairytale heart-shaped face, with rosy cheeks. Precocious, arresting eyebrows. An irregularly swollen wet, mauve underlip --

"Hey, you guys! Pick up the pace!" Lucy pointed pantomime-fashion to the oversized Swatch on her wrist, a gift from students.

Damn Lucy. The girl had the profundity of a jellybean.

"I, uh, think I dropped my pen in the hut. Guess you better get busy." Micah teetered to his feet only to find Beebe bounding to hers and fondling the prized Mont Blanc clipped to his shirt pocket.

"It's right here!" she warbled, a glittering sorceress on tiptoes.

"A different pen," he snapped, and walked stiffly off to the clammy depths of the garden's ramshackle hut, whose cockeyed stork he and

Watkins had temporarily moored more securely for the Tour. Gravity and the next spring squall would soon restore its familiar skew.

Securing the padlock from the inside, Micah was able to keep an eye on the whereabouts of both his companions through shutter slats. Sun filtered through clouds bearing the last lavender and gilt edges of dawn as Beebe bent to bury her face in a jam-colored tulip and Micah succumbed to the irrational demands of Eros.

* * *

Ignoring the flower harvest beyond Beebe's bedroom window, Althea reproached herself for leaving her full-length mirror behind. Already such a loss of *esprit* seemed unimaginable.

Resigned to wrinkling during the few frantic hours before Tour Day opened, she inspected her plain dress and 1920's Mary Jane pumps. The essential green shawl awaited them in Millefleurs. Linnet's obsession with fringe, Althea thought guiltily, would not be a problem today. After checking the torque of her Bakelite earrings she searched for the time. Did no one in this place rely on more than the grandfather clock? She couldn't be expected to wear Casper's watch invariably!

Hammering across the wooden floor into the hall, she realized Linnet had already puddled in her carrying case. The uniquely disheartening odor seemed confined to the case so far, where jailed Linnet huddled on a drenched towel.

"I'm so sorry, Linny, no time to fix things. You can get spruced up once we get you to the spa." A nauseous-sounding moan and muffled floundering issued from the case as Al grasped the handle. This would be Linnet's debut at "the spa;" Althea had martyred herself for years, making Casper take scenic business trips solo and painfully cultivating potential cat-sitters so her coddled neurotic need never know the baleful click of a veterinary boarding pen's latch. However, the Annual Tour's potential for feline disaster required stiff upper lips.

After a few staggering forays at the top of the stairs Althea sat on one step after the next, plunking the case down beside her. Linnet maintained an ominous silence. Al checked to make sure she was still breathing.

Three-quarters of the way down Althea heard a fumbling key. Aphrodite came barreling toward the door. Tad and Gloria, each stacked to the nostrils with greasy white boxes, found Al clutching her hem above them, wrapped around the cat carrier.

"Do you think you could call off the dog, dear? She's after the family jewels," Gloria asked, a caricature of patience.

"Sorry. I was afraid she'd scare the cat. She's already puddled."

"Well, we can rest in the knowledge that the worst is over. The dog, darlin'?"

Sweaty and flushed, Al got Linnet onto solid ground and rescued Tad from Aphrodite's attentions.

"Thanks, Althea." He escaped to the kitchen while Al clipped on the dog's leash and secured her to the banister. She relieved Gloria of three uppermost boxes in icy silence.

"I'll be right back, Linnet," she cooed over her shoulder, imagining Gloria found her syrupy and inept as well as potty. They hurried back to the kitchen, where Tad piled cartons into the refrigerator.

"Must run!" Althea smiled into the empty space over one of Gloria's shoulders, whizzing back to Linnet. If Aphrodite had gotten loose and molested the cat, it would have been that divorced, aging hippy dessert diva's fault.

By the time she got Linnet loaded onto the back floor of Casper's – no, *her* – car, dread oozed through her. The white-knuckled drive downtown, Linnet's betrayed outrage when she found herself shoved across a counter like so much lunch meat, the menacing undertow of stage fright she'd have to face as today's Millefleurs "docent," even

Bakeoven's well-meant, complacent encouragement seemed like so many stations on the way to the guillotine. She couldn't imagine surviving the day.

Noting the feel of her lips out of sheer habit as she sank behind the steering wheel, Al sought just a moment's refuge inside the aliveness of her arms and legs, her back against the seat, her cramped toes. She fought to manage at least three relaxed, thought-free breaths.

Did she have a problem *now*?

It occurred to her that only her ego anticipated a series of wretched events. Overwrought as her body had become, her mind was the source of the problem. Might she not take a holiday from her personality, or at least accept, even surrender to its habitual high jinks with a measure of equanimity? Her breath, the whispering fizz in her hands, the puffy clouds in a porcelain blue sky suggested this detour from dread.

Hence it was a slightly worn-looking blonde with an adventurous smile and firm step who negotiated Lilybanks' steep driveway, deposited her roommate at the vet's "Bed 'n' Breakfast" annex with brisk gravity and honked (in a tentative, strangled manner that improved with repetition) below the Professor's window.

Warned about fender-to-fender cars on Tour Day, she parked two blocks from home. Bakeoven had gamely refused to be dropped off. He wore a suit and a funereal lily-of-the-valley boutonniere. A thread of panic coiled in Althea's stomach – surely jeans would do for a mere house tour? Of course this wasn't just any Tour Day – Lilybanks was celebrating its centennial. Her memorized prattle began taking on the importance of a graduation address until she remembered to accept her customary traits as she would a zebra's, and pass on.

According to Marian's agenda, Althea was to take Bakeoven straight back to the garden. A quaint, sweet scent of pollen and fruit, nearly a palpable presence, met them in the hall and intensified at every room they passed.

"What on earth?"

Bakeoven grinned. "An annual rite. Marian had half the neighborhood potting up narcissus bulbs all winter for today. A yellow variety called "Soleil d'Or." Marian claims it's the quintessential scent of Lilybanks. Nostalgic. Nothing like those nasty paperwhites. Whole fleets of them on windowsills in every room today, you'll see. Must've been delivered after you left. You've noticed a weakness for theatrical effects?"

As if on cue, Marian materialized in the living room doorway, bristling with savage-looking hair curlers and leaking Kleenex from the robe she seemed to don as a sort of artist's smock.

"Very dapper, Bakeoven. He's our social gadfly, Althea, dispensing witticisms or scholarly gravitas as needed amongst the weary and restless out on the sidewalk."

"What she *really* wants me for is preening and fawning. Influential guests with ties to the University's historic preservation board need to be sufficiently appreciated," he smiled.

"Bosh. He hands out paper fans to ladies and recites Elbert Hubbard aphorisms through the house like a minstrel. But we're squandering precious minutes. Come along." Marian herded them toward the back door.

"Enchanted fragrance, Marian. 'Eau de Lilybanks,'" Althea ventured, wondering if the enthusiastic curtain of scent might induce seizures among allergy sufferers. The smell of Windex mingled with narcissus as they reached the back door.

"Bakeoven, just relax. Tell us if the blackberry lemonade's too tart. You can rest while standing; we don't want you getting wrinkled..." Marian's flutter continued out onto the dappled terrace. The door to the garden had been closed, enhancing its mystery. An expensively rustic picnic table – lent by a Waldorf family – occupied half the cobblestones. Aphrodite lounged proprietarily beside cartons of what looked like baby blue shower caps. Beyond her Micah Fennel crouched in the daycare sandbox, just filled for the season. Making a mental note to bring up sandbox hygiene at the next household meeting, Althea made out the domes of two familiar carapaces. Clumber and Cleo lurched and yawed, getting the hang of their sloppy new terrain. Apparently they, too, had been evicted.

"You're going to leave the turtles out here?" she asked no one in particular.

Marian was engrossed in Bakeoven's swilling of lemonade. Its purple clouds in a cut glass decanter suggested a chemistry experiment. Micah ignored her. She'd thought he looked rather sullen, but it was hard to tell; Al liked to imagine him wearing a monocle. She tugged at Marian's sleeve.

"Are the turtles going to be alright out here, do you think?"

"Quite alright, dear. We bring them out for every Tour. Micah's our garden proctor today; he'll check up on them from time to time." She didn't turn her head. Bakeoven seemed to be gargling.

From what she'd observed of Micah, Althea imagined he'd be too busy pontificating amongst herbaceous borders to patrol a sandbox.

"Just thinking of how curious unsupervised children can be, Marian," she soldiered on.

"No antsy, sticky-fingered toddlers, Althea. Tour's for ages seven and up. Ought to have a break from babysitting on Tour Day, eh, Marian? My congratulations to the kitchen – this is the archetypal Tour brew. Full-bodied, yet impish." Bakeoven raised his glass in the direction of the back stairs, and Althea saw Lucy emerge.

"People are getting out of cars, Marian. It's 9:30, but you know how they love to sit on the steps. Maybe you should get dressed. Beebe and Tad and I need to get things set up out here." Lucy steered Marian back up the steps like any daycare charge, saluting Bakeoven, smiling at Micah's preoccupation with her turtles and whispering to Althea on the fly that she "might want to inspect Marian before letting her loose." Marian just had time to yodel something about making sure

"Tad gets the booties onto the front porch in time" before she was pulled inside.

Althea reflected that none of the crew could witness any gaffes in her Millefleurs presentations; they'd all have their hands full elsewhere. A certain *esprit de corps* possessed her. Breathe...

By the time she'd held the back door open for six more decanters, platters mounded with pastries and a couple of overwrought cakes, Bakeoven was sending her meaningful glances, tapping his watch and pointing upstairs. She recalled Lucy's anecdotes about Marian greeting the president of the university with a blob of striped toothpaste on her chin, and something about wearing a new dress backwards. As she went inside Lucy and Beebe arranged a banquet's worth of napkins alongside a spectacular Grueby tureen brimming with lilies-of-the-valley. It struck Al that Lucy's wedding reception could scarcely be more lavishly appointed.

Peeking through a kindernook window she saw Lilybanks' listing, fissured sidewalk clogged with Tour-ists; several faces looked familiar. The early birds tended to be neighbors for whom the Tour was a tradition, Bakeoven had said; they often dressed up, sometimes in period costume, and expected their share of the friendliest welcomes, most intimate anecdotes and freshest fare. They knew to show up while the picnic table remained photogenic, the bouquets dewy, tempers genial. Al noted several women in long skirts and hats like deep, lacy buckets. Was that Mrs. Throckmorton emerging from a taxi?

She dropped the lace curtain and shut her eyes. Here and Now. "Did she have a problem now?" Yes, it was called stage fright and its voltage threatened to cancel any rarified communion with an "inner body."

But a tendency to stage fright was just a facet of that amusing, predictable rogue, her personality. She could accept it without letting it run the show, couldn't she? Attending to her breath, she felt jiggling under her increasingly cramped Mary Janes as someone thundered toward the front of the house.

Tad, in rolled-up sleeves and military school tie, gave her a grave, bovine nod as he trudged up the stairs wreathed in velvet ropes and wrestling with an armful of brass stanchions. Al followed him up at a safe distance, her offer of help having been lost in the clatter. One of these contraptions was destined for the doorway of her own room.

Althea had been more deeply gratified than she'd let on when the Sisterhood agreed her antiques enhanced the "Balcony Studio." She'd thrown herself into Tour Day preparation of her sanctuary with enthusiasm, making room for Calla Morrissey's easel and musty old painting kit, to Linnet's displeasure. The banished bust (Marian said it was Swedenborg) was resurrected improbably on top of the tansu chests. Althea's modest share of contemporary clutter – a makeup mirror, magazines, the cell phone she still thought of as Casper's – lay jumbled in the closet with Linnet's litter box and shredding bambam. She'd spent an hour polishing the leaves of the venerable philodendron. The new shades sported freshly stenciled nasturtiums.

She gazed wistfully over the fat velvet rope across her doorway as Tad clunked to the far end of the hall. A muffled clamor swelled against the front door. In a few minutes the walls would reverberate with the laughter and idle conversation of strangers. Marian had told her to think of Tour Day as a sort of birthday, an exceptional but normal part of the house's cyclical round, "a season, not a breach," when Al worried about the wear and tear and intrusion. Marian confided that she'd been reluctant to open Lilybanks' doors for daycare, but now felt the old house delighted in festive pandemonium.

Sighing, Al headed toward Millefleurs and nearly collided with Lucy's slightly unsteady advance from Marian's bathroom. The Wellies had perhaps unfitted her for heels.

"She's allowed one silk hanky in her breast pocket. No tissues up the sleeves, down the bodice, dangling from her belt." A fleck of saliva glued one of the sharply tapered tips of Lucy's coiffure to the corner of her mouth. "I've got to get out there. Bakeoven's patter must be wearing thin."

Al pulled the hair out of Lucy's face, which seemed to waken her; she lost the glazed look and focused on her housemate.

"You'll see, it's going to be fun. The first hour's a bit of a tidal wave, but once you get your sea legs it's a hoot. I'll ask Tad to bring up a slice of Gloria's kirschtorte before it's demolished. If you need anything, remember Tad's our troubleshooter. He'll be circulating. Enjoy yourself, sweetie. As soon as Marian's downstairs I'll open up. Remember to breathe." Lucy gripped the banister as she went downstairs.

Althea found Marian placidly depositing hair curlers in an old shoebox. She'd dressed compliantly in a pale tweed suit that drained the color from her eczema.

"I'm to inspect you and encourage you to assume your post, Marian. Hold on, the chain on your glasses is wrapped around your anthers." Having emancipated Marian's corsage from the tangle and checked for fugitive curlers at the back of her head, Al propelled her into the hall, marveling at Marian's composure. Of course, chatting about marquetry and grasscloth with the avid bungalow set must be small beans compared to the podium in the English department's tiered lecture hall. Clutching at the memory of her own successful presentation for a handful of new daycare parents, Al watched Marian recede down the stairs as though to let the dog in. She'd patted Althea's cheek and reminded her not to let anyone pluck the harp strings.

Permitting herself one little tic of micromanagement, Al straightened the bathroom's construction paper "DO NOT ENTER" sign the daycare kids had contributed, and limped into the mural room. The Mary Janes' suitability seemed to be expiring.

Eau de Lilybanks

Shoals of yellow narcissus lined the sills of Millefleurs' diamond-paned windows, exhaling their fruity "eau de Lilybanks" above reedy leaves.

The garish harp loomed in the nearest corner; a temporary carpet runner framed the floor a yard from the walls, affording a good view of the murals. Marian's Murphy bed had vanished into the paneling; all traces of rabbit fur had been expunged from the settle pillows. A whiff of orange oil and lavender polish mingled pleasantly with the flowers when Al stood in the center of the room.

Alternating between trapped panic and childish glee, Althea dutifully followed the runner back out into the hall and approached the landing. She could see Lucy in the entry handing out flyers to a crowd beneath the chandelier's lily lamps. Shower caps covered their shoes with a uniformly doltish effect that might serve her nerves well. Lucy was to let fifteen people in at a time and welcome them with a brief history before letting them loose in the inglenook rooms and the kitchen. Once Marian's tour of the sitting and dining rooms was underway, Lucy would tackle the next bunch. Wondering if fifteen would still look like a mob at eye level, Althea fled when Lucy cleared her throat and unbolted the front door.

Her hands shook as she poured herself some water. Her index cards were smeared with perspiration already. How could she fail to disappoint, after Lucy's nubile cuteness and Marian's command?

She was more rattled than she'd hoped, and the only way through was going to be not mere acceptance but celebratory, wallowing surrender.

A full-fledged attack of stage fright deflated her lungs and discharged a jagged current through her middle. She tossed some water down her throat, careful not to smear her lip gloss, and banged the tumbler on its tray. Bring it on! She embraced stutters, vacant pauses, quivering notes, sympathy – all so much treasure she could possess by bartering away her hoards of resistance, pride, numb despair. She exulted in the fearful glory of the Here and Now.

The shawl skimmed her icy arms like cobweb, a deficient security blanket. But no matter! Breathe, no matter how raggedly. Feel lips, however frozen in a smile. The "inner body?" No such thing, just unmanageable appendages…

In the midst of this struggle dawned a conviction that it didn't matter what happened. Futile, unhappy thoughts still churned in the background, but all was well regardless of what awaited her.

The fleeting silence had become eloquent, and empty space an active, friendly presence.

Instead of reviewing her notes Althea limped to the windows, resting her forehead against the lattice. Micah had yet to open the garden door, saving the dramatic effect for the first arrivals. Cleo and Clumber had been given a salad; most encouraging. A cluster of iced buckets chilled the lemonade *de la maison*, with its curious pousse-café clouds of plum and pale. In the far corners of the garden billows of flowering crab and mock orange vied with plump clouds against the enameled May sky. A fly on the other side of the glass launched a series of trial arabesques before whizzing toward the garden.

Althea turned to find an appealingly meek pair of youngsters (teenagers? twenty-somethings?) hesitating in the doorway. The girl wore leggings under a shred of skirt more suitable for a ballet lesson. A fetching circlet of cherries trimmed a straw hat that sat on her head like a paper plate. The young man's smile told her he was unaware of how to use those dark good looks, attractive in spite of the chain-gang buzzcut.

She received them as angels.

"Good morning, how lovely to see friendly faces. I've been waiting up here for what seems like ages. Have you escaped your flock, or are they hot on your trail?"

They laughed politely; he looked to the girl for a response.

"We're friends of Tad's. He sent you a drink."

Al clicked over to them, ignoring the runner.

"He's a love, thank you so much. I love your hat," Al ventured. Perhaps they were classmates, perhaps they were bankers. She prattled on.

"Did you see the first group downstairs? I'm nervous as a cat; never did this before. I hope they won't eat me alive," she smiled, knowing she was inviolable now anyway.

"They're alright. I think they're all housebroken," he grinned at the girl.

"It's mostly his family. And the Elmwoods – they're first in line every year. And some tourists."

The sound of an actual last name reassured Althea; she'd be dealing with mere mortals.

"I suppose you've been here before. I'm Althea, by the way."

"Sure – I'm Matt. And this is Rachel." He was engrossed in the mysteries of texting as soon as Rachel started chatting.

"Yeah. I used to play with Beebe when she was little. Young, I mean. When she first came to live here Marian was always inviting kids over to keep Beebe company. She was really cute. Always disappearing into the garden, or the attic or the shrubbery."

Al and Rachel laughed, in tacit accord.

"I suppose you just saw her in the library."

"Yeah. She tells about the cat book now. But she used to refuse to leave her room. None of the kids liked to come on the Tour; it was embarrassing. You could tell she hated it. She'd pretend it was fun for Marian's sake. But she looked like she was in a cage at the zoo."

"I feel a little that way myself," Althea beamed, and then changed the subject when Rachel looked uneasy. "So, you have childhood memories of the mural?"

"Marian let us play in here if she was around. I guess she was pretty nice about it, considering it's kind of famous and everything. I mean, we could have finger-painted out whole panels of art history."

"Well, it's not exactly *The Last Supper*. But it's pretty special. I envy you getting to know it when you were little."

"I guess." Rachel had begun to glaze over, however politely. "We felt sorry for Beebe, though. No parents. No TV, no video games or even a computer." She sounded accusatory, as if any adult should have been able to provide something more soothingly conventional.

By this time the early bird enthusiasts had all made it upstairs. Waves of aftershave and weekend jocularity wafted towards Al. She gave silent thanks for cherry-topped texting angels, and for the ministering banality of everyday people. How helpful her situation had become, once she'd surrendered wholeheartedly. She took a swig of lemonade, giddy with relief.

"Swirl it around so the blackberry doesn't stay on the bottom," Rachel counseled.

"Come in, come in, everyone," Al found herself booming. "If you'll all just stay on the runner, please, and distribute yourselves a bit, we can get started"...(This was really more like managing the kindernook or Libby's menagerie than the brittle formality she'd pictured.) Having left her notes on the settle she was forced to mince back up the length of the room to fetch them, sticking to the runner as an example to her public.

"Welcome to the Millefleurs Mural Room, named after the wildflowers in Calla Morrissey's fantasy landscape. Intended as a ballroom where Calla could perform for guests or give dance parties, the Morrisseys characteristically parted with convention by surreptitiously including Lilybanks' master bedroom at the far end." Feeling like a flight attendant, Al gestured "upstage" as rehearsed.

"My name is Althea Athnos, and it will be my pleasure" (unrehearsed) "to share some of the charming secrets of this celebrated room with you today." Al realized she was panting, and tried to slow down. "I'm told many of our guests are familiar with Lilybanks as friends and neighbors. The tour has become a rite of spring in Rutledge. Any newcomers?" Four or five hands fluttered up, including those of an attractive pair of men jotting notes on their brochures and a tousled young couple whose blue booties appeared to cover bare feet.

The more deeply tanned note-taker flashed an easy smile of film star caliber.

"Sure. I'm Terry; this is my partner Keith; we're from Santa Rosa. We saw an article on the murals in Style 1900 magazine and promised ourselves we'd include your centennial in our travel plans." A vaguely familiar old lady with a steely blue French twist patted his arm.

"They've restored a wonderful old bungalow on the Russian River, Althea. Tell her, dear."

Terry giggled, managing to be whimsical and ruinously sexy at once. "Our first owner was a friend of Bernard Maybeck, who may have had a say in the plans. And we discovered an original mural – a river scene – on a dining room wall after excavating seven layers of wallpaper and paint."

"Haven't decided whether to have it restored or just let it be chipped and weathered, *au naturel*," Keith added, intense. Althea hoped they were *both* undecided. "Anyway, we're already planning to make Lilybanks an annual pilgrimage. The hospitality – it's like the Garden District parties during Mardi Gras." His William Morris bow tie's russet and olive wings quivered.

"You're gushing, darling," Terry grinned. "Let Althea hear the Frisby-Wienholtzes' story."

The uncombed Frisby-Wienholtz party blinked and coughed from the humid depths of multi-zippered parkas.

"We're here for the history. We're riding our bikes across the country to raise money for a wildlife sanctuary outside our hometown in Ohio. We made sure to include Lilybanks on the route because of Calla Morrissey's ground-breaking work on behalf of animals. This afternoon we're meeting with managers of her park about their experience with humane population control. So we're excited to be here," Ms. Frisby-Wienholtz yawned. Althea refrained from inquiring where they'd camped last night.

"You'll certainly find kindred spirits among the current

inhabitants of the house," she smiled, reluctant to become mired in fervent conversation.

"As I was saying, the ballroom concealed the Morrisseys' bed-chamber. Calla enjoyed cavorting about as the spirit moved her, day or night. Sleeping in the ballroom allowed her husband to keep an eye on her in the wee hours. The Murphy bed disappears into the wall, keeping the room's handsome simplicity intact. Note the marquetry garlands and butterflies framing the entire floor, and the fireplaces of Grueby art tiles in Calla's favorite shades of cucumber green and blue. The beamed ceiling's inset panels were stenciled with wildflower garlands by Louisa Erikson, a set designer in the university's theatre department. The Morrisseys often strung paper lanterns along the garden wall and tree branches, creating an enchanted glow for par-tygoers who looked down from these windows."

"Calla Morrissey was a woman of many talents. She wrote and illustrated *The Cats of Lilac Corner*. Created to amuse her daughter May, the book briefly became "all the rage" in the late 1920's. (Don't miss Samuel Yellin's beloved weathervane in the garden, featuring characters from the story.) Calla designed many of the "Liberty"-style dresses she preferred, as well as the diaphanous Grecian tunics in which she performed *à la* Isadora Duncan. She delighted in painting and stenciling doors, brackets, screens and bric-a-brac throughout Lilybanks in a style that complemented the interior's nature motifs... *usually* without overwhelming the overall simplicity of the Arts and Crafts ideal." The old lady rolled her eyes. "Her embellishments cre-ate an impression of imaginative whimsy that reflects the bohemian tastes of its lively proprietress at the time and continues to charm present-day visitors." Althea gulped for oxygen as discreetly as she could, awash in the deluge of run-on sentences. The Santa Rosans beamed, a clutch of neighbors nodded, Matt and Rachel seemed mildly interested, the glazed campers-for-justice hovered patiently.

"Notice the wall panels are ornamented at intervals with carved columnar facades. Their detailed oak leaves, acorns, squirrels and birds are very unusual for an Arts and Crafts interior. A handsome example of the nature-inspired ornament for which Lilybanks is known, they were created by Samuel Ruffey, a friend of Calla's during her youth in California." She had to squint at her card for that one.

"In 1913 Ruffey departed for Italy, having completed the carved ornamentation up to the bank of windows on your left and the fireplace on the right, a natural stopping point. Having no plans to return – nor indeed did he ever, having been killed while helping defend his Italian wife's village in the last summer of World War I – the balance of the room was finished with plain oak panels above a waist-high dado, its plaster glazed a rich leaf green. (When we continue to the far end of the room you'll see that the dressing room and bath tucked into the alcove around the corner still feature the original plain green dado.) Calla's restless inventiveness soon led her to consider the dado as an empty canvas. Its color suggested greenery; the marquetry and ceiling patterns and the rather covert creatures on the carved columns called for a woodland meadow theme. Calla seems to have been inspired by Celtic braidwork, with its intricately woven patterns and organic forms. Her still extant plans for the dado express this artful – one might say mischievous – Celtic tradition of local flora and fauna half-concealed in labyrinthine decoration. One of her notes in the margin of a sketch reads, 'tuck a meadow mouse up this foxglove's sleeve.'" Althea smiled and winked at Rachel, who fielded the gesture with an insider's grin.

"Calla saw herself as an amateur. She referred to the appealingly eccentric, unsophisticated drawings for her children's book as 'scribbles.' I hope Calla's great-granddaughter was able to show you at least a few of the drawings in the library's original edition downstairs?"

The blue French twist nodded approvingly, as if Beebe were her obedient retainer; the Californians murmured happily, Keith looking as though he might levitate.

"The drawings of Fez are brilliant. We've got Fez, Bonnet and Gompy beside the roadster enlarged and framed above a Stickley bureau in our den."

"Not to mention our similarly improvised Fez mugs, aprons and refrigerator magnets," Terry crowed. "We think Calla would understand," he added in a stagy undertone from the side of his mouth, setting off ripples of laughter.

Ms. Frisby-Wienholtz waggled a finger.

"How much research has been done on the real Fez? For instance – "

Althea cut her off.

"You're in luck! Micah Fennel, our docent in the Lilybanks garden, has all the available facts about Fez, not to mention Gompy and Bonnet. He'll be happy to bend your ears," she smiled.

"Let's take a moment to discuss the harp behind you."

Everyone pivoted most satisfactorily as if choreographed.

"As popularized for Calla's generation by the iconoclastic Isadora Duncan – and lampooned by Hermione Gingold in *The Music Man*, Calla performed interpretive dance. Clad in minutely pleated tunics *à la* Fortuny," (Keith gratified her with a discriminating nod) "wafting and vaulting by turns as the music moved her, Calla edified, offended or bewildered her Midwestern audience, as had her notorious prototype Isadora. She danced for charity teas and private soirées, often accompanied by a string quartet, but preferred to dance in the Lilybanks garden or here in the ballroom to a flute or harp. You are looking at a large pedal harp. It's remarkable for its heavily ornamented forepillar, which, as Mr. Morrissey is said to have commented, resembles "an Aztec headdress fit for a steam calliope." We have no record of Calla's opinion, but the harp was a gift from an important business associate, and became a fixture in this room. It is in need of restoration," Althea concluded demurely. She considered the peeling, out of tune behemoth an eyesore that undermined Lilybanks' image as a living treasure.

A couple of newcomers jostled through the doorway. So much for her painstakingly timed script and Marian's assurances of "flow control."

Unable to contain her group any longer, she authorized their decorous stampede up the runners on both sides of the room, trilling, "I'll be right with you!" to an assortment of backs and heels.

"Hello there, I'm afraid you're a bit early. Would you like to –"

"That's alright, dear. We're neighbors from down the street. Come every year. We'll just take a peek and be out of your hair in no time...You've protected your floors this time, I see. I've told Marian for years..." The ample neighbor steered her anguished husband past Althea, urging him to turn his hearing aid back on.

While Althea struggled to observe a few breaths Tad stuck his head in the door.

"Sorry! Those two got away from me. Shall I escort them back to their group?" He scowled in the couple's direction as he leaned forward with one hand on either side of the door, his collar and tie already loosened.

She relaxed.

"We'll let it go this time. I suppose it doesn't matter, but keeping people in groups is designed to prevent forays into the attic and silverware drawers."

Tad nodded and went back downstairs. The remainder of group number two seemed reverently docile. On the pretext of having a word with Mrs. Morrissey on the advisability of a parting reminder to stay with one's flock, he joined them as they entered the sitting room.

He watched her in a sort of receiving line with gloved old ladies and their descendants; her enormous hothouse lily's tentacles quivered in its nest of homegrown lilies-of-the-valley with every gesture. Everyone clustered round in a deferential, elbow-jabbing hush.

License to Boast

"Welcome to Lilybanks' sitting room. The first generation of bungalow owners grew up calling it a parlor. Americans traded that fussy word for 'living room.' We Lilybankers say 'sitting room,' an older, more accurate term, though just as silly." Marian's opener seldom changed. Tad noticed folks exchanging smiles. This did him good, as he sometimes felt Lilybanks could crumble around the sisterhood's ears without their Hill District neighbors heeding anything but the market value.

"How good of you to join me here indoors on this first lovely morning of May. The spring sunlight sifts down through the terrace crabapple, dappling the rug's hieroglyphics, illuminating chair slats and dim corners, spangling the dark wood with ephemeral, dancing leaves and blossoms, just as it did when I sat reading in this window seat as a young girl visiting her Grandma Calla." Mrs. Morrissey almost looked beautiful – though certainly not pretty. Why had they stuck her with that ungainly corsage?

"The windows are shut to help our guests sense the stillness in the room. (There'll soon be a 'madding crowd' on the terrace.) We may regret the breeze from the garden, yet feel that Nature's rude health, harmonious hues and unerring composition have followed us inside. She resumes her sway on this side of the windows, does she not? Surrounded on all sides by glowing, quartersawn oak from our native savannahs, the hammered metal, gleaming pottery, handwoven textiles and bouquets from the garden all sing, kindled like so many jewels by the soft, dusky radiance of this hospitable room." Mrs. Morrissey smiled, distant and enigmatic, as if addressing the stars and planets.

"I have license to boast, as very little in this room or the dining room beyond has been rearranged since the days of Calla and Martin

Morrissey, the original owners. We will admit to scuttling a cuspidor, replacing the timeworn wooden blinds with happily similar new ones, and hanging a couple of pleasing landscapes in oils by our gifted contemporary Carl Chilstrom. Note that none of the chairs are upholstered in leather, but rather in velvet or twill, somewhat the worse for wear after coming in contact with three generations of Morrissey *derrières*. We've removed the vintage cushions' more modern covers for you. Calla Morrissey was ahead of her time as a champion of animal rights, and was vegetarian, as were several in her circle. Hence leather was considered unacceptable for Lilybanks' décor. Calla avoided fur for her own and her daughter May's wardrobes, and only reluctantly concluded that leather had to be tolerated in her family's footwear, no really viable alternative then existing 'except,' as Calla wrote to a young friend, 'bare feet and gutta-percha galoshes.'"

"From its beginning – one hundred years ago! – Lilybanks was a hub of idealism and new ideas about how life might be lived. Martin Morrissey's banking associates jokingly referred to his home as 'Grahambanks,' that wholesome, rather rustic variety of flour – already old-fashioned in Calla's day – being much in evidence at meals. Calla's style of entertaining caused a few raised eyebrows but no shortage of appreciative guests in her comfortable, stylish home... Excuse me, please..." Tad gaped as she seemed about to abandon them, making her way through knots of visitors to his place in the doorway.

"No, don't move, Tad; you're fine where you are." Marian fussed with the chain on her glasses, which seemed to snarl around the corsage every time she looked down. He decided against trying to help and drawing attention to her plight. (No wonder she'd looked like a hypnotist's subject when she crossed the room. Perhaps he could get Beebe to fasten the thing on Ditey's collar...)

Extricated, she cleared her throat and waved. "Seems only cricket to move around from time to time. My grandmother was born in San

Francisco in 1889, an only child. Her father, Matthew Jessam, was an assistant professor of Classics at the University of California in Berkeley. Her mother was an amateur painter and taught piano. Calla began dancing at her mother's feet and graced many recitals."

"I like to say heaven and earth moved to throw Calla and Martin Morrissey together. The Jessams were in Berkeley for a funeral when the San Francisco earthquake struck in 1906. Unable to get home – and when her father eventually did he found an eerily cockeyed, un-approachable house – they stayed in Berkeley. There Calla first encountered my grandfather, whose eldest brother was the Jessams' new landlord. The Irish Morrisseys had modestly 'struck it rich' in the California gold rush – or at least 'struck it respectable,' and invested in real estate with great good luck; Martin was able to be launched in banking thanks to these windfalls. Handsome, obliging and a quick learner, he rose through the ranks at a speed unheard of in the more caste-conscious East. He was accepted as Calla's suitor by the Jessams and their bookish, artistic set."

"In 1909 they were married in Berkeley's First Unitarian Church – now the University's dance studio, a bit of serendipity Calla would have fancied! – and departed for Chicago where Martin had been offered a position with First Trust and Savings. His bride spent their first summer shopping at Marshall Field's and touring the Art Institute, but when Martin had the opportunity to help establish a bank here in Rutledge she encouraged him to do so before they'd even visited the community. The chance to build their own home, the University, and, perhaps, an opportunity to be bigger frogs in a smaller pond all appealed to the energetic twenty-year-old. Moreover, Calla's letters indicate she missed the Bay Area's fresh air, hills and unspoilt scenery. Assured that Rutledge had a hill or two" – Marian paused to savor the Californians' glee – "Calla urged Martin to accept the position."

"They chose to build at what then seemed a generous distance from the campus" (titters) "and had perhaps more foresight in purchasing 2,200 uncleared acres behind their homestead. This of course eventually became a state park, Moraine Woods."

"Martin left much of the planning of the house to Calla. She'd grown up amidst the Arts and Crafts movement in the Bay area – the family tableware consisted of one-of-a-kinds and "seconds" from local potters; they picnicked in the steep Berkeley hills where artful, redwood-shingled bungalows and roughhewn cottages with a touch of the medieval or Japanese about them were springing up among the pines; she and her father had helped hoe a communal vegetable garden with prominent local poets and artists. Calla wanted a home that would inspire her neighbors. Determined not to be homesick for California, she hoped to recreate the bohemianism and creative ferment she missed in Chicago."

"Calla did her homework before hiring an architect. The unerring choice proved to be John Crumrind, a professor of architecture who also possessed a degree in botany, then on sabbatical from the University of Chicago. An eccentric middle-aged bachelor who was said to sleep on the roof of his Hyde Park apartment building even in blizzards, he was seldom without his three massive Leonberger dogs (who traveled, took their meals and entered the classroom with him). Crumrind's work was deservedly popular. One of the first American architects to marry Swiss chalet configurations with bungalow and cottage designs, Crumrind had a penchant for tucking plants and animals into his plans. Somewhat like Charles Rohlfs' furniture, Crumrind's bungalow interiors featured as much ornamentation as he could get away with! He was receptive to idiosyncratic requests along those lines, and courted talented artisanal woodcrafters. When my grandfather mentioned his new contract with Crumrind at a 1911 dinner party an associate warned, 'Keep the fellow in check, or you'll be living in a costly cuckoo clock.'"

"Calla and her more conservative husband compromised: she was to rein Crumrind in on the exterior, that imagination might hold sway indoors. Thus, diamond lattices, blue-green trim and riotous window boxes aside, Lilybanks' austere lines and almost dour dark shingles evoke Puritan Salem as much as Dionysian Berkeley."

"The sitting room is the most restrained in the house. Its walls and peaked, beamed ceiling of dark oak echo the exterior's chalet design. The amber glow from the central beams' lanterns invites and enchants…To my mind, this room's our pearl!" Marian, startled by her own affectionate blurt, lost track of her well-ordered thoughts. Blank, she resumed at the wrong place.

"Crumrind, who by several accounts became rather infatuated with his assertive young client, obliged her by instructing his foreman to leave the site's flourishing lilies-of-the-valley undisturbed whenever feasible. One could smell them all the way down to the muddy track now known as Corrie Street. They still grace our home." Tad shoved his hands in his pockets. Sometimes it felt like home to him, too.

Oriented again, she ignored a few raised hands. Tad had heard about Mrs. Morrissey's horror of dwelling on any particular private possession; she found it tasteless and awkward. Beebe said the Stickley cabinet alone could send her to college but she'd never permit her aunt to sell. It was the sort of thing he wouldn't mention to his dad.

Mrs. Morrissey migrated toward the French doors into the dining room. Tad watched people goggling over footstools and plant stands with pegs and slots that made them look like Boy Scout projects.

Mrs. Morrissey cleared her throat again. The glasses were behaving themselves, but Tad noticed she'd managed to acquire a forbidden Kleenex. Maybe she'd hidden a few among the Teco pots the guys to his left were swooning over.

"These doors nearly disappear when folded back against the dark walls, as they usually were in Calla's time. Bungalow design favors wide access between living and dining rooms; these quietly elegant doors were mostly used during Martin's business meetings in the dining room. Note that food from the kitchen must enter through the sitting room; Calla rejected a standard dining room entry from the hall, preferring peaceful seclusion to practical considerations." A few feminine brows knit, uncomprehending. "The dining room looks out upon Corrie Street, a fairly busy thoroughfare by the 1920's, but Lilybanks' elevation and long, relatively narrow front yard muffle the traffic and ensure a surprisingly pastoral effect."

"Please join me in the dining room," she commanded, surreptitiously blotting her nostrils with the tissue from behind a door she'd unfolded. Tad could tell the regulars from the tourists; the latter approached on tiptoe. In spite of a few minor collisions, Mrs. Morrissey seemed to keep things under control pretty effortlessly – just a few more students, subdued by paper booties.

"This striking room, with its burnished built-in china cabinets, sideboard and wainscot of oak has been a family favorite for three generations. John Crumrind commissioned a gifted art student, Ruth Mapes, to create the lovely frieze below the crown molding. Lilybanks having been named, a design suggestive of springtime and emphasizing Calla's favorite soft greens and blues was requested. Miss Mapes' choice of native hawthorns, elms, bluebells and lilies-of-the-valley was a happy one, was it not?" Enthusiastic grunts. "Her patterned clouds, indeed the design as a whole owe much to the work of Walter Crane, the celebrated English designer whom Miss Mapes admired. If you look closely at the hawthorn just above me you'll glimpse a shy river otter peeking around the trunk. Calla added it to amuse her young daughter May, born in 1915 in this house. You'll have time to look for it before you go upstairs," she soothed, as two girls in matching skirts strained at their parents' grasp.

"The leaded glass cabinet doors, hammered copper chandelier with heart cut-out lanterns by Gustav Stickley, and Crumrind's signature marquetry along the top of the wainscot (its interlaced tendrils complement the frieze, you see...) all enhance the room's almost ethe-real – some have said PreRaphaelite – charm."

Tad, accustomed to making himself smaller, listened from the sitting room. A movement in the hallway mirror caught his attention; he heard Lucy stage-whisper something about seeing how this group was getting on. They collided in the doorway. Tad felt her bounce off his stomach; he found yellow fuzz from her dress in his belt buckle that night.

Instead of giggling, Lucy maintained a frozen, onstage smile as she rubbed her nose, which had taken the brunt of the impact.

"Tell Marian Dr. Leiby's party is here."

"You mean, interrupt her?" he said, doubtful. He heard his words thunder through the silent hallway toward a cluster of people just inside the front door. They seemed to be observing Lucy's and his tableau attentively, though he couldn't make out faces with the light streaming in from behind them. Tad flinched at the thought that Beebe probably heard his famous un-whisper in the kindernook.

"Yup. Now." Lucy's smile looked as though it might shatter and have to be swept up off the hallway floor any moment. He watched her bounce back up the hall, cheerful and rubbery, reminding him uneasily of Mr. Bill in Saturday Night Live reruns.

"They'll be going upstairs any moment," he heard her warbling. "We can wait in the inglenook, where Calla Morrissey's great-grand-daughter is our docent today. You remember Beebe, Dr. Leiby?" Tad grimaced.

Lucy deposited the distinguished guests on the benches around the hooded fireplace. Its mantelpiece jardinière overflowed with lil-ies-of-the-valley, whose perfume floated through the clinging aroma of wood smoke. Dr. Marcus Leiby had seemed taken aback when a very composed Beebe had extended her hand; he'd probably looked forward to dandling her on his knee for a publicity photo.

After opening the front door just wide enough to misinform the bootied crowd on the porch that it would be "just a few more min-utes," Lucy dashed up the stairs. The heel on her shoe caught and tore a worn spot in the ancient gingko runner halfway up. Her hands trembled as she patted the carpeting back into place; she might have broken her ankle. Why did they all pretend Tour Day was such fun? Poor Althea wouldn't be happy to hear she had to deliver her spiel to royalty. By noon she should probably spike the lemonade and have Tad innocently hand it round to the sisterhood and Bakeoven. He could have some, too.

Unannounced

Althea had just drawn her audience's attention to a salamander peek-ing from a fenny thicket "whose stylized treatment prefigured Art Deco" when Lucy appeared out of nowhere to whisper in her ear.

"After the next group comes a private viewing for Rutledge's English Lit chair – can't remember his name – Carbuncle? – and President Leiby, plus a literary personage from England who will make Marian's day – name's, um, Rufus – no, Lionel Woodruff. And that arty local couple who did the mural on the university library's ceiling. Let them take as long as they want. Maybe Bakeoven could do a striptease for the teeming hordes. In the meantime, we have to get a move on."

Althea surprised her by grabbing her shawl and wrapping it round herself with a "let's do it" flourish. Maybe someone else had spiked the lemonade.

Lucy twirled among the Morris chairs. "Ladies and gentlemen, this concludes the tour of Lilybanks' second floor. Please follow me down to the terrace, where refreshments await you before or after your visit to Lilybanks' historic garden. Thank you so much, Althea!"

Lucy led Al's debut audience from Millefleurs exactly as she led the daycare kids in from recess. Terry blew Althea a wistful kiss, pantomiming angst, and Keith slipped his leash long enough to vow to Althea that they'd sneak back upstairs if it took all day. She told him where to look for Gompy Morrissey's grave. The small granite boulder near an elderly linden on a secluded knoll was unmarked; only trustworthy favorites got to pay their respects.

A bit let down but in need of a break, Althea plopped on the settle and hoisted her numbed feet onto it, one at a time, by hand. This must be what Bakeoven had complained of: the university president's sporadic, unannounced assaults on Tour Day, eminent guests in tow. Bakeoven said Marian tried to avoid the resultant mayhem by sending the president an invitation with an RSVP and hourly time slots to be checked off, but he never complied. Marian graciously imagined the fault to be that of his secretary. Bakeoven agreed that Leiby's secretary was too busy handling the paperwork for his show-off cars purchased abroad. But he suspected Leiby of taking a spoilt, naughty pleasure in kicking the ladies' punctilious arrangements to bits.

Thrilled by her successful negotiation of the day's challenges thus far, Althea forced herself to keep her mind on her breath, then to feel her lips, ears, eyes, the saggy skin under her chin, her heart, her stomach (which then unclenched); she even detected a subterranean fizz in the leaden arches of her feet encased in their museum-quality sarcophagi. She tried to acknowledge and be grateful for the empty space in the room, tried to sense some hint of unity between herself and the bouncing blue sky beyond the lattices, even between herself and the limp file cards. The floral fragrance had receded; she must finally have become immune to its witchery.

Rather than going outdoors her group seemed to be creating a tumult at the bottom of the stairs, interrupting Althea's visualization of mutual acceptance and serenity for all the day's guests, including President Leiby. As the buzzing and trampling intensified she hobbled out to the hallway. Several children were fighting their way upstream through the descending crowd; several apologetic parents politely clutched and bellowed in their wake, struggling to keep their balance. Lucy's playground signals failed to police a swelling bottleneck as Al's group inched toward the back door through Marian's stragglers. Al caught a glimpse of Beebe's frilled cuffs grasping either side of the doorway into the inglenook in a heroic effort to preserve the inner sanctum for Dr. Leiby's entourage.

Disarmed for combat by her shoes, Althea retreated to the settle. She knew better than to try to extricate herself from the depths of a Morris chair in public. She'd drunk all her water; too late to ask Tad for a refill. There'd been no sign of him in the melee; perhaps he'd been mowed down.

A triumphant child whose tutu-like skirt's elasticized waist now clung rakishly around her knees trotted into the room, panting. A second, chubbier girl in a less flattering tutu and a boy with scintillating braces emerged. Althea pretended to examine her notes while the winner of the staircase obstacle course was forcefully returned to the bosom of her family.

"Good morning! My name is Althea, and it's my pleasure to..." Looking from face to face, glancing at notes only occasionally, Althea floated easily through her tour. She could sense a still spaciousness within as she discarded unkind judgments and let go of the desire to cut a handsome figure.

They'd progressed all the way down to the Murphy bed and Althea had allowed the unruly sisters to operate its hidden mechanism. As though on cue, just as the creaky bed made its dramatic appearance a sort of shrill, rhythmical keening unfurled in the distance.

Guessing it came from the increasingly lively staircase, Al's first thought was for Skippy. Didn't rabbits emit a ghastly shriek when cornered by a predator? Unable to recall Skippy's Tour Day agenda, she tried to hang on to her breath, as though doing so for him, as well, might avert their mutual panic. At the same time one of the more reserved middle-aged women went rigid and ashen, crying out, "My God, is that a smoke alarm?"

"Certainly not!" Althea shouted, not certain of anything. Her eyes met those of two of the abler-bodied men. The three strode out of Millefleurs, though one of the men had to tackle a runaway child and return her – braying over his shoulder with her tutu up around her ears like a clown's ruff – to her mother. Meanwhile the almost human shrieking continued unabated. Urgent voices could be heard far below.

They reached the top of the staircase in time to see two strangers arrive at the bottom. As though in a dream she watched a wiry little man with a goatish beard and a pink fedora pause on the bottom step. A graying redhead in overalls sprang past him with strangely calculated grace, as though rehearsing a pas de deux. She landed mid-stairs next to a flailing human broomstick in a disreputably baggy suit, whose metronomic bleating continued to issue with the pitch and projection of an operatic soprano.

As Althea and the two men stared, rooted to the spot, the lady in overalls gave the twisted creature a smart slap in the face. The shrieking stopped.

"Get me a pillow!" she yelled up to them.

Al bolted, knocking the stanchion in her doorway to the floor. She yanked the embroidered case off her pillow with instinctive fastidiousness before tossing it to the less reluctant of her two attendants. After helping to stuff it behind the victim's head, he came right back up.

"Is there another stairway? If not, we're all going to be up here awhile. That's the worst injury I've ever seen. Compound fracture, she says. Guy in the hat says there's an ambulance on the way."

"No other way down. I mean, well, we do keep chain ladders that fasten over the windowsills in every bedroom in case of fire, but…" Althea vacillated, wondering vaguely if the wrong answer might result in scandal and fines. Feeling terminally silly and more flustered by the accident than she liked to admit, she groped for command.

"If you'd both please urge everyone to stay in the Mural Room? I should make sure Mrs. Morrissey and the others know what's going on. I'll be back and we'll continue the tour – if only to keep the children occupied till the ambulance is gone," she added, lest her compassion be in doubt.

As the two burly fellows stalked back up the hall she reflected that her compassion was mostly missing in action, buried under shock, dismay, ego-bound feelings of incompetence and, most distressingly, a vile shred or two of resentment toward the anonymous bungler who had to go and ruin the morning, not to mention the ambiance. How like the ego, she thought, steeling herself to run the gauntlet past the injured person. No sooner was harmony restored in its absence than it crept in the back door, began taking credit for everything, and then bawled at the first inevitable change!

Trying to salvage some glimmer of awareness for the victim's sake, Althea groped her way down the staircase. The trendy-looking redhead, whose swaying earrings resembled assemblages of Swiss army knife implements, seemed familiar. She knelt on the stairs, cooing into the waxen face of the broken guest clutching her wrist.

"I'm sorry; would it be possible just to squeeze past? I'd like to alert Mrs. Morrissey's tour. I've asked the upstairs guests to stay put until the ambulance arrives."

"Sure. Beebe's warning Mrs. Morrissey. My husband's gone to get water. Could you talk to the people out front? I think the driveway's clear, but an announcement of some sort might be helpful."

"I'll do that right now," Al said, glad to escape. She'd stolen a glance at the poor man as she passed, careful not to focus on dark stains. He'd stared straight ahead without noticing, a gaunt, pale fellow in his 30's or 40's with a thin beard and dark, girlish hair that receded from a high forehead. His shiny chocolate suit dwarfed him. She thought he might be a homeless person in pursuit of refreshments who'd strayed upstairs. (Leave it to lovable Lucy to simply let him loose.) Yet the clenched hand bore a handsome ring and the only odor she'd noticed was a queer, pleasantly sugary scent of cucumber. Perhaps an elderly neighbor? Even men dyed their hair these days.

She heard voices in the sitting room but didn't see anyone. The self-possessed redhead seemed to know Beebe...Althea tugged the front door open. Every pair of eyes in the queue coiling through the yard seemed to meet hers; the bootied group that slumped on the steps and against the urns stood with alarming alacrity. Lucy's perkiness looked a little worn, probably depleted of colorful anecdotes and architectural minutiae. Reluctant to pull her inside for fear of provoking a siege, Al settled for a *tête à tête* in the shrubbery.

"Some poor man's broken his leg on the staircase. They've called an ambulance. I'll keep my group in Millefleurs till he's gone. I'm guessing you'll have half an hour at the very least before the next bunch can go inside, Lucy. Maybe an hour." She hoped Eckhart would say that her conscious self-importance as the bearer of ill tidings was a sign of awareness – but surely she'd always watched herself like that, fruitlessly...

"I can't give them their money back; I've hardly got any cash. Almost everyone buys tickets ahead of time. I'll just have to take the names of people who don't want to wait. Bring me Bakeoven before you go, will you? He can spread the word." Lucy made an effort to maintain some composure while extricating herself from mulch and prickly twigs.

Though it took Althea longer than she liked to interrupt Bakeoven's diatribe about the pros and cons of gentrification with a polite young couple, she appreciated the way he cupped her elbow on their way back to Lucy. As she slipped back inside she saw the two of them gesticulating; Bakeoven looked more distressed than she would have expected.

No one seemed to notice her amidst the uproar in the foyer. Marian, Beebe, Tad, the gentleman in the pink hat and two sportcoated, sixtyish men – one pudgily suave with a showy watch, the other more rumpled and spectacled – appeared to be debating the mishap in varying tones of conciliation, chagrin and menace.

"Make sure they take him to the University hospital, not the clinic downtown. From there we'll get him airlifted to Prentiss in Chicago. My God, I know he looks like a vagrant, but he takes tea with Prince Charles."

"We became kind of fond of him at breakfast. Sort of an elusive, elfin fellow, sprinkling the conversation with poetry. My wife noticed him slip out of the sitting room during Professor Morrissey's talk, and thought we'd better follow him." The fellow in the pink fedora seemed to be married to Arty Earrings.

"Thought he might pilfer something? More likely to slide down the banister. Hell, I'll bet that's exactly what happened. He went missing at our little dinner for him; found him on the neighbors' swing set. No kids around, thank God. You never know."

"Careful, Marcus. He may hear you."

"Oh, dear. Mr. Woodruff lives on another plane; I'm sure he's not interested in our little anxieties. Perhaps I should go speak with him? Assure him of our tender concern, and faith in his recovery..."

"Ah...I think you'd find the gymnastics involved pretty daunting, Professor. The stairway carpeting's a mess. You don't want to end up on a stretcher yourself. Polly's got things under control."

"Could I go up?"

"Yes, he was quite taken with Beebe. She could accompany him out to the ambulance. It might sweeten his departure. The authentic spirit of Lilybanks – "

"He's unlikely to doubt the authenticity of the visit. Crippled for life if they can't iron him out at Prentiss."

"You and I can drive to wherever the ambulance takes him, Marcus."

"They'll take him to University or I'll sue their fuckin' asses."

"I think we're going to have to strip the carpeting off a step or two, Mrs. Morrissey. I'll go get the tool box."

A siren whined; as it grew closer they heard the unmistakable belch of a fire engine's honk.

"Never miss a chance to make a circus of it, do they," Doctor Leiby commented to no one in particular as he made his way to the bottom of the stairs.

"We'll have you in a top-drawer hospital in five minutes, Woodruff. Holding up alright, are you?" Leiby fled out the front door without waiting for a reply. Althea watched him cut across the lawn to the driveway, where a dark sedan glittered in solitary splendor. By the time his nonplussed colleague decided to follow, a team of medics with a tangle of paraphernalia clogged the entryway.

Feeling nauseous and anxious to be out of earshot, Al retreated to the depths of the kindernook. Her group would just have to stay stranded in Millefleurs till Tad secured the wretched stairway runner. She couldn't bring herself to peek through the lace curtain. Bakeoven was doubtless garnering a year's worth of anecdotes about a gaping, gossiping crowd wanting all the details, not to mention refunds and refreshments.

Sinking into the "story time" rocking chair, Althea closed her eyes. In, out…she envisioned a young head wedged between harp strings, and the slow, creaking, ominous tilt just before the bloodcurdling parental scream and the splintering, twanging crash…In, out, breathe in, out…

Having taken a detour out to the garden to alert Micah of the situation (he'd crossed himself solemnly, then coaxed his admiring coterie of ladies to cleave to the serenity of the garden instead of scattering to stare and cluck), Tad returned with a pair of rusty shears and duct tape. He nearly collided with the redhead in overalls. She'd glided out of the scullery bearing a teacup and saucer with both hands like a priestess. He suspected she'd conducted some kind of art workshop at Stubblefield last fall – students had to show up with an old book they'd soaked in the bathtub, then allowed to dry.

"I hope Marian likes Earl Grey. It's all I could find."

Tad could hear the fire truck pull out of the driveway as the two of them maneuvered up the dim hall; the exiting medical crew blocked the light from the window and doorway. Marian stood alone near the banister; Lucy and the pink hat hovered in the inglenook doorway. A stretcher surrounded by medics and Beebe floated down the stairs and out into the May breeze at a funereal pace. The ashen victim stared at Beebe worshipfully and fluttered his IV tube at the chandelier in an apparent farewell to everyone else.

Tad heard him whimper something like, "Why'd you ever laugh at us?"

Beebe smiled down at him. "Oh, Lionel..."

Tad gulped.

As though onstage, the redhead patted Mrs. Morrissey's shoulder, and poked the tea under her nose like smelling salts when she finally opened her eyes.

"This will do you good, Marian. I added a little sugar and lemon."

Marian nodded blankly.

"He was quoting Vaughan. 'Bright shoots of everlastingness,'"[12] she croaked.

Stiff Upper Lips

Touched by Lionel's childlike interest in *Lilac Corner* when she'd let him thumb through a first edition, Beebe had thought to bring it along. Throughout the afternoon, as he floated in and out of consciousness, Beebe read to him. This required both hands, as the pages were fragile and many had come loose from the binding. Lionel gripped the hem of her pinafore in a beatific daze.

*   *   *

He was too late. By the time his eyes adjusted to the darkness Bezique saw a human silhouette making its way back into the daylight. He followed lickety-split past stacks of lumber and buckets.

It was the grocer's delivery lad, headed toward the back of the house. Gypsy was soon at Bezique's shoulder. Neither tried to keep out of sight. The fellow nearly tripped over Gypsy but paid her no attention.

"I got 'em both, Missus," he beamed, holding a wiggly potato sack well out in front of him.

"Oh, the poor little darlings. Bring them in, Gus. Mr. Bunting made a pen for them in the cellar. You've earned your fifty cents."

He headed up the back steps. Gypsy broke into urgent cries, answered by pathetic peeps from the depths of the jiggling burlap. As she gathered the courage to follow them inside, the screen door banged shut on Gypsy's nose.

Beanie trotted over, having seen it all from across the yard. He and Bezique watched helplessly as Gypsy paced back and forth along the bottom of the steps, uttering involuntary cries of distress over and over again like a wind-up toy. She raced back to the front of the house and careened through the violated lair, calling frantically. The little side door remained open; she sniffed it, dashed around to the back again and began digging crazily in the grass at the bottom of the steps.

When they caught up with Gypsy Bezique cuffed her.

"You'll tear your paws to pieces. You'll need them to catch up with Leo. Your plan is still good, love. I'll go inside, and never let Twinkle or Scholar out of my sight. Mrs. B. thinks she's helping them; they'll be given lots to eat and a warm bed. They won't be frightened with me by their side. You and Beanie can go parley with Leo knowing these two are safe."

Gypsy hadn't looked at him or replied, but she'd stopped digging and begun an energetic manicure. Beanie blinked, relieved.

Nuzzling the warm pulse at her throat, Bezique murmured in Gypsy's ear. "And take care of yourself, darling, or I shall have to come for you."

She slapped him on the nose to even the score, but kept her claws sheathed, and then touched his nose with her own.

"Make sure Miss Snowball knows you're unavailable."

"C'mon, Gypsy, the sun's already high. Unless Leo's moved off a lot farther than I think, I expect we'll be back by the time all the stars are lit, Zeke."

Bezique watched them sidle through the pickets in the front yard, cross the street and fade into foreign territory. They looked so small. He hoped Leo realized *Gypsy* was unavailable.

*   *   *

They found Leo easily enough because he wanted to be found.

Beanie had decided Leo would stow the kittens somewhere in the flat, thinly settled territory between their lair and the woods. Uninviting, it was foreign to all but the most uncivilized cats. They passed the half-built house where the kittens had encountered the bricklayers, a smithy and a lumberyard, a few cabins. As they approached the first oaks the land became hilly; they took a rest.

"He wouldn't hide them in the woods, Beanie?"

"Of course not. Leo's no fonder of mink and foxes than we are. Don't worry, Gypsy. They'll turn up. We're not so terribly far from home. This is where children come to fly their kites; I've seen them from the orchard hill. If we -" Beanie broke off, and began grooming a paw.

"Look calm and businesslike now, Gypsy. Leo's watching us from the top of the rise behind you. Don't turn around. He knows I saw him."

"The kittens, Beanie?"

"Probably not far away. Now listen, Gypsy. We might be able to get one kitten away from him, but not both. So we'll have to negotiate."

"Nego –?"

"Lie. String him along. Bluff." Beanie saw Gypsy had no idea of what was coming. "No matter what you hear me say to Leo, he can't have what isn't his. Zeke and I won't rest till everyone's home safe and sound. Are you listening?"

Fear flickered over the little black cat's face and was gone just as quickly.

"Of course. Let's go."

They turned toward the knoll. A gust of wind rippled its grass and roared in their ears. Leo's ugly sneer and savagely fringed head, seemingly disembodied, loomed from the crest.

Beanie sighed. "Easy does it."

They trudged upward, Gypsy forcing herself to accommodate her friend's more deliberate pace. Leo gloated down at them, having chosen the summit with just such a deferential approach in mind. His pungent odor hit their nostrils as they came within earshot. Gypsy tried not to flinch in disgust.

When they were only a few yards from the crest, Leo came forward. His ragged tail twitched at its tip.

"Greetings. Bimbo, isn't it? The carpenter's pet. You're right on time. Prompt and eager to please – commendable. A pleasure to do business with you." Beanie didn't react.

"And here we have beautiful Feather's plucky daughter. Your mother was the finest she-cat in the district. Welcome. Surely you haven't entered into a regrettable alliance with our mild colleague here? No doubt you make a good protectress." Leo turned back to Beanie.

"State your business."

"We've come for the two kittens."

"Yes, they're most anxious to be reunited with their auntie. Very good of you to accompany her here. You may go now, Bunny."

"Piffle, Leo," replied Beanie, looking more relaxed than ever. "I wouldn't have thought cradle robbery was in your line. Nor bribery. You've had your little joke. The kittens must be reunited with their brothers. And Gypsy's life would be a hard one out here with you in the wasteland. Surely she deserves better."

Leo looked nettled. "What would you know of the pleasures of the wild, Soft-paws?" He turned to Gypsy.

"Stay, Plucky, and visit with the little ones. I'm thinking of moving out of the territory altogether. These two kittens take after you and your mother. I'll raise them to be sturdy adventurers on the frontier. Stay with us tonight. We can speak of your sister once they're asleep. And, who knows? Perhaps you'll decide to join our expedition. You'd be very welcome." Leo gave her a long, deep look and started back up to the crest of the knoll.

"Don't believe a word of it," Beanie murmured. "No cat in his right mind wanders far beyond the human circle, especially not a clever old devil like Leo. And there's no guarantee he knows a thing about Willow. It's just bait to get you alone with him. And then he'll use every conniving threat he can think of to keep you with him."

"I'm not afraid. Come back tomorrow, Beanie. By then I'll have set Leo straight. You should go now, so you're home by dark."

Beanie caught the tremble in her voice.

"I'll be back alright, Gypsy. With friends. Say hello to the little ones for me." He gave her a fond cuff on the shoulder. "And Gypsy? Do what he tells you. Especially if you hear coyotes."

"Yes. Tell Bah-seek I'll see him soon?"

"Of course."

Gypsy turned and trotted up the knoll. Beanie watched her and Leo's tail-tips disappear over the horizon.

*   *   *

Once again Lilybanks' ancient wicker suite of *chaises*, loveseats and high-backed queen and king chairs crowded the terrace, full of battle-weary Tour Day veterans. Once again frothing bottles of champagne passed sloppily from hand to hand as limping Lilybankers savored the battered remnants on the picnic table. The ice sculpture – this year a pair of romantic swans, now melted into neckless lumps – had overrun its bounds and gently irrigated the grass between the cobblestones. The tiered cake from Maven Alley had been reduced to rubble oozing mocha Bavarian custard. Skippy, newly sprung from his sanctuary in The Cygnet's Nest powder room, hunched behind the turtles' sandbox, athletically consuming something.

"Ah...Lucy? You might want to check on your rabbit over here. He's into something." Tad sat on the cobblestones, pinned by Aphrodite, who'd had a long day.

Lucy lunged from her chair. "I hope it's not chocolate. He's eager to party..." She returned with the black and white bunny scooped into the crook of her arm. "Nothing toxic. Just a bootie," she said matter-of-factly. "He hadn't gotten to the elastic yet."

Althea smiled weakly, too drained to summon much concern. Skippy seemed to have fared better than some. She did think to pick her shoes up from under her *chaise*, in case he needed dessert. To the left of her throbbing feet Marian, Bakeoven and Polly continued to confer. (Althea had eventually recognized Polly, who presided whimsically over the Highbutton Art Gallery with her perpetually pink-hatted husband.) It seemed that Bakeoven and Polly were alternately inflaming and soothing Marian's distress over what she referred to as "The Mishap."

"My husband revered the Empyrean Society. Carberry, my department chair, mentioned that he expected a brief visit from Lionel Woodruff, one of the Empyreans' darlings. He said he hoped to persuade him to give an evening lecture; he'd keep me posted. The next thing I know, here are Leiby and Carberry in the doorway with the genius – misunderstood, I grant you, but genius nonetheless – firmly in tow between them, like a Jack Russell on a short leash. Oh, how Geoffrey would have enjoyed communing with him! We could have put him up in the Temple." Polly raised her eyebrows, wondering if this was how Marian referred to Lilybanks. "They'd have held forth all night, forgetting to eat, pacing in the garden beneath the stars, reciting – well. At any rate, of course I encouraged Lionel to feel quite free. One can't expect the ardent creative spirit to remain shackled to convention!" Marian adjusted her spectacles, accidentally elbowing Bakeoven's diminutive nose; all three hunched over a table that tilted clunkily when any of them leaned on it to make a confidential remark.

"He wandered through the sitting room poring over things," (Bakeoven grimaced; everyone knew the Tour was strictly, if cordially, "Hands Off") "holding them up to the light, smelling, brushing things against his lips – and then disappeared." Like an unmanageable chimp, thought Althea, who'd found little Lionel Woodruff distinctly simian.

"That's alright then, Marian. Just tell that to the police in the same way," Bakeoven broke in. "Quirky little fellow interprets your generosity a bit too liberally, takes off on his own through the house. His hosts soon discover his absence, and simultaneously hear cries of distress from the staircase. It's alright so far. What do you think, Polly – any chance he tore up the rug on his own, cutting capers? Sounds like the type to test the banisters with his backside to me. No offense, Marian." Polly looked at him ruefully; Marian blanched.

"The carpet's worn terribly thin around the edge of the tear. Even if he were doing backward somersaults on it, the stair's runner looks like an accident waiting to happen – at least on those particular steps," Polly added, seeing Marian close her eyes. "You mustn't blame yourself, Marian. He ought to have been able to negotiate an empty set of stairs, frail carpeting or not. He's quite spry. Call it an act of God."

Marian groaned.

"So God wants us all on the street?" She looked over at Althea, who seemed not to be listening. "Well, no point in fortune-telling. Stiff upper lips. I'll take the poor man an armful of flowers tomorrow."

"He might be in Chicago by now, Marian. You heard Leiby," Bakeoven chuckled.

"I'm sure Beebe will keep us informed."

Aphrodite snuffled noisily as Tad unburdened himself of her to rescue his legs, which he could no longer feel. She sleepwalked over to the loveseat where a somber Lucy and Micah snuggled. Lucy grabbed the dog's head with both hands and kissed it.

"Sleepy-tight, Thunder-buns." Her throat caught at the notion of the huge old dog ambling unconcernedly along one of the neighborhood's busier avenues. Apparently she'd taken advantage of the household's upheaval to snoop through a few of the enticing neighborhood yards, then gotten disoriented. A pair of fifth-graders on skateboards pulled her out of an intersection and got her address from her tags. In the meantime Tad had realized she was missing, and swung feverishly from one knot of guests in the queue to the next, canvassing for clues. Ditey and her benefactors weren't visible till they turned in beneath the trumpet vine, due to the elevation of the yards above Corrie Street. Appreciative splutters of applause became a festive ovation as the news spread through the yard. Lucy watched the triumphant return from the front porch, utterly baffled; Tad had carefully avoided distressing her with the predicament. He'd later reported having sent the boys off with fistfuls of petits fours after hosing Aphrodite's glistening drool off their arms. Lucy snuggled more deeply into Micah's armpit, watching Tad affectionately.

Micah stared at the turtles, feeling dour. He'd had to interrupt his botanical lectures three times to investigate tender-hearted matrons' frantic reports of turtle abuse. They seemed to have survived bored, inebriated husbands and inquisitive preadolescents perfectly well.

"Beebe will need a ride home soon. I could take care of that," he boomed across the cobblestones in Marian's direction, startling Lucy.

A cell phone began warbling the first measures of Bach's "Where Sheep May Safely Graze".

"Bakeoven. Hello Libby. Oh, the usual. We're all still alive. Never a dull moment, though. Yes, she's right here. Occupied, however…I see. I'll have her call you tonight." (He winked at Althea, who slumped back with relief.)

A remote background noise – the first serious lawn mowing of the season? – intensified, and it eventually became apparent the source was overhead. When the turbulent buzz grew loud enough to interfere with conversation, Cleo's and Clumber's heads simultaneously withdrew from the public domain.

In the brilliant blue gap between the pines and crabapples a helicopter sliced the air. As it hovered alarmingly low above Lilybanks before disappearing, everyone but Marian could make out the letters on its flank: MEDI-FLEET. Marian didn't need telling.

7

Foreign Outpost

Beebe sat up straight at the bottom of her bed in the dark, eyes closed to enjoy the caress of a breeze from the garden. She'd rinsed her hair in linden blossoms the night before; the wind caught the faint scent as it prowled, pushing tendrils of hair across her bare shoulders and puffing out her gown as though caught in a ship's sail. Songbirds' trills tumbled in on the air. Beebe felt she sat at the stern of a ponderous, venerable vessel making its way along a verdant canal, the first hints of sunlight barely indicating copses and cottages on the bank as Lilybanks headed out to sea.

Absent to time and plans, absent to her outer self, she poised on the tumult of bird calls and currents, wind chimes and rustling boughs, till a quavering halo on her dresser heralded the climbing sun.

Beebe slid out of bed onto cool, scuffed planks and opened her door, making less noise than the robin pealing from the hut's gable. Gusts from the hall windows rattled Bubo's office door, flirted with the passage's stale wintry scent, and bore news of the lilacs along the garage and a young family of wrens established above the gutter.

The new carpet still felt odd beneath her feet as she crept down the stairs. It smelt like withered grass cuttings, subdued and blameless. Reaching her roost, the third step from the bottom, she sank into the nightgown's ample folds and hugged her knees.

Below her Aphrodite sighed in her sleep. The hallway clock

thrummed from its cavernous, warped casing. Lilting patterns of light and shadow struggled for purchase on the walls and figured floor before lapsing into the gloom. She watched the first concentrated gold of the morning simmering in the front door's empty keyhole. Motes percolated through a wan shaft from an inglenook window. The great dark hull of Lilybanks, resonant in the silence, received the morning's blessing as Beebe kept vigil from its prow.

*   *   *

Disoriented for a moment – Saturday? – Althea let the swirling debris in her head dissolve, eluding any more words, emotion or memories. She stretched, flopped onto her back and attended to her breath, gradually checking in with her body from the inside. She felt radiantly light, as though merely hovering on the mattress, until Linnet stalked over and boarded the bedding. She lurched purposefully up the length of Al's legs, punching one decisive paw after the next into the yielding flesh of stomach and breast. Undeterred by Al's shriek and charade of a spank, Linnet hopped back onto her and uttered a sweet, monosyllabic breakfast order.

Althea rumpled the fur between her ears.

"You want toast with that?"

She fed the cat and straightened the bedclothes with the vague good humor belonging to a weekend. Al thought of Lucy as she settled Cooky in his meticulously authentic hoodie between the kiwi and otter. Oddly insistent, Lucy'd been last night, about Al joining Micah's churchy plans for the afternoon. Al had remained firm; she couldn't think of anything she'd less rather do with her day than take orders from that pious egghead while negotiating some rickety stepladder and dodging Mary Lou Kishko's attempts to embroil her in more parish affairs...Besides, the day was forbiddingly cluttered with people-pleasing obligations as it was, she realized.

The front door's bell clanged. Fully resistant now, Al ducked below the windows and froze, reflecting sourly that Dr. Leiby had been dropping Beebe's bug-eyed admirer off increasingly early. She sympathized, but wasn't up to fussing over them while clutching her kimono closed.

Inhaling, Althea plummeted back to the here and now, where she cringed absurdly on a sunny morning because of some words and pictures in her head. They'd distracted her like so many mixed nuts strewn before a chipmunk. Refusing to indulge in a torrent of self-criticism, she straightened up and headed calmly for the stairs.

Marian, who'd been shedding her bathrobe and decrepit slippers earlier than usual, had beaten her to the door. Deciding to steal back to her room, Al could hear Dr. Leiby issuing curt instructions about pills and sunscreen over Marian's conciliatory murmurs.

*   *   *

Beebe had managed to walk Aphrodite, breakfast with Tad, revise some unsatisfactory cookie dough and meditate upon favorite passages from *The Cloud of Unknowing* before her guest arrived at 8 a.m. Now she perched on the porcelain garden stool, tackling the hangnail on her big toe among daisies and hyssop. Probing with her tongue while trembling from the extravagant effort to maintain her balance on the diminutive seat, Beebe presented a portrait of pure concentration as Woodruff and Leiby rounded the corner of Lilybanks' garden door.

Dr. Leiby, who'd wakened with a headache and had stubbed his shin on Woodruff's wheelchair twice in the driveway, felt his cares evaporate. The enchantingly precocious little Morrissey girl's obvious command of an arcane yoga posture captivated him. One felt one had surprised a rare species of butterfly basking in the sun. He'd be all too happy, for once, to oblige Professor M. by oiling the machinery to get her niece into Oxford early. A professional courtesy, as well as a pleasure to check up on his protégée during overseas conferences.

A gust of wind worried Beebe's petticoat and blew a strand of hair into her eye; she relaxed her attention and noticed movement from the terrace. Lionel waved eagerly. She carefully lowered her leg.

To Leiby's annoyance Woodruff immediately activated the pricey wheelchair's controls and shot beyond his solicitous grip. The girl hopped down from her seat – which looked about as comfortable as a medieval saddle – and met Woodruff on a posy-lined path with a handshake. Rather winsome, with those bare feet, Leiby thought, suppressing the disagreeable impression that she and Weirdy Woodruff were a matched set.

"Lovely morning, Miss Morrissey," he called, choosing an old-fashioned formality he thought would appeal to her. The sunlight made him wince. "I'd be happy to continue our discussion of Oxford in your delightful garden, but duty calls – summer session starts on Monday. I'll be back at one, Lionel." Gazing at Beebe just one second too long, and noting that his ward didn't bother to make so much as a half-turn in his direction, Dr. Leiby withdrew. A glance at his watch suggested there'd still be time for a pre-golf Bloody Mary at the country club bar after he entertained himself a little with Professor M. Compulsively scanning the garden once more before circling the house, he suffered a distasteful view of Woodruff holding the tip of Beebe's braid to his nostrils as she daubed sunscreen on his domed, balding head. A pair of grooming baboons...

In a frenzy, he jangled Lilybanks' atmospheric damned doorbell, each metallic stroke detonating a shock wave through his skull. By the time Marian opened the front door he'd composed himself, apologetically holding out the verdigris chain he'd yanked from the weathered bell's orifice.

"Yet another Lilybanks casualty, I'm afraid, Marian. I wondered if I might take you up on that offer of a glass of water after all? Things are heating up." He'd passed her on his way into the cool, dark vestibule before she could reply, and tossed the chain gleefully onto the nearest toddler's chair.

"I see we've got a functioning staircase again," he commented, unwilling to grant a compliment though the handsome new runner must have shattered her piggybank to smithereens. Marian led him through the scullery, since he seemed unwilling to wait in the hall. She didn't allow herself to linger over his unsettling use of the plural pronoun. Aphrodite, who'd been pried from the bathroom once Marian had thought her coast clear, followed balefully. She disliked Leiby's aura of spleen and dry-cleaning, and stared disapprovingly from beneath a corner of the tablecloth like a matronly chaperone while Marian poured Leiby some water.

"Kind of you. Spacious kitchen, isn't it? Imagine your grandmother had quite a staff. Love those double sinks, and the drain in the floor. But not quite up to regulation for entertaining the public. Of course it's only once a year, and the Tour's a Rutledge institution… I may as well tell you, Marian, I'm hearing whispered scuttlebutt to the effect that the Board of Health's taking an interest. Dog wanders freely through the kitchen, does he?" Leiby extended a hand toward the Newfoundland but thought better of patting it when the dog stonily refused to acknowledge him.

"The Maven Alley Bakery supplied most of the goodies this year. I suppose we could patent the lemonade; bottle it up. Perhaps it would bring the Ravens luck if we hawked it in the stadium at intermissions," Marian parried. The university's football team had had an abysmal season. Leiby produced his tight, managerial smile.

"I like your attitude, Marian. No harm in exploring some creative entrepreneurship, in your position. The University understands the plight of guardians of aging landmark properties. (You know we've shepherded several worthy acquisitions into our safe harbor.) It costs a pretty penny to maintain sufficient structural integrity to interest investors willing to be passed the custodial baton. Keeping up with petty regulations, nickel-and-diming makeshift solutions that prove fatal to the structure's welfare – very stressful. We've thought you girls very high-minded, generously exposing Lilybanks' situation to the public for the sake of art. Gives youngsters a chance to see an historic interior that may not be available to the next generation. Of course youngsters take their toll – speaking of which, I hope your preschoolers aren't going to pull the place down around themselves? You'll want to keep your safety inspection paperwork up to –"

Marian's silvery chortle of delight at the man's ingenuity interrupted his flow.

"We appreciate the University's interest, Doctor," Marian smiled, steering him back through the pantry. "May we accompany you out to your car? Older dogs need to be urged to keep moving...I'm always coaxing her out for a breath of fresh air..." Of one mind, Aphrodite and Marian conducted their guest to the door with exceptional alacrity.

Having gathered his wits by the time they'd propelled him to the bottom of the front stairs, Leiby turned a lethal smile on Marian.

"Nice of you to take Lionel off my hands again this morning. You know, this whole fiasco may yet be turned to good. If your niece keeps playing her cards right, it looks to me like he'll move heaven and earth to smuggle her back to the scepter'd isle with him. I imagine academic plans will pale compared to the great School of Life!" Giving her a wry, worldly nod and wave Leiby marched off to his Peugeot.

Dragging the confused dog back up the steps by her collar, Marian kicked a kinderchair out of formation; the front door was too heavy to slam.

"Who would have thought that stinker'd have such perfect aim? I guess that's how he wormed his way to the top of administration. Oh dear. Come along, Ditey. Please forgive me."

In the scullery Marian pulled the last three Smart Dogs from the daycare mini-fridge. While the elated dog had her back turned

Marian stole a furtive glance through the scullery window's screen of ivy. Lionel Woodruff appeared to be examining an inaccessible clump of columbines from his wheelchair, clutching Beebe's binoculars with characteristic intensity. Beebe, hands on hips, seemed to be expatiating on their charms. Innocuous, certainly.

Lionel and Beebe inhabited a different plane than poor bloodshot Dennis Leiby's. Or perhaps two different but neighborly planes, Marian decided, watching Lionel prattle to himself. He seemed to swing between two modes: a silent, manic, pop-eyed euphoria reminiscent of Harpo Marx, and an intermittently accessible glossolalian soup of poetic composition, private remarks and questions addressed to no one in particular. Accustomed to the tics and quirks of brilliant colleagues, Marian found him only mildly disconcerting, though Lucy said Micah thought he was schizophrenic. Whatever the case, Lionel Woodruff's cryptic pantheistic sonnets and exquisite essays on landscapes and botanical minutiae inspired reverence in certain spheres. He was admired by the Empyreans, an Oxford-based crusade of poets, environmentalists and gurus of various persuasions hoping to revitalize a sense of the sacred in nature through the arts. They appreciated his gifts as a *provocateur* and coiner of memorable phrases.

While some poked fun at the Empyrean Society as a precious, upper-crust pack of sentimental reactionaries, Marian had grasped at once upon hearing of the Society's formation that Lilybanks possessed a kindred spirit. It was as a modest ambassadress of an unsuspected foreign outpost that she had recently submitted an essay on life at Lilybanks to the Society journal, enclosing a few brochures for good measure. The published article had netted her promising Toronto tutee Jacob Engelbright, a pleasing assortment of erudite correspondence and a curious weekend with a potty viscount and his lady – owners of a celebrated Suffolk garden – who'd mistaken Lilybanks for a bed and breakfast. As the university's English Lit headquarters, Professor Carberry's office had received a few inquiries from doctoral candidates who mentioned the article; he'd politely rapped Marian's knuckles for her failure to "coordinate her private efforts with the Department's." She suspected that had more than a little to do with the lack of notification regarding the Woodruff visit.

She sighed, wiping Ditey's slobbery jowls with a tissue.

"Tut tut. We mustn't think ourselves into a dither, Ditey. If Beebe's meant to study at Oxford no petty egoic intrigue can stop us. Her."

All the same, she reflected, leading Aphrodite back to her basket, one could see in which direction Leiby was pointing his cannons. It was clearly time to address Watkins' occasional muttering about Lilybanks' wiring not being "up to code." (Of course *he* was the one who gleefully insisted his makeshift bandage on the furnace pipe would last as long as the furnace. His double meaning had only just occurred to her...) And time to let Bakeoven's eager architect friend submit some hypothetical drawings (and, she shuddered, a hypothetical bid) for an unobtrusive fire stair from the second floor.

By the hallway clock she had twenty minutes to prepare for the first of the Saturday morning tutees. Tremendous success, the new stair runner. Still the familiar fretwork of green and gold gingko leaves, on a soft blue-green that Mr. Chobanian had revealed as the original color before a century greyed it. To be paid for in theoretically affordable installments, full payment upon receipt having been waived in return for rights to publicity. She pictured a glossy magazine ad with Aphrodite posed at the bottom of the staircase: "As seen at historic Lilybanks."

Jumping its rails, her imagination went her one better and suggested an expensively "preserved" Lilybanks. She saw a small but scholarly bookshop with postcard stand in the inglenook library, the latest "no-touch" paper towel dispenser in the downstairs bath, a NO ANIMALS, PLEASE placard at the garden door. Upstairs, Beebe's room would be the likely choice for staff, with a humming copy machine, coffeemaker and the telltale glow of a computer screen or two.

Windows would be permanently closed for security; EXIT signs glare above thresholds…

A whited sepulchre.

She sagged against the banister, eyes closed.

Had she missed her cue? Failed to surrender? Was it time to let Lilybanks expire gracefully?

Bah, words. Marian took a deep, grateful breath and let them go. The scents of lavender polish and sweet orange oil, a silence punctuated occasionally by footsteps overhead or distant wheels, the press of bone and flesh on stair step, a dog hair fluttering in her nostril – awareness in the here and now was her true home, her refuge, which could never be lost. She pulled herself up, headed for her office. By force of felicity, through Lionel's "starry door" into Traherne's Estate of Innocence,[13] all things would work together for good.

Animal Allies

"Pass the brownies, will you, Libby?"

"Sure. Hey, what's this?" Libby pulled her arm back, frowning.

"An adorable green inch-worm. Probably fell out of your arbor onto the tinfoil. Be right back." Althea commandeered the foil-covered pan of brownies, extricated herself from the picnic table and was crouching beneath the grape arbor before Libby could intervene. Charmed by the celery-colored little creature's tiptoed humps, Althea settled it on a grape leaf in the shade. In her experience very few people could be trusted to deal fairly with stranded insects.

Al fought her way back to her seat through several ice cream-dazed dogs. Libby looked amused, but not scornful.

"I see you've caught the Lilybanks mania for compassionate micromanagement. Beebe would have included a prayer."

She had. Nettled, she studied the jiggly tiers of flab beneath Libby's tee-shirt, reflecting that Libby's fourth brownie was a self-medicating anesthetic. Little waves of disapproval and envy surfaced, reminding her that she'd also had a brownie and that dark chocolate tended to unhinge her.

Taking a deep breath, Al reached for a tangerine instead.

"Actually I was already infected when I moved in. I'm just wired this way, Libby. Thin skin, deep thoughts, myopic concerns."

"That's why we're having this tea party – so the callous realist can light a fire under the dreamy introvert's butt. Animal Allies needs you. We need your reedy elegant person to swell our body count at protests and parades and meetings."

"I know, I know. We've discussed this. It's not as if I've never been to a protest rally. I give to the charities when I can. I read the liter-ature – however sketchily – the horrible descriptions aren't really aimed at people like me, you know. Total overkill." She raced on, seeing Libby open her mouth. "I realize I need to stay informed on the issues. And I know you need bodies, and emailers and volunteers for the 'shitwork' as you call it. You know I can't go into the kill shel-ters; I'd come out with several unmanageable, expensively unhealthy animals I couldn't afford to keep and Lilybanks couldn't weather..."

"No one's asking you to risk a single precious quartersawn tooth-pick at Lilybanks, darlin'. And I'll provide your transportation." Al imagined arriving in state in Libby's prestigious old tub, the closest she'd been able to come to an armored car. Apparently she'd bought the Mercedes for a song from a wealthy old widow whose cat she babysat.

"We want you at puppy mill busts and fur rallies – mainstreamers need to see that college students with rings through their lips aren't the only citizens who care enough about the issues to go public. Look on it as a creative outlet as well as an ethical obligation; you can write up your own handouts, design your own placards...and you'll meet other members of your tribe, Althea. I'm sure your preschoolers and their moms are fascinating, but – "

Al rolled her eyes. "Stop. You seem to think I have these luxurious amounts of free time you need to manage for me, Libby. In fact, what with living in a cooperative and working from dawn through lunch five days a week – not to mention having had my whole life turned upside down less than a year ago – and being a person who needs plenty of private time – "

"Althea, I'm not asking you to join the army, or have a baby, or go back to grad school for Pete's sake. Just a few meetings and events that will enable you to live out your own professed –"

"ALRIGHT. Yes. Sign me up. I'm not on Facebook; you'll have to print me out the monthly schedule if you want me to show up for some of this stuff."

Libby let out a war whoop, pulled her orange "Animal Allies" sunshade off her head and plunked it down backwards on Al's. The dogs gathered round with panting smiles and cocked ears (except for Captain, who was discreetly barfing his ice cream at the bottom of the stairs.)

"Frisbee time, Sox! Come on, Althea!" Libby hurled a tooth-marked red disc into the center of the yard and struggled up out of the picnic table debris.

"Sorry. My sports are croquet and badminton. I get agoraphobic just looking at a Frisbee, Libby." Al pushed the sunshade's band out of her eyes, secretly pleased. She didn't see herself as the kind of person someone dared to muss.

Eckhart Tolle implied activism was counterproductive if one failed to keep ego out of it. Al pictured herself marching, handing out brochures and speaking at meetings with a serene detachment, powerful even if no one noticed. Immune, imperturbable, committed but never rabid, she'd be vigilant about not succumbing to obsession, superiority or hatred. While Libby tumbled about with the pack, Al fell into a gratifying reverie. She should get to the library and do some research on Gandhi.

A tipsy, grape-inebriated wasp fumbled off the edge of the picnic table into her lap. She coaxed it onto one of Libby's brochures and released it with conscious virtue. Pinky the puppy mill poodle, also abstaining from team sports, kept an eye on her from the shade under the table. He looked skeptical, even hostile.

Realizing that she'd just emerged from a transport of self-indulgence (Saint Althea!), she snorted.

"You're right, Pinky. Deluded and dangerous. But maybe not all the time." He continued to glare at her, his eyes kindled to a glassy garnet. Al tried to think of him as her teacher, and sighed. She struggled to follow her breath despite the mayhem of the barreling, yipping, swerving dogs. She felt grass tickling her ankles, heard Violet barking excitedly from the distant sidelines, tasted the salt of perspiration on her upper lip. Here, now. Let go of the egoic picture show in one's head. Grateful just to let it all be – Libby's can of diet Pepsi, the roaring fart of a motorcycle above her head at sidewalk level, her rising anxiety about the fact that she'd just given away more of her meditation time – Al rose almost contentedly to dissuade Scooter from cleaning up Captain's mess.

Leviathan
[*1912*]

Calla's and Martin's eyes met, triumphant, above Eugene Ringgold's splendid hothouse camellias. Initially cautious, Martin's favorite colleague had not only risen to the occasion but waded right in by the time Calla and Ruth removed the soup plates. His well-informed praise for Crum's talent had been acceptable; even by candlelight Calla noted the telltale pink at her guest of honor's earlobes and beak. Clearly taken with Louisa Erikson, the belle of the Drama Department, Eugene had already suggested that his fellow dinner guests make up a party for the Ibsen play her husband was directing at Hull House.

After a few misfired volleys with Miss Ruth Mapes he'd found his level, that of impish elder brother. (Fetching more wine from the drafty back hall he'd told Martin the sari-clad Miss Mapes needed a good pinch in the bottom if it could be found.)

Fragrant steam from the makeshift sideboard behind her enveloped Calla's shoulders; her audience might inhale a hint of sage or fennel as she gamboled past their tuxedoes tonight. Cook (Olive? She couldn't decide, though Martin thought it too obvious) carried in platter after platter of the wedding Roycroft, mute and anonymous as a mime. Craning to catch what Louisa was laughing about, Calla took in Crum's increasingly frozen smile. She'd arranged safe harbor for him at her side and across from Sam, only to realize now that his distance from the manly, moneyed camaraderie surrounding his convivial assistant Merrick was the crucial consideration. Ruth's increasingly riveted disdain for Eugene at Crum's other elbow didn't help.

Reading Calla's face, Sam produced an able anecdote about the mayor's mangled conception of botany's role in architecture that captured the entire table. Seemed their civic leader was intrigued by Alpine shallots. Crum's waxen grip on his napkin relaxed. Merrick Field's talents rose even higher in Calla's estimate as he began including his mentor's views on various topics with a friendly ease that drew no attention to itself.

Her evening saved, Calla drifted. How strikingly Ruth's hand-woven tapestry masked the expanse of plaster where built-in china cabinets would soon preside. Martin, who'd said she might as well have tacked up the scullery doormat, had been wrong. A loom might be –

Sam tapped her wrist.

"Miss Cook."

Olive, the marvelous new necessary evil, saluted Calla with a serving spoon just beyond the French doors, then thrust it under an arm, pointed toward the hall clock and held up eight fingers.

Crumrind observed her quiet sleight-of-hand with admiration.

She'd been the Marshall Singer Pratt family's Astor Street pastry chef before Calla lured her from Chicago.

Seeing Calla rise, Eugene consulted his little menu card. His hostess's plump, childish handwriting promised a cheddar soufflé and sorrel *gratin* enhanced by the season's first asparagus.

Ruth sidled behind the Meister to her assignment beside stacked dinner plates.

"A little more, Merrick?" Martin poured champagne, relishing Ringgold's good-natured astonishment at the arrangements – curiously bohemian, no doubt, by Chicago financiers' standards. Martin himself had been enjoying Calla's erratic minuet with the new cook all week; having spirited her away from the Pratts' munificence, his democratic wife veered between fussy pride in Lilybanks and the dilatory chattiness of an uprooted schoolgirl. Miss Cook seemed to possess an oriental pliability. But close, he thought. Probably a desirable trait.

Delighted with her party, Calla heaped food from the crowded sideboard onto plates that Ruth directed down the table.

"This one's for you, Louisa." The theatre department's set designer shared a contented smile with her hostess.

Crumrind marveled at Calla's careless grace. She intended to dance for a curious throng in a few hours, but thought it vulgar to change clothes "like a chorus girl." Here she was dishing up one of her dribbly concoctions in a filmy Fortuny that might dissolve in the halo of herbed steam rising from the platters. If he lifted his arm he could touch the tiny puckered pleats.

"If you'll just carry 'round the sauce, Olive."

"'Cook,' Mrs. Morrissey," she corrected, so low that only Crumrind caught it. Amused, he watched her accept a gravy boat and ladle from Calla and proceed to expertly interrupt one conversation after the next with minimal word and gesture. In spite of the butchered black hair that lent her probable Irishness a disconcertingly Egyptian look, she displayed a dignified self-possession. Tall, thin, colorless, she lacked Miss Mapes' stiffness, wielding her ladle with supple authority. When their heedless host shot up to propose a toast, she salvaged the sauceboat at his elbow with a nanny's vigilance.

"Hear, hear. A toast to Lilybanks and her Meisterbilder. John, your tireless dedication to detail in both chamber and garden renders our home's innermost soul as comely, as expressive as her visage. Calla and I thank you from the bottom of our hearts, and on behalf of our children, our children's children, and those for whom we'll be but faint shades. May --"

Calla recognized her mother-in-law's lilting, lyric talk. It haunted Martin's tongue when he was deeply moved, or only finagling. This was for his wife. Yet there slumped Crum, bashfully inspecting his forks with a sheepish delight quite incongruous in a man of his professional stature. The public display of his endearing vulnerability repulsed her. From their end of the table Ringgold, Merrick Field – the watchful understudy – and Martin savored her lover's susceptibility like schoolboys in a lavatory. Sam saw none of this, blinded by lovingkindness.

"...worthy of our adopted prairies and ponds, woods and meadows, the simple --"

An anguished bellow severed Martin's soliloquy. Crumrind watched his and Ruth's place settings shiver, bounce and topple as the table tilted into their laps. Something warm and wet soaked his right arm. Fearing an explosion involving the gas, he forced himself to look, and, as in a dream, Monk's proud head emerged from under the table. Before Crumrind could assemble his thoughts his eyes met those of Olive Cook. Above the gasps and exclamations her dark eyes telegraphed amused rapport as the last of the Hollandaise dripped from her gravy boat's lip onto his sleeve and thence onto one of his favorite shoes. Monk licked this clean as Miss Mapes took charge, their joint efforts a bastion of calm amidst embarrassment, forced hilarity and broken china.

"This way." Ruth seized the Meister's lapel with one hand, her silken hem in the other and propelled him along the sideboard, out the doors and toward a sink.

"Forgive me. The dog," Olive fretted, knowing her place. "I –"

"I'm so sorry, Cook. I'd forgotten he was in the room; they're always so reliable," Calla whispered. Her smile looked taut. "You should have been warned. Don't give it another thought. The fault lies entirely elsewhere."

Having cleaned up the Turkish carpet with sorrowful dispatch, the dog looked to Calla for his cue and followed her into the scullery as though anxious to be of further service. They met Ruth returning with towels, broom, dustpan and Martin's evening Tribune in tow.

"We'll just get the worst of the broken glass out and blot up the spills. No red wine, how lucky. Might we continue in the sitting room? I hope –"

The voices faded as Crumrind and Olive retreated wordlessly through the pantry and into the kitchen.

"Alright, are you? You've gotten the stuff on your shoes, too, at least. Write down your size for Mrs. Morrissey and we'll order some new ones." He tore off his jacket and settled it on the back of a chair, wrinkling his nose at the coagulating crust forming on the sleeve. "The evening's performance began earlier than expected." Crumrind pulled off his shoes and socks and sat on the kitchen table, swinging his legs. He watched Olive clean their shoes with a rag, expecting his meaning to be ignored. Instead, her shoulders began to shake. Perhaps he'd gone too far. He owed it to Calla not to reduce her only servant to jelly tonight.

A musical giggle with only a hint of attempted suppression echoed through the kitchen. He could see her breath; she looked quite deranged.

"Like Leviathan rising from the depths..."

"I'd keep it down, your employer won't – why in heaven's name is this open?"

She darted between him and the nearest window, whose curtains pouched with the night breeze.

"The ices. I have to take them out on a tray."

Olive was all deft expertise now, making Crumrind the eccentric derelict to be humored.

"Leave one out. Tell Mrs. Morrissey I'll be back with dessert. And bring me news of Leviathan." He banged the window shut, watched her disappear through the pantry.

The ice was pineapple, and perfect. Weary of the social endeavor, Crum lay back on the worktable with his knees in the air. Calla would probably give his seat in the living room to Monk. Olive Cook seemed to have left her "sirs" and "ma'am's" behind with the Pratts.

Finally irate, Crumrind stood waiting in his shrinking shoes for her return.

"The dog's keeping company with its mates in the shelter of the carriageway, Professor. They have their blankets."

"Excellent. You stepped on the dog's tail deliberately. Would you care to explain yourself?"

Companionably close, Olive held her ground. Her long, oval face, the color of weak milky tea, turned an alarming dark pink as though scalded. Nearly his height, she seemed determined to hold his eye whether she turned red, white or blue and expired. Moles on her flat cheeks and upper lip nearly disappeared against the flaming skin.

"Don't make yourself ill, sit down. I'll get some water."

She prevented this, gripping him hard by the wrist.

"I'd sooner step on your face than on any dog's tail."

Relieved, he smiled. "Clearly."

She let go.

"Oh, the pity of it. What made you think such a thing? Never mind, it doesn't matter. I thought you were quite different. I thought I'd get on here so well. What's brought you to this?"

Captivated by this strange familiarity, Crumrind felt they'd suffered a similar mischance elsewhere in time. They'd be forced to make up so they might resume some consuming game.

"The dogs have brought me to this, that's all. I know them. They oblige me with exquisite decorum at dinner parties, lectures, train stations. You might have served Mr. Ringgold his pineapple ice on Monk's back with complete confidence. He has a fine sense of his size and would never permit a stray appendage to impede your royal progress, Miss Cook."

"The poor beast must have jammed itself betwixt the chair legs tighter than a pig in a pew."

Crumrind backed up a little and folded his arms, smiling.

"Snugger than a cow in a custard cup, Miss Cook. My point."

"Mine. I believe you trod on the beast yourself, fidgeting while your praises were sung."

Crumrind sat back down and massaged his forehead while staring at the floor.

"Do you know, you may perfectly well be right. Entirely possible. And now it's I who must ask you to forgive me."

The man looked sad and tired. He had the unruly, peaked eyebrows of a pixie. Changeful. The thin lips suggested spitefulness, the eyes, clemency.

She extended a hand.

"I do, from the bottom of my heart. Will you help me with the cake? Mrs. Morrissey says you're fond of hickory nuts; we've put them in the filling."

"Did you." His handshake was merely perfunctory; she saw he'd already moved on.

Muffled noise in the hallway was followed by Calla peeping around the corner of the pantry.

"My quartet's here. I'll take them upstairs and get them settled, then we'll have the cake. And sherry, Cook." Calla smiled at them, checking for ruffled feathers. Crum rose to occasions unpredictably;

he seemed to have emerged from the mishap intact. But he'd need help returning to the party.

"I'm sure they'd enjoy meeting Lilybanks' architect, Professor. Won't you join us upstairs?"

"Time enough for that; I want to check on the dogs." Calla fluttered behind him as he loped through the scullery, slowed down at the sight of a musician's back, then executed a sharp left turn at full speed. He was out the back door before most of the music students realized anyone had entered the hall.

Olive hummed to herself as she smoothed a dent in her icing with a warm knife. No need to call him "Professor" on her account. She wished Calla better luck with the man than her former employer had enjoyed.

Archangel Gabriel

Micah commended himself for assigning Lucy the balcony garlands; the ropes of linden and ivy were being unfurled with artsy-craftsy proficiency. And he knew she was happy up there on her own with Tad. Archangel Gabriel Orthodox Church made her exceptionally nervous, in spite of friendly babushki charmed by their engagement, in spite of his attentive mentoring.

Beebe beckoned to him with both hands from the top of a wobbly old ladder in a side aisle. The parishioners who'd shown up to help decorate for Pentecost had been reluctant to let a reputedly unchurched visitor adorn icons, but Beebe's childish appeal and obvious reverence won out. Besides, she could negotiate the ladder. Gabriel's was an aging flock.

Micah tossed a dust cloth onto the candle desk and picked his way across mason jars full of vines and boxes of silk apple blossoms. Cleaning utensils and a vintage vacuum cleaner clogged Beebe's aisle.

In the meantime she had become engrossed in a conversation

with the deacon's wife, who was showing her how to remove wax from the candle stands. Beebe had to stand on tiptoe to reach the highest sockets. Mrs. Zilkovich apparently found that unremarkable. She treated Beebe with incurious patronage, like a niece who lived around the corner.

"Will you excuse me, Matushka? I need Micah's help with Saint George." Mrs. Zilkovich was famous for high standards of comportment. She'd once conspicuously admonished Micah for failing to eject a mildly intoxicated old man from the front steps. She released Beebe with a look that verged on the affectionate.

Reestablishing her perch on the creaky ladder, Beebe brandished the handful of purple beech she'd selected.

"This will be lovely poked behind the icon. Can you just lift him up a little while I slip the twigs under?"

Micah obeyed. The result – a smoke-obscured icon with dark leaves lapping at its borders – achieved just the artless effect wanted. He nodded, unwilling to show his pleasure.

"Okay, we need to fill two big vases with flowers, one on either side of the analogion." He pointed to a lectern. "That little room inside the front door has a sink." Micah didn't bother to steady the decrepit ladder for her, watching with amusement as she clambered down unconcernedly in the prim Miss Muffet dress. He made a mental note to ask the church council to fund a new ladder.

They bustled past a clutch of old-timers in headscarves who were on their knees to pick candle wax off the prized scarlet carpeting. Their obvious approval of Beebe filled him with pride, which struck him as ridiculous. He chose to ignore the thin but distinct tendril of regret winding through his gut.

He set Beebe to filling the heavy vases from the utility closet sink with a coffee can. Under the bare ceiling bulb's heat a smell like wilting flowers rose from her scalp, its straight part disconcertingly far below him.

"I'm fine," she grinned above the roar of water hitting tin, and he left at once, annoyed with himself for having loitered in the cramped space. He kept an ear out for the water while he polished woodwork, responding distractedly to the head of the women's guild's pleas-antries and excusing himself as soon as the gush stopped. He found Beebe flushed, sweaty, delighted with her work. No wonder the old folk wanted to eat her up with a spoon.

On impulse Micah gestured that she follow after he picked up the nearer vase. Absurdly she chose to interpret this – as he'd guessed – by lifting the other vase a few inches off the floor and painstakingly heading toward the icon stand in his wake. Leaving her to it, he placed his vase on one side of the stand and began poking droopy clusters of blossoms into it. The gymnastics required to harvest armfuls of black locust flowers from his landlord's trees had become an annual gam-ble. Spectacularly fragrant though ephemeral, these would only make it through the vigil service. He'd have to replace them with a second batch for tomorrow's feast day. Appearing to admire the perfume, he kept his back to Beebe's halting approach across the nave.

In the balcony Tad held segments of a garland for Lucy to mend with florist's tape. He could see Beebe's excruciatingly labored pro-cession and Micah's squatting, studied fiddling with his twigs. He conceived an unformulated but confident reassessment of the man.

"Hey, Tad, you can let go now." Lucy had followed his eyes and smiled, seeing only Beebe's painstaking concentration and Tad's ab-sorption. As though coming up from the bottom of a lake he met her eyes and glanced away again.

While Lucy groped for a hook over the railing's edge she watched Beebe position her vase, heedless of the discreetly admiring parish-ioners. Thanks to Micah Beebe seemed to have found a place where – however oddly – she fit in beautifully. Lucy felt happy for her friend, and had accepted her own malaise here as a mere inconvenience. Micah assured her he loved her as she was.

Everyone watched Beebe approach the crowded jars of foliage at the base of the wall of icons separating the altar from the nave. She chose some locust blossoms and impulsively curtseyed before the tiered images of saints. Beebe returned to the analogion with eyes only for the bouquet she held with both hands.

"A little bride," Mrs. Shomoliak whispered to her neighbor.

"Maybe a bride of the Church," returned Mrs. Groczynski.

Much later at home that night several spoke of their visitor's humility and poise.

"So Russian," someone said.

With wise restraint none of the sharp-eyed commented on Micah Fennel's naked absorption in the little bouquet-bearer's every movement.

Tree Hugger

Bakeoven's rather preposterous new red pickup, ostensibly acquired to cope with Rumba's jaunts, rumbled in the Lilybanks drive while he pried Althea from The Cygnet's Nest. She and Lucy wanted him to try on a smoking jacket.

"No time, ladies. The library parking lot fills up fast on Green League night. I don't want my new toy out on the street. See you there, Lucy."

"We'll save you a seat." Althea had made an effort all afternoon not to take Lucy's moony silences personally. Bakeoven held the door open, bowing deeply and flourishing a hand toward the stairs. She scurried out.

"I'd need the hookah as an accessory," he called over his shoulder to Lucy. Bakeoven had been trying to acquire the Nest's favorite fixture for a couple of years, but Lucy looked vacant.

Al let him open the passenger door for her, an embarrassing pleasure that Casper had never offered. She tried to suppress the moment's similarity to a date; Lucy wanted to walk to the meeting and Marian had a ride, which Bakeoven had ascertained before showing up with the two-seater. And the Green League was one of his impassioned commitments, like chess night at Caffe Luigi and wine-tasting fundraisers for the university's Bach Fest. His desire to get Al into the League was partisan rather than personal.

"We've invited Laura Pritchard and Kip Rusk, the most sympathetic city council members. Also Dr. and Mrs. LeMoyne, Lewis Hah, the Basketts – of the property owners whose land borders Bodie, they're the most committed to maintaining it as woodland rather than some kind of outdoor rec room like Powell Park...Or condominiums," he added at a stop sign, looking over at her with a grimace.

Much as she loved Bodie Woods, Al suspected this budding crusade of Bakeoven's was a tempest in a teapot. The number of comments he'd heard about deadwood, fire hazards and malingerers hiding in bushes seemed to have reached some critical mass; suddenly the woods had to be saved from insidious plotters. On the other hand, she reflected, glancing over at his tasteful shirt and tie, his competent hands on the steering wheel (though of course *anyone* else's hands looked capable to her on a steering wheel), Bakeoven certainly knew more about the way things got done in Rutledge County than she did. She and Casper had sat quietly in the back of enough of the county board's "public hearings" to grasp that by that stage of the game the Powers That Be already had the bulldozers hired, the hunting season's dates chosen, the inconvenient old mansion's chandeliers promised to allies, and sufficient support in the peanut gallery.

As Bakeoven concentrated on Saturday evening traffic, Althea tried to focus on Bodie Woods: the yearly miracle of resurrected mourning cloaks in March, Casper coaxing her out into the middle of the pond when it froze solid, her favorite confidante hickory, the rare disoriented deer grateful for an oasis. At bottom, *any* public interest or intervention in Bodie made her uneasy. She'd wandered through its green tangle for years; its faithful shared a tacit agreement to keep their refuge an insiders' secret, nodding to each other when a meeting on a path was unavoidable.

Marian's attendance comforted her. She wasn't so sure about Lucy, whom she could imagine supporting swing sets for toddlers in the woods, or Bakeoven, who might be influenced by wealth, especially from the academic quarter. He liked the idea of a woods in the middle of town, he walked his dog there or "took exercise," but did he commune?

Feeling a little ashamed of that last thought, Al reminded herself she was supposed to be judging what was best for the woods, not other people's inner lives. It would be a rough evening if she were going into the meeting ego-first. She wished she could screw her head off and carry it in under her arm.

Bakeoven had stopped talking; she hadn't really been listening to his patter about the difference between driving the pickup and his car. When they pulled into the library's lot it was filling up. Having attended a few meetings years ago, Althea had concluded she had neither the clout, science nor rural property to make her a useful League member.

As she strode along the library's air-conditioned corridors next to Bakeoven and his stylish attaché case, Al practiced feeling porous, flexible and delightfully unimportant. She'd begun using the technique for social situations that were likely to be hazardous. The less heavy, insecure ego she brought along, the more skillfully she surfed over potential slights and humiliations, and the quicker she recovered from tumbles. It could actually be fun to survive normally ego-bruising encounters with this newfound buoyancy.

It seemed they were early after all. Half a dozen members stood chatting in pairs. Marian sat alone on the long side of a table. No sign of Lucy. A substantial ring of folding chairs circled the upholstered chairs at the table.

Bakeoven claimed a seat next to Marian. Al chose a folding chair behind them. A few faces looked familiar. Barbara MacDuff from Euclid Street trudged in, panting, with a stack of books. She settled in out of view at a table end.

When Bakeoven finished conferring with Marian he looked around the room, eventually discovering Althea seated behind him. He pushed the chair next to his out for her.

"I'm fine here. As a newcomer, you know."

To her surprise he looked quite testy. He patted the upholstered seat and she plunked her purse down on it obediently.

"First come first served," he said, giving her an opaque look.

Removing her keys from her purse she escaped, ostensibly to the water cooler, and met Barbara MacDuff emerging from the ladies' room.

"Hello there! Nice to see you here. So you're still in town?"

"Oh yes. I'm renting a room in the Hill District. Much simpler, none of the pressures of home ownership, though of course it's all been an adjustment," Althea smiled, proficient by now. She'd liked the good-natured MacDuffs well enough, though she knew Barbara was groping: 'Ethel? Alice?'

"Oh, I'm *sure* it's been an adjustment," Mrs. MacDuff repeated, glad to gloss over widowhood and the loss of one's home.

"How's Euclid Street doing?" Al asked, eager to change the subject. She realized her mistake as the words escaped her.

"Street was repaved. You were lucky to miss that. Remingtons got one of those ground-level swimming pools. Beautifully landscaped, but every time Marigold's missing I think of that pool. Oh, and the Augsbergers – your new owners – got their zoning waiver from the council for the two-story garage. He'll have an office on the second floor. The Bishops aren't happy about the Augsbergers' driveway going in right up against her pampered hosta border – the exhaust fumes, I suppose, and so much less private, but I told her..." Mrs. MacDuff faltered, realizing from the drained, agonized face before her that she'd not merely blundered but ravaged. "I told her she'll soon get used to it...I'm so happy that you're still in the area, dear!"

"Some of the trees had to come down, I suppose?" Althea croaked with a ghastly smile.

"Not yet, no," Mrs. MacDuff answered like someone held hostage on a window ledge. "I suppose a few will have to go, but the Augsbergers are having a landscaper in from Chicago. I'm sure they'll replant." In fact, Mrs. Augsberger's plans mostly focused on a semicircular drive of trophy pavers, which seemed to be the way landscapers made their money these days, but Mrs. Augsberger had also invited the MacDuffs to dinner next week. Awkward if the inscrutable Mrs. Athnos became unhinged about her yard and indulged in an abusive phone call in which Barbara's name came up.

"They'll spare no expense; I'm sure it will be lovely," she continued. "It's Bodie Woods I'm worried about – apparently so much deadwood has accumulated that one vagrant's match could reduce the surrounding houses to ashes!" She looked at her watch, pleased to have shifted gears seamlessly. "We'd best get in there. Good to see you again, dear."

Althea followed and resumed her seat in a daze. Lucy had arrived, sitting next to Marian out of earshot. Someone outlined the evening's agenda, read minutes.

Every time Al resolved to be present and follow along she was besieged by memories that reduced her to digging her fingernails into her palms. Damn Bakeoven for forcing her into a conspicuous seat! Casper had planted the cherry tree in the middle of the backyard the same month they'd moved in. How many times he'd patiently coaxed Tutu into his arms and lifted him down into hers from a ladder after the cat got stuck in the tree chasing plastered waxwings and robins, drunk on fermented fruit. And the walnut along the Bishops' side – such a loss for the squirrels. Generations had fed from that tree, leaving furrowed shells to sprout tiny trees in gutters, on window-sills – they'd even found them wedged under their windshield wipers.

A man in a green park district shirt had assumed the mike. Something about insufficient funds (of course) and recommendations. "Blah blah County Conservation District…" She'd meant to visit the squirrels long before this, but somehow Euclid Street had dropped off her map. Her chest hurt at the thought of Biggy, her favorite catcher, who stood swaying from haunch to haunch like a baseball outfielder and revealing the curiously corrugated family jewels while waiting for her to pitch a peanut. She'd had to leave so much behind forever; at the time of the move the loss of the local squirrels had been just one more ripple on a tidal wave. They'd have to find new trees now. A dangerous business. She imagined them peering down from neighboring rooftops in dismayed wonder as the "tree service" trucks pulled into the yard. The catchers would probably cope, but the dizzies might run rashly out into –

"This is our man," Bakeoven whispered, elbowing her and nodding at the fellow in conservation district khakis who'd just reached the podium. Grateful, Althea tried to transfer her attention to the speaker, but floundered in his preliminary generalizations, repeatedly yanked back into her miserable swamp of nostalgia, despair and a growing, wounded fury at the Augsbergers of the world.

By the end of the meeting she had taken in very little except Lucy's blank reticence when asked to stand and display her new poster for the Green League's recycling program. Same lovable girl, but drained of twinkle. "Pithed," Casper would have said. Marian arranged a ride for Lucy; neither seemed accessible.

Al marshaled her reserves to make suitable noises as Bakeoven held forth on the way home. She'd expected him to linger after the meeting, hashing over various points with fellow Leaguers. But he'd steered her out of the room with facile efficiency, in the self-contained, dismissive manner he sometimes assumed, that of a person with important affairs to attend to, such as claiming his nightly glass of sherry.

She gathered that the League wanted the county conservation district to step up their desultory caretaking of Bodie Woods – benign neglect punctuated by rashes of "controlled burns" – and, with the permission of the Rutledge City Council, do a full-fledged restoration. Apparently the district had agreed, and sympathetic city council members promised to push the plan. Bakeoven seemed optimistic.

"We'll have the original oak savannah back, Althea. It's being strangled. We're going to save the oaks and hickories for future generations." Without having looked away from traffic, he added, "What's wrong?"

Grateful if somewhat alarmed that he'd sensed her distress, and unable for once to think of any reason to keep it to herself, she felt the tears rising again.

"The people who bought my house are about to rip out most of the trees...it seems. I ran into a former neighbor just before the meeting started...The Augsbergers certainly kept their plans to themselves. Butter wouldn't melt in their mouths! 'Oh, we love the house, the yard, perfect for us!' With a few major changes in mind, apparently. Mrs. MacDuff says they're putting a semicircular driveway on that tiny property. Like running a freeway though a thimble! They're going to have a two-story garage behind the house. There will hardly be room for grass, much less trees. A desert of trendy pavers, with a couple hibiscus in urns, that's what it'll be..." She realized her voice was breaking, but surely he needn't pull over to the curb.

"I'm alright, for goodness sake. It's just that one becomes so attached. Not very skillful, I see that. But..."

Bakeoven had turned off the motor. She cringed, expecting impatience or even hostility. No doubt he saw her as difficult, "emotional," a whiner who didn't face difficulties head-on. Fine! Who needed him, anyway, with his horrible little white mustache? How dare he pull over as though she were a naughty child! Not everyone could be as imperturbable as Marian.

Absurdly, quaintly, he wiped his face with one of his impeccable hankies. Poor old man; she was bad for his blood pressure. Here was the opaque gaze again.

"I stopped to talk to the new owners this morning, Althea. I happened to drive by and couldn't miss the orange X's on the trees." She flinched.

"They were out in the yard talking to the hardscaper. I pretended I was shopping for pavers. It's five trees. All coming down tomorrow."

Now she was really crying. He handed her his hanky, which she took reluctantly for lack of anything else to stem her running nose.

"I tried to mend the mischief a bit, Althea. Told them I had a friend who'd like the trees if they'd spare us a couple of days to make arrangements. No interest. Fellow wanted his crew out there tomorrow morning while it's still cool. This is why I've been pushing for the League to buy a tree spade. They're damned expensive, but some of our members wouldn't miss the money. If we had a tree spade we could respond to emergencies like this at short notice...They are going to plant something, Althea. A Japanese evergreen, I gathered. Weeping, no doubt. They're going to be permeable pavers. Good for the earth. I mean, it could be asphalt, or concrete."

She emitted a choked, gurgly giggle. She'd seen those outlandish, alien trees huddling oddly askew against various McMansions and public buildings. They looked silly, and would look doubly so on Euclid Street.

"I appreciate your efforts, Bake." It was the first time she'd attempted his nickname. Her words sounded queerly wooden and disembodied. How thoroughly extraneous she was! How unessential to anyone's happiness! Polite concern was the most she could ever expect from anyone now that Casper was gone, and she'd be lucky to have even that. Ashamed of imposing, she traded one misery for another.

"Useless to be so grieved about it. I'm glad things are working out for Bodie, though."

When they pulled into Lilybanks' drive she extricated herself from the truck immediately, clumsy but resolute.

"Thanks for everything." She knew it sounded dutiful and hollow. He nodded, raising two fingers from the steering wheel, looking mildly sympathetic but glad enough to leave.

*   *   *

When obsessive peeks at Casper's watch finally turned up midnight, Althea silenced Linnet with a forbidden nighttime bowl of crunchies and stole downstairs. She had a tiny flashlight, a wad of tissues and her driver's license in case she was arrested.

A distant glow from beyond the scullery suggested Beebe might be perfecting some tricky confection; Marian and Lucy were probably in bed. Running into Tad would be a first; he seemed to have a horror of being underfoot, plus his approach was invariably signaled by mild tremors along Lilybanks' frame. No sign of Ditey. She paused to double-knot her sneakers on the outside stairs. Maybe her housemates would imagine a dalliance with Bakeoven if her absence were noticed.

The misshapen, waning moon helped illuminate the shortest route to Euclid Street. Nearly all of Rutledge's crime occurred downtown or in the seedier student quarters; Althea's only fear was of tripping.

When she reached the house the night disguised it; it seemed neither her home nor the Augsbergers', but some momentary stage set. Relieved to feel somewhat alienated, she reminded herself of her mission. No time to commune with this dissembling building.

A sleek car had been parked at the top of the driveway. The only light came from a yellow bulb on the side porch; neighbors' lights were similarly sparse. Al wedged her sneaker between pickets, hoisted a leg over and found her footing on the inner horizontal rail just above the lawn. She relaxed as much as possible, surrendering a vivid fantasy featuring tinkling dog tags, panting, and a savage, delighted growl. The shrill vibrato of a mosquito hovered over her shoulder, then vanished.

Using her flashlight as little as feasible and continuously buoyed by the absence of a dog, Al fumbled into the backyard. She avoided smashing into a wrought iron table and chairs topped by an umbrella awning ("Pretentious! Clownish! Let go of judgments!") where her little clothesline used to be; skirted the car widely lest some sensor erupt; doubled back briefly to confirm an impression that her ladybells no longer fringed the front path.

Feeling slightly numb and all the better for it, Al sought out the trees along the Bishops' property line in the spirit of a guest in a receiving line. She'd promised herself she'd send them off – no need for drama. Trespassing in the middle of the night seemed a sufficient mark of her esteem. Already she longed to get back to Linnet, her pillow and the calamine lotion in the Lilybanks bathroom.

Day-Glo paint defaced the trunks of the condemned, no longer safely anonymous even in the dark. Already they'd ceased to be the friendly individuals she'd known; impossible to pretend they were anything but doomed.

Althea moved from one to the next, grateful for time and privacy. The lanky cherry – somehow still a comparative teenager – the venerable walnut, two memorably lovely ash trees, one of whose sheaves of tear-shaped seeds she pocketed, and the roly-poly blue spruce planted on a wedding anniversary: each received an embrace or caress.

"I'll miss you. I'm sorry you're going so soon. I know you forgive, and I'm trying to forgive. Thank you so much for everything you've given me. This is just a small moment, isn't it, in our eternity. I'm so glad to have shared this place and time with you. Go with God...with the spirit of the universe. I'll be going soon enough myself; some of our old friends are gone before us; we're here for just a short while. How patient and helpful you've been, benevolent presences. How I've appreciated you; so have the birds and creatures and the wind. Apparently our true essence can never be destroyed. I believe that; I can feel your energy will continue. We're always together, somehow. Thank you, loves."

She moved from tree to tree, trying to communicate the same incantation, weeping, hugging, stumbling, laughing. If mosquitoes nibbled she hardly noticed, sitting at the foot of each tree to watch stars dance among its branches or turreted crown one last time.

Drained of grief, happy to have managed her clandestine meeting, Al could scarcely believe the trees would vanish. Nor could she fully grasp her own demise though it was closer than ever, and Casper had demonstrated its reality.

She and the trees shared a peaceful, flourishing stillness that seemed more fundamental than tomorrow's temporary dramas. She wanted to believe – in fact, did believe – that the trees were glad of her loving visit, though how that could be was a mystery. If the notion was just a fairytale then her very essence and soul were mistaken.

Preternaturally attentive, managing the pickets as though they were allies instead of "stuff" to be manipulated, Al reached the sidewalk. She threw her friends a jaunty wave that felt as much a cryptic greeting as a farewell.

Walking "home," which seemed to be a fluid place, she realized she'd communicated with the trees and with something else, both beyond and inherent in them and herself. Her sentimental, inadequate words had encountered a reality more reassuring and profound than the language that helped to obscure it.

She let herself in the front door of Lilybanks, accompanied by serene presence. Aphrodite's barbaric, unfathomable features faced her beneath the chandelier's soft halo. Althea's skin crept; she'd never really seen the dog before. Aphrodite stared past her, rapt with some foreign wisdom.

"She's in one of her trances. A fugue state, Bubo calls it."

Too taken with the dog to be startled, Al hesitated to move or raise her voice.

"What is it? She looks so different!"

"We're not sure. I think she just forgets to flip back to her 'people' channel sometimes, and we can eavesdrop on her parallel universe." Beebe held a candlestick. Al often worried Beebe would burn the house down around them, though with the best of intentions.

Aphrodite heaved a great sigh, as though some apparition had departed, and waddled toward her basket.

"You're out late. Stargazing? If you're not sleepy come keep me company a bit. I've got milk and rusks."

Leave it to Beebe: "rusks" were something a forlorn Dickensian child might pull from the depths of a pocket. Unsure whether she wanted to share her encounter with the trees, Al reckoned Beebe's otherworldly plane wouldn't jar her own pensive mood. Moreover, the dog's odd state appeared talismanic. The night seemed thin, penetrable and impish, prone to glimpses of revelation.

"Alright. For a little while."

Al followed her upstairs, feeling surprisingly vigorous. Beebe's nightgown wafted up ahead of her, less spectral and antique than usual. This one smelled like laundry detergent rather than withered roses in attics.

Her door stood open; the coveted van Erp lamp lit a squat pitcher and napkin-topped basket on a bed tray. Binoculars spilled from a battered case on a corner of the bed. From the threshold Althea saw Beebe's lattice window open, and wondered if some nightjar or saw-whet owl might join them. Lilybanks had been home to a wood stork; surely a winged midnight picnic might still be attempted.

"Binoculars?"

"From Mr. Smeltzer, my friend the groundskeeper at Moraine Woods; he got a new pair. We're going to look for otters together. Have a seat, and then you can hold the milk while I get aboard." Beebe nodded at the far end of her bed closest to the window. The pitcher felt agreeably frigid; a peek beneath the warm cloth revealed crusty browned trapezoids dripping butter.

Beebe poured milk into the sole mug and thrust it at Althea, then rummaged for a cup in her bedside drawer.

"Have the saucer. I'll use my lap. I'll empty my nightie out the window. Micah says what's left of the unconsecrated bread gets sprinkled on the church lawn for the birds. I think that's just right, don't you?"

Reluctant to respond from her pleasant, shadowy mess of buttered fingers and milk mustache, Althea nodded.

"What about the thing the priest says at the heart of the liturgy...I heard it when we visited with Micah – he raises the chalice before communion and says 'Thine own of Thine own we offer unto Thee, on behalf of all and for all.' Everything...all creatures, all Creation. Stones!" Beebe's eyes shone.

"Yes, I love that too. But some stingy smarty-pants always has to say it's open to various scholarly interpretations."

"Micah says the saint who wrote the liturgy, John... Chrysanthemum?...the one with the beautiful name, meant it like it sounds to you and me."

"Chrysostom." In spite of her reservations about Micah, he knew what he was talking about. Al smiled...and then frowned.

"I forgot to tell you – we had a hummingbird in the tiger lilies this afternoon! I wish you could have seen – what's wrong?"

"Oh no. Tutu. They're going to cut down a bunch of trees in my old yard. Who knows what they'll do next. Our cat, Tutu, is buried in a corner of the backyard. He's not safe. *Nothing's* safe." Her face crumpled; she hid it with both hands, then furled into a tight knot against the bedstead and sobbed.

Beebe lurched over on her knees and grabbed Althea around the shoulders, pulling her towards herself.

"There, there. There, there..." Althea felt her head petted, inhaled the nightgown's laundered scent, noticed how strong Beebe's arms were. She felt the old-fashioned nursery phrase more than adequate.

"Did you forget? 'Nothing real can be threatened.'"[14]

Al nodded, but cried harder.

"*That's* where you were. Oh, dear. How was it?"

Al sat up, sniveling and rubbing her eyes, and saw Beebe pulling the lamp chains for her sake.

"It was WONDERFUL," she laughed, hiccuping triumphantly. "A conversation beyond words. They know I love them and I'll miss them but that it's ultimately inconsequential – somehow we can't be separated and in spite of chain saws and chippers and funeral homes everything's alright. Not lost. And all forgiven. Impossible to put in words, Beebe, isn't it? Like trying to walk with two left shoes." She laughed delightedly, and so did Beebe.

"Listen Althea. Tad and I will go get Tutu this morning. We can put him in the garden, if you like."

"Good God, Beebe. I don't know if he's even...transportable. I mean, it doesn't bear thinking on. Poor Tad. And how would you persuade the Augsbergers?"

"It'll be fine, you'll see. Stop resisting what you want! The Augsbergers will be sweet about it, and we'll offer to plant the bare spot with something from Lilybanks. Tad will be very matter-of-fact about the whole thing. He'll get the job done. Watkins is going to be here all day. He owes Tad a couple of favors. He can give us a ride back and forth. So relax."

Althea squeezed Beebe's hand, flooded with relief and exhausted now.

"Thank you so much. And thank you from Casper, too. He and Tutu adored each other. When my husband had to travel he'd send Tutu his own postcard, and another for me. I have to go to bed this second, Beebe." She struggled off the bed, inhaled deeply at the open window and shuffled out.

Beebe plumped her pillow, straightened the sheets and reflected that she'd have to rearrange Lionel's visit. Now that Tad's morning job as a substitute library page was over they needed a new arrangement anyway. His presence seemed to provoke Lionel's prankishness. Yesterday had been rather trying.

At the window a breeze scented with pine and lilies ruffled and ebbed. Beyond the garden raccoons' queer trills punctuated the cicadas' chorus. No longer Beebe Morrissey but alive awareness at rest in the night, she savored the stars.

Diplomacy

Scholar and Twinkle watched wide-eyed through chicken wire as an ample feline posterior ballooned over the edge of the cellar sink. A tail the color of pale moths swayed eerily above it. This was all the kittens could see as Applesauce stood on his head to catch a few tantalizing drops from the leaking spigot.

Bezique turned his head away in distaste, having caught his colleague's memorably ripe scent. That came of squalid grooming habits. "Aim it somewhere else, will you?" he'd been about to call, but remembered that kittens must respect their elders – even the tiresome ones.

"Applesauce! Are you down there? Come up at once! Appul-appulappulapple!" Mrs. Bunting had devised highly distinguishable calls for each of her cats. Applesauce lunged from the sink, knowing that yodel promised praise and a spoonful of cream or a sprig of window box catnip. Scholar shrank against Twinkle as the pale, roly-poly apparition thundered upstairs.

"Who was that, Bah-Seek?"

"I'm sure he'd want you to call him Uncle Applesauce. One of the other two cats who live here. Ah, here comes the other." White paws minced down the stairs. "Best behavior now – lift up your chins for Auntie Snowy," he whispered.

Not quite as alarming as the upside down moth-cat, but formidably puffy, Snowy inspected the homesick boys.

"What handsome fellows, Bezique! No wonder Mrs. B. thought they deserved a special room of their own. How proud your charming mother must be of you both!" Bezique's tail twitched. Snowy was laying it on a trifle thickly, but kindly. She looked giddy, almost sparkling.

"See what I've managed to bring you gentlemen – a catnip leaf. Your first?" Twinkle politely tweaked the shriveled morsel with his paw, releasing an irresistible odor.

"Now do share. No gulping! It will last longer if you rub your cheeks on it."

In a moment both kittens were on their backs, wrestling with each other and pungent bits of catnip.

"Over here, Bezique." Snowy slinked behind her mistress's washboard, out of the kittens' earshot. "Your friend in the beret gave me a message through the window. You're to meet him in his yard as soon as possible. Gypsy insisted on staying with Leo and the kittens overnight. She thinks she can talk him 'round. Oh, and she said to tell you she'll see you soon. He asked me to keep the little ones here company in your absence, and of course I was happy to oblige. Bezique? Be careful." Alternately eager and anxious, Snowy seemed to have the catnip jitters herself.

"Beret? That was Beanie. If you're down here babysitting how can you handle messages?"

"We'll have to enlist Applesauce. Or Delilah. I understand Mr. Beanie comes from a musical and artistic background."

"What!" Bezique's ears oscillated, trying to keep up with all this nonsense. Couldn't females stick to one subject? "Some accomplices! At least Delilah likes me. But I wouldn't bet on her remembering any message that doesn't have the word 'supper' in it."

"I'm quite capable of managing everyone. You mind your own tail and whiskers. If anything happens to you Miss Marjorie will cry her eyes out."

Bezique licked her forehead. "I'm going now. Tell the kittens I know I can depend on them to stay here till I return. Thanks, Snowy." He loped up the cellar stairs. Snowy turned to see Twinkle and Scholar staring into space in a happy, herb-induced stupor.

Bezique had only to scratch at the door to be let out by his mistress. He tore through Beanie's garden to find his friend had company. Three unfamiliar cats interrupted a conference to look him over. Beanie came forward and touched noses with his friend.

"Good timing, Zeke. I've assembled the cream of the neighborhood to help us bring Gypsy and the kittens home. I left them behind the first rise beyond the flats. Leo will guard them with his life."

"After considering several plans of action we've settled on one best suited to Leo's nature." Beanie looked a little nervous.

"He's just not sure we can talk you into it." A lovely old green-eyed tiger cat, clearly a belle in her day, emerged from the shadows.

"I hear Gypsy's your sweetheart. Congratulations. Couldn't do better. To hear Mr. Beanie tell it, she's a lucky girl. From the looks of you I can't disagree. So listen to the counsel of your elders, not your own young blood, and we'll get her and the little ones back in one piece."

"I'm in favor of striking swiftly, of course. How good of you all to come to our aid. Many thanks for gathering allies, Beanie." Bezique turned to the other cats, hoping to convey respect for the fuzzy old matriarch while appealing to the more useful young Toms. The grey fellow stopped grooming now, perking up.

"Happy to do it," bumbled Beanie, taken aback by Zeke's formality. "We want to strike swiftly too, Zeke. But it's a little more, ah, complex than that." Beanie frowned, then lightened with a happy thought. "We've got a secret weapon."

Bezique gave a nicker of impatience. "What's going on, Beanie?" He examined the other cats; the young grey was grooming feverishly; Madame Fuzzpot gleamed; the white and brown fellow seemed eager.

"His name's Star, but those of us who knew him as a kitten call him Gompy," purred the smug tiger cat over Beanie's shoulder.

"Star? Gompy?"

"He has a nice white star on his chest. Just never you mind about the Gompy, young man."

The grey cat looked up. "I've heard Gompy means "hero" among the Indians."

"Fiddlesticks," the she-cat snapped.

"I'm sure you agree that diplomacy is preferable to force, Zeke," Beanie continued. "There's only one cat in the apple hill territory who could summon Leo to a parley and be sure the slippery fellow'd show up. He and his humans claim all the land behind their house clear down to the water lily lake. Star wanders like royalty through the rabbit thickets, past the beavers' timber yards and mink dens. The bitterns in the fen recognize him, and the river otters."

"He goes where no other cat dares," supplied the she-cat.

"Beanie's been to Leo's camp himself; we hardly need this hero's fancy scouting."

"You don't understand, Zeke. Star has the gift of kingship, and he reigns peacefully. He's free to come and go in tangled woods and lakeside strongholds. They say foxes look the other way should he cross their path. We have this from the busybody swallows and squirrels, but Star's bearing is the strongest testimony. We cats of the barns and bungalows are lucky to count him as a friend, however remote. He serves his mistress faithfully and seldom has time to linger among us. He lives in the lone house at the top of the ridge. It has a pointy face with flowers up its nose. Its shingles still smell."

"Tell him the rest!" broke in the brown and white cat, wriggling with impatience.

"His mates? They're a curious crew. Florrie's the only one of us who knows them."

They all turned toward the old tigress, who narrowed her eyes. "Star's mistress is something of a handful. Twirls through the garden when the fireflies arrive, frolics through the halls like a mouse on holiday, capers up and down the stairs and out onto the lawn while people tweet and drum and clap. Gets Star to pose while she paints his picture. Very fond of creatures, his lady is. Star has to put up with a sulky pair of peacocks. But he's great friends with her other two favorites. They're a close-knit trio."

"A fluff-brained bitch and a giant cone-headed bird on stilts with a pocked face like the man in the moon!" erupted the wriggler, who looked like someone had dipped him in waist-high cocoa and splashed a bit on his face.

"Thank you, Britches. A lovely motherly collie who rescues baby birds blown from their nests..." The young grey cat made a retching moan. "Got a hairball, Hooligan?...And an elder wood stork, very curious in these parts. It lives inside the house. They both wander where they please as part of their mistress's tribe."

"A fine tale, but I don't see how this helps Gypsy," snapped Bezique. The dawn's fading while we're lullabied like squint-eyed kittens. Can you arrange to have this Star fellow meet us in the first oak grove beyond the flatlands?"

Mute with pique, the she-cat would have trampled the young grey's whiskers in her imperious climb to the top stair if he hadn't dived into the snapdragons. She began a manicure, both ears flattened.

"Ah...Zeke? That's not the plan. Florrie's going to take us up to the ridge so we'll be there when Leo arrives. Trust me, he's not going to pass up a summons from Star." Beanie glanced anxiously up at Florrie the she-cat, intent on her claw polishing.

Bezique's tail twitched. "Summons? There's no time for pomp, Beanie. If we don't show up soon Leo may move clear out of the territory with Gypsy and the little ones. It's alright for a farfetched back-up plan, but I want to leave now. Come along, and bring your two friends. I'll beat the tar out of the old derelict while you-all give Gypsy and the kittens a convoy home."

Beanie curled his tail around himself more tightly, staying calm.

"You don't understand yet. Once Leo has an invitation from Star he's not going anywhere but up the ridge, Zeke. He's not had an easy life, but in his own line he's a tremendous success. Leo knows just about everything there is to know about this territory from a cat's point of view. Never going to win any popularity contests, though. Not like Star, who's celebrated, respected, loved even by the meadow mice and, by Leo's standards, coddled. Star's the only creature Leo would meet as an equal, the only one so worth impressing he'd risk losing this latest game of wits with us. I chewed this over all night, Zeke. It's our best shot. Otherwise someone loses an eye or an ear and we only get one kitten back. Or worse, Zeke, because Gypsy wouldn't tolerate that."

Crumbling, Bezique mewed softly. "What will she think when we don't show up? By the time you get an invitation to Leo --"

"Oh, I believe he's received it by now," Florrie announced crisply from her stair. "Gompy sent a colleague off to the flat-lands while the whippoorwills were still flitting. He liked my suggestion that she carry a gift basket of tidbits. Crayfish in minted cream sauce was mentioned."

Camouflaged
[1912]

She's been sitting here on the church steps since the landlord's boy nearly cudgeled her as she slept, tossing firewood into a slum yard while the last stars winked. Sitting while Matins rang out, watching a whiskery vole chew the last of her potato peels, salted by the frost. Sitting through footfall, swish of skirts, hinge rasp. Sitting while the sun shrinks the damp stains on the concrete and traces the lacy railing's shadow onto the steps. The lady with dimples in both cheeks has pressed a loaf into her lap; the pigeons will feast. Naked creeper vines rattle against the wall in the wind that pinches her fingers with a twinkly bite; she has stars beneath her skin. The vole squeezes back to its chamber. She looks up to see her keen, quick Olive balking and dawdling toward her like a horse with a crooked bit. It's a gentleman making her shy away like that. His hat's as wide as a collection plate. They make it to the corner by the grace of God, like leaves tumbling in a gust.

"You needn't have been so fey, Miss Cook. I know the place quite well. Sullivan's Russian church." She ignored him, turning in at the open gate. A beggar had parked herself on the threshold, probably one of the sympathetic older priest's protégés. Father...Theophan?

"Caterina." Olive rushed up the steps, sat next to the tramp, took her in her arms tenderly. Crumrind fumbled with his hat. This was what came of meddling.

"Caterina, this is John. He insisted on squiring me about this morning. John, my friend Caterina."

The woman leaned on Olive to stand, offering Crumrind a grin with several rotten teeth. A cat scooted out from under her skirts like upturned vermin; he recognized the odor of unwashed streetcar passengers.

"A great pleasure to meet you, Caterina. Miss Cook's – Olive's – friends are among the elect." The hand that acknowledged his felt strong; the grey eyes seemed to appraise and forgive simultaneously. She was almost certainly laughing at him from her superior stair; somehow he felt it was the suppressed mirth of refinement encountering savagery. Intrigued, even curiously smitten, Crumrind suffered a risibly sharp sense of exclusion when Olive's pantomime urged him into the building. Inside, he moped beneath the star-spangled dome until his admiration for the place quelled his annoyance.

Only after lounging cross-legged in a cramped balcony seat above the silent nave for nearly an hour was he fetched. Miss Cook's increasingly thunderous throat clearings and gesticulations from below managed to scatter his meditation on the six-winged seraphim hovering in the spandrels of Sullivan's arches. Crumrind jumped up and banged his head on the balcony ceiling just as he had the last time he'd visited. Miss Cook waited by the candle desk, observing him with more favor than usual. She started for the door, clearly unwilling to violate the silence again. He pushed it open to find hail bouncing on the concrete, and blocked her advance.

"I hope you'll let me invite you to lunch? We can get a cab on Division Street. I see neither of us has an umbrella – optimists, weren't we – so if you'll wait inside I'll – "

"You're very kind. I'll walk down to the corner with you. No doubt we're going in opposite directions. I've more errands, Professor."

"I'll not release you as meekly as I did your Caterina – quite reluctantly, by the way, she interests me. And you'd better call me John, now that she does."

An impressive head, in spite of the dripping nose, yet she could imagine him preening discontentedly before his mirror.

"I'm afraid Mrs. Morrissey has instructed you to improve my day off. John."

"Calla surrounds herself with rare specimens whom I might well overlook; I'm more inclined to notice the botanical variety. So I plunder her spoils, being too stiff and bookish to sniff them out on my own. Calla merely told me we'd be on the same train this morning, that you're irreplaceable, and that I mustn't trip you."

Pleased, and aware that his need was somehow the greater, Olive managed to look grave.

"I don't hold still long enough to make a good specimen. So I'll benefit from my rarity and offer to be a friend."

His jaw dropped ever so slightly; pink stained the rather long face's dainty cheeks and a shy smile surfaced. She never failed to marvel at this transparency on the part of more than a few men of consequence. Perhaps they could afford it, like everything else – at least around her.

"Then you'll join me, so I can know my friend better."

"Yes, if you'll let me pay my way. Having dishonored your dog and vexed your valet I'm in no position to take on more debt."

"Agreed, if you let me choose the restaurant."

"Agreed, if you don't require the Palmer House."

"No, no, nothing so mundane for the Pratts' pastry chef. We'll find something more alarming." How tall she was; he was used to looking down at women. Not pretty, but very much alive in a stealthy sort of way. "Votes For Women," no doubt.

Warmed by his dry smile of complicity, she took his arm in good faith. As they bent their heads against the March wind Olive imagined what it might be to let oneself cling. Under no illusions as to her fate, she recognized one of her lambs.

When they reached the thoroughfare he gave up and put his great cartwheel of a hat beneath an arm, to her relief. The sun was already shining again. Her black serge coat was of the plainest cut; he'd not notice someone might think she'd sold herself to him.

"I don't recall seeing you at the Pratt home, though I all but lived there for months." He stepped down from the curb to squint west-wards. Crumrind made it a rule not to bandy clients' names about in cabs or clubs.

"I've the gift of invisibility, an advantage in my station."

"I shouldn't have thought so. Mrs. Pratt noticed you. Astor Street's a plum."

"The housekeeper noticed me. The Pratts' Italian wanted to go into business for himself, and she persuaded him to train me as his replacement. I never served, but she had me out occasionally to supervise grand presentations. So I had a glimpse of you, the despot who made the lights flicker and filled our lungs with plaster dust. I had the honor of lighting the old gentleman's birthday candles." Mrs. Pratt had given her a collar of Venetian lace for the occasion; she kept it pressed beneath the Book of Common Prayer in her Moss Street room.

Happy to change the subject, he hailed a cab too distant to make the gesture practical. They waited in silence.

"Clark and Harrison."

He looked as out of place as she did at their destination, a messy street full of Chinamen, indecipherable signs and unpromising smells. The first store window contained a crate overflowing with pulsing black frogs.

He stopped at the very next storefront, urging her ahead of him through a sticky door painted a dingy, peeling red and up a dim staircase as narrow as any to an underservant's attic. Olive made herself climb confidently; women went first only in calamities and doorways.

There was no landing between the top step and a heavy portière that nearly grazed her nose. Hesitating just a moment and receiving no instructions from Crumrind, she pulled it open.

A modest dining room lit only by windows onto the street met her eyes, its sole occupant a gaunt cat lounging brazenly on a tablecloth.

"Good afternoon, Madame," Crumrind's voice rang out.

A portly, dignified little woman in a high-necked robe without a waist appeared from behind a screen, nodded and led them to a table beside the windows. As she vanished behind a further screen with their coats Olive's choked laughter erupted. Crumrind's eyebrows rose.

"I thought you were addressing the cat."

"I was."

Helpless now, Olive sagged back in her chair, then kicked his ankle in warning and bent toward the window, having seen Madame already returning with a tray.

Perplexed, Crumrind nearly sent the tray flying as it materialized over his shoulder.

"Thank you, thank you." The cat jumped down and followed her mistress out.

"Don't you look at me like that, I was merely trying to tell you she was coming back. You must explain all these mysteries. The only thing I recognize is rice."

He cleared his throat.

"You don't know either, do you."

Crumrind started to protest, then shrugged and pulled at his cuffs.

"Of course not. She doesn't speak a word of English, except for 'tea' and 'bar-gick,' whatever that may be. Calla tells me you've taken to her vegetable regime wholeheartedly. I think these rubbery bits are fish; the rest is safe, I believe. Dip the little pillows into the relish. These jellied slices taste wonderfully like flowers. Not afraid you'll be dead by midnight, are you? I've eaten all this several times with no ill effect... The entrée's going to be a sort of lacquered rice with unidentifiable vegetables mixed in – mostly roots and stems – it may arrive in three minutes or thirty...Those are chopsticks. You'll get the hang of them. I'll demonstrate while you tell me about Caterina."

"They *are* like flowers. But sticky. These people don't use napkins?"

"She'll bring something better. Hot towels. How did you come to befriend Caterina?"

"Is there nothing to drink? Surely some water..."

"I wouldn't. There'll be Chinese tea. We're not on Astor Street, Olive."

She bridled. "You needn't feign polite conversation, *John*. That's a wily smile and you're determined to wring every drop of Caterina from me. I'm not accustomed to entertaining employers with tales of an immigrant's trials. You've sniffed something out that may prove diverting at one of your banking barons' soirées. It will be at my expense. The facts of their servants' private lives discomfit the rich. Kindly interest is apt to shrivel into qualms. A gaudy, well-employed butterfly flitting from his privileged students to one smart household after the next needn't concern himself."

She'd gone too far, as usual. But she'd buy her own lunch.

Crumrind offered the mild smile she would come to recognize as the marshalling of everything he'd got.

He pushed his plate away.

"You disappoint me, Miss Cook. In my butterfly-brained way I'd hoped you might be a camouflaged kindred spirit. You have intellect, and the diction of a self-taught, enterprising person bent on rising above her mediocre station. So does my favorite shoeshine boy. Yet something about you, some glimmer in your eye (doubtless of my own sowing) suggested an ability to live above or beyond the facile, pigeonholing prejudice you're hiding behind. I thought you might be an artist of life, 'flitting,' as you say, over the heads of convention and dullness on the wings of intuition, 'the meeting of true minds,' even genius. Such are the perils of my high-flown imagination...and my solitude. Do you suppose the mathematics of class, gender, and money govern the universe? I hear that they govern *your* world; you're welcome to them. You seem to have your figures well in hand."

Having met her eyes initially, he began gazing out the window and Olive felt he was talking to himself by the end of the harangue. Her initial impression of the man returned irresistibly.

She reached across the jumble of queer food for his lively hand, strong and elegant. The jade ring had a story she wanted to know.

"Then be my friend and help me be that kindred spirit."

Instantly bashful, painfully transparent, he nickered like a wallflower finally asked to dance.

"I'd like to try." He squeezed her fingers, turning pink with delight about the ears and craggy nose.

Her laughter rang through the room, making it congenial and intimate.

"I have no idea what I've just agreed to. But I look forward to it. Here come the roots and stems."

Reassembled as a man of the world he mimed a request for more of the fiery relish while Olive transplanted bowls and cruets for Madame. When she'd vanished again after the briefest of friendly, curious glances at Olive, Crumrind pushed up his starched cuffs and tucked in.

"You'll starve to death poking at the rice that way. Watch."

"I've known Caterina for twelve years, since I came to Chicago. She's Flemish. Left on the steps of a church as an infant."

"Is she simple?"

"Not at all. Well, not really. Perhaps she's an artist of life, unwilling to participate in pigeonholes, John. I feel responsible for her, yet she manages well enough on her own terms. Like an alley cat, really – cruelly abandoned, she's invented a life for herself."

"Pretty poor terms. Those teeth must hurt her. Her skin's like a rind. Sturdy shoes – you provided those?"

"No. Father Theophan, the retired priest attached to the church looks out for her. Won't let finicky parishioners shoo her off the steps, keeps her shod and gloved. She's nearly oblivious to a lot of necessities."

"I know him. Rustic but tremendously refined. He lets me prowl around, study Sullivan's thinking, snoop in the belfry."

"He's good."

"Why do you feel responsible for her?"

"We shared a room. We met filing registration papers with the city. A spittly leech who sniffed around the clerk's office preying on newcomers installed us in a storeroom at the top of an empty office building; it was all we could afford between us. Prison might have been healthier. We had a glass-paned roof, cracked and leaking. No beds, just a low table. It got us off the street behind a locked door; we were thankful for that. Caterina had worked in a chemical laboratory for university-trained scientists in Ghent. Someone got her pregnant. Imagine! She was sixteen or so, gangly, boyish, ignorant about all that and no friends to warn her – and they bundled her off to the New World lest someone at the college of sciences get wind of it and cut off their stipend. She'd lost the baby before I met her; wouldn't talk coherently about it…"

"She has the look of a constitutional degenerate, Olive." Crumrind wiped his mouth with a moist towel; it smelled like the jasmine in the Pratts' conservatory.

"No!" The urgency intrigued him. "I'm sure she has at least average intelligence. Or had…It's something else…She's some kind of experiment brought into the wrong world. Her strengths are…unrecognizable. I think by the time she'd gotten to Chicago she'd stopped trying to adapt. We were so young. I think I was the last person she spoke to, John. She's mute now. She had some English but I think she may have let go of it. It's like talking to an animal. You know, the way you sense they know a lot of things you don't, and may be superior in some way, but words are useless…She's not in a stupor, you know. I think she's highly observant but she takes no interest in normal concerns. She's drifted further and further out over the years since our ways parted. Always happy to see me but I had a terrible time keeping track of her until she washed up at the Russian church. You must think she's a brutalized guttersnipe, no more."

"And you think?" She'd stopped battling with the meal; he felt continuing to eat would be like belching at a funeral.

Her eyes filled with tears, but not for Caterina.

"I think she's thriving, flourishing in a world beyond ours. Or rather, the same world, unobscured by personal cares…I do believe in heaven..." She felt the tears slide down her cheek, realized he was being put to a test too soon.

Crumrind cleared his throat, tried to summon the stance of solicitous mentor that came easily with gifted students. Instead, a lifetime of longing scalded his throat and eyelids.

He turned to gaze out the window again, but not before she'd seen his face.

"Then she wanders in the Garden, happily afflicted by felicity... How shall we follow her?"

Madame padded back in with teacups on a tray. They sipped in thoughtful silence, like lovers, or like soldiers summoned to the front.

8

Extra Early

Beebe sighed and tossed all through the night, wrestling with joy. At dawn she tiptoed downstairs, managing not to waken Ditey.

She paused in the hall to watch dust motes revolve in sunlight slanting through the sitting room doorway. Disrupting their tiny orbits, she found the new day stenciling leaves and tendrils from the backyard across the sitting room's oak-paneled walls. The shadowy foliage trembled, faded, reappeared and crept along the oriental rug. Across the room softer light from the street filtered in through the dining room.

A cavern-like cool prevailed here at this hour even in July. Surrendering turmoil to a stronghold of stillness, Beebe let herself become one with its space, its denizens, its aliveness, a transcendental tourist.

As she moves, scent stirs from linens washed in lavender water, from orange oil in furniture joints, from pots of basil and thyme plundered by cooks. Century-old glass warps the view of the backyard, where jubilant spires of prairie dock and mullein rise against the garden wall above a tangle of yarrow, black-eyed Susans and flourishing weeds. A Japanese beetle – a stowaway from a jar of roses – looks like a mislaid jewel on the windowsill. Matte glazes on clusters of yellow and blue-green pottery gleam dully against their foil of dark wood. Fretty dill and late tulips billow from a vase on a wooden pedestal.

The scrolled lights perched above landscapes in tarnished frames bear a thin coat of dust. Below these stands a cabinet with hammered pulls and strap hinges. A trio of birds roosts on its shelf. Smirking, hunchbacked, beetlebrowed, they huddle together, beak to massively nostrilled beak. A few chipped appendages have been neatly glued.

The glass lampshade on a nearby table shelters a harvestman, suspended in its rude net. Below the lamp tendrils of creeping Charlie wave scalloped, heart-shaped leaves amid a bouquet of Queen Anne's lace in a squat vase. A pioneering filament descends from the harvestman's net into the flowers, whose tiny dead petals powder the tabletop.

Limp pillows of pale linen with faded embroidery slump along the window seat and backs of chairs. The baggy canvas cushion of the Morris chair nearest the windows bears a hollow imprint and cat fur.

A straight-backed chair stands against the folded wing of French doors into the dining room. It has been pulled forward, away from the cockeyed oval doorknob, so its back legs have turned up the edge of the rug. An open package labeled *MAPLE NUT GOODIES* sags against a front leg. The chair's dark polish smells of citrus. Where the sun lies brightest the red, ochre and blue patterns on the rug smell faintly acrid, like distant burning toast.

Drifts of shriveled plant fragments, dust and fur laced with an occasional thread or ladybug carapace have sifted down into corners and behind furniture. Sickle-shaped cat claw sheathes, particles of cookie and spirals of hair have secreted themselves among the rug fibers and cushions. Pollen sprinkles the floor beneath a plant stand crowned with sunflowers in a sturdy turquoise vase. A soft silver stubble covers their thick, ribbed stems; where they meet the water a slimy film clings to them, reeking faintly below the ripe odor of sunflower.

A small table with mortise and tenon joints has been pushed away from the windows, leaving faint grooves in the rug. Its philodendron strains toothed leaves toward the light. A chunk of milky quartz lies nestled in the pot for ballast. Two young, toothless leaves brush the back of the neighboring sepia photograph. Here a handsome woman in a shapeless, ankle-length coat and a shorter, broader man in suit and tie stand in front of the garden wall beyond the windows, smiling into the camera. A pipe protrudes from the side of his smile; a dog parks at her feet. To their left a large weathervane looms beyond the wall. Above its compass points perch three silhouettes – a collie, a cat, and a stilt-legged bird. Someone has written "Calla Morrissey and Samuel Yellin, 1935" on the photo's margin.

Beebe stands on the bank of seats to lower a window. A breeze from the garden pushes through the gap, sending kaleidoscopic patterns of light flitting across the interior. They spangle panels, planks and rungs made from oaks that lived on nearby savannah and once dappled carpets of bluestem and switch grass.

Enticed, she tugs the door in the corner open and hovers on the threshold. A cricket carols from the shade. Paradise continues to unfurl wherever her attention wanders. She has no need to be "in love" with someone in addition to all this peace and plenty. An embarrassment of riches seems to be her lot.

*   *   *

Lucy hadn't slept well either. Damp strings of hair had glued themselves to her flushed cheeks furrowed by flailed pillows and wadded sheets. She sat up to find Skippy, exhausted by her agitation, sprawled across the bottom of the bed, asleep after dawn for once.

As though in a dream she slid out of bed, opened the French doors between her bedroom and the adjoining nursery and tiptoed over to Tad. He slept on his stomach, his head on an angled arm, breathing heavily. She plopped onto the clashing concentric circles of a flea market rug, dazed.

Several shelves of battered Morrissey Teddy bears, one-eyed sock monkeys and yellowing plush dogs rose above Tad. Maxfield Parrish prints in glowing cobalt and amber hung from the dado moldings. A pyramid of scuffed vintage alphabet blocks printed with animals sat on a cabinet, "O is for OSTRICH" on top. A pair of Tad's socks lay crumpled beside the sleeping bag on an air mattress that he insisted was comfortable.

His awkward presence in the hall-side half of her rooms was to have been a temporary solution till school ended. By the time word arrived that his father had to be overseas all summer the stopgap had become routine. Tad's and Lucy's schedules seldom clashed; both were conscientious in a carefree way; Lucy had begun spending three nights a week at Micah's. Marian's scrupulous inquiries at sisterhood meetings never materialized. Lucy's insistence that things were fine as they were – no need to put up a tent for Tad in the ballroom end of Millefleurs, or shoehorn him into The Cygnet's Nest – met with no resistance. Beebe, who seemed increasingly dazzled by some inner vision, appeared to take little interest in where Tad camped.

Beebe's indifference had struck Lucy as noteworthy, but she left it unaddressed. She and Beebe had drifted imperceptibly, amicably apart this summer, though outwardly affectionate.

For weeks Lucy's head had felt stuffed with cotton candy; she was unable to keep a grip on anything much. Attending to her breath seemed futile; she felt tone-deaf in eurythmy class; the "kinder" had stopped rushing to sit by her at lunch as though they sensed her absence. So had Althea.

Micah tried to be supportive, insisting on St. John's wort drops and restorative naps (which he supervised while poring over the homeopathy pamphlets and tomes on theology and Renaissance madrigals he'd abandoned during what he now rather clinically referred to as their "courtship").

Marian made kindly attempts at reassurance, apparently suspecting cold feet about "commitment;" she'd stopped talking about which kind of champagne glass to rent for the reception and white satin nuptial collars for Skippy and Ditey.

Lucy sucked on a strand of her hair, rocking back and forth on the rug. Its tufts of raffia scratched at her through her p.j. shorts. She watched herself rise, cross the floor and kneel by Tad. His white tee-shirt was spotless. His short dark hair had been mashed by his pillow and a thin line of drool leaked from the corner of his open mouth. He looked guileless to the point of imbecility. She laid the back of her hand against his cheek and pulled it away, disturbed by the roughness.

His eyes opened.

"Tad!" she stage-whispered. "Sorry. I've been trying to wake you for five minutes!" The words seemed to form without her volition. "I'm afraid I need your help with a carpentry project over in the Nest...I've got an important customer coming extra early for a fitting and the three-way mirror's come unhinged. Do you think you could fix it up, at least temporarily? Watkins won't be here in time. I hate to ask you..."

He rubbed his eyes, glanced at her, looked away.

"Sure, sure. No problem. Right now?"

"She's due at eight. Can you meet me over there in fifteen minutes?"

He groped for his watch. "Yeah, sure."

"I suppose it's silly, but a three-way mirror looks more professional."

"Right. No problem. Fifteen minutes." He looked like he was coming up for air at the pool.

*　　*　　*

While supervising Ditey's early morning meander through the garden Beebe noticed someone had left a light on in The Cygnet's Nest. Second time in a week; she'd have to mention it.

After Ditey had played hide-and-seek with a pair of mercurial squirrels, kicked up mulch to celebrate a successful digestive process and squashed some luckless pachysandra, they recessed to the scullery.

"Carrots and rice with mozzarella," Beebe announced. She could hear Ditey's earthenware dish passionately jouncing across the tiles as she stole out the back door.

All summer this had been the hour of Lionel's arrival. She missed the eerie hum of his wheelchair speeding across the cobblestones. Lionel had nodded solemnly when she'd explained that the change in Tad's schedule made further matutinal trysts tactless at best. His dark eyes glowed like garnets when he was deeply moved. (Tad had rather abruptly referred to Lionel as "goggle-eyed" recently; while this was undeniable, his hyperthyroidism merely increased Lionel's distinctive charm in Beebe's eyes.) Magnanimous and uncharacteristically restrained, Lionel had kissed her hand as usual and hummed away to Dr. Leiby's impeccable Peugeot.

Beebe settled in on a mossy garden bench, folding her legs under her. Nodding pink cosmos and stalks of starry sky-blue borage leaned toward her. Lionel had had Bubo take her photograph here last week. Thrilling with affection, Beebe imagined the effect Lionel's forthcoming announcement would have on Bubo as she absorbed all its implications. Bubo was terribly sentimental about "the scepter'd isle" though she didn't like to own it.

The configuration of leaves and light above her shifted almost imperceptibly. After a moment she realized the light in The Cygnet's Nest had gone out. Perhaps Watkins had put the Nest lighting on a timer during one of his fits of security-consciousness.

A glorious green katydid landed on her knee. Beebe gave herself over to admiration of her delicate feelers, rocking horse legs and queerly scrolled brown posterior. In the distance sparrows chirped and flapped at a bird feeder. Her entire body felt effervescent.

* * *

Having put all her eggs in one basket, so to speak, Lucy tried to concentrate on her image in The Cygnet's Nest bathroom mirror. She looked rather hectic, like a circus artiste just shot out of a canon. But her unctuous lip gloss glistened on her pouty bottom lip, and one of the lacy little straps on her 1930's teddy had slipped down her upper arm deliciously. Since Tad seemed to like vintage clothes so much she'd show him the inside story. He'd profit from a little context should Beebe ever get around to dazzling him with her mothbally knickers. She saw her nipples protruding beneath the peachy-pink satin; she was rigid with fear. Her fingertips were icy; she warmed them on her forehead which seemed unusually hot. Hopefully reck-lessness was alluring; she certainly didn't feel amorous...Did she ever? With a muffled pang she imagined Micah at breakfast, praying over his granola and flaxseed capsules. Struggling to see herself as the mysterious Older Woman, Lucy pulled the door open with bravado and stubbed two toes so violently she saw sparks.

Tad, who'd begun fiddling with the unwieldy mirrors without giving much thought to muffled noises in the ladies' room, found her silently writhing on the linoleum.

"Lucy?"

Unable to accept defeat, she summoned a crooked smile and thought fast.

"I'm fine! Really! Fine!" She wiped a tear away with the back of her hand. "I'm just sort of...beside myself. I've broken things off with Micah; we're just not right for each other. But my body still feels so passionate sometimes. Isn't that silly? Just a physical craving for a man. What are you doing here, anyway? Oh that's right – the mirror. You're so sweet, Tad." She smiled up at him and began tracing a pat-tern on his knee as he crouched over her. She was pretty certain both straps had fallen by now, and maybe more.

"What's wrong with your foot?"

The top of her foot was indeed now pale blue and puffy.

"Oh, I just stubbed my toe in this wretched little bathroom. It's stopped hurting," she lied, "but could you help me up?" Lucy realized she'd bungled her way into a brilliant ploy of such shameless simplicity she could never have planned it.

"Sure. Just keep your weight on the heel," Tad managed to get out. With set jaw and moist forehead he took her hands, sensed he was trying to catch a flamingo by the beak, and settled on her elbows, which only brought his face perilously near her modest but highly accessible décolletage. Something like laughter filled the air – hers delirious, his desperate.

"Just let me grab your shoulders and you can pull me up," Lucy instructed in a whisper she hoped sounded breathless. She'd suspected she'd have to get clinical at some point, but this was unpromisingly early on.

Steeling himself for one last trial, Tad felt himself succumbing as her hands wrapped around his neck, only to be stabbed in the eye by a sharply angled wing of hair. He winced, tearing up, but managed to steady himself against the doorjamb as he hoisted Lucy, who clung to him like a koala on a telephone pole.

Assuming that she'd wrapped her legs around him to keep her weight off her foot, Tad edged his way with one eye closed over to a weather-beaten, low-slung brocade couch once rescued from the curb.

"The sofa? Yes! Yes! I'm so ready for this, Tad!"

"Let me get you some pillows," Beebe offered, unable to think of a better way to announce her arrival.

Tribe

Guiltily delighted that family vacations and a case of strep had decimated her "earlies," Althea had stolen into Millefleurs with Linnet as soon as the coast was clear. Curled in a corner of the settle she sipped at the pistachio-colored green tea latte she'd bought the previous evening with just such a retreat in mind. She'd had to steal down to the refrigerator to extricate it from its hiding place behind Beebe's pampered collection of sourdough starters and pastry flour. The *matcha* powder tasted like goldfish food, but seemed to discombobulate her less than coffee.

Linnet had flung herself into the far corner of the settle to groom her hindparts with splayed seraglio nonchalance. Someone had piled Granny Smiths into a ribbed, robin's egg blue bowl on the stand between the chairs.

Just this moment, at least, it seemed impossible to feel bereft, doomed or stale. The mural's whimsical, confiding creatures regarded her charitably from their plaited thicket. Rendered in rich colors that time had mellowed and unified, the enchanted tangle struck her as a refuge in spite of its apparent impenetrability. And beyond the windows a pair of barn swallows careened above the garden. Al felt "filthy rich," as she and Casper used to say when they'd come home from the library laden with books and warm Maven Alley turnovers, or woke on a weekend to a fairytale snowstorm with Tutu and Linnet snuggled against them.

She started to cry, not at all what she'd intended.

This was what came of inattention – reveling smugly in a comfort zone one minute, at the mercy of any random emotion, any chemical reaction the next. She'd been relying more and more heavily on caffeine, neglecting presence, "talking the talk" without walking the walk. No wonder Lucy had been avoiding her. She could probably smell ego-bound thoughts all over Al, like some cheap, rancid perfume – Eau de Me. It had been weeks since Lucy had brought Skippy in to play with Linnet, or caught her eye when one of the "kinder" gravely mispronounced the dog's name, or teased her about tortuous vintage shoes.

In fact, most everyone seemed to be avoiding her. She'd not heard from Bakeoven for over a week; Marian seemed preoccupied or un-reachably egoless. When it came to a tally, none of her several poten-tial friendships since moving into Lilybanks had materialized. Sally Osterman had failed to follow through two or three times on "let's have coffee sometime," a formula of which Althea had grown wary. She'd gone to dinner and a film with Evvie, but Al's exuberant emailed exposition of another film's charms and shortcomings was ignored by Evvie. Al felt she had not quite gotten the hang of the email code of conduct. Apparently enthusiastic, extended responses of a subjective nature were gauche. Then there'd been the friendly fellow customer at the craft store with whom she'd shared a witty appraisal of cross-stitch patterns. They'd realized they shared the same veterinarian. Daisy was an acupuncturist, an offbeat, compassionate profession; Althea had been sure they'd "clicked." Daisy suggested they meet again and they traded phone numbers. She didn't get a call. They ran into each other at the bank and Daisy had been about to walk right past her when Al forced herself to say hello. Daisy had smiled blankly and chirped something about the new bank hours before disappearing.

Everyone was too busy with grandchildren or work or an ample circle of old friends to take an interest in an unprepossessing, finan-cially wobbly widow who seemed a bit intense.

Althea had been content to let a handful of warm friendships fade away after her marriage. One trusted intimate had felt abandoned and preferred other single friends; one had gone back to school – fi-nanced by a husband who earned considerably more than Casper – and moved into a high-status profession with exciting new colleagues. A cocktail party for these that included Al and Casper had been mem-orably uncomfortable. Her oldest friend had moved to Manhattan and found a new confidante in a yoga class whose name was, oddly, Althia. After a couple of years Al's mail from New York began, "Dear Althia," followed by exultant tales of acquiring an art studio in Tribeca, with only the most cursory references to Al's news or interests.

Having married late, she and Casper were used to having single friends. When they'd moved to Rutledge they'd had no luck finding compatible couples; at best only the wives or husbands were a suitable match...

The drawn-out woodwind call of a mourning dove on the garden wall interrupted the familiar script. For thirty seconds life expanded, words receded, beauty and peace flickered like lamps in a mist. She twirled her latte, tweaked the kitty's haunch.

"Who needs shallow socializing, anyway. Right, Linnet? You and Cookie are my best friends. Human friends just dig me deeper into Ego. I suppose I need Here and Now to be my friends, too, don't I?" Linnet yawned with a Zen master's acumen.

"Okay already. No words." Al rose to wander through Millefleurs, tricking herself into wordlessness with Eckhart's advice: "I wonder what I'll think next..."

For a few noteworthy seconds the labyrinthine murals, the view outside, the empty space around her were liberated from self and judgments. They were simply as they were, uncategorized and leveled on the same plane of curious satisfactoriness. Shadows, distant sounds and ignored, mute parts of her own body acquired interest, having virtually not existed a moment before. Trouble evaporated; a feeling of being at home that transcended familiarity or comfort materialized.

Then some impulse of urgency found voice and Althea remembered she was due at an Animal Allies demonstration that afternoon. She succumbed to the flood of details, fantasy and resistance without putting up a fight. After all, she'd "checked in" with presence, hadn't she? Now she needed to organize her schedule, her emotions, her clothes. The caffeine humming along her nerves agreed. She'd be due down in "Kinder on Corrie" soon anyway.

She scooped Linnet up off the settle and crossed the room, making her steps more conscious when their self-important thuds struck her. "Lighten up" was a byword at Lilybanks. A play of light and shade on the floor filled her with wistful regret. Some days she still turned presence into a personal project and then rebelled against the tiresomeness of "trying," "practicing." Like trying to turn on the lights with a pencil sharpener.

Linnet, beginning to scrabble in her arms, allowed her one quick survey of the mural's tiny bubbling spring near the central fireplace. Segmented like jewelry, a damselfly clung to a weedy leaf. Behind it a frog's tongue arched decoratively. Althea knew that if she got down on hands and knees she'd find a tenantless snail shell, half submerged in the puddling, secret trickle.

*　　*　　*

Her daycare morning proved unusually trying. Marian had been stuck upstairs, advising an electrician whose reasonable rates and reputation among Hill District rehabbers absolved his capricious availability. Beebe – technically free as a bird and unpaid, but usually dependable for an hour or two of "cajole and patrol," as Al thought of it – ran out the door gabbling something about an appointment.

Lucy was nowhere to be found either. Althea ended up alone with seven preschoolers, one of whom had chewing gum in her hair. Mayhem was avoided by relaxing the curriculum to the level of babysitting. To distract from the absence of recess she permitted a spree at lunch: fistfuls of carob-covered raisins and yogurt-frosted pretzels disappeared from the kinderbins.

By the one o'clock pick-up sugar-shocked preschoolers either staggered into cars with glazed smiles or rocketed past their au pairs onto the lawn, forgetting newly liberated cell phones and high-tech gadgets under chairs or (to her confusion) in the dog's basket. Little Harry's father was the only client to comment on the dearth of staff; he seemed concerned.

"Lucy's not here today? We had sort of, ah, an appointment. I was going to take her out to lunch to discuss getting my neighbor's kid into Stubblefield...She probably forgot." Looking crestfallen, he remembered to add that it was "no big deal."

Althea escorted them through the back door with some annoyance. Harry was a manly little sugarplum; his daddy was clearly well remunerated for his suit-and-tie profession (something dull she couldn't recall), gentle and sensitive in an acceptable, all-American way, handsome but not intimidating – and quite married. Couldn't Lucy attract anyone suitable? In spite of Marian's approval Al continued to think Micah much too unbending, stingy and cerebral for Lucy. She suspected Lucy could only park in front of a fire hydrant, lapse into one of her stuttering, tic-ridden spells or show up at the cathedral in red Wellies during deepest Lent so many times after the nuptial zenith before her gamine charm palled.

Happy to leave daycare behind, on the bus Al silently dedicated her part in the Animal Allies protest to presence and humility. She dismounted at the first campus stop, head high, only a little nervous.

Libby had reneged on a ride, coming late because of Violet's obedience class. Althea knew no one else likely to be an Ally. She had the sisterhood's blessing *in absentia*. Lucy disliked "agitating," preferring to teach children to love their "furred and feathered family." Beebe favored private acts of sabotage, surveillance and nonviolent mutiny, refusing to elaborate. (Althea delightedly suspected Beebe was the celebrated culprit who'd sprung a doomed veal calf from its scorching fiberglass hutch on an outlying farm last month. The incident had sparked a community controversy and the anonymous purchase of the calf for on an out-of-state animal sanctuary.) Marian was quite willing to participate, but Libby intervened. Apparently last year Marian had doggedly handed out leaflets against Kentucky Fried Chicken near campus until she sank onto a curb in a woozy daze. Bakeoven, a financial supporter of the

Allies, quietly threatened to cancel his membership if Libby continued to "squander" Marian.

Althea found a cluster of women and a pile of placards at the designated intersection on the campus's most urban edge. More placards leaned against the Department of Digital Media building; they featured raw, crumpled dogs that Althea realized had been skinned alive. After the briefest of investigations she averted her eyes from the photos for the rest of the afternoon and resolved not to point hers at children.

A clean-cut young Asian-American fellow in white shirt and tie and a sprightly girl with purple hair and plenty of tattoos seemed to be in charge. They ignored her. People were chatting, but only casually; she didn't have the sense of a tightly knit group of friends. There were women her own age who might have been shoppers, younger, hipper women, a sprinkling of students both male and female, a lesbian couple. A woman nearby looked approachable – sensibly shod, fifty-something, beauty salon hair.

"I've never done this before. Think we'll get many more people?"

"Oh, good for you! We might. My name's Frances. Welcome." Her smile reassured.

"Althea." She decided against mentioning Libby.

"I'm one of the puppy mill group. Six or eight of us meet on Tuesdays to picket Hamm's Pet Store. Unbelievable abuse – the mothers bred repeatedly till they're worn out and exterminated...the sickly pups...and once in a while there's middle-of-the-night illegal trade in Chicago pit bulls in the alley behind Hamm's. We're assembling documentation. We'd be happy to have you join us. Ten o'clock every Tuesday."

"I'm afraid I'm teaching pre-schoolers at that time. But I appreciate what you're doing." Al was interested in targeting the most overtly violent crimes against animals. She couldn't turn out for everything; fur trappers and cat boilers had priority in her nightmares.

For someone else it might be the crime on one's doorstep that had to be addressed first. Animal Allies claimed 1,000 members on their website. Not bad for a smallish university town, even assuming a fluid student population made up half the members.

The purple-haired girl was passing out wads of leaflets while clutching a megaphone under one arm.

"So what exactly do we do?" People seemed to be assuming positions along the curb.

"We stand here. You can hold a sign or pass out information. Technically we're supposed to stay at least a yard away from the building. The university's pretty friendly towards us." Frances patted Al's arm, waved at a passing car. A young woman with lots of eyeliner and immense hoop earrings offered Al and Frances some of her brochures.

"Yeah. They can afford to be friendly because of their lackluster science department. No fat grants for sadistic experiments on animals," she commented.

Al grimaced in agreement. Across the state border her alma mater funded scandalous, sickening experiments on baby monkeys and had provided accommodations for a "professor" who received federal funds to "study" the effects of firing tasers close-range at pigs.

"My name's Carita." Althea followed her to the stack of plywood-handled placards, choosing the least graphic and grappling with her fistful of brochures. Several flew under the wheels of passing cars as she struggled to keep her sign visible and still be able to thrust information at the public.

By now perhaps fifteen Animal Allies lined the sidewalk, some aiming posters hoisted overhead at traffic, some chatting and paying no mind to their buckling homemade posters, some beginning to leaflet pedestrians. A grumpy fellow in a campus security uniform spoke briefly to their clean-cut, suited leader and disappeared, smiling, back into Digital Media.

"WHAT DO WE WANT?"

"Rights for animals!"

"WHEN DO WE WANT IT?"

"*NOW*!!!"

Althea, unable to negotiate the smallest wine and cheese affair confidently, added a sonorous voice to the easy chant. The chance to unload a little rage, disgust and inconsolability onto the public airwaves was just as bracing as she'd anticipated. Forgiveness, non-egoic presence, detached teaching, yes. Passivity, no. Not on this subject. Every squashed family of raccoons ("road pizza") along the highway, every dancing bear with a ring and chain, every frostbitten abandoned cat, every bulldozed meadow renamed "Deer Hollow Condominiums" rose up inside her.

"You look really wonderful. Powerful. I love your earrings," Carita said. Al knew it was a way of saying she made getting old look alright, as well as reassurance that Al looked dynamic rather than dotty. From tall, shapely, hip Carita this was gold.

They chatted between pedestrians. Carita's in-laws lived in Rome; her mother was born in Columbia. She thought most humans were thoughtlessly cruel and that couples should have to acquire a hard-earned license to have kids. She knew the names of the latest vegetarian restaurants in Chicago. Al scribbled these down on a damp bus transfer. She began to taste her melting sunscreen.

It took her a few pedestrians before Al developed a fast, intuitive reckoning of probable sympathizers. Tight-faced women in high heels with tissue-filled boutique shopping bags ignored one icily; parents with grade schoolers sheltered them as though encountering a bloody traffic accident. Lone women often took a brochure hastily, head down, probably choosing the lesser of several evils. Others stopped to listen briefly; their brochures might stay out of the wastebasket a while. Students in pairs or in groups laughed or flashed thumbs up; students on their own stopped to talk or passed impenetrably, as though on their way to an exam or suicide.

Surprising and gratifying was the number of twenty-something fellows who gestured or shouted friendly support from cars or bikes. Their good-natured response brightened everyone. Enthusiastic honks were prized.

Most Allies let the posters and leaflets speak for themselves. Althea preferred adding hasty explanations:

"People around the world are protesting Korean abuse of dogs and cats this week."

So saying, Althea offered a leaflet to an immaculate, stern young man in a suit who stopped dead in his tracks. Dressed as though for a date, the woman on his arm stared blankly ahead.

"I don't care. I respectfully disagree. What do you want?"

"I want you to read this information." She looked up at him without hostility.

He put both hands up as if to block all communication.

"No thank you. I just don't care." Their eyes met one last time and he strode off with the young lady who continued docile and vacant. Al imagined they were on their way to some pricey, heartless restaurant. Le Boeuf Bleu, perhaps.

He'd stunned her. She'd anticipated indifference, hot debate, jeers, scorn. Not deliberate, considered unconcern. He'd decided from a position of relative affluence, power, education, that animal suffering was irrelevant. And he'd deliberately taken a moment to inform her of that very clearly.

Shocked and desolate, she turned to a nearby Ally who'd seen the encounter.

"Don't mind. It happens all the time."

That was hardly consoling, but a growing sense of belonging to a tribe, however anonymously, countered her distress.

Some people did thank her for the leaflet, in spite of its dismaying photo of tightly crowded, caged dogs in a meat market. A turbaned cabby honked at them and flashed a peace sign above his window;

two people in the back leaned out theirs and skirled approval. A mild academic put down his bulging briefcase to scan her proffered leaflet. He listened to her recommendations to boycott Hyundai and Kia cars and contact the South Korean embassy. He nodded and placed his carefully folded brochure in a breast pocket when she told him not to lose the photocopied insert.

"It tells you how to check online for their latest contact info because they change it all the time to block us."

"Alright. Thank you very much. I'll do that." He nodded again – almost a bow – before collecting the briefcase and disappearing into the crowd.

Al felt something change. Some unconscious, minimal but meaningful goal had been met. She thought he could even be depended on to contact the embassy.

The demonstration broke up on schedule; the Asian fellow and his purple comrade briskly collected posters and paper. No one lingered. Althea shared a few friendly goodbyes and headed toward her bus stop, tired, proud of herself. Libby – who'd never shown up – had put her on to a good thing.

Brimming with reflections on her afternoon – not least of which was sober doubt as to whether they'd made any difference for the animals waiting to be tortured and eaten in Korea – Althea collapsed onto a bus seat. It wasn't till she'd trudged a bit smugly up Corrie Street's hill toward number 707 that she remembered presence.

When had she last really attended, embraced the here and now beyond distracted ego concerns, really inhabited her inner body, breathed consciously? Mortified, she sagged onto the concrete steps up to Lilybanks, reluctant to enter the yard.

Undoubtedly she'd last been at least intermittently present just before Carita's comment that Althea cut a handsome figure.

Since then she'd been watching herself. Oh yes, an orgy of self-consciousness. Every forearm raised to a sweaty temple, every fidget with unruly papers, every stance assumed as a bus passed the demonstration had been scrutinized by her double. She'd let one well-meant, supportive comment plunge her into a movie, blot out real existence. Apparently her ego was hopelessly starved for affirmation – and on what a vulnerable point! Irresistible! It had turned an effort dear to her heart into a preening masquerade.

Something about this grandiose critique rang hollow and familiar. She found herself breathing, clear and calm, then laughing.

"Oh, no, you don't."

A hummingbird whizzed past her head as Al navigated the trumpet vine's unruly profusion. Fresh caulk marked Watkins' latest patchwork assault on the sidewalk the vine regularly heaved apart. One of the round, rayed nasturtium leaves from a window box had floated down onto the porch landing. The cavernous cool beyond the urns looked homely and soothing.

Delicate

When Marian pulled the door open unexpectedly, gave Al's hand a squeeze and murmured that she'd "thought it might be Lucy," Althea felt only gratitude and wonder.

"Come up to my office, could you dear? How was the demonstration, you must be exhausted, I've got some shortbread fingers in a drawer, we'll – "

Micah Fennel appeared on the stairway, surveying Althea glumly and muttering something abrupt to the effect of "Didn't think so," before stamping back upstairs.

Marian sent Al a grave, pointed look over the rim of her bifocals; Al decided against iced tea and followed up the stairs. In Marian's study she found Tad folded tortuously into one of the delicate old rockers. Immobile, he suggested a tableau in a wax museum and didn't meet her eyes. Beebe waved and patted the seat of the adjacent rocker for Al; she looked serene in contrast to "Bubo's" distracted shuffling through a desk drawer. Micah's exaggerated swinging of a crossed leg as he chewed the end of his reading glasses and stared into the garden from the window seat struck Al as affected in the extreme.

"It's alright, don't bother, Marian," Al said, wishing she'd plundered the candy bar stash in her bedroom. She'd begun to feel quite drained, and plunked down obediently, careful not to look at Tad.

"Yes. Well. Micah's come in hopes that we might be...be hiding Lucy in the attic, so to speak. From him. Isn't that it, Micah? Because she's missing, Althea." Marian looked particularly blotchy; pencil shavings and a broken rubber band from the drawer dangled from her midriff. "She's never missed a day of work here, never just disappeared like this...Of course Beebe saw her briefly this morning in The Cygnet's Nest. Too soon to call the police; they'd think us quite naïve..."

"A lovers' quarrel. Only there wasn't one," Micah muttered, continuing to stare out into the garden with inexplicable hostility.

"It's just that we all know Lucy can be...delicate," Marian observed.

Beebe broke the careful silence that followed.

"Unless you know something, Althea, maybe we need to do the difficult thing and just *wait*." Al shook her head, calculating that little Harry's father's disappointment could only add a futile embroilment. She'd mention it to...Marian or Beebe later, and realized with her first real pang of worry that Lucy was the confidante to whom she usually "mentioned" curiosities.

"Perhaps she's already turned up at your place, Micah," Marian suggested, not wishing to pry as to whether Lucy had a key.

"Yes. I'm going." Micah rose, cooperative but not eager, which struck all three women.

Beebe rushed out after him, which even the moribund Tad noticed. Al looked over at Marian, seeking clues if not enlightenment.

"Someone needed to see him out."

Althea took this as a reference to Micah's status as Lucy's fiancé, but as soon as they heard his car backing out of the drive Marian continued,

"Finally. Beebe doubtless prevented him from searching the shrubbery. Something's awry there; he clearly thinks Lucy's had enough of him. But you're in the dark, Althea."

Beebe pattered back in, flushed. Bustling back to Tad, she patted his shoulder and felt his forehead like a nurse, which Al found disconcerting. She'd suspected clandestine ardor between the two of them since Tad had moved in. Perhaps what Tad really needed was a little mother. Al wriggled at the image of herself as a frustrated busybody and tried to redirect her attention toward Marian, who'd risen from her desk, a sure sign of an impending lecture.

"When Lucy failed to materialize by mid-afternoon, Althea, Beebe and I – and Tad," she added, throwing him a kindly look, "felt we must delve into the matter. Now that you're home from your very worthy cause – we're proud of you, dear, and look forward to an eyewitness account – let's bring you up to date."

Althea melted, not having realized how much the praise and attention meant. She listened in earnest, resolved to help this odd, ephemeral little family of hers as best she could.

"Tad understands the sisterhood's tradition of openness in matters that affect the household. It needed no persuasion, therefore, for him to agree to share a very possibly relevant incident involving Lucy this morning. He and Beebe – who also missed Kinder on Corrie, as you know," (Marian shot Beebe a quizzical look which Althea imagined expressed some hurt) "came to me with the information after our children had departed. Did you want to tell Althea about your predicament this morning, or shall I, Tad?"

Marian employed a daycare "show and tell" intonation that Al thought most unfortunate. Marian treated her "tooties" straightforwardly enough, but seemed unequal to Tad's disconcerting adolescence. Yet again Al found herself wondering about his age – or for that matter, Beebe's. She'd once asked Lucy and been offended by a masterfully dilatory evasion.

"I think we'll leave the two of you alone for that, Bubo. Tad needs some good hard work. He's going to make our supper." Tad, who looked as though he'd been recently treated with leeches, seemed surprised but comically eager. He beat Beebe to the door, aiming a humorous, heart-wringing knit brow at Althea.

"I'll be right back. And I want to hear about your afternoon, too, Althea!" Beebe sailed out with roses in her cheeks.

The minute the staircase creaked beneath Tad's sneakers, Marian let out an alarming groan, threw down her current Kleenex and plummeted towards the floor behind her desk.

Terrified and ready to dial 911, Al tore around the furniture to find Marian arched over her shabbily carpeted portion of the cosmos like Nut the Egyptian goddess. It looked as though a crane had hoisted her baggy derrière heavenward while she executed a rigorous push-up worthy of a decathlon. A yoga drop-out, Althea recognized a "downward dog" veiled by a dangling hem.

"Marian?"

After a rather long silence punctuated by an occasional wheeze, Marian's thick rubber soles squealed on the oak floorboards as she sank to all fours.

Still suspecting some sort of seizure, Althea hovered.

"Can't I get you a pillow?"

Marian declined further into a stubby half lotus that revealed a garter belt. She nodded at the rubbery white tabs matter-of-factly.

"Pantyhose and I don't agree."

Althea sat down on the floor across from her.

"Curiouser and curiouser, Marian. How the hell did you manage that?"

Marian's glee revealed all her bridgework, and Althea realized she was quite likely lonely, partly due to Al's own circumspect deference. By assuming prior arrangements Althea had colluded in excluding Marian from the pajama party nights. How much the sensitive, hypervigilant Althea Athnos missed.

"I was Rutledge's women's field hockey coach for twelve years. Used to play on a women's curling team Saturday mornings for years, too. We had our own rink, paid for the rent by pooling our paltry book royalties – mostly academics. Geoffrey and Bakeoven used to sit in the bleachers with thermoses of cocoa laced with rum; game always improved after half-time! Always been something of a tomboy, really," she said demurely, groping for a tissue under the desk. Geoffrey and I found a yoga instructor in Chicago after we fell under Krishnamurti's spell for a few years – the 70's, that would be. Geoff pooped out but I discovered a natural affinity – though my instrument's more oak than willow. Gruesome aftershocks on the way, no doubt. Must remember to pile on the hot water bottles tonight. But I digress. Oh, the slings ands arrows of outrageous fortune, Althea! All these suffering egos. Lucy's hard-won strength dismantled – I fear she's coming unstrung, Althea, wait till you hear – sweet innocent Tad having rings run round him while my cherished niece sips nectar from forbidden chalices, perhaps – so trying to let go of a child!"

"Yes. I think I haven't realized…I mean, not having raised a child myself. I've let you down that way, perhaps. Blind."

"Certain paths must be walked alone, dear. And I rely on you, Althea; you're a pillar."

Abashed, Al saw that Marian meant it, if only from a kindhearted myopia. Buoyed and embarrassed, she changed the subject.

"Not such a pillar that I can contain my curiosity much longer. Spill the beans, won't you? Tad's predicament." She pulled her knees up under her chin.

Marian straightened her glasses, askew from gymnastics.

"Lucy tried to, well, molest him this morning! She lured the lad up to the Nest on some janitorial pretext at dawn and simply glued herself to him. Mercy, I'm being unfair. Perhaps she only needed some-one to talk to" – she lowered her voice – "about Micah. I've begun to suspect that Beebe is the last person she'd approach on such a theme" (leaning forward) "and I've been too enthusiastic about the re-lationship, not making Lucy's real needs my priority. She's a deep one, Althea. One can test the wind repeatedly and still not guess where her ship will sail....At any rate, the poor thing banged up her foot and Tad had to carry her over to that silly divan. She 'didn't seem to want to be put down,' as Tad put it." They both began to darken with suppressed mirth and Marian's eyes widened and watered – "and as he became increasingly, if reluctantly, embroiled, Beebe materialized. So difficult for everyone," Marian sighed, looking truly regretful, which undid Al. She snorted treacherously.

"Maybe it was entirely impulsive. Once he had her in his arms, I mean – the experiment seemed irresistible?"

"Oh, I think not. Beebe said Lucy was quite scantily clad."

Althea suppressed her desire for a detailed description, hoping Lucy had at least done The Cygnet's Nest proud. Perhaps the *eau de Nil* 1930's slip with black lace trim and nothing underneath? She might get the lowdown from Beebe, if only by expressing concern for missing merchandise...

A glittering thread of fear began to weave through her enthralled impression of the morning's events. Lucy's appealing vulnerability had an ugly history and probably no one at Lilybanks had consid-ered her potential for some act of blind violence. (Although she could imagine Casper's "I told you so.")

"...distressed but also very confused," Marian continued, not hav-ing noticed Al had stopped listening for a bit. "The sleeping arrange-ment in the nursery – whose oddness became customary, and I very much blame myself for that – will change at once. Predictably, Tad blames himself – a train of thought that can only yield poisoned fruit.

Tad has offered to move out immediately. I simply forbade it, at least until Lucy returns and we can straighten things up." Marian paused for air, blotchy again.

"One sympathizes, of course, with his farcical role in a piece of marionette theatre. But I think much more troubling to Tad, who will easily forgive Lucy, is Beebe's attitude."

Althea's eyebrows rose; she imagined the anarchical Beebe angelically giving Tad away at a revised wedding, then setting out for Holy Russia, barefoot in the airport. Mere red-blooded jealousy seemed unlikely, though the image of the sturdy young lady stripping down to her bloomers and tackling her competitor in a half-Nelson as Tad looked on, slack-jawed, was entertaining. Catching herself, and wincing, Al glimpsed the tangle of envy and bitterness that animated her imagination.

"All solicitous, sunny concern. Superficial, to my eye. She's betrayed not a twinge of jealousy or irritation. Reading between the lines of Tad's account I gather her serenity fell little short of cheering them on."

(Typically perverse *and* angelic, thought Althea.)

"The poor fellow. For that matter, she seems pretty sanguine about our Lucy's absence as well. I must say her attention seems elsewhere. I've never been one for idle conjecture... oh, dear." Marian looked at her as though for assistance.

Althea reached out to pat the toe of Marian's veggie Oxford.

"This morning's mischief will blow over soon enough for everyone but Lucy. I have a very bad feeling about that," Al said. She savored Marian's solemn attentiveness; maybe gratified ego would recede if her focus included her buttocks against the floorboards, her breath, the tea bag string dangling over the edge of Marian's wastebasket.

"I think we should phone Evvie, Bakeoven, anyone you can think of, without creating a panic. After all, Lucy may stroll in any moment. What does Micah say? Does he know about the Tad escapade?"

"Good heavens, no," Marian wheezed. That's entirely up to Lucy. Micah said Lucy turned down their standing arrangement to sleep at his place. Said she needed solitude to work on her concept for the first semester eurhythmy recital."

Althea could imagine Micah saying it exactly like that – "the first semester eurhythmy recital" – in his pedantic, humorless way while his distraught fiancée hitchhiked penniless into deepest Idaho or tap danced along some high-rise window ledge.

"Micah said he didn't think anything of it. A bit truculently. He went so far as to suggest I'd gotten befuddled about the daycare schedule, that perhaps Lucy had notified me earlier of some appointment. He would have been more genuinely concerned last year. Something has soured. I was too preoccupied with my foolish, romantic plans for the wedding to see it. Hand-painted Lilybanks napkin rings for every guest. Folly."

Althea refrained from commenting that Marian had been wise to enjoy herself, as Beebe seemed an unlikely candidate for the traditional fuss. She'd probably elope. On a different continent. Al crawled over to the desk to pull herself upright; the afternoon's militant posture had begun to make itself felt along her sciatic nerve.

"Here and Now, Marian. Would you like a hand?"

*   *   *

"You've come undone," Beebe said, crisscrossing the strings of Tad's apron behind his back and retying them on the firm curve of his belly, turning him back and forth like a giant rag doll as he peeled sweet potatoes at the scullery sink. She thought he still looked a little shell-shocked.

"I should get going. You on top of things? Just remember the cans of black beans in the pantry, and the directions for making rice are taped to the inside of the crock's lid. And you'll really impress everyone if you squeeze a lime over the potatoes and then sprinkle them with cilantro." He frowned. "You know, the stuff that looks like parsley. In the fridge."

She leaned her head against his bibbed chest a moment.

"Just embrace whatever happens, Tad."

"Very funny."

"Hmm? I mean everything's okay. It always is. And, Tad? I have wonderful news. Lionel made me promise not to tell without him, but I can't help giving you a heads-up. He's coming over early tomorrow morning, and we'll share it with everyone. I guess you should set your alarm. You look a little tired. I'll set the table for you."

She kissed him on the cheek and all but skipped from the scullery. One of her braids had come loose.

"Better open three cans, in case Lucy shows up.'"

Once she was out of earshot Tad hurled the potato peeler out the window after impaling the last vexatious tuber.

Stardom

After praying for Lucy, Beebe read herself to sleep.

*　　*　　*

"Auntie Gyp! Look! It's a great big dog got its head in a trap!"

Gypsy and Leo swiveled to see a nimble Scotch farm collie picking her way down a slope tangled with arching blackberry canes. Prairie dock's yellow-crowned masts towered over her tawny head.

"Be quiet! Get down, both of you! The dog's not hurt; it's carrying something," Gypsy hissed. She'd observed enough gardening to recognize a basket, and was secretly charmed by its pink calico cloth and the sweet-faced bitch, who reminded her of Delilah.

Leo, more suspicious, wondered who was in the basket. He extended a few well-honed claws experimentally and considered. The visitor looked hopelessly mild, the type of dog who'd defend a helpless charge to the bitter end, fatally handicapped as a lifelong non-combatant. As for the nincompoop hiding under the napkin, he'd be delighted to give him a warm welcome. Bugstink, or whatever he let the humans call him, couldn't think up anything better than this? Leo felt almost disappointed. He was at the top of his form this morning; too bad little Plucky couldn't see him trounce opponents of a higher caliber than this. Perhaps she'd appreciate his own fine points after watching him tenderly tuck what was left of her suitor back into his hamper.

Seeing she had their attention, the collie's tail rose and waved. Daring a heartfelt, split-second calculation, Gypsy shot toward the dog, tossing a "Follow me!" behind her.

The half-gleeful, half-terrified kittens careened sloppily behind her. The three all but skidded into the collie, who wagged and smiled and put her burden down carefully with – alas – no apparent purpose except hospitality.

Leo gloated as he strode toward them.

"My companions are eager to welcome a new face! What brings you to these lonely parts, artful one?" He kept his eye on the basket, which looked less threatening up close. Gypsy lashed her tail, mortified to have sought refuge with this silly dog. The kittens took turns executing mock attacks on the pink napkin that fluttered and dimpled seductively in the breeze.

The collie drew herself up with dignity and, after an effort, stopped panting.

"Have I the honor to address Leo the Wanderer?"

"You have."

"My name is Bonnet. I come from the home of the Star on the hill. He requests a parley. Something about gypsies and babies – he said you would understand," the collie explained, feigning ignorance. "If you agree to grant him this I am to escort you." Bonnet cocked her head, trying to get the next bit exactly right, as Gompy had emphasized its importance. "Your companions may join us; I am to entertain them on the estate during your conference should you choose to bring them along." Bonnet tried to look indifferent; Gompy had assured her she wouldn't need to twist the tomcat's whiskers on this score.

Leo forced himself to appear only mildly pleased, having succumbed immediately to the flattering invitation. He had complete confidence in his own freedom to come and go. The Star would lay no trap. At worst Leo might lose little Plucky, which gave him less of a pang than he'd expected in light of a private chat with his sole peer.

"The kittens are welcome to make the journey in the hamper," Bonnet offered, turning to Gypsy with her merry collie smile. Gypsy laid her ears back, mistrustful.

"It's not so far, but mostly uphill and more thickety than the flatlands you crossed," Bonnet explained. "Just let me know if you think little paws are flagging, Ma'am." Gypsy realized her mistake and blinked cordially.

"Star thought you might want refreshment before we travel. He sent a picnic, courtesy of our mistress's kitchen." All eyes turned back to the hamper, to find little Pippin covered to the shoulders in pink calico, his hind legs scrabbling for balance on the wicker rim. Bonnet gave a soft, delighted yip and pulled the napkin off with her teeth, revealing a big white blob on Pippin's nose.

"Mmmm!"

Gypsy mewed reproachfully, but Leo marched right up and helped Pippin clamber out.

"Thataboy. Eat your fill." He stuck his claws into a bowl heaped with fishy morsels in green-flecked clotted cream. "Delectable. Garden mint – my favorite." He gobbled noisily. "But I forget myself. Come, you must be hungry." He nodded to Gypsy. "My thanks to the Star."

Gypsy squeezed her head beneath the wicker handle. Scout and Pippin poised acrobatically on the basket's rim, alternately wading into the bowl and falling back onto the grass to suck their delicious paws. Bonnet admired the kittens with a motherly eye.

* * *

Florrie kept to the humans' soft, winding footpath up to Star's stronghold, not wishing to startle some mink or grumpy badger into a show of strength at the proud young toms' expense.

By now Bezique perceived that Florrie had sent a messenger up to the house on the hill without informing the well-intentioned, dilatory Beanie. The kindly chap had sincerely thought they were all waiting for Bezique's approval of the plan. Meanwhile, the imperious old fluff-ball had assumed command of the situation. Too late now to do anything other than cooperate and hope the hard-boiled Leo was as dazzled by Star as Florrie was.

He watched her portly tortoiseshell breeches waddling upwards just ahead of him. She seemed an able scout, confidently choosing one path over another at a fork in the trail.

"We're on his estate now," Florrie told them without pausing.

A low stone wall appeared on either side; the dust beneath their paws gave way to newly-laid cobblestones. A brilliant morning sky opened up.

"We're to meet him behind the house," Florrie mewed.

Happy to trade the woods' whispering shadows for a tender, dappled lawn and human comforts, all five cats paused to polish their whiskers and stretch in the warm sun. Smoke rose from one of the dark, shingled house's chimneys. The cobblestones led to a terrace and a high wall; around its corner they could see flowers and shrubbery. When a breeze stirred an overpowering billow of perfume hit their noses. Eyes crossed.

"Mistress of the house never does anything by halves," Florrie sighed. "Lilies of the valley."

Bezique was startled to realize a black cat had been sitting in the shadow of the garden door, perhaps for a long time. Now the cat sauntered towards them.

"Happy to see you all! Hope you didn't wear your stripes thin getting everyone up here, Florrie. Just like the old days... Sparks under her tail," he added, turning to his other guests. "Known her since nursery school." The two young toms had to bury their noses in each other's flanks to hide their amusement. Florrie swiveled an ear in their direction, but her chest puffed.

"I see you've brought a good crew. But I'm hoping it won't come to that. Thank you all for coming. Plenty to drink by the back door – Cook's just watered all the flowerpots till their saucers filled." The Star touched noses carefully with each newcomer.

"...You must be Bezique. Very good of you to fall in with my friend's scheme. I'm sure you had a bolder one. Don't know Leo personally, but I've hoped to bump into him for a long time. Every territory needs a wily, seasoned rambler. A tremendous resource, but they don't usually care to mingle."

Bezique was on the verge of sharing his opinion of Leo when Florrie bustled over.

"Excuse me, Star. Perhaps we should get organized before Bonnet returns?"

To Bezique's surprise Star accepted her interruption respectfully and rose.

"Quite right, friend...Best that everyone's at ease and a bit familiar with their whereabouts." Star had assumed a graver, more vigilant air now and all the newcomers sensed the meaning behind his words. The young grey shook his head as though evicting a flea, and the others quietly groomed in an effort to revive their customary cattish cool on unfamiliar turf.

"My humans are well-disposed towards our tribe. But

neither's at home at the moment. Just as well, I think. Cook is here, up to her elbows in dough; she won't mind us. Screen door's off the latch; she's been beating rugs this morning. Will you come inside? Have a drink on your way in, won't you."

Star stuck a paw into the cracked door, wedged his muzzle in, then worked his shoulders through the opening. Beanie leaned into the door to open it further, and Florrie marched inside like a familiar guest. The younger three lapped at the pansy dregs before following her.

"You go ahead, Beanie. Many thanks. Getting one's tail out of the way before the door smacks shut requires practice."

They found themselves on cool flagstones at the bottom of a hall so quiet that the merest click of a claw resounded. A distant, rhythmic thumping could be heard far away to the right; every cat except the bachelor carpenter's Beanie recognized it. He looked to Star.

"Just Cook kneading her sourdough." Star crossed a threshold on their left.

"Feel free to come along. Looking for a friend." A fly fussed above a long bank of windows. The place smelled of lavender, honeycomb and daffodils. Bezique noted that many of the chair legs bore Star's musky signature. While he and Beanie followed their host into an adjoining room, the toms tailed the fly across the window seat and pounced at fluttering shadows on the sun-drenched floorboards.

"Manners!" Florrie mewed, and both retreated to the doorway.

Star strode back into the hall, Beanie and Bezique on his heels.

"Perhaps the library."

A mountainous staircase loomed on one side as they approached a door at the top of the hall. Light filtered through lace. Bezique admired a chandelier like a king-sized cluster of honeysuckle far above the strange dark patterns beneath their paws.

The Star's upright tail flickered toward a gloomy doorway opposite the staircase.

"The Inner Gook," he announced solemnly. When no one cared to enter this dark chamber first, the Star led the way, melting into the shadows.

Sunlight struggled down through small windows flanking a fireplace. Its massive stones were armored with a hulking copper hood that glimmered at them through the murk. Only the cozy scent of wood smoke reassured as their paws met the chilly flags.

Someone cleared his throat, or scuttled; something like a ghostly parasol unfurled without warning; Bezique wondered confusedly if Star's mistress was home after all. A winged apparition materialized above them, creaking and sighing. Gaping, claw-like pincers groped in the cats' direction. Bezique heard the tomcats scrabbling frantically down the hallway.

"Heavens to Betsy, Fez, you've scattered our forces," Star gurgled, emerging from the inglenook's shadows and looking not at all cross. "Your tassel's askew," he added, as though that detail were the only source of consternation.

Ashamed to have forgotten Florrie's account of the wood stork, thinking mostly of Gypsy, Bezique realized he'd need to recover the heedfulness that is every cat's lodestar.

Forcing himself to examine the dreadful curved pincers, he saw they formed the ungainly creature's formidable bill. Bezique's eyes had adjusted to the gloom sufficiently to realize the bird was balancing on the settle in front of the fireplace; in the dark its knobby-kneed black legs had made it seem to float eerily above them like a great snowy bat. The tremendous black and white wings whooshed like flapping laundry as the stork spread them the length of the settle, then cupped them to keep his footing. Gnarled pink claws clutched the cushions. Star's mistress must be tolerant indeed.

"Caught me napping. Sorry to have alarmed you folks.

Awkward. Splendid to see you, Florrie," the stork gabbled. Its breath smelled swampy.

While Florrie puffed her chest with pleasure, Bezique sidled over to their host.

"What's wrong with your friend's head?" he asked, damping his meow. A scarlet carbuncle disfigured one side of the bird's naked head.

"Nothing. That's his smoking cap. Foible of the mistress's; she worries about ague what with that bald head and neck. Fancies himself quite rakish; sheds it most reluctantly in July. Claims the tassel attracts fish."

By now Beanie had retrieved the toms. They observed from a prudent distance behind the she-cat. Stouthearted cats at bottom, they were soon intrigued and then amused.

"Friendly fellow. Think he'd fly me 'round the garden?" Britches purred.

The Star leapt onto the back of the settle.

"Beanie, you've assembled a top-notch crew here. I'm hoping Leo will prefer a businesslike approach, but a show of strength never hurts, does it, fellows? Let's have some introductions. Fez, make yourself agreeable. This level-headed cat is Beanie, the companion of Mistress's carpenter."

The wood stork, who'd managed to straighten his headgear by bunting it against Star's flank, perked up considerably.

"Oliver Goodfellow's yours? My compliments. We've enjoyed many a little lunch break concert amidst shavings and sawdust when he's up here fancifying some cupboard or other. Mistress drops everything to prance around to his pennywhistle. Why, –"

"Yes, and this hot-headed gallant is Bezique Bunting. His professor's a lecturer at the University."

Fez's bill dropped open, quite like a smile.

"Professor of classics, I believe. So you're the beau with a damsel in distress. We'll have her back safe and sound in no time. Best way to settle this interloper's hash is to..." Star appeared to lose his balance and wobble against the great leathery legs. "Ahem. Yes. And these sturdy lads?"

"This is Britches, an expert farm ratter. Very sound. And the young gentleman in grey is Hooligan. Faster than a cottontail crossing fox turf, I hear."

"Excellent. Deeply regret that spectral first impression. Terrible timing on my part. So glad you could...I say."

Six pairs of ears swiveled in the direction of the stork's gaze. Leo sat in the inglenook doorway, composed and smug. In the half-light his burning eyes and warped whiskers glowed above the perpetual sneer. Bezique thought he resembled the pirate in a book of Marjorie's, forbidden to the younger girls. Before Leo could capitalize on this *tour de force* Star took over.

"Leo? Thank you for coming. Sorry you had to find your own way in; meant to welcome you in style out on the lawn. Let's all move on out of the gloomy Gook, shall we? Much better out in the fresh air, eh, Leo?"

"After you," Leo grinned, and sat as if in review while the others filed past him down the hall. Bezique watched him nod curtly at Beanie's polite mew of recognition, and exchange cursory, ceremonial sniffs with Florrie. Leo was thin to the point of flatness, like the sunfish the neighborhood boys brought Mrs. B. Striped, sooty fur fringed his ears and cheeks lavishly and gave his angular face a foxy cast. His tail rivaled Snowy's plume, but his everlasting grimace made him the ugliest cat Bezique had ever seen. Leo ignored him.

Once they were all out on the cobblestones Florrie insisted on giving everyone a tour of the walled garden as if on cue. Bezique watched over his shoulder with regret as Leo and Star strolled around the corner of the house, thick as thieves. Leo seemed willing to tolerate gawky Fez trailing close behind.

After an interminable exploration of each mossy cairn and babbling grotto, even Florrie looked impatient.

BY FORCE OF FELICITY

"I suppose it's not possible the Star's come to some harm?" Beanie finally asked her, voicing the others' concern.

"Nonsense," she snapped, a little too shrill.

And then, most wonderfully, the Star appeared in the garden's doorway with a spring in his step.

"Leo and I are going fishing. Fez has flown on ahead. Hope you'll all stay for lunch. Florrie, you know Cook. We'll have to roll you fellows back down the hill. Plenty of time for naps before the sun gets low. By the way – memorably solid, all of you. Beanie, a real pleasure. Britches, Hooligan – the affectionate nose of friendship will always be extended when you visit (which I hope will be often). My congratulations, Bezique."

Baffled, Bezique approached.

"You make it sound like a good day's work, when we haven't even gotten started."

"Yes, yes; everything's sorted out beautifully." The Star gave Bezique a fraternal lick on the forehead. "Your little friend's probably on her way up here already. Fez is leaving word that all is well. Bet those kittens will drop their knickers when they see his wingspan!" He lowered his voice. "I'll get the story on the little lady's sister. That chap doesn't miss a thing."

"But Leo... you mean..." Bezique stuttered, teetering on the brink of joy.

"Your charming friend's a bit too frisky for Leo. And he knows what little cockleburs the ladies can be. On the other paw, I prize his hard-won wisdom, I admire the old devil, and I'm a humdinger of a playmate, if I do say so. Leo feels he has traded up."

7

Ravening

[1912]

Olive pelted across the studio, vaulting over the sleeping Bruno and nearly felling the mannequin.

"No you don't, sir! S-s-s-s!"

Gompy wheeled away from the new loom's enticing tangles only to be seized by Calla, who hoisted him onto her shoulder.

Mollified, the black cat sniffed the breeze from the balcony hungrily. The peppery scent of nasturtiums mingled with the faintest hint of something more provocative.

"His lordship's about to discover the treasure in the teacup, Calla."

"Come along, love. Keep an eye on Uncle Fezzy for me." Whisking the cat out to the balcony and onto a rain barrel, Calla shut the doors on him.

"Fez is hoping for more casualties from poor Martin's aquarium."

Olive adjusted the elderberries on the mannequin's hat. She sympathized with the cat's disapproval, having recently interrupted her vigil at a soufflé's side – with a party in full tilt – to pry the stork's beak from the far side of a window screen. She was also expected to remove the creature's calling cards. Calla feigned nonchalance after the miserably disoriented bird nearly maimed her; her shrill new insistence on bleach and dustpans failed to eradicate an undercurrent of dread. Mr. Morrissey wouldn't put his foot down, admiring his wife's pluck instead of exiling Fez. John lured the bird off the premises whenever possible.

Watching her employer caper around the room in a fit of self-expression, Olive reflected without malice that she might add "nanny" to her skills along with cook and confidante. Perhaps her true peers at Lilybanks were John's dogs, three obliging, vigilant papas.

"I'm starved. Let's go down to the garden."

Calla's transparency fused the two women for an instant. Their eyes met without jealousy.

"Yes." Olive smoothed her skirt, suddenly less sallow. Calla glimpsed a tremendous vitality, more recessed than her own.

"Take the teacup, will you. Go ahead; I'll get Gomp back in."

Olive clucked to Bruno and they processed down the stairs with the cup held before them like a grail. A pale goldfish sagged within, its dead eye fixed on Sam Ruffey's fretwork.

Calla found Gomp punctiliously covering up his use of a window box; she knew better than to interrupt and paused to enjoy his sunlit iridescence.

Fez, all weathered skullcap, horny maw and wings, preened in the shade beyond the small concrete pool Crum had devised for his meals. The bird's ornamental presence, alternately whimsical and nightmarish, possessed her. Calla thought of it as her totem, crossing forbidden thresholds, a hazard to itself and others, outlandishly genuine in an alien world.

Satisfied with his arrangements, the cat strode over to her with glistening, slightly crossed eyes and something relaxed and velvety in his bearing that conveyed ardor. She crouched to stroke his head and shoulders, hot from the sun. The cat's nostrils flared at the scent from her moist armpits. The enticing spice of bruised nasturtiums wafted around them.

"Let's go play."

She clapped the mannequin's hat on the back of her own head.

About to hurry down the stairs, Calla made herself slow to a luxurious swagger. The window by the front door had been shorn of its lace; washing day. The landscaped young yard was empty of workmen now; she missed the clamor, the reticent attention...When she halted Gompy tilted his tail to caress her calf.

Calla turned to find the back screen door propped wide open, doubtless to let the dogs come and go. Crum had droll notions of Lilybanks' compass, putting his tenet of transparency to nature into robust practice. The garden served as his office, the ballroom his camp. Yet he was no woodsman; his flat in the city possessed a dressing room the size of Martin's office; she'd dubbed it "The Chapel."

Calla lingered on the cool flagstones in the hall, reluctant to spend the day's treasure just yet. She came to life most keenly now through anticipation, her intoxicated defense against unspeakable want.

How typical; he'd opened the house to all comers and closed the garden door behind him. Gompy sat in front of it, willing her across the cobblestones. Scampering over the terrace with a finger raised to her lips as though the cat might otherwise announce their arrival, Calla hoped for a chance to spy. She twisted the purple glass knob, her touch of Berkeley bohemia. Gompy slunk around the door but went no further, an accomplice.

Through the aperture she could see Monk and Blitzen flanking her red wheelbarrow and basking under the sun's zenith like a pair of idling walruses. Crum couldn't be far. Eventually she detected his spare buttocks swaying against a horizon of dill and angelica.

Wrenched from both mischief and threatening melancholy, Calla waded across drifts of tansy and Queen Anne's lace, hat now shyly in hand.

"Have you found our lunch?" she called, not caring. Crum straightened slowly and turned to find her beside him. He squinted down at her, returning from some reverie. The dogs huddled round, excited. In the sun the hairs on his forearms were golden. Once again she marveled that this particular person should be the object of her passionate devotion – the sharp, old-ladyish chin, the professor's fussy self-assurance, the dry smile, the dry scent occasionally varied by a whiff of plumcake tobacco. Reflecting that the wizard of her realm need hardly conform to worldly standards, she smiled up at him.

He offered her a freshly dug parsnip, pulled off his gloves, wiped his face. They never touched each other outdoors now.

"Here's Olive."

Calla turned to observe her stride toward them, Bruno at her side. She had long, boyish legs; she and Crum were built so similarly they might be brother and sister. Olive could be very *chic*, though never lovely, if only she chose to subdue the hair and flatter her assets. She clearly knew that Calla and Crum were lovers, though this was neither discussed nor displayed.

As she approached, erect as a queen in the baggy, greenish-black shroud she favored when free of the dining room, Calla wondered again if Olive and Crum might also be a couple. They had plenty of opportunity; their rooms in Rutledge were around the corner from each other. It seemed a matter of indifference. Confident of her place, it entertained her that Crum liked thistles with his lilies.

Olive hurried toward them, grateful for these improbable peers. Calla's necessary audience and John's respite, she knew herself welcome. On such terms they offered her rare companionship.

Yet wasn't she simply tending two gifted children – protector of John's sly, unquenched anarchy, and Calla's spoilt determination to have her father? So said the light of high noon.

"Mr. Morrissey's fish is dispatched; Fez stalked off toward the orchard," she reported before meeting John's eyes.

"Mr. Morrissey." All three colluded in preventing Martin's full knowledge of their camaraderie to keep it inviolate. Calla did so in spite of believing he'd tolerate the egalitarianism; her husband was no silver-spooner.

"Look at these tomatoes! I say no cooking for lunch. We'll fall like ravening rabbits on our spoils here. Help me rescue the topmost wobblies, Olive, and we'll unload the rest of the barrow at the back door. Do we have a loaf of your walnut bread?" She tossed a lettuce at Olive. "We'll have a Bordeaux from the cellar...white," she added for Crum.

The women waited at the door, rocked by wave after wave of dog, only to see Crum roll the harvest right up to the sitting room windows. He knocked hard on the glass.

"Open up!"

Calla nodded at Olive and they rushed inside to unfasten the bank of windows. Calla tore pillows from the window seat and dragged tables and ottomans out of the way in a frenzy of exuberance while Olive plucked figurines up and away. Perhaps exaggeration was an artistic foible, but it seemed to Olive that Calla had begun to feign a joy she required.

Gompy materialized on a sill, eager to patrol any gap in his fortress; the dogs pressed into the room to participate. Calla fielded the produce reverently, receiving a swollen bulb of fennel, three bristling cucumbers and a crock of beautiful peas like relics in need of curatorship; Olive held her skirt taut before her, an improvised basket, so Crum might pelt her with new potatoes and kale bouquets.

"My black radishes are ready...Make way or I'll break my neck... We'll need a plain white loaf for those, Olive, and plenty of cold hard butter." Crum shucked his shoes and shinnied carefully onto the window seat, handing her two dark tubers. "And salt."

The anise scent of fennel lingered after the women bore his treasure off to the scullery. Crum fondled Blitzen's ear absentmindedly, thinking he should go wash his hands but unwilling to let the dogs experiment with plunging from the window.

The heat oppressed him now. In cool, berried September his honors seminar would resume. And a recently deceased client's son wanted him to turn the family estate on the North Shore into a cultural center. The finances would be unbuttoned by autumn. Intriguing fellow...He saluted Gompy, who peered at him from under the wheelbarrow's shade with cattish exasperation as the dogs panted in his direction, waiting for the next round of entertainment.

Aubade

Marian took a deep breath, decided it was really a sigh, and tried again. By the glow of the cracked lithophane nightlight Beebe had given her for a long-ago Mother's Day, she monitored Clumber and Cleo. They'd parked like stalled carnival bumper cars – cozily hinge to hinge – in front of her toilet. Having performed the gymnastics necessary to accommodate them, Marian had felt entitled to a flush. The turtles remained unruffled. Reminding herself to alert the household to their unpredictability in Lucy's absence, she'd just turned off the light with a self-congratulatory flourish when she realized her slippers were squishing.

With a sinking heart she pulled two chains; Calla's reverse-painted hummingbird shades revealed a subdued cascade of sewage puddling around the turtles on its way toward the hall.

They'd have to be sterilized somehow. Boiling? No. Bleach? Imagining the turtles eventually floating down the stairs while the Crumrind marquetry warped if she didn't take charge, Marian began splattering back into Millefleurs, thought better and shed her slippers, then plundered her drawers for every available towel with which to stem the tide.

Sacrificing even Geoffrey's Egyptian cottons with the stiff upper lip she fancied Churchillian, Marian swabbed the tiles while trying to recall the whereabouts of the mop and rags. Perhaps the children – the youngsters? – never get it right – had commandeered them when the vintage malted milk contraption had erupted a few weeks back. Tad had been so tickled to stumble on all that old stuff from Lumley's soda fountain, free if he lugged it out of the real estate agency's basement. He'd presented Beebe with forty fluted sundae cups and an industrial-sized blender. The latter had rattled like light artillery before disgorging a half gallon of milk and powdered chocolate all over the stove and toaster.

"Mr. Lumley would have been appalled. He used to give extra maraschinos upon request."

Unable to discern any correlation between Marian's remarks to herself and the scene at hand, Althea paid no heed, accustomed to the apparently slender thread by which Lilybankers dangled from the fabric of everyday reality. She cleared her throat emphatically.

"Problem with your toilet, Marian?"

"You're up early, dear." Marian sounded perfectly placid, as if sandwiching herself on hands and knees into the least wholesome corner of the tiny Millefleurs bathroom at 4:30 in the morning, robe wadded up around her waist with what appeared to be the late Professor's suspenders, were routine.

"Couldn't sleep," Al rejoined, deciding to match platitude for platitude. In fact, she'd wet her pajamas racing to the other bathroom after the usual struggle to stuff Linnet back into the bedroom. Too much salad for supper. The light at the end of the hall and Marian's remarkable slippers projecting from the doorway had seemed odd. Visualizing a stroke or armed robbery in addition to untimely whim, she'd thought it best to investigate.

"Oh, I couldn't either, Althea!" Marian lurched to her feet, audibly loosening the ceramic towel rack she'd grasped.

"Bother...Talking to myself again, wasn't I? Sure sign I'm not present," she panted, hoping to avoid explanations. Althea had been looking increasingly pinched lately, like some friable, desiccated orchid. Best to spare her the import of the toilet's resumed congestion. Watkins had informed her last month that he'd rodded out the sewage line in the driveway "as best as humanely possible;" further problems before winter would indicate the celebrated old willow gracing the top of the drive had infiltrated the system so thoroughly as to require expensive excavation and the city's involvement. Oh well, to every cloud a silver lining: too late to solve the problem by cutting down the tree.

"Mine's frozen eyes."

"What's that, dear?"

"You know. When you're so lost in thought you can't move your eyes. My surest sign," Althea babbled, trying not to reveal her dismay about the evident state of affairs. Watkins had spilled the beans about thousands of dollars' worth of potential intervention. Lucy, Beebe and Al had been exhorted by him not to flush "female supplements." Al had found herself simpering; it had been a long time since anyone had underestimated her age.

"Yes. Let's come back. Look at these wise innocents, sound asleep. Marvelous, aren't they." Al tried to concentrate on their reptilian housemates' mottled humps with neat piecrust edges and the shadows they cast. A car passed slowly along Corrie Street; she listened for the thud of a newspaper hitting the sidewalk. Marian smelled of the ancient "Oh! De London" talcum powder she insisted on using up at a glacial pace, a kindly joke among her housemates. Althea felt her breath rise and fall, felt her tense abdominal muscles relax. Marian lowered herself onto the toilet lid, majestic in her happy indifference. The William Morris flowers above the cracked dado seemed to pulse; the diminutive radiator's sculpted coils assumed the significance and interest of a living thing; the tiny craters in a puddle of dried soap lather on the edge of the sink declared an engagement with the rest of the universe irrespective of size and human opinion. Al sat down gingerly on the edge of Calla's pocket-sized clawfoot, unwilling to jostle this tenuous hold on the nature of things.

"Scaling the heights 'By force of felicitee,' as Parr might say? (Very minor poet but not without insight. Can't hold a candle to Traherne, of course.) The 'faerie casements' of presence will still be here if you tumble into the tub, Althea. Lighten up."

"Did you have to break the spell by talking, Marian?" Al bristled. "I was deeply --" She caught herself, and managed to laugh. "It's just letting things be as they are, isn't it? Not some special little guided tour for adepts. Not a hobby."

Chenille muffled Marian's giggle as she rubbed her nose on her sleeve.

"Goodness, I'm getting as rheumy as the dog...As Eckhart always points out, you have to experience presence. Mere believing is a poor substitute indeed. That said, indulge me by admiring the ravishing silver vapor on the tip of...Skippy?"

As though posing for Beatrix Potter, Lucy's roommate balanced on his hind legs in the bathroom doorway. He strained forward, working his nose in the direction of the signature "Oh! De London" scent.

"Poor fellow must be wondering where his roomie's gotten to. I thought Beebe said she'd watch over Lucy's menagerie until..."

"It's alright, I'm back."

Lucy dropped the uncharacteristically high red heels she'd been carrying and stooped to grab the rabbit by the scruff of his neck, delivering him up to Marian, his ardent admirer in spite of her rashes and sniffles.

"Stop trying to look sheepish, Lucy. You're incandescent." Marian peered up at her from between Skippy's delicately veined ears.

"It's good to see you!" Althea ventured, ending up in a powerful embrace. Lucy felt as firm and defined as an apple.

"You, too! I'm so sorry, both of you, really! We're so happy. I've been so lost. No, I mean, I didn't get lost – Micah and all that. The silliest part was wanting to please all my girls, my Dorfies, with their fairy-tale expectations, 'happily ever after' and all that...It was like a crypt. Wax museum Micah and his penchant for little girls. But God bless him, it hardly matters now." She blushed, yet looked becomingly older.

"My lips are swollen. And that's not all that's swollen!" Lucy rhapsodized, slumping against the doorjamb in a shorter, more rumpled suit than Al had ever seen her wear. Fond as she was of sweet, obliging, ever so slightly askew Lucy, this carnal version was superior, more fully realized.

"But what's going on? I was trying to tiptoe into my room, and Skippy barreled up the hall here the minute I opened my door. Someone sick?"

"Just the plumbing. All is well."

Lucy took in the pile of sodden towels.

"Oh, Marian. Listen, I'll bet Chip would take care of it for you. We're going to build a home, with my own dance studio! He'd love to help."

"Chip?" Marian looked blank.

"Chip Kretschmer. You know, Harry's daddy. 'Charles and Hannah Kretschmer,' it used to say on the checks we received – until six months ago. She left them. Wants Harry every other Christmas."

Althea quickly shot a shuttered, dubious look at Marian, who simply continued to observe Lucy while kneading the rabbit's shoulders.

"Sounds perfectly decadent, I know. Another mistake. But we're perfect for each other. In a *good* way," she added, when Althea failed to coo, or even smile. "When you stumble on the right person you just know. Didn't you find that to be true?" Lucy kept her eyes on Skippy, realizing she was prying.

"I think I figured it out over time. Casper was so insistent. No overnight epiphany," Al said slowly, also glued to the rabbit.

The turtles had begun to stir, peeking out through tentatively lowered drawbridges and swaying as first one, then another set of claws hit the slippery floor. Marian put their companion down in their midst and lurched upward with a hand on each thigh.

"So happy for you, love. Delighted."

Lucy dove into her arms, managing to miss everyone when she

dropped her spiky shoes. She surfaced with a reddened nose and glistening eyes, and accepted the linty, seasoned tissue Marian proffered.

"Which sounds better? Lucy Murgatroyd-Kretschmer, or Lucy Kretschmer-Murgatroyd?"

*   *   *

It had not been a good night. The inglenook settle – in spite of occasional Kinder-generated crumbs and Aphrodite's devoted drool – offered a satisfactory, manly refuge from unpredictable females. Tad even liked the clammy reek of the fireplace. Regardless of these amenities, the infallible military watch his dad had given him read 5:06 a.m. and he'd never really gone to sleep. Fretful visions of Beebe and Lionel Woodruff had flickered beneath his eyelids like some jumpy, incoherent old film played over and over. Beebe bestowing Lionel with a trophy cup as big as Lionel himself on a tipsy podium. A priest who looked oddly like Professor Bakeoven reading the banns (wasn't that what they called it?) for Beebe and Lionel from the top of one of those lollipop red double-decker tourist buses in London.

His head felt like a sandbag; when he grimaced the sludge at the corners of his mouth came unglued and his parched lips cracked.

"Just embrace whatever happens, Tad."

Oh yeah. He was up for embracing Lionel – President Leiby's Bugatti-class wheelchair and all – like a grizzly bear messing with a vole. Tad leapt to his feet, and reeled into the fire screen as his sleeping bag zipper got tangled in a pajama leg. The screeching metal and clomping broke the inglenook's monastic silence, but not even Ditey appeared. Sound sleepers, Lilybankers. Sighing, he rubbed his face, did a few tentative shoulder stretches and pulled on his khakis. Maybe a cup of coffee, just to keep himself company.

Tad's stop in the hallway bathroom did galvanize Ditey, who padded into the scullery behind him. In the window above the sink a pretty, peach-colored smear glowed above the garden wall. As Beebe never failed to remind him, crummy days were as sweet as the pleasant ones; people just failed to tune in. Subtle but unmistakable movement beyond the open garden door (open?) put him on guard. Glad that he hadn't turned on a light, he held still and squinted, ignoring the dog's wagging request for breakfast.

Clutching the sink's chilly rim ever more tightly, he made out Beebe and Lionel, decided he was hallucinating, contemplated dialing 911. What would burglars want in the garden? The weathervane! Hesitating to abandon his concealed lookout in order to place the call, he caught a profoundly familiar, angled gesture on the shadowy terrace. Beebe had tossed back a braid.

Now Lionel, that maggoty troll, reached up and pulled her face down to his. They remained in some kind of forehead-to-forehead fondle long enough for Tad to feel his stomach turn inside out. Then Lionel – unmistakable now by the amber glow of the back porch lantern – wheeled out of view, clutching Beebe's hand at his side. She had that peaceful, self-contained look he always loved.

Muffled noise at the back door sent Tad darting through the hall and up the Lilybanks staircase two steps at a time, leaving a sadly baffled Newfoundland wheezing beneath the extinguished chandelier. He couldn't throttle even Lionel in a wheelchair.

Vaulting like a fleeing, oversized doe, Tad whisked around the top of the staircase into the murky upper hall toward some dimly envisioned refuge. Warm, humid flesh thwacked into his at chest height, releasing a familiar scent of honeysuckle which he associated with disaster. A slender female form teetered backwards from the force of the collision. Tad reached out instinctively to steady it.

"We're really going to have to stop meeting this way, Tad Bramble. Assault just isn't the Lilybanks approach," Lucy chirped. Before he could absorb the words she'd administered a sisterly thump to his shoulder. Adjusting to the dim light from further down the hall, he took in a thoroughly relaxed, confident Lucy in a jaunty little skirt and bare feet.

"I was just on my way to the loo, as Marian says. Hers is terminally clogged. Oh Tad, I'm getting married! We'll probably stay in Rutledge...Isn't it wonderful?" she squeaked, and threw herself into his arms.

Tad gave her a warm hug, thought better of it, went limp and backed off just as a shimmering, quivering thunderclap surged up from the hall below, enveloping them.

Marian came shambling down the hall towards them, followed by Althea who clutched an upside down Skippy as if bolting to an air raid shelter. She thrust him at Lucy and looked toward her own room, debating the efficiency of trying to bag Linnet.

"Not the Apocalypse, Althea," Marian panted. "Gustav Stickley." Althea stared at her like someone fighting down claustrophobia in an elevator.

"I mean the gong."

Giving the horrified Tad a wink of pure deviltry, Lucy bounded to Althea's side, grabbed her round the waist and breathed into her ear, "You know. In the hall cabinet so the kiddies don't deafen themselves."

Pacified, Al remembered the massive, oak-framed gong locked away behind glass. Beebe had told her it used to announce birthday cakes, recovered errant pets, even taxi cabs till silenced by the constraints of day care.

Grateful for the diversion if suspicious of its source, Tad tucked in his tee shirt and applied a little spit to his cowlick. He squared his shoulders.

"I think that's probably Beebe, Mrs. Morrissey." Taking in the lopsided bathrobe and mushy slippers he forced himself to add, "And possibly Mr. Woodruff."

At this Lucy and Skippy took off down the stairs, followed merrily by Marian leaving a trail of damp blotches on the new runner. Althea had recovered sufficiently to toss Lucy's spiky scarlet heels down to her with studied *esprit* when she turned back for them. Tad trailed behind, increasingly sullen.

A dark, empty hall greeted him, none of the squealing ladies having bothered to switch on the chandelier. Even faithful Aphrodite seemed to have taken off for the dining room, the apparent source of all the light and babble. He faltered a moment by the cabinet, from which faint dying reverberations still pulsed as he leaned his head against the glass.

Someone tugged at his sleeve.

"There you are." Flushed with good fortune, poised, already a woman, Beebe smiled up at him. Someone had tucked a rose behind her ear.

The enormity of his loss – no longer subject to misinterpretation – pressed in on Tad from all sides, rendering him curiously insubstantial. He seemed to be floating, sustained solely by the force of his admiration.

Acknowledging some nearly tangible barrier, Beebe stepped back, leaning against the sitting room doorjamb with her hands shoved into her pinafore's pockets. She appraised him from her unintended ascendancy: the small, warm eyes under the Neanderthal brow, the secretly stubborn lips – their natural pout qualified by a tendency to drop his jaw as if perpetually nonplussed – the stubby, capable hands dangling at his side as though his sheer size precluded self-defense. Impossible not to compare this with the hothouse bantam two rooms away, controlling his twitches and stutter for her sake, impeccably dressed (which had cost him pain to achieve), captivating Lilybanks with his European cufflinks and erudition, curiously enhanced by the goggling spaniel eyes and shooting spittle.

Dampened, unable to lead him by the hand, Beebe made herself smile encouragingly.

"C'mon."

A peace apart from pledges or festivity filled and surrounded her. Lamblike, Tad followed.

Enthroned on his chrome-plated buggy behind a towering pyramid of buns and an expanse of white damask, his rival preened and blinked, twirling a hand in greeting. Tad's grunt was swallowed by feminine twitters.

"Over here, Tad!" Mercifully that was Mrs. Morrissey, not Lucy.

He felt himself passed from Beebe to Gloria to Marian like some high-maintenance guest.

"Some sort of announcement, I gather?" Gloria probed, pulling him down into a chair between herself and Marian as he watched Beebe float over to Woodruff. Someone should tell her the hem of her dress was turned up in back.

Gloria followed his gaze with glittering eyes; she'd chauffeured Lionel as requested but the ride hadn't yielded the hoped-for scoop. Once folded into the passenger seat by Dr. Leiby (who was all savage silence and bad breath) the petted poet who supposedly enjoyed royal favor had lapsed into impregnable, sugary-scented rumination. Perhaps he'd conceived some ode to opacity in her Honda. One thing she was sure of: poor old Tad loathed the fellow and Beebe was playing them off against each other like an expert while the "sisterhood" continued to dote on her inspired sanctity. Gloria had successfully bullied her grad student into opening the shop after receiving Beebe's last-minute invitation. She wouldn't have missed this for the world, whatever it was.

Althea stretched toward Lucy, eager to make contact in spite of the insular ecstasy Lucy exuded as she leaned back in her chair, rubbing a foot and humming to herself.

"Profiteroles stuffed with frangipane cream, with an orange glaze," she whispered, having inquired.

Lucy gave her an enormous, fixed smile. Althea resolved upon no further forays. She watched Beebe pluck a dripping rose from the pretty floral miscellany someone had shoved into a sterling vase, and swaddle its thorns in a napkin. As usual, all eyes followed Little Miss Magnetism (as she probably assumed they would) – oh, God, why couldn't she leave her friends alone and enjoy herself? Could she escape this gibbering ego? She found relief, release, with a few breaths that lit up her whole body.

Conversation ceased as Beebe squeezed behind Lionel's wheel-chair and presented her increasingly blotched and beaming Bubo with the token. Not a word passed between them – only a long, dear look while Lucy and Al sniffed. Even Gloria felt a lump in her throat though she felt nutty about it, anticipating anything imaginable. Beebe embraced her aunt, kissing her on the top of her unkempt head, and resumed her seat while Marian patted Tad's hand and fumbled in the pocket of her robe.

Lionel tugged at one of Beebe's braids like a bell rope, which lac-erated Tad, and she hopped up again, sweetly obedient.

"Lionel and I have an announcement that we hope will please you all." Beebe kept her eyes on Marian. Gloria surveyed the table. Tad, Althea and even Marian had assumed variously disguised cringes. Lucy conveyed an anarchical, "bring it on" quality; perhaps she'd underestimated yesterday's tizzy about Lucy's whereabouts? Lionel seemed on the verge of tears, or perhaps a seizure. Aphrodite's head floated at table height next to Beebe. Her huge, unruly tongue lolled in Lionel's direction, aimed either at his throat or the cream puffs. Her domed forehead bore a distinct if unfortunate resemblance to his.

Beebe gave the poet a fond little poke in the arm. He cleared his throat.

"My charming Beebe and her family of friends: You will forgive the hour, and suffer this hasty *aubade*; we have a plane to catch. By force of felicity, with some pulling of strings and various machinations, we learned only yesterday that our dear friend here has been admitted to next year's newly created Masoncup Seminar in Transcendental

Poetics at Oxford. You can be very proud – to be admitted to this elite group of scholars at our Beebe's tender age is an unprecedented honor. Mrs. Morrissey, your tutelage has doubtless been instrumental. But the glory must go to Divine Providence, which has chosen to crown our friend with genius." Here Lionel wiped his glistening face with his napkin, and collapsed back against his chair, spent. Beebe dipped a napkin in champagne and moistened his temples as tentative squeals of delight erupted.

After Lionel had conspicuously enjoyed her attentions, Beebe called the table to order with a spoon.

"He only just found out, after working on this for weeks...Oh Bubo, isn't it wonderful?...There wasn't time to collect everyone – Bakeoven will forgive us I hope – Lionel's due in Stuttgart for an important symposium on Wednesday. We're so grateful to him." She raised her glass; Gloria followed suit and the flustered gathering toasted Lionel. Tad had sagged back in his chair but made a limp effort.

Beebe fumbled for the watch inside her neckline while gesticulating to Gloria. The latter gave Tad's forearm a perfunctory pat, walked around the table and skirted Ditey's rump to begin dismantling the stacked cream puffs onto plates. As an animated Lucy dispensed these like Frisbees, Beebe dropped a strawberry in Lionel's champagne and held a gooey puff to his lips as though he were in high chair and bib. He gurgled, purled and goggled as the windows behind him filled with a pinky-mauve light transfusing the horizon above Corrie Street.

"Could he have some more frangipane, Gloria?" Beebe whispered, and scrambled round the table evading embraces to pull Tad from the room.

Marian, very pink, shuffled over to Althea.

"Trip anyone who tries to follow them, dear."

Flattered, Althea spent the next ten minutes devising stratagems while appearing to make giddy small talk. Marian went into a huddle with Lionel while Gloria and Lucy eavesdropped. Aphrodite acquired a frothy mustache and crumby forehead intercepting Lionel's stealthy tidbits.

In the inglenook, Tad sighed and sat on the edge of the settle, leaning forward with elbows on knees as if the solution to his troubles lay inside the fireplace.

Beebe pulled the chains on the mica lanterns flanking the chimney. He winced.

"Congratulations Beebee. It's a great opportunity. Perfect for you," he told the fireplace as Beebe sat down beside him.

"You sound a little sepulchral."

He managed half a smile. She'd use gaudy words in the eye of a hurricane.

"Yeah. It's a lot to get used to, that's all. When's your plane leave?"

Little fingers, familiarly moist from nail biting, found his.

"Lionel likes to affect the royal 'we,' Tad. He just meant *his* plane. *His* plane leaves O'Hare at noon. Dr. Leiby and Professor Carberry will see him off. *My* plane leaves in October. Lionel's arranging for me to visit Oxford and sit in on some of the first Masoncup sessions, so I'll feel more comfortable next year. A year from this autumn."

Tad groaned quietly as though someone had cured his headache by hitting him over the head with the andirons. She pulled the great fleshy hand – unusually cold – onto her lap.

"Those tickets for Russia – I traded them in for tickets to London for you and Bubo this October." The lilt had gone from her voice. "How could you think I would ever, ever leave you behind, Tad?"

He finally turned. Tears welled; first one, then another spilled.

"Everyone tells me how clever I am. Brilliant. And wise. Divinely inspired." The voice shook just a little; she wrinkled her nose. "I've certainly gotten one thing right. I belong with you."

He wrapped her in his arms. She nestled, feeling him tremble, and laughed through tears.

"Tad, I think you're going to break me..." He relinquished an arm and they looked at each other shyly.

"We're gooey messes," she giggled, dabbing at his eyes and her nose with a tatted hem.

"I've got another surprise. After we visit Oxford – Bubo's going to be in paradise, it's over a decade since she's been back – Lionel's connections will open all sorts of literary doors, she'll swoon..."

Tad darkened. She rumpled his hair.

"Oh, Tad. Lionel lives on another plane. Sort of half William Blake, half..."

"Ape. Half ape."

"He does have a primitive streak. He's a child, Tad. A balding child genius. There was never any danger. Now listen. When we get back from our trip we'll have a whole year before my eight months of seminar..."

He groaned.

"I know. We'll talk to your dad, see if there's some British apprenticeship program or something he'd be pleased to have you in. But listen to the surprise! Gloria's moving to Florida right after Christmas. She's gotten an offer to run a fancy bakery in St. Augustine, with the option to buy at a give-away price if she likes it. An old lady who wants it continued with style after her death. I can try managing Maven Alley while she settles in down there, Tad. I talked her into it. Maybe somehow we could buy it, Tad! She'll be so happy to be warm she may not care about a lot of money...Well?"

He smoothed back her hair, cradled her face in his hands.

"I guess the sky's the limit, huh?"

She sniffed. "After we're married – I mean – will you? Marry me?"

He gaped, grunting. "Could you let me catch up, honey?" He started to laugh. "Yeah. Will *you* marry *me*?"

"Yes, Tad."

He tugged at the hidden chains around her neck, disentangling his locket proficiently for someone with thick fingers and arranging it outside her lace collar. Tad had the feeling he'd said and done all this once before, somewhere else – maybe a long time ago.

"There. We'd better get back in there, huh."

When Beebe stood up the rose fell from her hair. She picked it up off the floor and tucked it into the pocket of Tad's tee shirt. He patted it carefully.

As they walked down the hall hand in hand, grinning, he asked out of the corner of his mouth, "What's up with Lucy?"

"Micah's out. Harry's dad is in."

"Improvement."

Althea was tremendously relieved when they returned; Mr. Woodruff's wheelchair had been making ominous buzzings as though preparing to zip off on reconnaissance. She'd had time to become self-conscious about her damp pajamas.

Marian, now on her second wind and jaunty in the devil-may-care bathrobe, bustled over to the couple.

"I see all is well." She made Tad bend to receive a kiss on the cheek. "Lionel's been intoxicating me with various splendors arranged for our visit. Tad, we'll consult Bakeoven about augmenting our wardrobes," she chattered.

"Yes ma'am."

Lucy came up from behind Beebe and put her arms around her.

"Gloria's spilled the beans about the bakery. You'll be great! You'll still do my wedding cake?" She nuzzled the top of Beebe's head and gave Tad a very kind and normal grin.

Althea slumped contentedly in her chair, out of conversational range from the alarming Lionel, for whom Gloria was assembling a doggy bag. She smelled something stale and turned to find Watkins breathing down on her. He brandished an old peanut butter jar before her eyes; the thing was crawling with insects. They resembled the winged decanters in Tenniel's drawing of the dinner party finale in *Alice in Wonderland*. Watkins snatched it back.

"Carpenter ants. Having a party up in the attic!" This shrill explanation slashed through the happy hum, leaving a jagged hole that Watkins filled with *brio*.

"Carpenter ants, people!" he cackled, holding the jar overhead and giving it a savage shake. "You'll have to call Pest Patrol first thing, Mrs. Morrissey. Could be too late – they may have escavated the whole house. Have to call the place Lilycrumbs."

"Thank you, Watkins. We certainly would have invited you for breakfast had we known you were on the premises. When did you let yourself in? I don't recall discussing any work in the attic for this week." Marian's voice was determinedly level.

Lionel put a cream puff on a plate and held it out to the nicotine-permeated old handyman, who accepted it doubtfully. Beebe rescued the hapless captives while Watkins contemplated how best to negotiate the unwieldy pastry with all eyes upon him.

High spirits rallied. Skippy endured Aphrodite's attentions while sprawled in Tad's lap. Lucy discussed the possibility of an October honeymoon in England. Beebe promised Althea (who felt a migraine coming on) she'd release the ants in some benign location. Lionel listened to Watkins grumbling under his breath between increasingly sticky interactions with his frangipane cream:

"Cuckoo, that one. Braids too tight."

Eventually Watkins paid his respects to Marian and shuffled out, never having determined whose birthday it was. When he crossed the dining room threshold Lionel, who'd wheeled into formation with forethought, lobbed the last cream puff, hitting Watkins squarely between the shoulder blades.

Versatility

Wakening after a triple-strength dose of Advil, Althea resolved to take a stroll through Bodie Woods. She'd avoided the sanctuary for weeks, reluctant to encounter evidence of the Green League's ruthless restoration.

Stooping at the entrance to empty a muddy beer bottle and carry it at arm's length to a trash can, she recognized rather wearily that she needed to stop resisting. The new life she'd cobbled together kept buckling and threatening to splinter. Surely the odds were that at least some changes would be for the better?...No, that line of thinking couldn't be right. One was to embrace everything in joyful surrender without calculation.

Tripping on even ground, she swore. Bakeoven would be horrified by the inelegance. They supposedly had one of their nebulous "dates" this evening; she considered canceling, knew she wouldn't. They were perfectly partnered. His frustrating pattern of mixed messages – thoughtful appreciation of her psyche here, coyly barricaded bachelorhood there – meshed snugly with her hypervigilant mistrust and throttled impulse to cling...

Casper must be feeling very stern about these cowardly fantasies of a second marriage. Some days her current refuge felt pretty rickety. She'd seen the look Mrs. Curtis had thrown Mrs. Montini's au pair when the kids babbled excitedly about all the lights going off on the same day they had to use the upstairs toilet while theirs was overhauled. What was the big deal about climbing the staircase by flashlight? Weren't Waldorfers supposed to grasp the timeless appeal of stuff like that? Priceless childhood memories were being forged at Lilybanks. The cool families fathomed this, but were they enough to keep Kinder on Corrie going? And who was supposed to hold down the fort this October? She –

Good heavens, was that the parking lot at the far end of the pond? She'd never been able to see its saggy metal fencing from here. As far as her eye could travel the woods' overrun thicket was disappearing, restored to bare savannah and mature oaks. The illusion of a sprawling, labyrinthine, cozy green kingdom was threadbare indeed in several directions. One could see farther, but the vistas opened up now included distant traffic, homes and other hikers once mercifully concealed. She sighed and shook her head, resolving to be tough and take it all in her stride. Her world had turned upside down and she seemed to have survived; she felt reluctant now to squander much difficult emotion on yet another unsought transformation. After all, they could have razed the woods for a housing development. Best to count one's blessings, lighten up, let go.

She already needed to go to the bathroom. Harder to control the floodgates these days – she'd wet her pants five times since moving into Lilybanks. Probably the result of sharing bathrooms, having to keep an eye on Linnet, daycare's exigencies...

On the other hand, she reflected, choosing the less pruned of two paths to the pond, perhaps the light tug of gravity beginning to have its way with an aging uterus actually indicated a tumor. The size of a cannonball. Riddled with malignancy. She hadn't been to a gynecologist in seven years. She imagined Bakeoven impeccably dressed at her funeral. No eulogy; not enough mourners. Half of them across the ocean, the others too jubilantly embroiled in life. Her cousin would dutifully arrange the sale of Al's worldly goods, culling a few of the less flamboyant antiques for her offspring, and take Linnet to Animal Control. My God, Linnet! She needed to make some kind of will immediately –

A chainsaw started up somewhere to her left. She doubled back to the other path and found a fellow in a Rutledge County Conservation District cap who turned off his saw and nodded.

Walking into the jaws of the enemy required cunning.

"Morning! Lots of changes around here! We're all so happy the oaks are being saved. Thank you for your work. I understand some other trees are being left to stand as well? These saplings with pink bow ties aren't all oaks, are they?"

He removed his cap and wiped his forehead. "The goal is to leave nothing standing but oaks, hickories and cherries. Give 'em room to breathe. Probably take another year or two to get the job done, but we're making progress." An innocuous young man, pleased with his world. Probably never set a foot in Bodie till paid to do so. Possibly saving up for a few nice rural acres.

"I noticed more wildflowers this spring after last year's controlled burns. Lovely. I do wonder, though...Bodie is home to a small population of mourning cloak and question mark butterflies. They're unique, you know. One of the few species that actually overwinter. With their wings on, I mean. Not as larvae. They spend the winter under the bark of trees or deadwood. And then they're the first ones fluttering through the woods here in spring, even with some snow on the ground. Have you ever seen them on a sunny March morning? A little miracle. My point is, those woodpiles you folks put together sometimes sit for months and months before you get around to burning them. They're ideal sites for overwintering butterflies. You may be incinerating them." She paused, imagining the quintessential spirit of the woods trapped in a funeral pyre. He waited, courteous and blank.

"Cloaks and question marks favor willow and poplar for their egg laying. Quite a bit of that at the pond's edge. Don't have to take those down, do you?"

He scratched his jaw and turned toward the pond.

"All that scrubby sandbar willow's coming out. And the poplars will all have to come down eventually. We're hoping the tallest will fall over into the pond on their own. Expensive to cut down the tall ones. They've got ten more years of life at the most, anyway, and if they fall into the pond it'll be good for pan fish."

Not wishing to linger over an elaboration of that mystery, she thanked him for the information and turned away in shock toward the farthest corner possible.

The dear musical poplars, whose shivering golden reflections she sat on a pondside bench every autumn to treasure up! Unthinkable.

Madness. No use begging Bake to do something; once the conservation district took over, science and industry ruled. The poetry, the
very soul of the place would suffer, and the oaks' solitary splendor
would irresistibly attract picnic tables, asphalted workout stations,
dog poop bag dispensers. And tidily regulated, fee-paying "pan fish-
ers" for whom safety railings and piers might be necessary?

Sobbing, for this was even worse than she'd expected, she trudged
over to Casper's favorite bench – the one closest to an exit – hoping
for solace. Earlier in the summer a red admiral had fluttered down
next to her, sunning on the seat, typical of Casper's vivid, economical
tokens of affection.

She sat down and leaned forward to realize that they'd uprooted
the sparse little stand of wild rose just across the path from the bench.
Every year she admired its meager offering of unobtrusive blossoms
found nowhere else in the woods. Culling a sprig of its tiny rosehips
from the withered debris, Al whispered, "I'm so sorry. But we're always
together. Go with God – and find new joy." She dropped the memento
in her pocket and left, reflecting brokenly on the various interpretations of "a healthy woods."

Ignoring the path to slog through weeds, Althea came upon a
downy woodpecker perched on a spike of mullein and pecking away
as though it were ten feet up in a birch. With this perky advertise-
ment for versatility the last twenty minutes of self-imposed tragedy
dropped away like so much sludge. She entered the street with light
feet. An opposing view of Green League purification merited an editorial essay as well as, perhaps, some creative interference. She might
even be the person to arrange both. But walking around under an
egocentric bell jar of doom demonstrated deplorable incompetence
on the part of a Lilybanker. Head up, shoulders back, Althea turned
to admire Bodie's profile stenciled against the clouds as always when
leaving.

On an impulse she decided to go check up on Libby, who'd phoned to cancel both Althea's animal sitting slots for the month, sounding as if she were calling from the bottom of a well.

*   *   *

Just as Althea turned from Libby's front door, debating whether to request a police wellness check from the Walgreen's phone while buying Band-Aids for her purpling knuckles, it opened a crack.

"It's you. I cancelled, remember?"

Controlling her anxiety at the very suggestion of Alzheimer's symptoms, Al smirked.

"So what are you up to, Grumpy? Drowning your sorrows in fair trade vegan fudge?"

Libby looked dumfounded, then smiled with what Al suspected was admiration.

"Where's Captain? Is Captain okay?"

"He's watching TV."

"What?"

"He's upstairs watching TV with the cats. Their favorite song-bird DVD."

"Oh. Are you going to invite me in?"

Libby stared down her freckled nose at her while dislodging something from a molar with an index finger. She pushed the door wider. Bigsby the beagle/lab mix tried to scoot out the door, and Libby dragged him back in none too gently by the collar. A steaming mound of dog poop lay in the middle of the kitchen's faux parquet; a second pile in a puddle just to the left of the doorway looked older.

Socks barely lifted her head from Libby's dumpster-worthy brocade loveseat, but Scooter and Bigsby mobbed Althea as though desperate for a walk, or even a word. When Bigsby slipped in the mess Libby's mouth began to wobble.

"We're out of paper towels."

"It reeks in here, Libby. The fumes have gone to your brain. Let's go outside and –"

"<u>NO</u>. Not outside."

"Alright, let's shut ourselves in the bathroom, and you'll tell me what's going on. You can be on the toilet, I'll perch on the side of the tub..." Al had her hand on the closed bathroom door's knob when Libby nearly knocked her over.

"Sorry. Pinky's in there. Resting."

They ended up in the small back room that served mostly as a path to the second floor. A battle-scarred Art Deco armoire and the lovebirds' aviary loomed over them as they sat on the bare floor. Libby leaned against the stairway door, knees to her chin, and Al assumed a meditation pose with the elderly Scooter's head on her thigh.

"Tell me what's wrong. Maybe I can help."

A hollow, cracked noise halfway between a burp and whooping cough erupted from Libby's chest. She covered her face with white hands.

Althea flinched.

The embarrassing, raw noises continued and Al got up to go hold Libby, wondering if she even remembered she was there. Scooter quailed and retreated; Al could hear a lot of panting and clinking dog tags behind her in the doorway.

Libby thrust both arms straight out ahead of her like a traffic cop.

"I'm better. That was good."

"How about I get some toilet pa –"

"Pinky needs his space. It's okay. Sit down, Althea. I'm glad you came. Lilybanks to the rescue." Libby sounded like she was under-water, but the familiar dictatorial style reassured. She wiped her face with the bottom of her tee shirt while Al pretended to admire the clouds out the window. Libby needed to put on some deodorant.

"I would kill for a cigarette right now...oh well, probably not the moment to resurrect bad habits. I'm going to be homeless in a month or two." The attempt at nonchalance was spoiled by a couple of involuntary, shuddery gasps for air.

Libby managed to wrench her gaze from the armoire to Althea's face for a few seconds; their eyes met.

Al made herself breathe deeply and consciously a few times, fending off the need to temper Libby's despair for her own sake before she even had the facts, which might be cruel. Socks made her way past and sniffed Libby's mouth, then licked it. Libby clung to her, then patted the floor next to her, where Socks lay down against her. Scooter came back in haltingly and settled next to Al, giving off comforting puffs of warm dog smell. Al's fingers tingled; she focused on the presence of the empty space in the room.

"You and your friends here won't be homeless as long as Lilybanks is around, Libby," she found herself saying with confidence. It was true, so why not say it, however presumptuous on the part of an insignificant boarder.

Libby hiccuped, wiping the outer corner of an eye with her fist. "That's probably not the long-term solution, Al...But it beats the hell out of warm milk and a blankie. Thank you." She smiled, then teared up and looked out the window. "I don't want to have to split up my tribe..."

"Shall I make us some tea? Something a little more bracing than the weedy stuff? I saw a box of Lipton's –"

"No, no. I can think better if we don't get the critters all riled up. They're putting up with plenty."

"Well, it looks a little like you're all holding each other hostage, but we won't deal with that right now. Let's hear what's going on. In an orderly fashion, please, for my thinning brain cells."

"I lost my little job at Alley Katz." Libby addressed the armoire. "Which has become a disaster – you can't imagine. Alright, I have to back up. Katz, that fucking asshole, sorry, sort of lost it because I relieved him of a set of antlers – you know, the mounted trophy type of thing schmucks hang over their mantels or garage doors. I found it leaning against a cobwebby wall in a storage closet. Almost impaled myself on it. Turns out he inherited it from his late brother Seymour "Kit" – don't get me started – Katz. Great big majestic spires, Althea. The skull and antlers of a lesser kudu the horrible Kitty Katz murdered on one of those canned hunts down in Texas. You know, the gallant hunter pays top dollar for the pleasure of hiding behind a wall to shoot at an exotic animal that's all but tied to a tree."

Althea winced. "Good for you."

"I buried 'em in a cornfield that belongs to an Ally's relative. Katz noticed them missing right away, claimed he'd planned to mount them above the snack bar. Next to the TV."

"That was worth losing the job, Libby." Al shuddered. "You'll find something else. I take it there's more?"

"*Oh* yeah. I got fired coolly enough, but it turned out the Katzes were both foaming at the mouth. She got him to circulate a petition through the neighborhood here claiming I'm a hoarder with dangerous animals and asking for signatures to request the city council get me out of here before children and small mammals are maimed or some kind of plague spreads."

Al's heart sank. "Is that why everyone's inside? The problem with that, Libby is that right now the house *does* feel like a hoarder's. Before I leave we've got to get it aired out. You can sit with some of the dogs in the car while I clean if you're afraid to have too many in the yard. We'll just let the best tail-waggers into the yard. If..." Libby didn't seem to be listening. "Okay. First things first. What else?"

"The Katzes went door to door telling lies while pretending to be concerned about me, what a joke, as well as innocent citizens. (I have reliable informants.) They got a couple dozen signatures. Enough to make it seem plausible for the council to consider, though hardly a landslide victory. It's coming up for a vote at a special council forum, less than two weeks away...I'm not letting anyone take my family away from me, Althea. If they vote against us they have to give me a month to move, my lawyer friend's guessing."

Libby seemed more demoralized than Al would have predicted.

"I can't believe you're assuming you'll have to move, Libby. The guy's just irate about his antlers. They want to scare you for revenge. Probably promised a bunch of tournament bowlers free Cheetos for a year if they'd sign the petition. There are some pretty decent, intelligent people on the council, Libby. Amy Newton, Kip Rusk...They'll probably think the whole thing's kind of humorous. And how about the Allies? We can pack the council room to the rafters with supporters. Do they know what's going on? It looks like you're isolating, to me."

Libby managed a wobbly smile.

"I guess it's that I've been on my own pretty much since always. And I'm pretty much an anomaly in the neighborhood. The pudgy butch witch in the crappy little house with all the dogs. I'm tolerated because I'm intelligent. The Hill District fancies it's fond of eccentric academic types. I'm a bit much for a lot of the Allies, you know. They're all buddy-buddy at puppy mill protests, but I don't get invited for dinner. Not a good fit." She smiled more fiercely, finally turning toward Al.

"I know what you mean. I'm not exactly the hot dinner guest of the season myself. But you're being awfully self-indulgent. Not to mention dumb, Libby. The Allies are an incredible resource in this situation. And you know it. Do you want to cling to a mental image of yourself as a victimized loner, or do you want to stay in your cozy little home with your family? Which one's more important to you? I'm wondering."

Libby let her head drop back against the wall a little too vigorously, and shut her eyes for what began to seem a long time. Al tried not to think at all, letting herself dissolve into the murmuring lovebirds, Scooter's toenails against her thigh, a pulse all along her own body.

"Okay. You're right. Lilybankers always are...Sorry. That didn't come out right. What I mean is, let's get going. Do you want to be involved?"

Al felt annoyance zip through her gut. "What do you think?"

"Thank you. You're a good friend. Not a word I use lightly." Libby embraced Socks, but smiled hard, reddening, at Al.

Unwilling to reveal her delight, Al patted Scooter and stood.

"Excellent. Let's get you a comb. Your hair looks like a worn-out Brillo pad." She strode toward the bathroom and had the door open before Libby had time to blurt, "Stop!"

Pinky stood cowering in the corner by the tub, staring at her with glassy, ruby red eyes that glowed with menace. Her legs were rigid. A low growl rumbled in the direction of Althea's shins. She shut the door carefully, sickened, and turned to see the hair along Scooter's spine on end. Libby placed herself between Al and the bathroom.

"It comes and goes. Sometimes he's just exhausted and curls up in a little ball on his pillow. I'm not ready to..."

"Yes you are ready. Call that Hungarian vet who gives Allies discounts. Get him to come over. You've done everything possible for Pinky. He's ready for a joyful transformation, Libby. 'Nothing real can be threatened; nothing unreal exists,'[15] like it says in *A Course in Miracles*. I know you're not into all that. But don't you think it's at least possible that Pinky's hardships will evaporate like a bad dream, while that eager, lovable spirit is indestructible in a way our limited brains can only guess?" She pictured the unappealing, irksome little fellow jouncing along determinedly on their walks, inevitably tangling his leash, shrinking from passersby, growling at shadows. "It's not a fairytale. Do you think this is all there is? Just dog poop and phone calls and whatever else our egos tell our brains to focus on? Look –"

"Yes, Althea. I do think that's all there is. If it's just a bad dream, well, I'm all for that. But what's the point of trying to alleviate suffering in that case? We could just wait for the dream to be over, and then we Wake Up to Enlightenment, I suppose?" Libby folded her arms, looking her most stolid.

"Hold on, Libby. No one's suggesting compassion's not a good thing. Just loosen up a minute. Let go of yourself in this situation, let go of words, try to just *be* for sixty seconds without clinging to thoughts and emotions that seem to tell you who you are, where you are. And then tell me you can't sense – I can't put it in words – some alive awareness in the air, in the living creatures in this room, even in this dumpy Deco armoire. (Sorry.) Look at the sunlight and shadow on the windowsill. Get connected, Libby, and then tell me you can measure that connection. Tell me it's finite, just another thing to think about and discard. Just stay right here, right now, without telling yourself narrow little Libby-Merchant-the-know-it-all stories. You might stumble on peace and joy, so watch out." Mustafa the iguana had stolen into the doorway like some angel of the odd. Al resisted the impulse to cackle.

Libby turned her back to look out the window onto the alley's utility poles, puny vintage garages and sparrows. Al found herself increasingly gratified as the silence stretched, dropped that like a hot coal and returned to quiet spaciousness. Eventually, as though on cue, Libby's cell phone bleated from the kitchen table. They let it ring. Socks whined softly, and Libby turned around to pat her.

"Guess what? The dogs know all about this. Okay, the peach-faces, too, and probably the plants. I'll work on keeping an open mind about the armoire. I'm not ready for gurus and prayer beads. But I definitely agree to try to be more like a dog." She advanced to gently push a loose strand of hair back from Althea's face.

*   *   *

"The cheese is a sheep's milk Brie with lavender, from a place in Oregon called Harlequin Hill...I'm familiar now with your artistic tendencies in these matters," Bakeoven added, seeing Althea perk up. He filled the glass she held out. "Can't indulge you regarding wines, however. No kitty cats on the labels...What do you think of that? Spanish. Hints of melon and coriander." He watched her, eyes narrowed.

Normally ill at ease under Bakeoven's gourmet tutelage, Al inhaled dramatically over the edge of what she considered a risibly large glass, sipped, sloshed, held it up to the light, sipped again.

"Mmmm...insidious, isn't it? Makes an equable first impression; then it sort of – burgeons. Beguiling, I'd say." Twining one leg twice round the other, she permitted her arm an unusually expansive stretch along the back of Bakeoven's reproduction Biedermeier settee. She'd made the remark up on the walk over.

His scrutiny became even more scrunched, the glitter in his pale eyes all but eclipsed as he sorted out various unprecedented phenomena.

Contempt and compassion dueled ever closer to a precarious edge as Althea considered telling him she resented being used in his homophobic masquerade. It wasn't an unattractive role, in her situation; what she minded was appearing duped both publicly and privately. Taking another sip, and then a gulp, she looked him in the eyes as levelly as possible.

"Bake, I know men usually hate talking about relationships, but I'd like to clarify a few things." He paled, predictably. Goodbye, Bries and benefit nights.

"Since our chemistry seems to be cordial rather than, ah, carnal..." (she'd worked hard on this one) "I'd just sort of like it to be official that –"

"DAMN it. You're recently bereaved, Althea. Gentlemen tread lightly on hallowed ground. Gentlemen of my generation, anyway. Our chemistry has yet to be explored. Nothing about your wary demeanor, my dear, has suggested that an aggressive scaling of your castle walls would be welcome."

Dumfounded, she felt her face redden, though whether from embarrassment, annoyance or flirtatious delight she couldn't tell.

He was smiling now, albeit a thin smile, and waiting.

"I see. Yes, I see your point. I suppose I'm glad I spoke up, though I feel like a great lumbering orangutan now." She saw him relax. "I'm afraid ambiguity's my middle name. Triple A. Frustrating, perhaps, from your point of view."

"I'd call it edifyingly complex." He inspected his glass. "Equable first impression, then...beguiling, I'd say."

"*Touchée*," she giggled, knowing she was crimson now, and how unbecoming that was with her coloring.

He offered a plate of water crackers. "Try the cheese." He was frankly appraising her now. She wondered what the correct amount of cheese would be, decided it was safe not to worry about that, and took another long drink, claiming her moment.

"I will say you come the closest to my ideal of any woman I've known."

This lavish compliment struck her as chilly. In a rare, gossipy moment Marian had told her Bakeoven was "married to a knave." Beebe had translated: he was self-defeatingly critical, sidelined by perfectionism. Al gave him a dubious, lopsided smile – just in case he'd thought the honor overpowering.

He put his glass down as though the moment were definitive, still staring at her with an unusually warm expression – the bottle had been only half full when she arrived. She quailed, unsure whether he repelled her, and unsure whether she cared about that just for an evening's experiment.

He pulled the small table between them aside, and knelt to remove her shoes. Thank heavens she'd had a shower.

"Lean back, lovely." He patted the tasseled bolster she'd always found so perfect for the Biedermeier, and so unpromising.

"No invasion tonight, Althea. Just an admiring salute."

Onstage

BLRAA! BLRRAAAA! Scout somersaulted backwards into Pippin as the fancy blue rooster with the tail of many eyes turned on them. Its caustic screeches were taken up by the second bird; their little headdresses trembled with rage. Seemed they didn't appreciate a good game of Pounce. They stuck their pointy tongues out at the kittens, hissing and posturing.

Seeing Gypsy on the verge of charging, Bonnet trotted toward the pair of peacocks, wagging. One cock managed a stately scamper into the hydrangeas; the other fluttered to the top of an ivy-clad column. The kittens began shadow-boxing below it, taking an occasional swipe at the feathery fringe hanging just out of reach.

"You're very young to be a mother, dear," Bonnet said to Gypsy as she settled back in among the remnants of luncheon. Her mistress's outdoor stage and its lawn – the midpoint of their ramble up to Lilybanks – had seemed the best place for a rest.

"I'm their auntie. Their mama's gone missing, leaving four little ones. I've lost track of how many days it's been...What my sister'd say if I'd lost these two to Leo – especially little Scout, the apple of her eye..."

Bonnet swiped at Gypsy's forehead with her tongue. "Now, now, don't fret. Star will have you all safely home very soon."

Gypsy purred and blinked, grateful for a little mothering. "The kind lady at home has a collie, too. Perhaps I've been wrong to steer clear of Delilah...She does love to sniff us so."

"Delilah? Delilah Bunting? I've met her on a promenade or two. House the color of cambric tea, with a picket fence and lilacs? A sweet dog; you can rely on her. Count your blessings, love. A bouncing, mild-mannered collie and a picket fence are treasures. Ask any fox. A damp little fanny from time to time's a small price to pay, Gypsy."

Resolving to be more appreciative, Gypsy flattened her ears in warning as Pippin looked over to make sure she wasn't watching. He longed to scale the steps to Mrs. Morrissey's stage, from which one might launch oneself into the midst of those gussied-up roosters.

"Plotting mayhem, isn't he. If a hawk spied him all alone on that bare stage it would make short work of your nephew. All apologies when it learned the tasty morsel was a protégé of the Star. Lunch first, ask questions later, those hawks. You're right to be stern, Gypsy..." Bonnet stopped, cocking her head.

Gypsy made out a faint rustling, from which direction she couldn't tell. Seeing Bonnet scanning the sky she mewed to Scout and Pippin, who raced, tumbling, to obey the unmistakable edge in her cry.

Flattened against the hamper by their growling aunt, who expected to be carried off by a hawk in their stead, the kittens missed the giant winged shadow on the stage floor. Gypsy followed Bonnet's gaze. Something big and white that cupped the wind like Mr. Bunting's shirts on the clothesline floated ever closer, dangling a pair of sticks. Bonnet seemed quite pleased.

"Not a hawk, dearies. And not an umbrella with two handles. A friend."

Merriment erupted among her relieved guests at the sight of the buffoon-bird wafting down to the stage.

"What is it? What is it?" Pippin wriggled his hindquarters, feigning an attack.

"A red-headed woodplunker!" Scout suggested saucily as the great bird thudded onto the wooden platform. It continued to flap its wings as though struggling to keep from falling over. The peacocks watched with disdain and stalked away; Bonnet clambered up the stairs of the stage to press her nose against the stork's breast. Its flapping and clatter increased.

"Come meet the little darlings," Bonnet panted. "I'm afraid we had them expecting a vulture, but they seem to have recovered."

Fez rubbed his head against her shoulder, and saw three cats grooming themselves with studied self-possession. Accustomed to the lukewarm reception his dull croak earned among newcomers, Fez merely stretched his neck in their direction, nodding cordially.

Little Pippin's tail lashed with excitement. "It's the great-grandfather of the cardinals!" Scout gaped at the stork's crest, deciding that Pippin was right for once. Gypsy thought confusedly of the smoking cap Mr. Bunter wore the night Bah-Seek had proudly pointed him out to her through a window. Cuddling and conspiratorial behind the window box geraniums, they'd watched wafting wreaths of pipe smoke circle his armchair. Perhaps this bird could also send smoke curling from its mouth? Bonnet had powerful friends – if peculiar, Gypsy decided, imagining how impressed Bah-Seek would be with these new associates of hers.

"All's well," Fez rasped into Bonnet's silky ear. "Star's won a new friend; I'm on my way to meet them at the Sandy Neck fishing hole. You may reunite the young lovers at Lilybanks. Star's had his way with Cook; our guests will feast before they go home. Their elders will have to roll these stuffed, tuckered little ones back down the hill."

The collie's pretty folded ears stood straight up; her dark eyes sparkled. "Let me tell her, won't you?" Bonnet plunged down the stairs.

"My friend Fez wants to meet you two, so pull yourselves together. I must speak with your auntie." Bonnet bustled off to Gypsy while the kittens groomed each other's rumpled faces.

"The kittens are safe now, dearie. Your beau's waiting for

you up at the house. Leo won't be up to any more shenanigans, you may rely on it...Look at them! Two wee sillies and one great big silly!"

Scout had been granted the honor of trying out the stork's headgear. Engulfed from the shoulders up, she wobbled about in circles, trying to maintain her dignity. Pippin prepared to attack from the rear.

"Tut tut! Not quite your size, I fear! Perhaps our mistress could order something smaller from the haberdasher – mind your stern! Pirate abaft!" Their flapping referee shifted from one gnarled leg to the other, his eye to the ground.

"Come along, little ones. We're going up to the house. Your auntie's in a hurry," Bonnet barked. "Fez! Get that dear child uncorked and find a lovely trout for our guests!"

Looking a little sheepish, Fez plucked his cap from Scout's head, mashed it back onto his own and peered down at his admirers.

"Perhaps you'll come fishing with me some day, friends. Clear the deck!" A few heavy, running jumps sent him soaring.

*   *   *

"Foxes, mink. Coyotes wander through now and then. One lonesome old badger. A few thick-skinned snakes who might enjoy coiling themselves around a kitten sandwich after a long hibernation. Hawks, of course. Oh, and snapping turtles: faster than you'd guess. All of 'em pretty cooperative about leaving our tribe alone, merely out of friendship, of course. They'll become accustomed to you, Leo. I'm assuming you're willing to give up hunting rights in return for the liberty of wandering our woods and fields undisturbed." Star surveyed Leo candidly, neither menacing nor coaxing. The tomcat's perpetual sneer had petrified over the years, making his a difficult map to read. Behind Leo's favored wily expression Star observed a hunger for friendship. Somewhere in there a sweet kitten peeked out through the sly mask.

Star tried not to sputter with amusement: Gypsy would have unstrung the poor fellow. What he needed was a bachelor comrade who grasped his true worth.

"Just stick with me for awhile when you're out and about up here, why don't you. The fierce ones will see you've permitted me an alliance of sorts, and recognize the wisdom of neglecting you. That way I won't have to worry about you...Worry about you beating the tar out of one of my neighbors, I mean," Star hastened to explain.

Leo lashed his tail and examined a front paw.

"It's alright, Star. Happy to comply. Stupid not to learn the territory with you. Already indebted to you for rescuing me from that misguided attempt to assemble a ready-made family. Sunstroke, I suppose. Speaking of that, wait till you hear about the time I found myself..." They continued, Leo gabbling and Star nodding sagely, till they reached a clearing.

"Honeysuckle's a little sparser here, you can get a glimpse of the lake. That white stain on the sandbar is Fez."

Leo crept through the greenery in the direction suggested, and contemplated the water. He looked doubtful.

"I've been meaning to ask you. How can you fish without getting..." Leo squared his shoulders – "well, wet?" The question itself was a major concession.

"Beavers felled some trees in the shallows down there. You just flatten yourself out along the log and Fez herds the fish toward the shore. On a sunny day like this you need only stick a paw in the water. After a little practice, of course...By the way, while we're alone – what's become of the youngsters' mother?"

Leo stared down at the lake.

"I found her under the last full moon, in a rinky-dink shack with half its roof caved in. Far side of the fen – foolhardy of me, but you know how a full moon can be...She'd dragged herself into a crate. Buckshot. Shoulder wound. Lost the end of her tail, too." Leo's tail went limp.

"Takes the starch out of a fellow, seeing something like that. Go on, Leo." Star's eyes glowed with anger.

"Trig little thing. Pretty once. Quiet, modest type. We'd met before...Did what I could. Little enough. Stayed till she'd entered the trance. No need for anyone, no fear, after you've gone through that gate. Just between her and her moon."

"Yes."

The lake's sunlit ripples held both cats' gaze.

"Kittens are luckier than many, having their auntie," Leo finally said. His tone suggested he'd been an orphan himself. "Best not tell her clan."

"I'll tell Bezique. Let him decide...C'mon. Let's get down there before Fez starts eating 'em. He won't be able to hold out forever. You'll see – this'll be worth the risk of a dunking."

10

Retreat
[1914]

Calla lay in the bedroom overlooking Corrie Street. The dome of her belly rose beneath a taut eyelet sheet from her trousseau. The delivery boy's bicycle bell tinkled through the open window... another crocheted blanket from a neighbor, or the eucalyptus ointment her mother had promised.

Downstairs the new Scotch collie pup clattered through the hall, racing Olive to the door. She'd filled Calla's temporary room and the adjoining nursery with lilies-of-the-valley; crocks, majolica and canning jars spewed the fragile scent.

Calla had considered feigning morning sickness to overthrow spring's dominion in here. But it seemed as impossible to escape one's home as one's fate.

She and Martin had run into their fashionable architect last weekend in the Blackstone Hotel, inauspiciously named after the meatpacking magnate. Afterwards Calla had astonished Martin by obeying stuffy Dr. Hargrave's entreaties that she take to her bed. Old-fashioned and unwarranted as this was – she was sound as a prize broodmare – the temptation to retreat had suddenly become irresistible, the rickety barrier between pride and fact breached at last.

Greeting them with a blitheness that bordered on hilarity as he edged his way through the crowded tables, Crum had frankly admired her condition with the detached license of an art connoisseur. Martin beamed proprietarily as usual, dependably missing any hint that the evening had shriveled into so much ashen wreckage for her. There was much reason for Crum's delight; he couldn't have fathered the child.

His wealthy North Shore brat of a client had probably been waiting for him in the bar. Calla had read that Anna Pavlova was expected to grace the Tiffany-clad salon Crum had designed for him this summer. A slave to the arts, her architect hadn't crossed Lilybanks' threshold in a year, and had been a rare and unreliable visitor for months previous.

A suggestive note – probably from that louche chauffeur, Letitia Pratt's barbed condolence at a charity raffle ("I hear our Professor has decamped, my dear, finding Russet Farm's temptations even sweeter than Lilybanks'"), Olive's inability to dissemble when Calla had broached the unutterable one night after too much of Martin's Scotch...John's every gesture, hesitation, regret – these had gradually penetrated her willful naiveté. It had needed only that one last unnatural response at the Blackstone. Her lover preferred men.

His genuine satisfaction with her lush, daringly apparent pregnancy had dismantled her own acceptance of its inevitability, its ponderous, primeval necessity. Bereft, and sick at the realization of the profoundly fatuous role she'd played in what she'd seen (still saw) as the love of her life, she'd come home bent on destruction. Impossible to kill herself, for Martin's sake, but a fall down the stairs would provide some perverse relief. The child's only appeal had been as the ripe fruit of her enchanted kingdom, blighted now.

She'd found she couldn't do it to the house.

Olive's tea tray rattled up the hall accompanied by puppyish panting. Gompy withdrew from Calla's toes to her pillow.

"This way, Bonnet!"

Olive bustled through the nursery, her irrepressible hair bristling around the starched cap. Dr. Hargrave insisted Olive don this and a cumbersome full-length white apron. She'd told Calla with amusement that he kept trying to persuade her to train as a nurse and head overseas to the front – while he enjoyed the Yanks' prosperous neutrality.

"We've brought you Melting Moments with your tea. Bonnet's learning to stay put quietly while I wrestle the dreadful eggbeater." Gompy hissed down over the edge of the bed, sending Bonnet back into the nursery.

"Now, now, love. She's just a little muffin, with a nose as black as yours."

Sighing, Calla made an effort to sit up straighter. Her intriguing domestic had retreated behind a tedious maternal mask since Calla had been unable to respond to more intimate, effortful conversation.

"Ruth brought her wedding sari round last evening after you'd gone, Olive. Threads of real silver, worth a ransom." Eugene and Ruth were to be married in Lilybanks' walled garden next month. Ruth had hinted she'd wait till the day before the wedding to mail Crumrind's invitation. Loyal, efficacious Ruth. Her worshipful Eugene had consented to honeymoon in Java.

"Mmm. Let me tuck this under your chin."

The puppy delivered a fusillade of gleeful yelps in Gomp's direction, bouncing backwards with every salvo. Its tail flailed the bassinet's flounce.

Lunatic Fringe

"I'm not sure it quite comes together as a piece of art. Lucy's kindergarten poster skills can't spoil the words of saints. Though I'm afraid they don't enhance them." Micah had been surprised by his church's participation in a controversial community art event; *he'd* certainly done nothing to promote the Lilybankers' latest shenanigans.

Micah appeared to consider the churchyard art installation

thoughtfully. In fact, Beebe had riveted his attention. Standing on the bottom rung of the fence with a wrought iron spear in each fist, she radiated heat and light. Passion surrounded her outline like a nimbus; Micah momentarily thought the air around her hair and shoulders roiled, contorting the parked cars and elms in the background.

"Love even for the demons..."[16] her voice choked. Tears threatened.

Horrified by a queasy brew of conscientiousness and pulsing exultation, he refrained from the tender pat he longed to deliver.

"Beebe?"

A car had pulled up to the curb.

Dennis Leiby's Italian loafers appeared below the door of his ambassadorial sedan as the president converted his glacial inspection of Beebe and Micah into the granting of an indulgent paternal audience. He joined them.

"Beautiful morning! I like to take time to make the rounds of our neighborhoods, keep up on local color – always glad to see familiar faces. Mr....Funnel, I think?" Micah shook the extended hand, feeling like a peasant waylaid by a seigneurial tour of the marches.

"Fennel," he corrected, too low to be heard beneath Leiby's silky exclamation of "Beebe! My old friend." He seized her hand also, sandwiching it in both of his and effectively prying her off the fence so her forehead slammed into his university tie tack. Micah watched her offer Leiby one of those long-suffering, apple-cheeked, radiant smiles whose sophistication he'd not fully appreciated till now.

Leiby feigned a discerning frown as he took in the churchyard display.

"'No Tree Is a Junk Tree.'" His guffaw appeared to be purely nervous, devoid of content. "Ah. Another salvo from the community dialogue about Bodie Woods. Love it. Glad to see the arts involved. Healthy debate of this sort's just the kind of thing you want to see in the wider community; we like to think a flourishing university infuses the public with the spirit of inquiry and self-expression we stand for," he churned, sounding increasingly wooden as he scrutinized the pile of fresh-cut brush and berries stacked against a large mock-up of a church marquee. The "Junk Tree" title and the quotations below it had been lettered in quaint, bungalow-style script *à la* Charles Rennie Mackintosh, an allusion to the church's architecture.

Archangel Gabriel Orthodox Church was the brainchild of an energetic apprentice of Louis Sullivan, Crumrind's idol. Gilt onion domes and steppe-style rusticity bloomed amidst a hodgepodge of Pre-Raphaelite stained glass, hammered metal doors and square-pegged corbels that made Gabriel's a darling of the historical preservationists. After much wringing of hands by the local historical society, that unpredictable, well-endowed body had offered generous technical and financial support for the salvaging of the church's moldering interior if the university would match its pledge. Leiby, ever eager to enlarge his domain, had seen to it that the board of directors came through.

Micah had become a rather high-profile convert, recognized by campus library patrons during festal processions around the church's exterior or when he dangled over the edge of a belfry window to touch up the paint. Leiby, among others, was gratified by Micah's presence as an indication of successful cross-pollination. The mostly elderly parishioners, second-generation Estonians and Russians, and the occasional stray Greek, welcomed him; Micah and his motley grad student guests bore as much symbolic weight for them as for the Hill District powers.

Leiby's patronizing remarks echoed tinnily. Beebe had enrobed herself in silence; Micah groped for an excuse to escape.

Reluctant to venture into art criticism – one had to be politic – Leiby progressed toward his objective.

"By the way – congratulations! I understand my efforts on your behalf have been pre-empted by my distinguished recent houseguest. Sure you wouldn't prefer to pursue a full degree at Oxford? These fancy seminars tend to have the impact of any old pedestrian junior year abroad on applications, regardless of the participant's age." He observed his loafers thoughtfully. "Always at your service should you change your mind, young lady. Though I'm getting that familiar swamped feeling with the fall semester upon us...Of course I'll make a point of looking in on you while you're over there. I'm scheduled to cultivate some promising academic liaisons in Europe next year; they've allowed me a generous budget...Foreign travel ever more expensive, eh, Funnel?" He eyed Micah's ink-stained, slightly threadbare shirt, then turned toward Beebe again, assuming a hushed, solicitous tone as he leaned closer.

"I understand the city's going to have to be involved in your water main situation. I'd be happy to arrange university housing for you and Professor Morrissey. Keep it all in the family. The Ravens' nest, as we like to think of it." He winked at her and waved chummily to Micah as his car tore from the curb.

Micah sighed. "Anyway. I'm glad you like Saint Isaac the Syrian's thoughts on a charitable heart: 'on fire for the whole of creation.'[17] A pretty exacting definition of compassion. Lucy copied out the lines to use for some Waldorf performance after she saw them framed on my wall. Someone else must've given her the lines from Dostoevsky... 'Love to throw yourself upon the earth and kiss it'[18] – now, that sounds more like a fertility dance from *The Rite of Spring*. Not chaste enough for Lucy," he observed, instantly regretting having revealed his meanness.

Beebe hadn't heard.

"'Love all of God's creation, the whole of it and every grain of sand. Love every leaf, every ray of God's light!...If you love every thing, you will soon perceive the divine mystery in things'[19]... Bubo suggested the Dostoevsky. We just want people to see that buckthorn and wild garlic are invasive, not worthless. Just as filled with divine light as the oaks. They could be restrained with love and respect, not reviled and mutilated." He felt she was talking to herself, having surpassed him. "Paradise is so close, just a breath, a choice, a pulse away...Grant me the humility to lay down my toys, my weapons...my 'me'..." She traced the wrought iron's flaking paint with a plump finger.

Micah's unease grew. She was uncontainable. Beebe would not be trifled with, though that was exactly what he longed to do.

"I should have realized you'd have read *The Brothers Karamazov*," he smiled, thinking of her florid references to that poorly documented laywoman – Katerina? – in whose "miracles" Beebe took such interest. "There's an important new biography of Dostoevsky just out. I'm done with my copy from the humanities library; haven't returned it yet. If you can spare the time to walk over to my house I'll dig it out for you. Just return it on time – even employees pay late fees."

*　　*　　*

Althea sucked hungrily at her contraband latte, then tied a French knot in a strand of Vintage Bordeaux. She'd resumed her tapestry seascape. One had to do something with one's time, after all, even after learning not to take egoic efforts quite so seriously nor confuse them with one's true Being. Having initially felt a little diminished by Lucy's genuine artistry (not borrowed, as Al's embroidery and stencils were), Marian's erudition, Beebe's mystical propensities (which alarmed Al in her heart of hearts, though she'd flattered herself a champion of eccentricity) – even Bakeoven's tasteful, modest affluence – she'd (mostly) stopped struggling to see herself as special. The key to peace, to joy, seemed to lie very much elsewhere.

She took another sip, enjoying her view of Linnet nestling in a compartment of the tansu chest. She could accept and share her inevitable personality, now that the possibility of transcending it had become real. Turning her ego into an archenemy just created a vicious circle. Maybe peaceful acceptance of one's egoic individuality made it easier not to let it have the final say.

She'd managed to rise to the occasion when the sisterhood had pushed her to air her misgivings about the essentially violent Bodie Woods restoration. Lucy had gotten Stubblefield involved and Marian had made calls to the university art department and Highbutton Gallery. All four Lilybankers had pooled ideas. But it was Althea who had – at first gingerly, then with accelerating passion – written and distributed a "Love Every Leaf" manifesto to the Rutledge Sentinel as well as the university paper, to potential kindred spirits among the Animal Allies, to interested artists and their likely hang-outs, and even (to Bakeoven's amused fury) the entire Green League mailing list. Theoretically anonymous, most insiders knew the underground "art event's" epicenter was Lilybanks, that genteelly offbeat, crumbling great-aunt of a mansion with its harmless clutch of ineffectual, high-minded dissidents.

Lopping off a strand of Burnt Sienna, she giggled. Bake had been apoplectic about the unofficial use of the League mailing list, to which she'd had access as his de facto secretarial assistant. The refined silver blades of his mustache had sprung loose from their pomade as he lectured Althea on the League's reputation for community-minded compromise when necessary. The county conservation district might interpret the "dissent" as a betrayal by the very organization that had requested their services.

By then her flyers were in the mail; she listened with wide-eyed sympathy to Bake's prediction of the toll this prank would take on his usefulness as one of the Green League's more versatile emissaries. Between the sputtered lines Al received the distinct impression Bake feared he'd be tittered about as an infatuated dupe. She'd savored his negotiation of the slippery slope between sympathy for her viewpoint and some fantasy of himself as a high-stakes diplomat.

Finally observing her gleeful, shabby attitude (not to mention her complete absence), Al sighed. No use wallowing in guilt about backsliding. At least earlier in the morning she and Linnet had wafted through Lilybanks in a quiet solitude that brimmed with friendly vibrancy.

Tad had flown to Washington to visit his father; Beebe had yet to come in from her night in the garden; Marian was asleep, making the most of Kinder on Corrie's annual Labor Day weekend closure. And Lucy now spent every available moment supervising Chip's plans for their dream house or weaning him and little Harry from those pernicious disposable diapers.

So Al had pattered through the house in a state of childlike suspense, observing. Nothing looked quite familiar; every gleaming doorknob, patch of scabby paint or void seemed an artful novelty – as long as she stayed free of words.

Eventually she'd been run off the road by a series of emotional distractions. Every time she felt a sinking sensation from out of nowhere she remembered her obligation to speak at this afternoon's special city council forum on Libby's potential disaster. And then there was that mulish feeling that preceded remembering she'd given in to Lucy and Marian's nagging and promised to make a doctor's appointment.

She stabbed her needle finger, lost in mortification. She'd brought it on herself: a painfully expensive, embarrassing probe by some assembly-line gynecologist. She'd given the sisterhood sufficient reason to insist: an impulsive, ill-advised confession to Marian of her heart palpitations (undoubtedly just a side effect of the multiple lattes!)...a door pounding tantrum when Lucy'd hogged the bathroom – Al had felt compelled to explain how frequently she wet her pants...Beebe had caught her pale and out of breath at the top of the stairs. (Aging and sedentary, one expected these things.) Al could feel her eyes locking and glazing over, a sure sign of being lost in her head, but plunged deeper.

What if she were due for the surprise of a lifetime? What if she were riddled with cancer? Her eyes filled at the vision of Linnet mourning her in the depths of the closet till she starved to death or, more likely, someone – Chip, she'd bet – decided to have her euthanized. All alone in a cold, clinical, chrome hell! As Althea herself might be in a few days. She sniffed. Who would be willing to oversee her last days? Her cousin, silent with repressed resentment? It would be too much to ask of Marian, an unlikely nurse who already spread herself thin ministering to the capricious needs of the ailing house. No, she'd need to be installed in a budget hospice, suffering dutiful visits from Lucy and Beebe, whose lives were only just beginning. Her cousin would fly in to catalog Althea's antiques and hire someone to dispose of them profitably. (My God! She needed to make a will at once!...And she needed to deliver a heartrendingly effective plea at the city council meeting so Libby couldn't refuse her when begged to save Linnet.) Bakeoven would screw himself to the highest pitch of conscientiousness, once or twice at most, visiting her with a discreet handkerchief dowsed in cologne...

A comparatively early death was no doubt desirable. What had she – primitive self-love aside – to look forward to once the sisterhood evaporated? Ten more years (her nervous system was unlikely to make it much past 70) of lonely penury in a series of alien, increasingly crummy interiors and "no pets allowed."

Ah, but faced with a terminal diagnosis she'd surely be grateful to be spared for even that kind of existence – grateful to touch someone else's dog's eager little muzzle on the sidewalk, grateful for a handful of Christmas cards from the ever-receding Lilybankers.

The dearness of life sparked against her heart, and presence returned. How good to feel her bones settled in her chair, to hear traffic and the noisy resident blue jay, to study the glint of sunlight on embroidery floss. To rest from drama, from thought's savage diversions.

*   *   *

"Have another *gougère*? They're so good with the Petite Sirah I can't stand it," Polly Barnable sighed, looking oddly mournful. Kip Rusk had been married long enough to realized this was probably a reference to calories, though Polly's supple figure was enhanced by the slight thickening of deep maturity. Her husband, a pleasant guy in spite of that pastel fedora Kip's own wife found so clever, seemed to appreciate her. They added a touch of offbeat class to Rutledge's downtown.

Kip plucked another cheese puff from the proffered abalone shell. (Couldn't artists ever keep it simple?) He gestured with his wine glass toward the mishmash of photos, collages, inscrutable assemblages and framed diatribes the Highbutton Gallery was fobbing off as cutting-edge social commentary.

"Fomenting civil war among the tree huggers, Polly?"

She offered another briefly knitted brow.

"It's actually a fascinating debate on the ethics, aesthetics, and spirituality of environmentalism, Kip. Articulate voices – and a lot of raw emotion – with an orientation the mainstream, capitalist media NEVER acknowledges. Uniquely local, too. Jack and I are honored and excited to provide them exhibit space." Her henna'd curls trembled with the fervor of proud patronage; he noted her dangle earrings seemed to be pencil stubs.

Kip polished off his Bordeaux.

"The chamber of commerce is happy if you and Jack are happy, Polly. I've gotta run – be nice to grab some lunch *once* this week. But I promised a few nettled folks I'd take a look at your show. The county cut us a deal on the Bodie rehab, Polly. They're not likely to do that the next time the city needs 'em if this lunatic fringe spreads onto campus and makes the conservation district look like evil incarnate. Just a thought." He hoped his grin looked meaningful.

On his way out he spotted Lynn Throckmorton bent over a macabre oil of immolated butterflies. Never wise to snub Lynn.

"Neighbor! Maggie tells me we're booked for the same cruise in December." She gave him one of her wintry smiles. "Not one of Highbutton's better shows, is it," Kip persevered in a conspiratorial tone. "I hear the esoteric ladies of Lilybanks are behind this ruckus," he offered, not certain what "esoteric" meant but sure it applied. "I guess babysitting doesn't occupy their active brains sufficiently." This was more than he usually allowed himself as a city council member, but Lynn was safe enough. All she cared about was her clothing allowance. Only noon and her mascara was already clotted.

"From the Historical Society's viewpoint Rutledge is extremely fortunate to have Calla Morrissey's descendants in charge of Lilybanks till we have the funds to move ahead. They're a goldmine of anecdotes. And they don't need decks or cable satellite dishes." She admired the rickrack on her vintage black jacket, then produced a clinical smile that revealed rather alarming teeth. "They're a creative force in the community and I've taken an interest in them. Hands off, Kip."

He bowed in surrender. As the door's Dickensian bell pealed in his wake, a deeply tanned woman with clanking jewelry took his place.

"Mrs. Throckmorton, isn't it? Pam Thompkins. My husband and I are so appreciative of the endowment for the library. Our oldest is shopping for colleges, and the expansion's likely to keep him in Rutledge, which we'd love, of course." She paused for an encouraging noise that wasn't forthcoming, then hurtled ahead. "Our youngest is in the Kinder on Corrie program at Lilybanks. I couldn't help overhearing snatches of your conversation and just wondered...well...if the whole scene up there isn't becoming a little..." (she cleared her throat) "marginal. I'm all for – what's Highbutton calling this? – outsider art. But building code violations are a different matter. I'm hearing rumors. Just wondered what your opinion is, as someone who's in the know." She checked her trophy watch discreetly but distinctly, in response to Mrs. Throckmorton's advancing rigor mortis.

"We're not going to allow the property to deteriorate." Little lines gathered at the corner of Mrs. Throckmorton's eyes, indicating an effort at humor. "I'd relax. All this intensity about preschool résumés!" she smiled, and clicked briskly toward the exit.

Sally Osterman, who'd slipped in to drop off more copies of Althea's "Manifesto" from the copy shop she managed, made a beeline for Mrs. Thompkins. Possessing a slight but useful insider standing compared to most other Kinderparents, Sally had begun to suspect the outsiders' gossip was more relevant now.

"Nice to see you! Enjoying your vacation?"

"One of my favorites. My husband choreographs the entire barbecue right down to the invitations." Sally tried to look envious.

"Hard to believe autumn's just around the corner. We'll be stumbling over each other in the dark for Martinmas in the blink of an eye."

"Townshend won't be back this fall. We think he's outgrown all the fairytale artsy stuff. He's been admitted to a new trial program on campus: bilingual Chinese/English immersion for preschoolers. They've got funding for three years, and if it fizzles out we can carry on with a tutor. Eric's ecstatic. Chinese will be indispensable in finance, he says."

Sally tried to imagine Townshend as a CEO.

"We'll miss you guys. To be honest, we've had second thoughts about Melody's return." (She counted on the unlikelihood of Althea and Pam Thompkins ever exchanging more than thin smiles.) "Melody's come home with stories about desperate pilgrimages to the top of the house to go to the bathroom because the kids' was out of order too many times – on top of malfunctioning radiators in the winter and crumbly ceilings. Someone said the place is probably crawling with lead, but I don't see why...do you?" She realized she was all but cringing with guilt.

Scenting blood, Pam gave Sally her full attention for the first time. Her nostrils flared as she flipped back her hair, tinted an improbable shade of bronze.

"The rustic candlelit crafty routine has its moments. Certainly easy on their budget. We thought it might stimulate Townshend's tremendous creativity." Unable to continue meeting Pam's gaze, Sally studied a collage over her shoulder. "Daycare providers sleeping around with clients is a much bigger issue, isn't it?" Pam's eyes skewered Sally, who blanched with dismay.

* * *

In spite of Althea's efforts Libby looked worse than ever. Her tense, bloated face had acquired a greenish tinge above a regrettable Madras plaid jacket that appeared to have been slept in, perhaps by the dogs. At least it covered the love handles.

The city council's snug chamber was packed to the top of its carpeted tiers. Althea thought she could guess the Alley Katz faction by their stony isolation and air of sullen righteousness. Animal Allies of various breeds dotted the tiers and swelled the speakers' ranks. Her favorite feature writer from the Rutledge Sentinel sat dead center; a campus newspaper reporter tinkered with his camera.

Amid the buzz the lissome Mayor Feldkamp floated, glad-handing cronies, troublemakers and nonentities alike with the urbanity that had won him a third term.

Althea thought she saw Mrs. Augsberger in a topmost corner and had to remind herself of her tendency to glimpse the woman from various unlikely eminences such as the double-decker campus trolley or the employee mezzanine at the pharmacy. She sighed, noticed how moist her notes had become, and turned back toward Libby for selfish relief from the feeling she was the most anxious person in the building.

Libby looked defeated and weirdly guilty in spite of Al's pep talks, cozy supportive suppers at Lilybanks, and a lawyer's advice paid for by Allies. The crew in the speakers' queue waved and smiled at Libby despite her comatose slump.

During the preliminaries Althea was too nervous to attend to the mayor's summary, already outlined in the agenda handouts. Libby's supposed menace required only a "yea or nay" vote rather than new regulations. When Al caught herself hoping Libby would botch her presentation so that Al's would have nowhere to go but up, she understood she had to surrender. The way out of her phobia was to embrace it, tremors and all.

Libby was at the podium now, reviewing her notes as someone adjusted the mike for her. Al felt it was cruel to keep watching, and pretended to examine her own notes. She heard Libby testing the sound – "One...two, three."

An excruciating silence followed, punctuated by increasingly elaborate coughs and throat-clearings among the audience. Althea followed her own breathing as if the practice were all that was keeping her alive.

"Mayor Feldkamp, members of the City Council, neighbors: I'm here this afternoon to ask the council to dismiss the petition circulated by Mr. and Mrs. Morton Katz, which impugns my character, my concern for the welfare of my neighbors both human and animal, and my common sense. Having chosen to blow an unfortunate but minor incident out of all proportion..."

Uninspired but adequate, and enhanced by her clenched delivery, Libby's remarks laid a sufficiently solid foundation for the pleas of her supporters – some of whom surprised Althea.

Among the first was a maddeningly familiar old woman in a black pantsuit. As she adjusted her reading glasses with the deliberation of one used to being indulged, Al recognized Stubblefield's dowager empress Mrs. Hassenpfeffer. Referring to Libby's "consistently high ethical stance," "independent spirit" and "imaginative lifestyle" as a credit to her alma mater, she reminded those present that citizens like Ms. Merchant enriched the vibrant community life for which "university towns worth their salt" were celebrated. She garnered spotty applause in spite of Mayor Feldkamp's energetically mimed attempts to quell audience participation.

A few vapid but pertinent remarks from Libby's next door neighbor to the effect that Spike and Violet made her own property more secure suggested a twisted arm to Althea. Similarly undemonstrative testimony from Libby's mailman as to her dogs' harmlessness created a rustle among the Allies; Al later learned an Ally who ran the no-kill shelter was his favorite niece.

Bake had offered to speak on Libby's behalf; he showed up with a pearl in his tie and the professorial, noteless *sang-froid* that impressed Al more than his wine cellar, first editions of Robert Frost, and Charles Rohlfs armchair combined.

"Libby Merchant is that most precious of Rutledge's assets: an intellectual with moral integrity," he proclaimed, mentioning his own credentials and "long years of friendship" with her. Al had insisted he bolster his testimonial with anecdotes. She'd had to provide them; Bake's approval of Libby and her tribe had never extended to actual interest.

By now the mayor's famously bouffant coiffure had begun to deflate; Althea had noticed him squirm every time he took in the serpentine speakers' queue. As though in a sweet dream of deliverance she heard him announce crisply that in the interests of time speakers pro and con would be limited to eight apiece; speakers near the front of the line could choose to cede to someone else. He expected them to sort themselves out "courteously and expeditiously."

As groans rose from frustrated Allies, whose quota was nearly filled, Althea realized she held the eighth slot and could effortlessly find an eager alternate. In fact, it would be wrong not to do so. Her evident stage fright would provide an ineffective finale. Libby'd be the first to agree. Besides, she'd wrestled this demon down for the Tour; it seemed unfair that she had to surrender again...and again...

In the whispering commotion that followed one face came into focus. Libby's stern eyes caught hers like magnets. She pointed to the podium. A wayward Rottweiler – maybe even a wolf – would have complied. Surrendering for at least the tenth time, Al turned her back on Libby and all possibility of reprieve. No point in wrestling further.

When Al's turn arrived she smiled at her trembling paper, accepted the awkward sound of her panting into the mike, welcomed the blubbery sensation in her lips and tongue as she struggled to form coherent words. It was what it was: Althea Athnos visibly floundering in front of dozens of acquaintances, strangers, the entire city council. Putting up no resistance, she felt light, buoyant, golden. No suffering – just full acceptance of the occasional break in her voice, the mayor's kindly, sympathetic gaze, her nervous giggle echoing through the chamber when she'd finished.

As Al picked her way back to her seat a few Allies gave her encouraging "thumbs up" or winks, but most people were already focused on the next speaker. Her epiphany had been utterly private.

The Katz faction's increasingly unimpressive quibbles ended on a ludicrous note – Mrs. Katz's dithery mother accused Libby of securing desirable curbside parade views with her intimidating "beagles." The mayor resumed command. He read the summary of an inspection of Libby's property a little too rapidly, having accurately gauged the growing sense of a media tempest in a teapot.

It appeared that Ms. Merchant's consent to an inspection by a sanitation officer, a couple of council members and an impartial veterinarian from two counties away had yielded only one infraction (failure to update her parking sticker, noticed by an energetic councilwoman) and an invitation to breed Mustapha. Mayor Feldkamp did not elaborate.

From the upper tier a gentleman in an Alley Katz team shirt (sporting their spherical, earless black cat face) managed a strangled, out-of-order bellow – "That pack of curs is gonna mangle someone's kid!" – and received an uncharacteristically savage glare from His Honor.

A brisk vote by the council, who unanimously waived debate amongst themselves, ruled out any attempt to curb Ms. Merchant's "extravagant but responsible" animal companionship. "As soon as that parking sticker's paid up," the mayor gleamed, securing the good-will of delighted Allies, who were easily the largest bloc of voters in the room.

Wheel of Fortune

Althea was pleased to find herself alone in the house when Bakeoven dropped her off after Libby's victory. Lucy had all but moved out, so cooking had been re-divided between Althea, Marian and Beebe-and-Tad. During Tad's stay in Washington Al would only have to cook for three. She had a new recipe for spinach rissoles.

Still energized by her euphoric bungling at the microphone, Al pulled her usual bunch of scribbles from a pants pocket, found what she wanted and picked up the kitchen phone. Not letting herself think, she left her name and number on Dr. Morgan Purdy's voice mail, re-questing an appointment.

Delighted with this triumph over procrastination, she resolved not to worry about the exam. Typically her anxious resistance proved worse than the dreaded event, exemplified by her speech that after-noon. Even her worst fears come true seemed less draining than their anticipation.

A shaft of late sun etched the sink's bottle of daisies onto the wall as she thawed blocks of frozen spinach under the faucet. The pattern of stars tattooed into the colander always reminded her of Lucy's Martinmas lantern. Maybe Lucy could drive her to the appointment. No, she'd rather go by herself. Asking for a ride would be self-indul-gent. "Drama," as Eckhart called it. Just because she hadn't seen a gynecologist in nearly a decade didn't mean she'd be diagnosed with a panoply of expensive diseases, all terminal. Beebe probably wouldn't mind if she used her crepe pan. Why should Beebe mind anything these days? The wheel of fortune had carried her high. Of course her own life didn't seem exactly flat today either. She'd had more than her fill of those prickly pleasures, attention and excitement. The mushy velvet of green puree between her fingers seemed more genuinely enjoyable.

These days she was feeling sexy, in a way that seemed to emanate from someplace beyond her own saggy charms. Getting in touch with her inner body had wakened an intimacy with the world she hadn't felt since adolescence. Teapots and shrubs and running water invited a physical response, some kind of reaching out from within, a mutual psychic embrace. Trying to put it in words smothered it.

Clearing her mind of monologue, she lost herself in inhalation, exhalation, awareness of the tingling pressure of her weight in the soles of her feet, the squelch of half-thawed spinach as her fist pressed it, Aphrodite's moan in her sleep as she waited for supper. The clunk and scrape of pots as she rummaged for the pan slammed through the kitchen's tranquil hush; she straightened to find Beebe in the scullery doorway.

They exchanged shy smiles, Al exulting in this new extension of quiet attention to comfortably include another human.

As the familiar taint of self-congratulation seeped into consciousness, ushering a return to the gush of me-centered words on a more cramped and familiar interior plane, Al's smile turned wry with self-mockery.

"Hi. Don't mind me. I've got a case of the Wobblies brought on by patchy presence." She heard her words, leaden with ego, extraneous, echo stupidly. Beebe continued to smile softly across the linoleum. Something was different with her hair; it ballooned over her ears in soft wisps like a rakish bird's nest. She thought Beebe's gaze held some hesitant invitation she seemed unwilling to voice. She'd recently taken to wearing elaborate cascading earrings; today there was only one, which seemed a trifle lopsided, though perhaps fashionable? She looked the tiniest bit stooped, as though buckling beneath an invisible weight, and clutched her beaded purse like a little old lady. Her breath looked wrong – too fast, or too shallow.

"Beebe?"

The girl just stood there with that small, fixed smile; when Al approached Beebe continued looking where Al had been standing by the sink. Where the hell was Marian?

"Why don't you have a seat. I could use some company." Al pulled out a chair, instinctively lifting the ponderous thing as though noise might burst Beebe's eerie bubble. She felt cowardly and wished herself elsewhere, certain she'd be unequal to whatever task lay before her.

"I'm making spinach rissoles?" she essayed, as though asking permission.

"Yum."

The distant, hollow syllable established conversation, however counterfeit. Al resolved to wait.

When Beebe sagged into the chair a whiff of perspiration hit the air. Aphrodite plodded over and collapsed heavily against Beebe's chair leg. Al turned to see her rest her hand on the big black head vacantly.

"This is really easy. Spinach, egg, bread crumbs. Like little croquettes. Let's just hope it holds together. Maybe I'll fry one just to see." Al found herself oiling the crepe pan and turning on a flame, mostly for the sake of an industrious charade. If Beebe were working herself into some kind of state Al was right here, wasn't she? Home safe and sound with a responsible adult, Al told herself, trying to stem the queasy sense of dread.

"Oops," she chirped over her shoulder. "Is it okay to use the crepe pan? I meant to ask." Realizing she really had to turn around, she saw Beebe's eyes widen momentarily with proprietary concern, then fill with tears. Or perhaps it was her imagination.

"You okay, Beebe?" she forced herself to ask.

"Uh huh." Spooky smile. Al hesitated.

"Sure?"

A ghastly damaged croak, like what Al imagined a death rattle might sound like, escaped through the addled smile. At this range Al could see a lavender lump rising on one of Beebe's cheekbones. Her hair wasn't mussed; it was a soiled tangle.

Al cleared her throat. "What's happened? You look like you've been wrestling."

"Pretty much." The shaky smile disintegrated. Beebe tried to laugh and began sobbing.

"Dammitofuckinghell."

Al flooded with relief. Words, she could handle.

"Oh, sweetie. Let's get some ice on that cheek." She started toward the freezer, then turned back.

"Beebe. How bad is this, sweetie? Do we need to get you to a doctor?"

A joyous cackle erupted.

"Nope! He might need to see one, though. A few stitches, and maybe a hernia."

"Look at your hands."

Beebe's vestigial fingernails were caked a rusty red; the knuckles were smeared.

Ditey snuffed and licked at the blood until Al grabbed Beebe's hand away.

"I think we should take you to the police...All messed up like this...*Now*, Beebe."

The harsh edge on Al's voice startled the girl. She pulled her hand back, staring at it.

"Okay...You want me to drive?"

Marveling, and finally able to put her arms around Beebe, to feel alive again, Al steered her through the scullery and out the back door.

As she fumbled for her key Ditey barreled into them and glued herself to Beebe.

"Sorry, babe. C'mon!"

"Let's take her with us, Althea."

Hardly hesitating, Al opened her car's back door before sidling behind the wheel.

"*I'll* drive. They'll have to take us as they find us. Ditey deserves to be at your side." Panting filled the silence. She started the motor, adjusted the mirror.

"One thing. Was he anyone you know?"

"Yeah."

For the first time since she'd gotten home Beebe looked truly sad. Tears threatened again; she raised a hand in a "halt" gesture, shook her head and turned away.

Horrified, Al put everything she had into getting the car down the driveway and headed in the right direction.

*   *   *

In less than an hour they sailed back to Lilybanks, trailing streamers of drool as Ditey's head and shoulders plugged a back window. Beebe had politely spurned a gynecological exam, a staff psychologist's ministrations, an officious attempt to track down Professor Morrissey – even Althea's protective presence during the filing of the report. The officer in charge of the case had told Althea to keep Beebe at home till they "apprehended the suspect."

Guessing Al's chagrin at being left in the dark, Beebe had given her a squeeze on the way out of the station and explained that "Bubo had to be told first." Between white-knuckled attempts to avoid left-hand turns, children's disconcerting waves at the mammoth backseat passenger and her subterranean review of potential rapists, Al drove right past their Corrie Street intersection.

"Alright, I give up. Close but no bananas. Where am I? It all looks familiar but which way's Lilybanks?"

"Sorry, I thought you went past on purpose. There's a row of orange traffic cones across Corrie. Just turn left up here and we'll go back around the block...Keep going left," Beebe counseled. "WATCH OUT!"

The Rutledge fire chief's red station wagon bore down on them from behind, flashing and wailing. Al's right wheels scraped, then mounted the curb as it tore past. Beebe kept silent; Al laughed weakly and sighed.

"Is this a full moon?" She planned to spend the evening locked in her room, hiding under a blanket with Linnet and a bowl of popcorn.

"Almost there. Turn left up here, and then one more left immediately. You'll know where you are by then."

Their final turn was blocked by a traffic cop who brandished his arms, fiercely shaking his head "NO" when Al rolled down her window to explain she lived three driveways up. They could see two fire engines with flashing lights bumper to bumper near the crest of the hill.

"Turn into this driveway! The Browns will know Ditey," Beebe barked, rolling the dog's window up beyond temptation and jumping out with an urgency that filled Al with dread...She got out herself and locked the car as she watched Beebe and the cop gesticulating back and forth in the street. Althea waited meekly on the curb, then raced across at a sign from Beebe.

They strode up the far side of Corrie. The trucks' roaring engines made talk impossible and blocked their view of the action. But Lilybanks was almost certainly involved.

No flames or even smoke could be seen from where they stood, and Althea began wondering if Marian had been taken ill – but there was no ambulance. Perhaps they'd left for the hospital?...Beebe had attached herself to the younger of two firefighters staying with the trucks, who pointed further along the street. Al trotted along behind Beebe, who hadn't looked back.

Past the trucks they saw smoke wafting from the side of the house. The windows had been opened rather than smashed; except for the ominous beige python of a hose extending up the front steps the scene looked almost decorous, as though Betty Crocker had burnt a cake.

"We're supposed to stay on the sidewalk," Beebe shouted, diving under its handrail and scrambling up the grassy embankment anyway. Al followed, wondering if Beebe would try to get inside and aware that she'd probably follow. She slipped and nearly fell backwards. The deafening clamor, her breathlessness, a glimpse of onlookers on distant porches muddled some chain of thought that struggled to surface.

Burnt cake. Jesus God. What if she hadn't turned off the burner when they'd left? She grabbed Beebe by the shoulder, but words wouldn't come when the girl turned around.

"It's alright. They must have it under control. Smoke's not very dark. It's going to be alright. Let's go back down." Althea looked queer, frozen. An ambulance had pulled up and Beebe tried to steer her housemate toward it, having abandoned her impulse to storm the house. But an upstairs window shot open; they glimpsed fluorescent stripes on a firefighter's sleeve. More windows opened. Their bedrooms, the ones above the kitchen.

Already in despair, Althea finally thought of Linnet hiding from the uproar in her closet, no doubt.

She ran diagonally across the front yard, eluded the young fireman who'd noticed a little too late and lunged up the staircase ahead of him into what she thought might be the suffocating jaws of hell. Someone grabbed her from behind at the top of the stairs. Althea still had breath to yell "MY CAT!" but couldn't point to her room because her arms were pinioned. A grey haze enveloped her but she could see sunlight ahead; they'd opened all the French doors onto the balcony, where a couple of firefighters knelt as though checking for flames below. One of the great philodendron's thrusting arms hung at a sickening right angle.

"We found a cat. You wanna cooperate? Or he'll take you back down, ma'am," a voice boomed behind her. Still held in an iron grip, Al turned her head to see a curly-headed woman emerging from head-gear worthy of an astronaut.

Al nodded vigorously. "I'll be good! I mean, sorry! I have to save my cat!"

"Hold onto her, Craig. What's your name?"

"Althea Athnos."

"Mary Jean MacNamara. Promise you'll NEVER run into a house fire again, Thea." Mary Jean shook her hand.

"I promise."

"There's a cat out on the balcony. Any other pets this side of the stairs?"

"Nope. A rabbit and two box turtles further down the hall," Al reported. "Can I go see?"

"Let her through."

Released, Al ran, imagining Linnet about to plunge over the bal-cony from sheer shyness. The sinister metallic stench she'd barely registered in the foyer hung in her room. Just be alright, please God.

The relative quiet and the fresh air ahead calmed her; it wasn't as bad as she'd imagined...

Like something out of a TV show or a dream Linnet sprawled on the weathered planks of the balcony near a shucked-off uniform jacket. A crewcut fellow in a black tee and suspenders knelt over her, pressing a plastic mask over her face. Black tubing coiled from Linnet to a wheeled canister with dials and gauges controlled by another fellow. Linnet's tail was limp; her front legs hung strangely floppy as the man jammed his fingers into her chest.

Knowing it was too late, Al crouched next to the equipment.

"I'm here now, sweetie. I love you Linny. It's alright...it's alright... it's alright." Surely touching her side lightly wouldn't interfere.

Couldn't be the first time they'd had to deal with a sobbing, dribbling bystander.

She realized a certain percentage of herself was calculating the height of the balcony. If it wasn't high enough she'd find another way. Tonight. Another percentage seemed disengaged, sort of transparent, and floating or something. It seemed to cradle the awful sensation of having her head in a noose and the box kicked out from under her feet. Something, or someone, held her tight...and safe.

Al felt a tremor beneath her fingers. Linnet's back legs kicked convulsively. A front paw curled.

"Bring it down to forty and keep her there."

"Stay back, ma'am. But keep sweet-talkin' her."

Linnet began sputtering and galloping on her side as though dreaming. The mask was lifted.

"Linnet! Linnet! *Supper time!* Supper time, Linnet!" The ears pricked.

The two men gave each other surprised, pleased looks over Al's head.

"Hold on. Let's see if she's steady on her feet."

Linnet opened her eyes, gave the nearer fellow a baleful glare with a touch of third eyelid and pulled herself into a crouched ball.

"Oh, Linny, thank God! Thank you both so much! I thought she was gone."

Linnet glanced at her and began licking a shoulder, obviously at a loss to account for this exasperating situation.

"Gotta make sure she's walking okay. No way to know how long she was out. Better have your vet take a look at her."

At this Linnet teetered toward the balcony rails, thought better of it and sallied more confidently into the shade beneath a cascade of nasturtiums where she applied herself to her toilette.

"This is the equipment the Animal Allies funded, isn't it?" Al beamed, accepting something resembling a windshield wipe for her nose.

"Some animal charity, yup. Brand new. Your cat's our third resuscitation. Drop her photo off at Station Number Two and we'll get her in our newsletter."

"We gotta get going, Jeff. You're maybe gonna have to check into a motel for a night or two till this place airs out. Kitchen's kind of a mess. Lucky we got here when we did. Someone left the flame on under a skillet. Coulda been way worse."

Althea began crying again, leaving that open to whatever interpretation they chose as she watched them clamber downstairs in a flurry of squeaky rubber, flapping buckles and clinking canisters.

"Kitty make it?" Mary Jean leaned into the doorframe.

"Yes! I'm so grateful to you all. I'll never forget how you helped us. Thank you from the bottom of my heart."

"Glad she's okay. And make sure everyone pays attention to what they're doing with the stove and all." Mary Jean waved and ran downstairs; the hollow, oversized beep of a fire engine's horn resounded from the driveway.

"Yes...Attention," Al muttered, and stashed Linnet in Marian's bathroom. An outlandish peace filled and surrounded her, somehow different from the joy of still having Linnet to squeeze against her heart. No disaster could touch this weird wordless refuge. It was like some tremendous angel – one she sort of recognized -- had knocked the wind and words and suffering out of her and she was breathing something better.

By the time she'd located Cleo and Clumber in Millefleurs, which seemed unscathed and minimally smelly, and tucked the bewildered Skippy into his drawer the engines were gone. Beebe was just coming in the front door. She smiled up at Althea, still halo'd by snarls and the prodigious unmatched earring. Her hem was coming down; she looked like she'd been playing football with the crew.

"Your Linnet's going to be on the front page! Mary Jean's cousin's a reporter for the Sentinel. We've been incredibly blessed. A fire truck was a block away when a neighbor smelled the smoke and called 911. I'll make her a pie...Or not. Have you seen the kitchen?"

"No, I've been upstairs...Have you?"

"Nope. That fellow you whizzed by tackled me instead. They let me use a phone to page Bubo at the library. I thought it best to warn her. About several things."

"Who was it, Beebe?" It wasn't going to be an evening for subtlety. Al took the stairs extra slowly, clinging to the banister which was coated with a grey film.

Beebe wrinkled her nose.

"Bubo's choirboy from Toronto, on his way home. I think he'd had the scenario planned for a while. 'Just happened to run into me.' The police are going to meet him at O'Hare. She's going to be a lot more upset about him than a smoky kitchen."

Her kindly smile brought tears to Al's eyes; she smudged her face wiping at them. Beebe could have no doubt about how the fire started. Al squeezed her hand when she got to the bottom of the stairs.

"That poor creep."

"You look like a raccoon. Let's go face the music." Beebe linked her arm through Al's and steered her down the hall.

"The clock's stopped. What if it's ruined?"

"It probably just wound down. It'll be alright. They didn't have to use the hose in here."

Ditey's wicker basket had been overturned and shoved against the wall beneath the stairs.

"My God, where's the dog?"

"I took her up to the Nest. She's probably sleeping off the whole experience on the divan. Everyone upstairs is present and accounted for, right?"

"Two turtles, one rabbit accounted for but even they may be having trouble being present."

Al could see the scullery sink's curtains had turned light grey, their crochet trim even darker. They billowed on the breeze; one of those clunky, single-minded firemen had unfastened the little window's fussy old-fashioned clasp. The floor looked wet and streaked with soot; a black ring encircled the sunken drain. An alien stench reminded Al of scorched blackstrap molasses and a rusty incinerator on her uncle's farm, with a sickly, almost floral overtone like a feeble attempt to disguise some vile medication. It intensified with every ginger step. Beebe moved ahead of her, leaving damp footprints with her sandals. Their shoes might be ruined. Of course Al herself deserved it. For a fleeting moment she foresaw her entire frail vintage wardrobe reduced to confetti at the dry cleaners' in a futile attempt to get rid of the foul smell. So what.

Then, inescapably, they'd passed from the pantry's wet, grimy ranks of cream-colored cupboards powdered with grey to the dark kitchen.

"No gas or electricity till tomorrow after an inspection, they said."

"Oh Beebe. All your set-ups. Your frangipane and the sourdough starter, the –"

"Most of that stuff's at Maven Alley now. Relax. Hardly anything's been destroyed. We can have a party or two. One for cleaning, one for painting. You can buy a cute pair of overalls...We'll get *Tad* a cute pair of overalls."

Althea sighed. "What will we be celebrating? A lunar landing? This room looks like the dark side of the moon. On 1950's black and white TV. I think you may be minimizing...You're twirling around so much I can't see a thing. How's the stove?"

"Um, not so good I guess. Sort of...melted."

Approaching, Al made out a congealed tarry puddle seemingly baked into place over much of the blackened stovetop.

"Probably the insulated handle on the crepe pan. I guess your spinach croquettes got REALLY hot."

"Rissoles," Al whispered. She cleared her throat. "I've single-handedly ruined the Morrissey 1911 family stove. The one Calla baked graham teething biscuits for Marian's mother in." For just a moment she felt like rabble, a menace to society. "The one you invented bird of paradise sauce on."

Beebe snorted. "Why do you get the starring role? Don't I get to be the naïve careless victim? We've had enough drama today to feed off of for the rest of our lives, Althea. I vote we skip it."

"I love you, Beebe. But who's going to pay to replace the stove? Without drama. Which doesn't address the fact that it's irreplaceable." She poked at the reeking residue on the stovetop. Obdurate and dully gleaming like volcanic rubble, the petrified goop had swamped the burners, choked the cute control knobs that resembled faucet handles and flowed over the edge, sealing the oven door and creating pocked craters and blisters in the black and white linoleum beneath.

"There's insurance."

"Does the coverage include addled inmates?"

"Probably!" Beebe's finger traced butterflies and flowers in the soot on the kitchen table. The Jadite sugar bowl and creamer had turned a uniform shade of snail-puke.

A flashlight's beam darted around the kitchen.

"Insurance agent's in the Bahamas for a wedding till Tuesday. But I should certainly think I arranged coverage for the addled among us." The beam sank to the floor.

"Incomparable obtuseness. One ought to have seen the two faces of Janus. Our little *Townshend* would have been more discerning. Vanity! I could never have forgiven myself if..." The saggy shape behind them sank onto a chair cloaked in velvety soot at the end of the breakfast table.

Beebe shuffled through the dank rubbish on the floor; careful arrangements of fruit, napkins, chopsticks, potholders and herbs had been catapulted by the force of the hose. A rack of mugs had been dislodged from the wall. They lay dismembered in the sink.

"I've already let it go. We'll let the police sort him out. How could you know, Bu? None of us saw the potential. At any rate, it was a *mauvais quart d'heure*, not a nightmare." She wrapped her arms around her aunt's neck from behind the chair.

Althea rolled her eyes in the privacy of the semidarkness. Joy kept unfurling around her. Linnet and she had been given a miracle; Beebe had escaped, drolly self-possessed; Libby and her furry family had been pronounced innocent. Now that Marian had arrived Al was able to let a vision of her dismissal by the sisterhood dissolve. And behind and between and around all this was something bigger, something more reliable that felt everlasting.

"Althea thinks we're attached to the poor old Oriole, Bubo."

Marian straightened up, patting her niece's arm.

"Understandably. It's quite alright, Althea. Lilybanks transcends nostalgia. If Lucy invites her flock of Stubblefielders to help, we'll have the place fixed up in no time at little expense, and any insurance money can go towards a new cooker. Althea, why don't you be in charge of finding one suitably archaic but serviceable. Good heavens. We'll all leave a ring around the tub tonight. By candlelight."

"Marian. I'm so sorry. From the very bottom of my heart." No use saying much of anything else.

"My dear. We all know how deeply you care for the place. Can't tell you how often I've thought myself a fool for choosing that unfortunate girl over you." She held out a hand, which Al rushed to squeeze.

"Did you hear about Linnet, Marian? She'd passed out from the smoke, being right above the kitchen, and they used the new equipment donated by Animal Allies to resuscitate her! She's going to be in the papers!" Al heard her own childish squeal and decided it was alright to need a mother occasionally.

"Well! Thank God. Lilybanks wouldn't be the same without the dear little thing." Marian dabbed at her nose and blackened it. "I suppose we'll all make the morning Sentinel's front page. That should cheer Doctor Leiby no end. He's not been looking very chipper lately." She regretted her slip. Leiby'd enjoy nothing more than creating a miasma of anxiety amongst the Lilybankers. She'd not confided much about his innuendoes to anyone except Bakeoven, who was under strict orders to keep it to himself.

Beebe fumbled for candles in a drawer. "Let's order Chinese. I guess the phone works?" The entire sisterhood enjoyed a profound vagueness about even the most familiar technology.

"Call Lucy first. She might want to join us. And Harry and Chip, if they haven't eaten." Althea could hardly wait to tell them about Linnet.

Clear-cut

"If she'd only come in sooner."

Lucy tried to say something about health insurance and found she couldn't speak. Althea sat across the otherwise empty waiting room with her back to them, ostensibly contemplating the aquarium.

"We won't have the test results back till Friday. And she'll need more. But I have to tell you Doctor says her situation's..." the nurse, whose fine wrinkles reminded Lucy of Beebe's crullers, cleared her throat. "...very clear-cut, I'm afraid. If she wants to try the surgery her best bet will be County General. This is their oncology department's number." She handed Lucy a business card. "We gave her the information, of course, but it's best someone else gets involved. The shock... Good luck to you." She appraised Lucy, trying to decide if she were addressing a sufficiently responsible party.

Lucy nodded in the numb, sleepwalking manner Nurse Farber recognized, and headed toward the fish tank.

"C'mon. Let's go, Althea." She touched the thin, stooped back, trying to avoid pathetic patting.

Al rose, scattering a sheaf of papers in her lap. Lucy crouched to pick them up for her. With a twinge she remembered Al had phoned her before breakfast to remind her about the promised ride. Lucy had breezily implied she hadn't forgotten, then rushed out ten minutes later without deodorant or socks.

Nurse Farber had withdrawn. They swept down two flights of stairs, eluding the elevator's silence.

Lucy gunned the motor of Chip's BMW and pulled out of the clinic's parking lot.

"How are you doing?" She'd meant to ask it before the car was moving, but the need to put the clinic behind them triumphed. Her eyes met Al's at the first stop sign.

"Not very well, apparently!" Al appended a thin laugh, shakier than intended. When Lucy was unable to respond to the joke, Al rolled her window down all the way.

"Just get me home. I want Linnet." She shut her eyes and leaned into the wind.

Messenger

Delilah's merry barks lifted her front paws off the ground. The fattest of Lilac Corner's squirrels occupied the young hickory, which had borne its first nuts this autumn. Its twigs clattered like buttons on a washboard as the plunderer ricocheted among the branches. His overweening manner delighted the collie, who matched his scolding with sneezy snorts of pleasure the Bunting girls called "snoodles."

Gypsy observed the encounter from behind a muslin curtain in the girls' room. Below her windowsill Pip, Scholar and Twinkle quivered with excitement at the edge of a game of jacks on the plank floor. The braided rug had been rolled up out of the way and Scout lurked behind it, intrigued but eager to keep out of arm's reach.

"My turn, Alice. Mind your ribbon. The kitty wants it." Twinkle craned towards the little girl's curls in a transport, swaying in unison with the straggling hair ribbon. His were the only feline eyes that didn't follow Alice's surrender of the little rubber ball to her oldest sister. When the ball began bouncing Bezique abandoned his seat on a rocking chair and joined Gypsy. He knew the echoing noise repelled his mate though she strove to preserve her composure. Daintily touching her nose with his, he tried to distract her.

"Likely little bunch of devils, aren't they. Pip's nose gets flatter every day," Gypsy mused. For weeks Bezique had been suggesting that Leo was the kittens' daddy. "Leo himself may notice the resemblance – if he could pry himself off that hill."

"Florrie and that bird in a bonnet must have him lapping out of crystal bowls by now. He'll come to show off."

"When he does, make sure to tell him not to say anything to --"

"I've already promised, dearest." Gypsy insisted on believing her sister was alive somewhere, and had led the youngsters to expect they'd be reunited some day. Bezique disapproved but held his tongue. He was proud they'd be indoor-outdoor cats, mentored by Uncle Beanie. Pippin had already successfully negotiated a solo trip to Beanie's cottage – without permission, which had earned him an ear-boxing from his auntie, but promising all the same. Mrs. Bunting had promised him to the piping family of the orchard and chickens, a fine post for an ambitious mouser.

Mrs. B. had a sensitive nose for personalities. The girls had been forbidden to chase Scout or pick her up. Her wild streak seemed unlikely to recede and a stubborn campaign to cuddle and kiss might dismantle the standoffish tolerance of rocking chairs, closed doors and laughter she'd achieved. She was to stay with the Buntings, the cat whose irregular presence at the hearth would be noted but respected. Gypsy, whose grasp of the human tongue was sketchy, listened with approval to Bezique's translation of these arrangements. Her niece was to inherit the wander-ground.

Twinkle and bashful Scholar were particular favorites of the girls. Their coveted attendance at dolly tea parties suited Applesauce and Snowy well. Difficult to be jealous of newcomers who took one's place in the baby buggy. Applesauce thought Scholar looked delectable in the wee bonnet festooned with plaster cherries.

Indeed, there'd been a bright side to the changes Bezique had brought to the household, Applesauce reflected as he strolled past the game of jacks. Bezique's babysitting and Snowy's mooning about the back porch windows allowed Applesauce to reign over the Florida room in heathen splendor.

Contemplating a sunbath behind lace curtains, he gathered all his pudgy force and lunged heavily onto Mrs. B's sewing table. Skidding into the window glass Applesauce found himself nose to nose with a ferocious sneer, raggletag whiskers and a pair of bearded, battered ears. Realizing this impressive rogue must be his own reflection, he sat down with relief only to find his reflection still standing and lashing its unfamiliar tail. Appalled, he crashed to the floor with a doily stuck in his claws and staggered upstairs, unable to free himself. Completely unhinged, Applesauce scrabbled into the Professor's closet trailing the wretched doily. He settled in the darkest corner.

Baffled, Leo heaved himself from the window box, spoiling several geraniums, and made his way around the corner of the house. He ignored Delilah's uproar. Bah-Sneak (that his name?) seemed to be saddled with several useless crew members. A motley arrangement of crockery in the side yard suggested the kindly humans he'd been led to expect. A breeze from the back of the house carried feline conversation. Leo picked his way forward around brittle fallen leaves, eager to spy.

"...not any old barnyard cat. I'd hate to catch a chill." A she-cat. The frilly type.

Leo could make out that harmless, rather clever cottage cat...Beanie. He sat at the top of the back steps in a doorway propped open with a brick. Leo hoisted his tail and strode forth.

"Well, now! A pleasure to see you again, Beanie." Leo turned and swaggered in the direction of a stiff-necked cat who permitted herself the briefest of uppity inspections before ignoring him. He turned back to Beanie. "I come from the house on the hill with a message for Gypsy. Any idea where I'd find her?" He kept his back to the princess. Not as polished an entry as Star would have managed, but an improvement on his usual.

Beanie looked momentarily flustered, a cue that Leo had stumbled on a tryst. Snowy feigned boredom.

"Inside. Miss Snowy, might we trouble you to let Gypsy know she has a message from the hill house?"

Thrilled by Mr. Beanie's exquisite tact – so rare in Toms! – Snowy unfurled herself.

"A pleasure to assist you, Mr. Beanie." With a swish of her magnificent tail she disappeared into the house.

When she returned, struggling to stay abreast of Gypsy, Snowy found her guests deep in fish tales.

"The bullheads are succulent. No scales. Of course they're apt to be muddy..." Leo's eyes glittered appreciatively as shapely little "Plucky" dashed onto the porch alongside the puffball.

"A message?" Gypsy trilled, and was nearly trampled by her mate's thundering entry. His eyes telegraphed suspicion to Beanie.

"I'll take the message, Leo. Gypsy, the kittens are calling for you."

Gypsy touched her nose to her mate's. "Let's the three of us take a stroll and leave those who were here first in peace."

Admiring her adroitness at dodging snoopy Puffpants while soothing her hotheaded mate, Leo followed Gypsy down the steps, making sure to let Bezique precede him. He threw Beanie a wink, who caught it with good humor. Snowy gaped for an unguarded moment, then rearranged her tail for a charming effect.

Gypsy stopped as soon as they'd reached the far side of a pile of raked leaves.

"What news do you bring?"

"A message from your sister. She's up at the hill house, well again after a long illness the hill folk nursed her through. Why, she's plump and firm as a fat little turnip now...I thought we'd lost her for sure when Cook first brought her up..." Leo's kittenish gush wasn't lost on Bezique, whose grudge softened.

A crashing avalanche of autumn leaves at their rear produced Scout, powdered with leaf-meal and ecstatic. She scurried up to her former captor with a leaf scrolled around one ear and sat before him squarely. Scout trembled with excitement rather than fear; Leo congratulated himself. She was a chip off the old block, if he did say so himself. Willow had set him straight about who the kittens' father was.

"Mother's found? She's alright?"

"Fit as a fiddle!" Leo raised his eyes to meet Gypsy's and Bezique's. "And well seasoned. A bit weathered around her edges from her travels." Gypsy flinched. "Lovely and mellow," he crooned to himself.

"Take us to her! I'll get my brothers at once!" Scout went so far as to bunt Leo's shoulder with her little black nose. He pulled himself together.

"Your mother's longing to see you all. I promised her I'd beg you to bring the kittens up the hill as soon as it can be managed...With Bezique's permission, of course."

Bezique found it hard to tell a beam from a grimace on the tramp's face, and he realized Leo knew there'd be no "permission"; Gypsy would trample anyone who got in her way to Willow. He met her gaze and read her thoughts.

"If you can spare a night here, I think we might manage to accompany you back up the hill tomorrow morning. That is, er… we'd be much obliged. Your presence would be a help."

Leo preened his whiskers as Scout somersaulted around her blithe auntie.

"Agreed. Will you spare me a saucer of milk? And an introduction to the dog. I'll wager the nose at the end of that long snout is mighty cold in the middle of the night."

Presentiment
[1918]

By the flickering light of paper lanterns strung round the court-yard Calla watched her daughter asleep in Martin's lap. May turned her head; a flushed cheek bore the imprint of Martin's shirt button. Gloating and glazed, he was satisfied with the evening.

How quick and lean the Ringgolds seemed. Once they'd gone she and Martin were content to sip their Benedictine in lazy, overfed thralldom to their offspring. Her teenaged caretaker had been taken home.

Through the garden door fireflies lit and snuffed their tiny floating lamps, so many random embers.

She'd not heard from Sam for half a year. Not heard from someone else for longer. Perhaps she'd take May to California come autumn. Martin would join them for Christmas after supervising the building of his coach house. They'd have to find a short-term caretaker – a student? – to mind the place; their young neighbor Ross Nicol had joined the war effort.

The night breeze flirted with her hair, even coaxed the heavily beaded hem from her ankle. Burning her throat, the liqueur annoyed her – what use?

Martin was saying something in a low monotone so as not to waken May.

"...thinks the board may be willing..." His and Eugene's eternal scheme to get investors interested in a new theatre and art museum for the campus. "...a question of assets. Now once they've..."

From behind her a faint, high-pitched series of squeals troubled the thick silence of woods, fields and a few tranquil yards.

She put a finger to her lips, which Martin eventually noticed. "What is that?"

"Saturday night session at the carpenter's."

"I don't think so. Too far. The orchard?" She had his attention.

"Godfrey." He smiled with amused admiration. "Pipes. Old Nicol's four sheets to the wind, and taking it out on the apples."

Obscure but insistent, a presentiment brought her to her feet.

"No you don't, Calla. If he mistakes you for a cougar or even a skunk I wouldn't count on his shotgun missing the mark."

"Don't be silly. I'll not go further than the well. I'll be back in time to sing lullaby." She was already moving off, tossing her satin mules onto her chair.

"Hamstrung by my womenfolk as usual," he murmured into his lap, half glad of an emissary.

Soon out of sight, Calla kept to the outer garden wall, stopped to catch her breath and listen, then plunged into the meadow. Its trilling chorus vied with the shrill echoes from the hilltop. The cold dew, her favorite coral chiffon snagging on brush, the clamor in the grass caught her giggling, a foolish girl all goose pimples in the dark. She cried out when her foot came down against the warm, yielding side of a nightjar. It rocketed into the night. Her relieved laughter hung in the air, alien and ludicrous against the elemental skirl from the hill.

Fleeing the self's inner mirror, shucking words, she let the foreign voice among the trees pull her towards it. Rather than melody she followed a haunting pattern, like a thrush's cascading notes...

It was Rorie, their young friend Ross's older brother, rather than his father. And no jig or reel, but intricate, bubbling trills – the music of burbling springs, fleeting thunderheads, furious regret.

Some banshee at her elbow in the courtyard had whispered true. They'd had a letter from the War Department.

She stumbled back down to Lilybanks, half-blind with the memory of a broad young back hunched over a pint of milk and a plate of Olive's hickory hermits while Bonnet worried his bootlaces.

]]

Candlelit

"Do you, Althea…"

Al listened more closely, realizing for a hectic moment that she had no idea what name Pastor Greely was about to pronounce.

"…take Kenneth as your lawful husband to love and cherish – "

Quelling the possibility of a hysterical giggle, she reflected on the naked vulnerability of one's name hanging solemnly in the candlelit hush.

Pastor Greely nodded at Al encouragingly. She felt Bakeoven touch her elbow.

Mortified, she rushed to respond, "I do!" too loudly, to no one in particular.

Bake's "I do" was crisp and firm; the glance she risked met pleased approval – even happiness? – peeking through his perfectly groomed poise.

This seemed permission, finally, to detach her gaze from the Murphy bed's outline in the wall ahead of them.

Their hands were being shaken. Pastor Greely's dark cheek against hers felt warm but careful; Bake's coolly genteel, familiar.

She thought to look around as Bake's arm encircled her, eliminating any need to confer.

Al's matron of honor, her pleased face patchy and inflamed, patted their hands approvingly.

"Well done, my dears," she glowed, adding "Much happiness, many years!" with the robust authority of the lecture hall. As though, Al caught herself hoping, those could be had.

Lucy twittered forth, resplendent in the red Wellies Al had requested and a clever, polka-dotted dress. Al recalled guiltily that she'd asked her to come alone; Chip and frisky little Harry seemed more possible now she and Bake had survived the ceremony.

Lucy doubled back, scooping Linnet out of a carrying case festooned with nuptial bows and ribbons. She brought her over for Althea to pet just as Bake's niece Stella, with Rumba in tow, lunged toward Bakeoven. Al submitted to it all gratefully; nothing hurt more than wary, tiptoeing tact. Linnet seemed to be coping well with her rhinestone-studded collar and Al was able to massage her ears tenderly before Rumba's panting shredded the cat's poise.

"Grace under pressure," Bake murmured, squeezing her arm a little and nodding in Lucy's direction. She'd discreetly retreated toward Linnet's "Pet Taxi" as the frantic cat tried to climb Lucy's face.

"*She's* going to have some puncture wounds to clean up," Libby cracked, kissing Al and pumping Bake's hand from within a frothy tent of mauve organza that rendered her unrecognizable. Martha, her new flame, followed suit with the heartiness of newfound happiness.

Beebe and Tad appeared next in the impromptu crush. She was letting him hold her hand; he looked removed from the human race, a colossal seraph dumb with bliss. In fact, Althea reflected through the detached ether in which she floated, the guests' joy eclipsed the wedding couple's. She let the predictable thought evaporate and tugged at Beebe's sleeve as giddiness encroached.

"I'll sit down for just a minute?" she interrupted, not sure why she'd made it a question.

Bakeoven winked at Beebe and steered Althea back to the Gustav Stickley dresser the Lilybankers had transplanted from a bedroom as a stand-in for Pastor Greely's pulpit. They'd crowned it with a pot of sunflowers, sumac and artistically droopy burgundy flowers. Althea had darkly informed him the latter's name was Love-Lies-Weeping. And when he'd explained that the Unitarian church he attended fitfully didn't use the cross in ceremonies, she'd quipped that a Blue Cross would have been apt. He'd have to address this attitude at some point, but now wasn't the time. She sank into his priceless Rohlfs armchair, an inheritance, all Gothic trefoils and turrets, Bake's handsome contribution to the exigencies of the day. He'd rented a heavily cushioned hearse to get it to Lilybanks and had sworn Beebe and Marian to secrecy, wearying of the tenor of his bride's attempts at humor.

Al arranged the drape of her Lilybanks shawl and realized none of the others had followed them; the isolation of marriage, already! Or perhaps they thought she might be surreptitiously vomiting behind the Stickley altar. The marvelous, savage sunflowers, straining toward a bygone sun, pulled Al from her thoughts. She was surrounded by beauty and kindness – how profligate to flee!

She reached for Bake's hand timidly, still not sure what it meant but certain he'd prize the gesture just now. They'd been married by a justice of the peace a week after her diagnosis, with only Marian and his attorney as witnesses. Till now that had changed nothing but her ability to pay her medical bills. Tomorrow she'd move into his guest room with its own functioning bathroom, central heating and a view that included the roof of the university hospital. She waited for the burning gulp that accompanied thoughts of leaving Lilybanks. It didn't come; her medications created a foggy moat between thought and feeling. Both seemed dispensable. Best just to commune here with the ripe scent of pollen and awareness of this benign, obliging creature who for whatever reason leaned towards her as though to proffer smelling salts.

"How about some water."

"No thanks. Just a little gimpy. It'll pass."

"Marian's herding people downstairs."

"Oh dear. That means we make a grand entrance?"

"It beats being knocked down by Rumba in the melee."

He'd been secretly horrified when she'd warned him she'd be wearing a knit cap for the ceremony as a hedge against the hair loss she anticipated hourly. To his relief Lucy had devised a burnished bronze helmet of silken chain mail sprouting genteelly whimsical tassels – samurai *cum* Chanel. It hugged Althea's head so that her candlelit cheekbones suggested Nefertiti. Perhaps Lucy could make several – he had no idea what lay under the cap.

Suddenly Beebe was between them, with a hand on his shoulder as he crouched, the other on Al's thin forearm. She gave off heat; her locket teetered over the edge of a stiff lace collar.

"Are you guys up to coming down? Bubo says to tell you 'we can send everyone packing and they'll be none the wiser.' We've been pretty enigmatic about anything more than the ceremony. Libby and Martha are out walking Stella's dog with her."

Al smiled at the delicately casual "you guys," in case one of them might be too overcome with emotion (regret?) to face a modest clutch of guests.

"No, no, it's fine. Isn't it, Bake? I'm fine." She'd requested the all-important cake be served in the sitting room, feeling skittish about the formality dining room seating imposed. One could faint more inconspicuously and comfortably in a rocking chair.

She patted the rosy cheek, an elderly gesture she felt appropriate.

"Come down with us, Beebe. So I can hide behind you."

They both enjoyed this; she'd set them at ease. Casper had never fully appreciated her sense of humor. She hoped he had one today.

Candles in the Millefleurs windows over the garden illumined windowsill vases of white asters and pink windflowers from the grounds. Parched petals too close to the flames had fallen to the floor.

"I'll be right back, and then let's go down, shall we?" She smiled at Bake and walked over to her favorite otter, giving the creature a conspiratorial wink before returning, all business. Bakeoven, used to Lilybankers' vagaries, merely gave her his arm. The Grueby tiles surrounding the fireplace quavered with reflected light. Flames snapped in the grate. Watkins' attempt to start up the ancient furnace on the traditional first of October had failed dismally. Marian was supposedly negotiating an affordable outcome. Al suspected she was being protected from knowledge of pending disasters.

As they descended amidst Beebe's warbling enjoyment of the moment her elders felt its decisiveness. Relying on the banister despite Bake's attentiveness, Al reflected that she was more in love with Lilybanks than she ever had been with a man. Aphrodite, sloppily wreathed in baby's breath, welcomed them beneath the lily chandelier.

Ensconced in Morris chairs behind the flawless cake for photographs, both rose to the occasion. Since it seemed as impossible to ask as to guess what medley of gracious pathos, humble gratitude, even coy expectancy Bakeoven wished her to display, Al relaxed into the celebration, blaming the medications for any lapses.

Completely indifferent but alive to Beebe's desire to please, Al had requested something elegant rather than sentimental by way of a wedding cake. The resulting polished square, fashionably enrobed in glossy white chocolate like a marble tablet, featured a spidery interpretation of the staircase's gingko leaf pattern in shades of sage and yellow. "FELICITY" served as salutation in fretted bungalow lettering.

"It's perfect. The perfect cake, Beebe. Won't you cut it for us please?" She made her tone more languishing than necessary to spare everyone a photo op of her and Bake in a dutiful clammy clutch with Calla's sterling spatula.

Marian, looking very pleased in spite of the dark under-eye circles and deeply etched lines that betrayed her lately, lurched to her feet with a punch cup.

Bakeoven startled Al by leaping to his feet and motioning Marian to sit.

"Marian, Althea and I want you to have a well-earned rest from the podium. I'm used to being master of ceremonies – I find I can't resist taking over. We thank you – and all the Lilybankers and our friends and family – for your deep generosity, your imaginative caring, your comforting ability to be genuine. And now, keeping it simple, please join me in a toast: To the health of my beautiful bride."

Pinioned, Al began weeping with all the sense of gratitude and trust she'd held at bay. Feeling she had nothing to offer this husband but decorum at such a public moment, she labored to stanch her runny nose. Kind murmurs and clucking filled the momentary quiet. Then Libby bellowed, "Hear, hear!" and began clapping, Martha chimed in loyally, Tad galvanized everyone by whistling through his fingers, and Beebe flung herself around Al's shoulders, smudging Bake's tux with frosting.

Congratulating herself on her foresight, Al struggled up to speak, veered forward precipitately and felt Bake grab her hips just in time.

Blushing, she raised an empty cup.

"To my husband, the 'parfit gentil knight' of chivalry."[20]

Stella, as tall as Tad, beamed and raised her cup high. She'd been warm and supportive ever since a luncheon with her uncle during which Al felt certain some delicate issues had been addressed. The prenuptial agreement reaffirmed that Stella was Bakeoven's sole heir, and authorized him to dispatch Althea to a hospice at any time he chose should her situation be declared irrevocable. Inconvenience would not be allowed to evolve into martyrdom, even the eager martyrdom of Lilybankers hoping to bring Althea "home" at the end. Bake would decide, and Al knew he was unlikely to permit her the unhygienic, primitive charms of Lilybanks after throwing in the towel himself. People would talk: "They'll be in England." "The house is in a tenuous situation itself." He'd even said, with memorable daring, "I'll know what's best." She'd barely murmured, anxious to spare the sisterhood a burden and grateful for his stunning generosity.

Someone had tucked dahlias into Calla's majolica pots; they made Al wistful for a walk in the garden. Bake's cologne was proving an impediment to such pleasures; leaning against him released a cloud of scent evoking urbane interiors and over-civilized imbroglios.

"Just plain ginger ale," Lucy whispered, pressing another fussy crystal punch cup on her. "For three o'clock." Al pulled her shawl closer and took it in both hands, feeling like a beggar receiving alms. The sisterhood had been alarmingly relentless in their supervision of her pills; Bakeoven was probably mistaken in thinking their threat to telephone in the middle of the night a joke.

Everything in the room seemed smaller and more distant than it could possibly be; she seemed to be floating, and the *andante* humming behind her left ear didn't appear to issue from her spouse. The word made her want to retch, but then so did the cake and the lamplight and blotchy Marian's surreptitious squinting at Stella's ankle bracelet.

Bake had promised that Linnet could be with her at all times. In just an hour or two they'd be left in delicious peace in a strange new bed.

Mysteries of the Heart
[1927]

Rorie forced himself to open the envelope with his brother's name on it, holding it away from his body as if avoiding contagion.

> *Ross,*
>
> *Thought you'd admire this set of chisels used on marble. <u>Stay home</u> and put them to good use. The story's for May Morrissey, give it to her Mama with Sam's regards if this makes it through the havoc here. – S.R.*

Reluctant either to keep the gift for himself or abandon what had been kindly meant for Ross, Rorie tossed the kit onto a heap of other stalemates in his suitcase.

Desperate to be done, constrained by the desire to do right by the dead, he rolled up the typed manuscript and jabbed it into his jacket pocket, crumpled the note and dropped it on the closet floor. The orchard's new owners had enough work ahead of them; a few dustpans more or less wouldn't hurt.

Their mother had refused to let the room be touched except as a shrine. His younger brother's taste for simplicity had spared Rorie much. Nothing to hack another notch out of him but these few closet shelves and some plaster dogs lined up on the bedside wainscoting. Did she ever think who'd have to do this once she and Father were gone?

Furious, he wrapped the dogs in a pillowcase and escaped.

At Lilybanks' front door he licked the lead of a pencil stub, wrote MAY on the sheaf's topmost page and lowered it silently into the mailbox, anxious to avoid humanity.

Just as reluctant, May had frozen behind the hazel bushes and only investigated the matter once the footsteps receded down Corrie Street.

*   *   *

THE RAVEN REVIEW October 16, 2011

Amid Controversy, Leiby Hints
R.U. Will Save Decaying Landmark

By I. M. Fitt
Exclusive Raven Interview

Rutledge University President Dennis Leiby indicated
in a series of informal remarks to this Raven reporter

while working out at the Mayhew Gym last night that he wants the University to intervene in an historic Hill District property's escalating domestic crisis. Recent water damage in the upper story of "Lilybanks," an Arts and Crafts mansion built for Martin and Calla Morrissey, Moraine Woods State Park's original owners, has the local historical society, university trustees, Lilybanks's current owners (Morrissey descendants) and an unlikely international cult of Lilybanks fans at each others' throats.

Rutledge's famously independent-minded Historical Society has earned President Leiby's wrath by backing the home's beleaguered female residents' desire to maintain ownership of their aging ancestral home. Leiby, who referred to Marian Morrissey, her niece and several other unrelated residents as "eccentric in the extreme," admitted Morrissey is one of his own employees, a tenured, semi-retired professor in the Department of English Literature. In response to this Raven reporter's reference to an undercurrent of hostility toward the university's Acquisitions team among some Hill District neighbors, who fear Leiby will "bully" Morrissey, Leiby snorted into his sweatband.

"If nothing else we can open Rollo up again for a while," he replied when pressed to elaborate on a comment that university housing (chronically in short supply) could be provided for Morrissey and her niece. Rollo Hall is scheduled for demolition next summer.

*　*　*

Althea made an effort not to groan out loud; Bake had been very good about letting her see the morning's campus newspaper. He'd declare a complete communications blackout if he detected "unnecessary stress."

Moreover, this amateur but high-profile exposure of Leiby's machinations, which likely told the truth more baldly than the Sentinel would dare, seemed heaven-sent. She'd never doubted the rumors of Leiby's drinking; these pompous indiscretions clinched them.

While the most she could manage on her own behalf was "Thy will be done, and help me to bear it," she daily resumed a threadbare prayer life on behalf of Lilybanks. Marian and, tacitly, Beebe, who embodied the spirit of the place, must retain possession of the property. And Lilybanks must age gently, a protected refuge. Some mundane miracle was urgently needed, and surely in the works. Althea refused to let herself imagine otherwise.

She'd insisted on accompanying Bake to the house after Lucy'd stopped by earlier that week with the news about Millefleurs. Impossible to witness, but impossible to refrain from doing so. Al had felt the same tender urge to suffer vicariously on the beloved room's behalf as she did when refusing to avoid thinking about the latest environmental atrocity. One didn't turn one's back on one's friends, animal or mineral.

Soggy puckers leached of color that disfigured three yards of the mural after a series of rainy days revealed, too late, the need for a roof repair. Nature had imitated art, or rather done it one better, reducing patches of the fenny dado to oozing pulp. Beebe maintained a taut, unsmiling silence; Lucy kept up a feverish gibber about some exclusive design studio that specialized in exquisite restorations, the owner of which golfed with Chip; Marian, looking alternately stricken and serene, was clearly struggling.

Most alarmingly, Bakeoven looked terribly sad. Althea, striving for best behavior on her short leash, had decided to trust in Chip's social skills until she realized a favorite, comically pert little kingfisher had been all but erased. Who could bring it back now that, rather like the Cheshire Cat, only its brash beak remained? She'd put her hand in Bake's and tugged; they'd simply left, though Al had managed to croak, "I'm sure there's a silver lining," to no one in particular.

Yet again an improbable savior, Bake had reminded Al that he'd made sure Millefleurs and the entire property had been thoroughly documented with camera and pen several years ago. He took pains to show her an excellent close-up of the kingfisher.

Thus reassured, Al at once found herself thinking, "Ah, but *my* little bird, the original that lived there so long, has vanished forever," and discovered herself unable to summon the requisite melancholia. The knowledge that mortality no longer waited graciously in the wings, as it seemed to for most people she knew, but had begun kicking in her back door, quickly exhausted her penchant for this kind of self-indulgence. If Casper's death had branded her heart with knowledge of the irreparable, her own suggested the wisdom of yielding. She had no time to assume and defend any but the most indispensable position.

Marian, a more familiar and welcome pillar than Al's "husband," visited almost daily. She referred to the invasive local interest in Lilybanks' woes as "Restoration drama." Though she shared droll snippets of the goings-on – "The Hysterical Society keeps alluding to 'secret resources;' do you think they're considering blackmail? Leiby thinks he's so discreet!" "Tad heard Watkins muttering about selling his story to the Chicago Trib…" – Marian mostly liked to sit and look out Al's window as they sipped the contents of Bake's Limoges Havilland teacups: English Breakfast for Marian, miso broth for Althea. Marian often contributed a pocket's worth of fallen leaves, the more crumpled the better, for Al had begun sketching their convolutions as a door into the Now.

After an hour of savoring the play of light and shadow, the din of waxwings in Bake's hawthorns, the musical clinking of Rumba's tags, Marian departed, seemingly as edified as Al. The much-anticipated trip to Oxford had dropped out of conversation, though Al felt certain it was only a week or two away. She hadn't the strength to bring it up, though soon she'd need to ask Bake to investigate. Dennis Leiby and a few worn-out roof shingles mustn't derail Marian's pilgrimage.

Memories of her honeymoon with Casper nudged at her heart; she bit her lip. How like life, perverse, comical, that now she finally dared feel how terribly she missed him.

Al sighed and punched her pillows into shape; she disinterred Cookie from the bedclothes where she hid him. Bake had eventually discovered the fraying cocker spaniel when groping for a hot water bottle. Althea had emerged from an unhappy trip to the bathroom to find Bake dangling Cookie by a hind paw as though interrogating a burglar. He gave Al an arch, quizzical look that seemed possible to interpret as good-humored; she'd shrugged, as eloquent a response as any other regarding mysteries of the heart.

Normally at this time of day she'd be policing the morning kinder-snack, ensuring the correct distribution of cups of soy milk versus cow's lest any child be scandalized. She missed sticky fingers clutching her own; runny noses and impatient, glazed parents somewhat less. Her diagnosis had been the final straw in the daycare program's demise. Amidst gossip, threats from the board of health and Lucy's reduced involvement a handful of loyal or under-informed families had signed on for the fall "semester" in spite of Marian and Beebe's announced two-week absence. Al, with help from a recent Stubblefield grad saving for college and a promise from Tad to coach recess during his lunch hour, had been slated to hold things together. That plan, which she'd been characteristically unhinged about, now seemed a shred of benign daydream.

In the wake of "Kindercrumple," as Lucy's Chip rather annoyingly called it, Bakeoven had remarked to Al over a glass of Chablis (and an illicit antique thimbleful for herself, already a married ritual) that Marian ought to consider throwing in the towel and remaining in England. Al had initially thought that possibility preposterous, then dismaying and finally creative, symmetrical and therefore impending. Neither breathed a word to the Lilybankers.

Preservation

Lynn Throckmorton squinted at the bracelet she'd instructed Lucy to fasten on her wrist. Massive vintage rhinestones: witty or awful? She felt inclined to take the risk, and thrust her hand out to Lucy.

"Wrap it up with the mohair suit, will you?"

"Beebe'll be happy to box it for you. I have to leave for my Stubblefield class. We'll look forward to seeing you there in November. I'll send you an invitation to the opening once we get 'em printed… There's more tissue paper in the cupboard above the toilet, Beebe." Deciding against giving their best customer a friendly little squeeze, Lucy twirled out the door of The Cygnet's Nest blowing a kiss to Beebe and devising a deferential twinkle for La Throckmorton.

"You don't have to run off somewhere, young lady?" Mrs. Throckmorton habitually assumed "Beebe" was a silly nickname and that having forgotten the correct name, it was too late to inquire.

Deftly sandwiching the fuzzy suit between two layers of expensive paper, Beebe didn't look up.

"Not at all."

"Excellent. I want to talk to you." She pulled a cigarette from a cloisonné case Beebe recognized from last year's inventory. "Could you open a window? I won't exhale on the Lilli Anns." It was all getting boxed up, anyway. She wouldn't miss climbing the fire escape steps in winter, but she'd regret the privacy, the almost clandestine atmosphere. Emerging with a shopping bag full of treasures just wouldn't be the same in a corridor full of sweaty adolescents whose crackpot parents fancied themselves European intelligentsia.

"I guess so."

Mrs. Throckmorton watched Beebe tie up her box, then make her way to the windows overlooking Lilybanks' driveway to tug one open. Mrs. T. observed with fascination; someone on the board said the girl wore pantaloons under her musty velvets. She lit up, considering her mission.

"I'm curious: why's your last name Morrissey? Surely the name went dormant since Calla's only child was female?"

"My aunt decided I'd be Beebe Bauer-Morrissey. Legally. But it's too much of a mouthful."

"I hear you're buying the Maven Alley Bakery."

"Oh, no. Nothing like that. Yet." Beebe cleared her throat. "After all, I'm a minor. I'll just be helping hold down the fort while Gloria decides if she likes Florida. Where did you hear that, Mrs. Throckmorton?"

"Oh, who knows. I hear lots of things. Most things. We're glad to hear the bakery's staying. If you encounter any difficulties give me a call." She handed Beebe one of the historical society's business cards, sank onto the divan and crossed her skinny legs.

"Dr. Bakeoven's a great admirer of yours. He says you're 'a young woman of parts.' I'm trusting his judgement." Mrs. Throckmorton indulged herself with a pointed survey of Beebe's Emily-Dickinson-straight-from-the-grave attire. "And my intuition." Beebe, armored with the light of her most guileless smile, clambered onto the edge of the lingerie table, swinging her feet so the Throck could examine her pre-World War I black cotton lisle stockings. Mrs. T. exhaled smoke onto them, suggesting fumigation.

"We've been in contact with the Empyrean Society." Beebe wondered if this was a royal "we" or the obscurely ubiquitous Rutledge Historical Society.

"Now, listen. Here's the offer: The historical society will contribute two thirds of the funds necessary to secure Lilybanks, and the Brits will come up with the rest. On certain conditions." Beebe stopped swinging.

"We'll own the property. Some international lawyer we've dug up at the university will draw up contracts giving the Empyrean Society fifty-fifty partnership status with us regarding management and use. We make all final decisions on historic preservation; they get priority bookings. Then –"

"Bookings?"

"Just listen. It'll all come together. You Morrisseys get to live in the house. Forever. Though eventually someone not of direct lineage would have to be subject to approval. I mean, fifty years from now a second cousin twice removed who's down on his luck – obviously not necessarily an asset. Anyway. You and your aunt and..." (Mrs. Throckmorton indulged in a prim cough) "...your descendants are guaranteed residence. And you get first right of refusal for the curatorship. (We're hoping you'll accept, obviously.) Lest there be any doubt, we're referring to the property in its current entirety." She referred to notes. "The garden. The stork on the steeple, uh, cupola."

Pausing for breath, Mrs. Throckmorton thought Beebe looked dazed, though whether from ecstasy or nausea remained to be expressed. She made haste.

"Lilybanks has become too expensive for your family to maintain properly. Feldkamp – the city of Rutledge fears the university wants to monopolize the acquisition of historic landmarks." A glance at her notes. "Diversity of ownership's much healthier for Rutledge."

She re-crossed her legs, took another drag on the cigarette, tossed down the notes.

"The historical society's become a key player in this community. We've got an enterprising, farsighted inner circle. And we're constantly networking. I'm sure you're a little surprised we've been in touch with the Prince's Empyrean Society. We're on our toes. 'A word to the wise,' as they say."

Beebe continued to look as though she'd swallowed a mothball and might turn a delicate shade of blue violet any moment.

La Throckmorton snuffed out her cigarette on a tray of cufflinks.

"Tell Marian it's time to surrender. All you have to do is turn a bedroom or two into guest facilities for an occasional bed n' break-faster, live with a few inconveniences like anyone else whose home's being rehabbed and collect your fee for supervising historical accuracy. We can't afford to cross your palms with silver, but would you prefer having Leiby turn the place into a frat house (after he safely retires to an island)? Or, more likely, run it as the historic district's tourist center, with a parking lot where the garden is – a "gift" from the university – and his latest girlfriend running the place? We're making you an extraordinary offer, and I need someone sensible to put an end to the water damage and potential lawsuits and tell us 'YES' before Leiby starts twisting arms. What do you think?"

Beebe slipped off the table's edge and began fiddling with the mannequin's thin Chinese robe, as though utterly absorbed in displaying its sleeves to better advantage.

"We're collecting bids for the water damage to the mural, Mrs. Throckmorton. And we have connections, too," Beebe said, picturing Chip in the Bugs Bunny boxers Lucy said he favored.

Misunderstanding, Mrs. T. dealt her final card.

"Lionel Woodruff's given us his blessing. I'm sure you'll be hearing from him soon," she purred. In fact, the prince's court jester (as Lynn had overheard Leiby refer to his houseguest) was reported to be irretrievably holed up in some Scottish patron's Highland aerie, completing his latest collection of odes in a creative frenzy. Sleepless, intransigent, the Rutledge Historical Society had prevailed, extracting 'an unintelligible but apparently favorable series of grunts' from

Woodruff regarding the advisability of the Empyreans rescuing Lilybanks, according to the Society's delightfully wry secretary.

"The decision is ours. I'm sure you realize that. Thank you so much for your interest." Beebe examined her chewed fingernails, fighting back an urge to gnaw. She met Mrs. Throckmorton's gimlet gaze.

"I think the meeting between our attorneys should be here at Lilybanks, don't you?" With the key players present. So many details to discuss. I'll make Calla's gingerbread."

"I'll bring the champagne!" Mrs. Throckmorton, disarmed by victory, extended her hand and then, overcome, permitted herself the arm's-length kiss into the air above Beebe's left cheek that passed for intimacy among her friends.

"Maybe a little prema –"

"Veuve Cliquot!" Mrs. T. sang out, bolting.

Private Things
[*1927*]

Calla smiled at her daughter's bulging coat pockets.

"Been through the orchard, have you?"

Cheeks and nose aflame, May tossed her a Golden Russet with a careful underhand. She sniffed extravagantly; a runny nose had left crispy streaks on her solemn, chubby face.

"What are you doing?"

Seated at May's desk, Calla gave an ingenuous shrug and leaned over to blow on the typewriter's dusty innards.

"I came in to air out the room and your jumble of papers flew all over. Just tidying up for you. Did you return that glove?"

"Yes. The lady said...to thank you."

"You're always so vague about names. It's Mrs. Guinness, you know." Calla sighed, certain May had fled as soon as possible. Her daughter's impenetrable shyness enveloped her more snugly with every year; even Martin's bland protestations that she'd eventually shed it had begun to sound artificial.

Stolid and bookish, May was the apple of her Grandpapa Jessam's eye. "Still waters run deep," he said. May had thrown herself upon his shipment of Greek and Latin primers with a passion reserved only for her precocious studies and Mother Nature.

The girl's face was all queer blotches; her eyes looked glassy.

"Come let me feel you. You look feverish."

May stayed in the doorway.

"Those papers with the green ribbon weren't flying around. They were in a drawer."

"Yes, I think you're right. I put a few things back in the drawers so you won't have to look for them in the garden."

"Those papers were at the very bottom of the drawer, Calla. You've been poking around in my private things."

"I suppose I have, in an absent-minded way. It must have been meant to happen, May. Why didn't you tell me you're writing stories? This is delightful, in its way. With some illustrations I think we might get you published." Calla picked the sheaf up again, and peered at her daughter over the reading glasses no one but May and Olive ever witnessed.

May imagined the desperation behind this motherly enthusiasm. Calla's dull, flatfooted bookworm of a daughter might finally make her proud, especially after Calla had smeared her charming self over every page.

While pity, shame, and something approaching hatred churned in her stomach May wrestled with a more delicate conundrum. She'd not been to the orchard. The apples were given her at Olive's. And *he*'d been there, Olive's troubling, kindly friend. Though Olive had never said so, May knew she wasn't to mention him. Something wasn't right; she had no idea what. He might well have written her Cat Tale, and she felt that couldn't be proper either, judging by how guilty she felt right now.

She took a deep breath.

"My story just came along by chance. It's not really *mine*. If you turn it into a book with my name on it I'll never forgive you. I'll ask Grandpa to come for me."

"May, lie down at once. You're not well."

Calla watched her daughter drop onto her bed like a toppled post, her face dark and congested – the way she'd looked as a constipated infant, Calla told herself with sour amusement. A venomous antipathy she refused to acknowledge wriggled alongside her sense of the need for prudence. She drew the desk chair to the bed and sat, but decided not to risk caressing the clammy cheek turned away from her.

"It *is* yours, darling. You're just not accustomed to being invited to dance yet. Your muse wants to fall in love with you, May. It didn't come along by chance: you're being courted. I – I'm sorry I pried."

Appalled and frantic, May held perfectly still. Did Calla mean she was to be a writer? At the same time she seemed to mean some other thing. Nothing was as it appeared – least of all, she'd long suspected, her mother. "Being courted." She thought of someone's fidgety eyebrows and parched laugh with revulsion, resolving never to visit Olive's rooms again.

Transcendental Fruitcakes

Althea had been forcefully tucked into one of the Millefleurs Morris chairs beneath a collection of quilts and counterpanes. When she fidgeted the layers exhaled lavender, stale milk and dust. She watched a drop of amber water plunk into a scarred old hip bath Watkins had consented to haul down from the attic should his temporary patch job on the roof deteriorate. It had.

Hollow pounding issued from somewhere distant beneath her. "Watkins seems to feel we'll have more heat in here after he batters the furnace into submission," Marian observed, urging the inevitable mug of miso on Al.

Beebe and Lucy sat in lotus position at either end of the settle with Skippy nestled on Lucy's hoodie between them. Marian installed herself in the remaining Morris.

"Let's just take a moment to become thoroughly present. Breathing. Here and Now."

After what seemed to Althea like twenty minutes of tiresome attempts to inhabit at least a few bits of her body, a shaft of morning sunshine glorified the peeling paint inside a nearby window frame. Immediately she felt herself to be at home, glimpsing paradise. After that she accepted her intermittent out-to-lunchedness during this ultimate convocation of the sisterhood as a mere phenomenon, like a passing cloud or the cluster of raisin-like droppings Skippy had just evacuated on the floor.

"Er, Lucy?" She pointed.

"I knew I'd forgotten something! Be right back..." Lucy pattered across the marquetry to fetch a litter box.

"The Nest's going to be alright at Stubblefield?" While Al recognized the necessity of relocating the shop now that its staff-in-residence had been decimated, she had doubts about the charms of a windowless school supply closet.

"You'll see. Mrs. Hassenpfeffer gave us carte blanche. It's not as small as it sounds," Beebe smiled. We can keep the divan and the mannequin, and I'm pretty sure I can make the gramophone fit. Mrs. Hassenpfeffer may draw the line at having the lingerie vanity in the corridor. But we're going to be more of an insider's secret than ever. The clothes horses will love it."

Lucy raced back to the settle. Skippy nibbled the toe of one of her knocked-over Wellies tentatively, then resumed his seat as well.

"Are we ready now? Beebe, I think we all understand the essence of Mrs. Throckmorton's, ah, tidings. I suggested we each keep our thoughts to ourselves until we could meet. So here we are…" Marian seemed at a loss for further words; her surreptitious dabs at her eyes hadn't deceived anyone. Lucy's tremor had started up; Beebe seemed to be on another plane. Eager to fill the turbulent silence in some benign way, Althea cleared her throat and raised a limp hand.

"Bakeoven suggests you make sure…I mean, if you decide on some version of the historical society's offer – make sure you're not expected to be open to the public all the time, or at the drop of a hat. Maybe tours and overnighters only on weekends? We think that would have to be very precisely laid out in any contract."

Lucy leaned forward eagerly now, pushing back a dark wing of hair. "You'll have to get all the details in writing. Like who can actually live here, or not. And whether residents can use the property for other business. I mean, once repairs and finances are on an even keel you might want to reopen Kinder on Corrie. And there's Beebe's baking. Even the "tooties," Marian – Chip's attorney is up on all this stuff. He's very pro-active."

"Bake recommends his lawyer. An old friend. Sorry; he insisted I put in a word."

"Thank you, my dear ones. It will be crucial to safeguard personal liberty should we proceed along the Hysterical/Empyrean path. A timely offer, quite generous in its way, with creative potential." Al thought Marian sounded enigmatic at best.

"It seems that Lilybanks is to be rescued from Dr. Leiby's unfeeling machinations as well as from my own good intentions." Marian's blotches darkened. "Everyone's unspoken assumption is that the Morrisseys' – and perhaps other Lilybankers' – highest aspiration is to live here. It occurs to neither friend nor foe that I might sell out for a tidy little sum and spend the rest of my days in the Bodliean. With holidays in the Lake District." Lucy's lotus came undone; she knocked over the Wellies. "…Or on the Isle of Skye," Marian considered, brandishing a linty tissue with an air of recklessness.

"And Beebe! The world is her oyster. She and Tad may travel around the world and open a patisserie in Kashmir...after she takes a first at Oxford, of course. Althea and Lucy are being married off to Rutledge's most desirable, responsible men – who dote on them and come well supplied with charming homes. I ask you, –"

"Ditey."

Marian broke off to look in Althea's direction.

"What about Aphrodite? Where would *she* prefer to be?"

Marian gurgled alarmingly and closed her reddening eyes. Lucy and Althea sobbed in harmony.

"Luckily she'd prefer to be here at Lilybanks with Tad and me. The curatorship should pay for a dog-sitter if we need a weekend in Kashmir. This is my home, Bubo. I'm staying."

Tad, who'd been trapped on the threshold of Calla's powder room for several uncomfortably intimate remarks, plunged forward.

"Sorry to interrupt, Mrs. – Marian – but can you identify these spoons?" Tad knelt and held a couple of teaspoons out for inspection, waiting gravely while she blew her nose. Utterly bleary, she'd recognized Tad by the way the floor shook as he approached.

That everyone present felt identification of a couple of spoons was urgent bore witness to Tad's humble good sense.

"Gobbledygook, Gothic script," Marian muttered, fiddling with the chain on her glasses. "That will be a 'C,' in spite of the vertical line," she said, squinting at the spoons' florid handles as though no other business lay to hand. "Crumrind rather foolishly married a spendthrift ingenue late in life and died penniless. A chest of sterling flatware was found in his rented room with a note to the effect that it was to go to the Morrisseys as partial payment on a loan. Poor devil. His wife clearly chose the pattern."

"I found one in the hallway and on a hunch went down to the furnace room. The second was sticking out of Watkins' tool pouch."

"They belong in the attic, in their chest. Grandma hung onto them for some reason. Design clashes terribly with the Lilybanksian aesthetic. Reactionary. Completely against Crumrind's principles. Call the police."

Lucy thrust her new cell phone at Tad. Beebe sprang to his side, grabbing his sleeve.

"Tell them no siren. Can you keep him busy till they get here?"

Tad nodded, threw them one of his "leave it to me" salutes and to everyone's fascination tiptoed out.

Beebe plunked back down on the settle, startling Skippy. She kneaded the thick roll of fur between his shoulders with vocational expertise.

"I'm staying. Our bed and breakfast service could be affiliated with the Maven Alley Bakery. We take over from Gloria on New Year's Day. That gives us nine months to train some Animal Allies and Stubblefielders to keep the bakery going and help Bubo with the B & B while I'm doing Masoncup. At the very least we could crank out a mountain of top-notch fruitcakes for the holidays and circulate lots of publicity about resuming regular hours. (That's our fallback position if we get strangled by red tape. Though I think Mayor Feldkamp may prove very helpful.) Althea, you're going to have to be my liaison; Tad's father is arranging a London apprenticeship with a metalwork studio for him during the seven months of my Transcendental Poetics – on condition that he accepts the architectural restoration trainee position his dad's arranging for the same period. (We'll only be together on weekends, but the Empyreans are springing for married housing on campus!) By the way, I think Friday-Saturday-Sunday, additional days at our discretion, sounds right for the contract. Wait till they hear Tad's career choice. Not to mention his hobby. Turning the weathervane hut into a metalworking smithy would really enhance it. And we really do need to get a potential daycare business – or whatever – into the contract."

Beebe was panting. The others waited to see who'd go find a thermometer.

"Married housing?" Of course; they'd discussed all this weeks ago. With her consent Beebe could be married next spring, Marian reminded herself.

"Transcendental...fruitcakes..." Lucy stuttered. She and Al looked at each other, telegraphing discomfort. This wasn't their Beebe. And while neither was surprised to be outgrown, it stung.

"Such energy, Beebe. I can see you've put a lot of thought into this." Marian's remark was surely barbed. Perhaps she felt hurt too, Al realized. So much for the Isle of Skye.

Yet the hectic laundry list of schemes and contingencies sounded increasingly desperate the longer it hung in the silence.

Beebe turned pale, then fuchsia, and popped from her lotus. She rushed around the settle and stood behind Lucy, who put a hand up to hold one of Beebe's.

"I can make it work, Bubo. You can go to Skye on our fruitcake money. You can spend your vacation in the Bodliean every year. The Society will put you up. You don't want to live in exile. This is probably our best chance to stay. For the rest of our lives. Please."

The last word, a quavering incantation, restored harmony to a waning mother-and-child alliance.

"Life's about embracing change, child. Seems we'll have plenty to embrace without leaving Lilybanks."

Just for a moment Beebe knelt and laid her head in the familiar tweedy lap, prickly with toast crumbs.

Muffled knocks at the front door punctuated by Aphrodite's uniquely sepulchral, booming knells made their way up the stairs towards Millefleurs.

"That will be for Watkins," Marian observed, tucking a strand of hair behind Beebe's ear.

Althea, galvanized, teetered from the depths of her Morris chair to a window with a view of the cobblestones.

"Get downstairs and guard the back doors!" she bellowed to no one in particular, startling herself.

While the more able-bodied half of the sisterhood vanished, Althea paced between windows, trailing a quilt, and Marian composed herself. By the time Watkins' ornery croaks ascended the stairs to the clink of police paraphernalia, she was able to receive him regally from the depths of her slatted throne.

"Mrs. Morrissey? I'm Sergeant Boyd; this is Officer Cziski. From the Rutledge Police Department, ma'am. We had a call from the young man who opened the door for us..." He checked his notebook while Watkins muttered and grimaced. "Tad Bramble? Says he's a guest living here temporarily?"

"Oh yes, Sergeant. I asked him to make the call."

"Suspected stolen goods?" Sergeant Boyd proffered the offending spoons. "These belong to you, Mrs. Morrissey? Bramble says he found one in Mr. Watkins' tool kit. Mr. Watkins says he has no idea how it got there. That right, sir?"

Watkins looked so unwashed, unsavory and incompetent with his mashed greasy hair, gnarled stoop and perpetual spittly sneer that the Lilybankers seemed as shocked as the police by his having the run of the house. Althea in particular felt ashamed, as if the household had been discovered distributing pornography or hoarding underfed animals or indulging some other dark, ingrown predilection. They'd just accepted Watkins as an amusing, necessary evil – the design's deliberate flaw to appease jealous gods. Or perhaps he was the perfect match. Studying Beebe's sideshow appearance, Lucy's vacant smile, Marian's lopsided glasses and the unsightly old hip bath, Al looked forward to giving the police her new address. She hurriedly folded the bed quilt she'd been clutching to her chest and tossed it onto the chair. Her clever little silken cloche must look like a nightcap.

BY FORCE OF FELICITY

Bedtime at the asylum. Snickering out loud, she attracted Officer Cziski's briefly raised eyebrows.

"I don't think I'll be pressing charges, Sergeant. But would you officers be kind enough to accompany Watkins and all of us to the attic before he leaves? I rarely go up anymore. Negligent of me. I'd like to acquire a sense of the state of affairs, however briefly. We mustn't keep you long."

Repenting her fit of meanness, Althea remembered her rabid ego still liked to pirouette, frothing and howling, across her inner stage. She slipped one arm through Lucy's and the other around Beebe as they exited Millefleurs behind the shuffling, stale-smelling handyman.

Guests

"Here you go, Sour-Puss. That face must've curdled your own mama's milk. Never mind, you make a fine watchcat." Cook tossed Leo a fat morsel of fish, which he accepted with dignity.

Cook watched intently. "Minnie," the weathered Tom's ladylove and the apple of Cook's eye, looked gratifyingly plump as she basked on the backyard cobblestones surrounded by the crowd of newcomers who'd appeared that afternoon. Handsome young cats, all of them. Mostly big kittens.

Minnie struck Cook as a shy cat, yet here she was licking these weanling visitors like she wanted to eat 'em up. The two black cats with them were older. Stunners. Wait till Mrs. M. saw them.

"Oh, Min. Do you miss your own kittens? Or are these little customers yours? Who's the daddy, I wonder. That one's got as flat a mug as your old Tom."

Cook stooped to pick up the platter of perch she'd offered the handsome guests. Not a speck left. Looked like they'd gotten loose from someone's yard and decided to explore the countryside. Steady nerves, taking Fezzy in their stride. You'd think they were *his*.

The wood stork, with his gaping beak and great knobby legs, had waded right in and lowered his head to the visitors' eye level for so long she feared he'd given himself a cramp. One of the braver little rogues had already speared his cap.

Gypsy and Willow had shared a single shadow ever since Leo had arrived with his longed-for caravan.

"Have you been in the house?" Gypsy asked, watching Cook disappear through the back door.

"Once. Leo insisted. And to please Cook. She calls me Minnie. I owe all this to her. We've had the wrong idea about the humans, Gypsy."

"Yes. Do you think you might ever come ho—come down the hill? Mrs. B. will be so glad to see you." Gypsy chewed delicately on her wrist, that Willow might not read her thoughts. Perhaps the sight of lovely Willow's stiff front leg and missing tail tip would be too sad.

Willow's ears perked.

"Of course. Star wants the path between here and Lilac Corner to be a thoroughfare linking the town cats and the hill cats. Star says the woods and lake will be let alone, but more and more humans and houses will come to the flat land. That means more cats. You see? There'll be more and more of those big motorcars coming, and we cats will have our road, too. We'll be neighbors, not strangers. Oh Gyp, you will bring them up from time to time, won't you? I've missed you all so." Willow laid her throat on Gypsy's warm side that the sun had lit with prisms.

"How round you've become." Willow sat up again, sniffing at her sister.

"Gypsy?"

"Yes. Yes, I think so. Very late in the year, but I'll have the run of the warm house, and if I choose our old burrow when they begin to arrive we can always tote them back inside if it's too cold."

Cook watched Minnie and the plump little black cat through her scullery window. Cats didn't cozy up with each other like that unless they were family. The two bore no resemblance to each other, but that was sometimes the case. Must've been parted for a long while. If she hadn't stumbled on poor Minnie hiding in that shed while the life eked out of her...Mr. M. liked to poke fun at her constitutionals. "Out filling her hat with weeds and wounded baby birds again?" she'd heard from the doorway, after rushing back to make sure tea was on time. Yet if not for her rambles surely no one but a fox would have found Minnie. Even Mr. M. doted on the pretty little half-wild she-cat, so clearly grateful for their help. And now it seemed she'd been sorely missed. Content, Cook dropped the curtain.

As her brothers wrestled between the wood stork's legs, Scout soaked up the sunshine that warmed the autumn breeze. She kept her eyes on her mother across the terrace with Auntie Gyp. Every trembling leaf, each floating tasseled seed, the elderbug seeking refuge on the sunny side of the house all radiated the joy she felt. The entire world seemed to be purring...especially from somewhere on the far edge of the lawn beyond the rooftop.

When the distant purr became an ominous rumble clearly advancing in their direction, the kittens drifted toward their mother and Gypsy, who'd stood up in alarm. Leo's attempts to explain the approaching racket were swallowed in dust and din as Mrs. Morrissey's new motor car chugged around the corner, lurching to a smelly halt.

Fez flapped to the top of the garden wall to escape the fumes. The cats held their ground behind Leo from the depths of the hosta border.

Mrs. M's passenger, in a chauffeur's cap and uniform, emerged ashen-faced. After removing the cap to wipe his forehead, he opened the burnished Ford's rear door for someone.

Bonnet tumbled out, her lavish tail wagging high. Spying the kittens, she bounded over to the hostas, yelping and cutting capers with her nose to the ground. To the amazement of everyone, including Cook at the back door, Scout barreled from beneath a fat striped leaf and batted the collie on the nose. Bonnet greeted this with joyful barks of admiration, beside herself with the beauty of the family reunion.

"Hush, Bonnet, you're scaring our visitors. I don't think they realize how smitten you are with them. Shush now! Parsons, please leave the Ford here for the night; we can't have you mowing down inexperienced kittens. Cook, where did you find all these darlings?"

Mrs. M. inched toward the hostas, cooing and asking for Scout, who'd retreated.

"Where's the little hero?" she murmured, crouching a respectful distance from the huddling cats.

Unsure of the words but eager to prove their hostess's trustworthiness, Leo emerged. Making a supreme effort, he puffed his shaggy chest and rubbed a cheek against the lady's silken knee.

"Why, you old *roué*, are they yours?" She patted his bony back, aware of the privilege. Her new Jacquard shawl, luminous with metallic threads and fresh from Paris, slid to the cobblestones.

"He showed up with them at lunchtime, ma'am. Four big kittens not quite fledged, and two natty black cats. I think they're family to Minnie one way or another."

Gypsy, followed by Pippin and Twinkle, had crept forward to sniff the lady's outstretched hand. Even Scout looked relaxed, and played furtively with her mother's docked tail within reach of Mrs. M.

"Aren't you lovely! Whose porch swing should you be sunning yourselves on? Someone must be fretting over you. Do you think they're lost, Cook?" The sunlight stenciled Pippin's pale ears in silver as she rumpled the fur between them.

"I think Minnie's Tom looks like the papa. And Minnie is mama. It's a puzzle how they came to be separated. You should've seen Minnie sniffing and licking 'em. I never saw her so lively." Cook folded her arms over her apron with satisfaction.

"Oh look, ma'am – here's number six coming through the garden gate with Star. Black as the moon's backside, and just as finely chiseled as a cut glass cruet."

Mrs. M. dropped to the mossy stones and tucked her legs beneath her, not minding her frock and stockings. She smiled, fond of Cook's blarney.

"We'll have to send Parsons around with handbills in a day or two, though I'm sure they're all welcome to stay." She nodded at Star, who caught their mutual "come hither" signal and strode forth. After clambering gracefully onto her hip he reached up and gave her the wettest of tender nose-kisses behind her perfumed ear, accompanied by a throaty purr.

"Mmm...champagne and roses. Friends of yours, my love?"

Star thumped his head beneath his mistress's chin, then looked back toward Bezique, who'd hesitated by the great garden door. Mrs. M. extended a hand toward the handsome straggler, coaxing.

"Princely, aren't you? Looks like he stepped down off a wall of hieroglyphics, doesn't he, Cook?"

Bezique gave her a wide berth and sat down next to Gypsy, which delighted Mrs. M. As her laughter rang out Fez cupped his wings and parachuted off the garden wall into their midst, sending the visitors scrambling.

"I must get them all into print, don't you think, Gompy?" Mrs. M. whispered.

History

Tugging a hanky from under her pillows, Beebe clutched the frail, peeling book to her chest. That last line was her favorite, the one that sailed right out of the story into Lilybanks.

God bless dear Watkins...Beebe unfastened the chain inside her nightgown. A medallion clinked against Tad's locket now, and she examined it yet again under the "Erp's" mica shade.

A newly polished sterling disc, embossed with wreathed lilies-of-the-valley, gleamed in her hand. "Star," read the delicate script in its center. Perforated at the top for a link, it had fit perfectly through a metal ring on the worn, bracelet-sized collar of red morocco in the Crumrind silver chest.

Through all her childhood forays in the attic she'd never done more than wonder what the stiff little bit of harness was doing amongst the runcible spoons and butter knives. And she'd never lifted out the gravy ladle to discover Gompy's tag in its tiny flannel pouch – not until Bubo had her tally up the silver chest's contents.

She'd held her tongue till Watkins – and then the police – left. Everyone had been so touched, and Bubo'd given her consent to wear the Star's tag around her neck. Why Calla would have hidden her beloved pet's only memento in an undistinguished collection of flatware seemed random but not irrational.

There'd been more treasure. Beneath a bundle of fruit knives lay a wax paper envelope. "From Sullivan's church," read an elderly, hesitant scrawl on a scrap of paper. When Beebe pulled out the gold paper star it curled like a shy invertebrate pried from its pool. Lucy and Bubo thought it must be a remnant from a restoration. Beebe preferred to imagine it floating down from the dome, a message for some solitary seeker.

Beebe restored her chain and snapped off the light. The waning votive for Blessed Katerina had guttered out with finality a bit before the equinox. She'd not replaced it. All those figments and phantasms with which she'd embroidered a dim history had faded like outgrown toys.

She never saw Micah these days. Maybe he was still ruffled about her awkward visit to his house. She'd realized Micah's insistence on loaning her a book was a pretext. He'd been preoccupied and tense;

she'd guessed he wanted to embroil her in some effort to reconnect with Lucy. The book got left behind in her eagerness to escape.

She'd told only Tad that Katerina's prescient, Eastern compassion for creation was mostly her own invention. He'd asked whether she planned on being Blessed Beebe.

From anyone else that would have been hurtful. "Of course," she'd answered, and stuffed a handful of soggy fallen leaves down his tee-shirt.

Appraisal
[1937]

Who'd have thought a blacksmith would be so picky. Calla had heard he'd demanded *truite au bleu*, turning up his nose at the caterer's Chateaubriand.

Crum's fatal amour, the banquet's waspish, freckled host, had sprained a finger while awarding the celebrated "devil with a hammer" a mawkishly inscribed marble anvil. When a fawning matron led him off to the kitchen in search of ice, Calla had lured the bored guest of honor to Lilybanks. She'd thought it quite funny as Bishop whisked her and Mr. Yellin away from the clubby North Shore arts center.

As her friend Ruth never failed to expound, Calla's covetousness had swiftly borne bitter karmic fruit. Yellin liked the house very much, enthused over his weathervane's setting, appreciated Sam's woodwork particularly, but ignored or disapproved of her embellishments. He'd summarized the murals as Lily-gilding, such a catchy pun that she dreaded his repeating it out East. At least she'd modestly omitted to claim them as her own.

Feeling a bit sullen, she led him down the hall, pulling on an old coat from the rack. They emerged into a bleak November afternoon. Brittle leaves eddied across the cobblestones like furtive rodents.

She'd not been able to persuade Gomp's grandson to have his photo taken. Cats. Where was Bishop?...

"Mr. Yellin's in a hurry, I'm afraid. His lecture starts at five. Rettiger Hall. Bishop will have you there on time, Mr. Yellin. Let's have the entire weathervane and at least a bit of the roof in the photograph...And try to get the garden door in..."

She turned to find her guest packing his pipe on a bench.

"Your woodcarver is still working? Ruffey?"

"No. He died in Italy, the last year of the war. Not even a soldier; married an Italian girl and got swept up...killed within a week of a neighborhood boy who enlisted..." She seemed to be drifting.

"A great loss of talent." He lit his pipe, hitting on a happier topic.

"The daughter for whom you wrote the little book – all grown up now? Brothers and sisters?"

"No. No more children."

He waited politely.

"May's newly married, somewhat to our surprise. An unpretentious, sober girl. Quite unlike her frivolous mother. To a doctoral candidate in archaeology – Rutledge's first! He was earning a few desperate pennies proctoring a field trip and wound up sharing May's lunch (these absent-minded, ascetic scholars!)...Well, each had the native wit to recognize a soulmate. We threw them a charming wedding in the garden here – puritanically secular, I'm afraid, the groom insisted on that – and May's beloved grandparents from California were able to attend...May's more like her grandpa than her parents... We crowned your weathervane with a garland of lilies, Mr. Yellin. But I'm gushing."

He smiled, relieved to find Lilybanks in the charge of a woman with her feet under her. This home was not one of the hollow showcases he sometimes encountered.

"Have your Crumrind make them a honeymoon cottage."

"Oh, they're perfectly ecstatic in a cramped warren on campus.

Oblivious Spartans absorbed in their studies. Lilybanks supplies more than their required dose of design when they stumble in from some dig for arrowheads in the fields."

Bishop coughed, and, catching Calla's eye, pushed the presiding mongrel's posterior in her direction.

"Ah! Well done."

Unsure whether she spoke to the shy, coltish dog or her chauffeur, Yellin preserved a cordial silence and joined his hostess against the towering garden wall. Thinking its height excessive, he mugged for the camera behind a succession of smoke signals till his companions came to rest.

"Pipe a bit lower, sir, please. MUGWUMP, SIT. I could take him for a walk while I wait for Mr. Yellin, Ma'am."

Ten minutes later Calla waved them off, her dog regarding her through the Auburn's back window as though of two minds about the excursion. Yellin had easily accepted her regrets about the inconvenient lecture squeezed between the art department's and his train's schedules.

"The hearth untended is no hearth at all," he'd said, and patted her hand.

She and Martin clung to middle-aged routine now. He caught the early train back when at all possible; she made dinner and would be waiting for him at the station. Never underfoot, May had left a breach in their days that responded to careful mending.

A honeymoon cottage from Crum could only be a grotesque pipe dream. One heard of increasing oddness and isolation; Merrick thought it began during the war. Crum had feared his dogs would be requisitioned. The majestic Mrs. Pratt had cleaved a sea of starched linen and tea services at the Drake for the pleasure of mentioning the architect's "deterioration" to Calla; she'd run into him on State Street looking "threadbare and glazed." Saddened but unwilling to become embroiled for Martin's sake, Calla had murmured regretfully.

By then she possessed the key to the strange virulence Letitia Pratt exuded if their paths crossed. When pressed, Olive admitted her staff believed *La Pratt* had tried to ravish the architect, who'd unflatteringly failed to rise to the occasion.

Calla had eventually let Olive go, a mutually peaceful conclusion without the merest fizzle of drama. She thought Olive might still maintain a friendship with Crum; at times she hoped so for his sake.

The self-absorption of youth! Everything had shimmered with personal significance. In her innermost heart she'd cherished even the dervishes' stark exaltation as a harbinger of earthly ecstasy. That impoverished appraisal, that missing of the mark, time had begun to correct even in spite of herself.

Behind her the storybook weathervane rattled. The wind had shifted.

At her feet she noticed a lobed oak leaf, caught like a fallen star with its pale underside skyward among desiccated weeds. It pulsed and fluttered in slow half-circles, pulling her into itself. Words, habit and memory retreated. Some vital communion rejoiced her.

Au Boeuf Bleu

Beating out the approaching waiter, Bake pushed Ginevra Hassenpfeffer's chair in for her. His hand lingered on her shoulder; she firmly suggested he sit down.

"Handsome wedding ring. It looks well on you."

"Yes."

"What does your wife think of my ideas?"

Casting aside Le Boeuf's menu, which he knew by heart, Bake cleared his throat, frowned.

"First of all, Althea doesn't realize Stubblefield's redoubtable Mrs. Hassenpfeffer is the youngest of Eugene and Ruth Ringgold's numerous offspring, Ginevra. Apparently it just never came up in conversation." Her expression told him how silly that sounded. A familiar pattern with Ginevra. "I simply told her that particular daughter still lives in the Rutledge family landmark, that you and I are old friends, and that you had an idea for a book."

"Old friends. So you've left her out of the loop."

He twiddled his knife and spoon, nettled. "I think I can assure you Althea takes little interest in my loops."

She offered the enigmatic smile specially reserved for him; did it indicate pleasure or disappointment?

"Anyway. Listen. It's time you write a history of Lilybanks. Something full of romantic disclosures, written from a sympathetic viewpoint. Maybe a little titillating, but not nasty. When I got wind of what the Hystericals are up to from Lucy and Beebe, I realized your opus is long overdue, Ken. Done properly – and it would be, if you apply yourself – the profits might be considerable."

Flattered and furious, he waved off the little fellow at his elbow. "That's the only impractical thing I've ever heard cross your lips. I've got a new addition to my household who's lost so much weight even I can carry her around. You think this is the moment to print up a bunch of moldering photographs and huddle over them creating tantalizing captions? And Marian hates showing old family pictures, won't even display a few for the Tour. Like they're captive souls. Everyone around here's heard the rumors about Calla's flirtation with her architect… we'd be serving up yesterday's leftovers. You surprise me." Hearing his own shrillness, Bake let up. "It's dear of you to be concerned."

She sat straighter, pushed a silvery-blue wisp back into the French twist with what could only be called a coquettish gesture. He felt better.

"You'll see. I think I'm right on this one. You underestimate the appeal of this stuff. Think BBC. I want you to hit the Hysterical Society right between the eyes with a book, and I've got a new angle for you."

Disarmed, Bake ordered their usual and decided to enjoy himself.

"Let me pour that. First of all, how do you propose I produce this bestseller instantly? Both sides already have attorneys breathing down our necks. They're planning some kind of little contract-signing fête just a few nights away." The wine was helping.

"Have your lawyer – Marty, right? – get you a trial period. Two years, say. So the Morrisseys can back out of the whole deal after that if your book pays off. And photos aren't essential. You don't even want to know what the angle is? Men."

He grinned, reflecting a little sadly on the hidden charms of Stubblefield's headmistress.

"Tell."

"Yes, it's time. Mother told me not to, but I know she'd want to help. Crumrind wasn't Calla Morrissey's only admirer. Samuel Ruffey fell in love with her out in Oakland at the College of Arts and Crafts and never fell out. He drank, sometimes, and told my mother all about it one night…Mother thought Sam was a bodhisattva. (Don't get me wrong, she preferred my worldly father!) All lovingkindness, no instinct for self-preservation."

"So I get to emulate him, canceling what's left of my life to write a soap opera?" He realized it sounded too freighted, made an attempt to stuff years of resenting her refusal to marry him back into their bottle. "I'm letting myself go off on a friend…my apologies, Ginevra. I do appreciate this. But it's fairly small beans." He stared at his starched napkin, weary.

"I agree. But it adds to the pile. And there's something bigger. Sam wrote the cats 'n' stork book. He wrote Mother from Italy. Said he consoled himself making bedtime stories for Calla's kid. He'd married over there, seemed happy enough for someone in the middle of a world war, she said…Would you like an aspirin, Ken? I think you're overdoing."

He needed to blot his forehead but simply leaned back out of the candlelight.

"You seriously think Lilybanks will benefit from being divested of her main claim to fame?" He poured himself another glass of wine with precision, weakening.

"Yes. Writing will be good for you. And by the way, Mother left no doubt as to the Calla-Crumrind affair. Definitely fire where there'd been smoke. Calla's only marital transgression, in spite of what people think. Now listen, *liebchen*. If the book fizzles I twist Throckmorton's arm. In return for keeping bed 'n' breakfasters out of Lilybanks, I leave the Hystericals my mint-condition historic family mansion. No need for her to know I've always meant them to have it."

Lilybanking

Althea stuffed another armful of windflower stalks into the yard waste bag, then paused to pull wisps of what was left of her hair out of her lip balm.

"Kind of goes against the grain, cutting stuff down early. I always liked to wait till the last minute." She thought of her garden on Euclid Street – probably an intimate swimming pool or cramped *boules* court with Euro-grill by now – with a muffled pang that subsided immediately. To everything its season.

"Me, too. The poor beheaded stems. But they'll come back next year. You'll have enough work potting up the herbs while we're gone. I hope you're going to make Bakeoven get himself a pair of gardening gloves," Beebe replied, on her knees to prune back a bank of baptisia. Bakeoven, for whom no detail nor expense was *de trop* when it came to pampering his pocket-sized "conservatory" full of droopy datura and ferns, abandoned his property's grubby yard work to hard-up horticulture students.

"Got your long johns packed?"

"Yup. Bubo's taking six pair. That's all we've been able to persuade her to buy for the expedition aside from a new briefcase with her initials on it and a magnifying glass that lights up for map reading in the fog. She's saving her "mad money" for an elegant lined umbrella from Harrods and rare old editions of poetry. Less predictably, Tad's bought matching bright yellow rain gear for the two of us. *He'll* certainly be hard to lose."

With a matching yellow leash, Althea thought. Beebe's encounter with the treacherous tutee had nearly unglued Tad.

"Bright yellow! A sacrifice for love. What are you really going to wear?" Althea noticed an unwitting slug navigating the debris in the bag and restored it to a secluded clump of leafy sludge.

"Your beige wool with all the passementerie."

Al suspected the prized, slightly moth-eaten 1890's coat, ornamented with so much labyrinthine braid it resembled a flying monkey's uniform, would draw more stares than the raincoat. She'd had a tailor whittle the sleeves and shoulders for Beebe.

"Perfect. And what's been decided about Aphrodite?"

"Lucy and Bubo decided against having Libby come by, though that way Ditey could stay home. Concerned about germs Libby might carry from all her dogs, and the lizard... Ditey's so old; it might not be such a crazy idea. And...well, they thought Libby might be less reliable than usual. 'The unpredictability of love's course,' as Bubo put it. So Evvie's having her, since Ditey'd never manage the stairs up to Chip's flat. Evvie's going to take her to Stubblefield on workdays. Ditey will love the kids."

"We could've taken her, you know. Only three steps at the back." Al regretted the words at once, having vowed to stop trying to read her future in others' words and arrangements.

"But I'm selfish. You've got to be at my wedding. Stop trying to take on more than necessary in the meantime. Just heal up."

Althea tossed down her pruners and trod on the last of the asters in her haste to take Beebe's cold little ungloved hand in both of hers. She had months to plan her dress.

Beebe rather than Lucy (whose Chip wanted a huge do at a hotel) would be standing in her wedding finery at the top of Lilybanks' staircase next year. Al realized she was looking forward to the festivities – surely a sign of health?

From its rooftop Yellin's iron menagerie creaked in a rush of air.

"It's going to rain. Let's have some tea. Grab the other side of the bag, will you?"

Al complied after blowing her usual kiss to the clump of black-eyed Susans where Tutu now rested.

Ordered to relax in the sitting room while Beebe put the kettle on a "new" old stove, Al piled pillows for herself on the window seat. With her cap and jacket on, the chilly little gusts eddying through rattling frames seemed merely bracing. One might be in England.

A basket of hedge apples had replaced the philodendron next to Calla Morrissey's photograph; they'd moved the plant closer to a window. Through the dining room doors she could see Calla's pair of Rookwood vases brimming with tansy and strawflowers. The candles on the table were stubby now; guests had been entertained. No doubt various members of the historical society required maintenance. She and Bake dined composedly beneath his restrained Georgian chandelier now; she'd graduated from trays and straws. Graduated, or merely been released. Who could say with certainty? She'd made it very clear she was not to be bothered with prognoses. Her dearest treasure now, along with Linnet, was the present moment. Though a slippery commodity, it provided immunity superior to all these costly pills and procedures.

"Here we are!" Beebe bustled in with tea, napkins and what Al suspected was a tea-drenched braid. How the child managed the precision her pastries demanded eluded Al. She accepted a delicate cup and saucer. Bake had thought Al's idea for a wedding gift very clever, and had begun looking for a magnificent samovar for Maven Alley.

They sipped in silence. Rain lashed the panes; the golden glow of lanterns hung from ceiling beams intensified in the gloom. Aphrodite, alarmed by the slightest suggestion of thunder though nearly deaf, shuffled over to them. She crumpled cozily between Beebe's footstool and chair; the footstool scooted out of range. The hall clock chimed the hour.

"I've got something for you." Beebe lifted the footstool's hinged lid. She pulled out a faded Edwardian album and placed it in Al's lap.

"It's a selfish gift," Beebe continued over Al's shoulder. I think we should have a chronicle of 'Lilybanking's' progress in the world. Without you the Trib never would have coined the term. A fitter tribute to life here than tours and postcards, as Bubo says. See, I've started with the editorial; then we've got all the articles about the woods...and here are the reviews of the gallery exhibit – I wish they could've gotten Lucy into the photo of the church marquee – here's the letter from the woman in Vermont, the one from the organic farmers in Ohio; Lucy printed out some of the emails...here's some more stuff in the back I've left for you. The shot of Bake looking helpless and dismayed at the Green League meeting's in there somewhere; I didn't glue it in."

Embarrassed, pleased and annoyed (her obituary could be tidily included on the last page) Althea closed the album and ran her fingers over the velvet cover and its dented swans, forget-me-nots and curlicues on embossed paper.

"Oops. Forgot the madeleines." Beebe hurried out.

Althea sank back against the pillows, grateful for silence. The red creeper vine on the garden wall jounced in the downpour. No doubt Linnet was still sound asleep in her new closet.

Regardless of how much her efforts had to do with it, some recognition of the pervasive, nearly unconscious insensitivity to creation, to its poetry, had stirred Rutledge in the wake of the Bodie Woods protest. Her idea of tying heart-studded ribbons around the trunks of Bodie's doomed buckthorns had spread to the campus; students had trickled into the woods to add love letters to the trees, poems, charms and amulets.

Bethke Hall, whose pigeon-encircled cupola had been an unsung pleasure for a century, made headlines beyond the campus paper when the art department, a humanities professor or two and Animal Allies had collaborated. Their revelation that the university had hired a pest control firm to gas the birds on account of their droppings had galvanized a surprising number of students. A lovely photo of the pigeons flying about the cupola's slightly listing Stars and Stripes at sunset made it onto a national news service.

The Rutledge Sentinel, fond of boosterism, had treated readers to a full week's worth of staff-generated cartoons. Al's favorite was that of a child crouching to rescue a worm from a puddle. Thankfully, no caricatures of the sisterhood had appeared. (Bake had been terribly touchy about his thankless, neither-fish-nor-fowl role in the clash between the county's conservation district and Althea's "contingent of Jainists." Even so, he'd threatened to file a libel suit if images of his rickety, tasseled wife, dumpy, mortar-boarded Marian, waifish Lucy and bird-sized Beebe in her antediluvian garb were hurled onto the neighbors' sidewalks some morning.)

More promising, the Empyrean Society had appointed Lionel and a colleague to assemble an international panel for a forum at Lilybanks on "Compassion, Creation, Creativity." Marian had off-handedly terrorized Al by mentioning she'd be expected to say "at least a word or two." Terrorized but also thrilled, she wondered if her hair might be presentable by then. "As soon as feasible," the Society had urged, in order to make the most of "the movement." Another outfit to plan, too. She *had* to live.

A characteristic puff of butter, almond oil, must and b.o. scented the air. A bit startled, Al looked up.

"Lilybank is a beautiful verb, Beebe. The commission of subtly nuanced random acts of compassionate solidarity with our unrecognized, devalued sisters and brothers. Including Things. With which we're actually one."

Beebe, glistening, leaned to kiss her on the cheek.

"I love you, Althea."

Bon Voyage

Elated, Al wheeled past a fen in Moraine Woods Park. A flock of mallards on a migratory break muttered amongst themselves; she wondered if they'd absorbed the local families she'd observed raising their young through the summer. They'd be leaving her behind, too.

Marian, Tad and Beebe might be dining in some Oxford refectory right now. Waving them off from Lilybanks' driveway as Bake drove them to O'Hare had been harder than she'd expected. Her own adventure was so much bleaker.

At the same time, she reckoned her wooded horizon, the fen with its cloisonné of sunshine on cerulean and algae, the autumnal clamor of birds and wind as the equivalent of her friends' faraway treasures – all the more so for her precious ability to navigate the trail on her bike. Only three of the perplexing gears had ever seemed to work, yet she'd already managed the worst of the hilly bits. If Bake found out he'd pretend not to mind she'd transgressed, then be politely glacial for a day or two. They seemed to be falling in love, or something like that but less stridently personal. Her fraying, no, wabi-sabi body had never been so responsive. Nothing surprised her anymore.

A great tawny bird rose from a field and circled just ahead. She'd learned to simply watch, to let the labeling rise of its own accord later...A sandhill crane.

The trail continued through a chilly, shaded alley of hickories and oaks, changed direction and ascended. Toiling, Althea looked up to see gusts of wind tearing the leaves from a birch at the top of the rise ahead. A joyful riot of yellow leaves exploded against a shard of sharp blue sky. She knew it to be a celebration, a gleeful surrender, an embrace.

Endnotes

1   Gerald Manley Hopkins, "The Starlight Night," *Poems and Prose* (London: Penguin Classics, 1985), p. 27/28.

2   All references to Eckhart Tolle's teachings are from *The Power of Now* (Vancouver, B.C., Canada: Namaste Publishing, 2004) and *A New Earth* (New York: Penguin Group (USA) Inc., 2006).

3   William Wordsworth, "Ode: Intimations of Immortality from Recollections of Early Childhood," §9, lines 163-66; in *The Norton Anthology of English Literature*, Revised Vol. 2 (New York: W.W. Norton & Company Inc., 1968) p. 153.

4   Hopkins, *op. cit.* p. 27/28.

5   Wordsworth, "Intimations" §1, lines 1-4; in *op. cit.,* p. 149.

6   "Intimations" §11, line 205; in *op. cit.,* p. 154.

7   *A Course in Miracles*, First Edition (Tiburon, CA: Foundation for Inner Peace, 1985) Introduction, p. ix.

8   Christopher Smart, "The Nativity of Our Lord and Savior Jesus Christ," final stanza; in Hollander & McClatchy (eds.) *Christmas Poems* (New York: Alfred A. Knopf, 1999) p. 62, reprinted with permission from Robert Brittain (ed.) *Poems by Christopher Smart* (Princeton, NJ: Princeton University Press, 1978).

9   Clement C. Moore LLD, *The Night Before Christmas, Illustrated by Arthur Rackham* (London: George G. Harrap & Co. Ltd., 1939) p. 16.

10 *A Course in Miracles*, p. ix.

11 *Orthodox Daily Prayers* (South Canaan, PA: St. Tikhon's Seminary Press, 1982) p. 5/6.

12 Henry Vaughn, "The Retreat" line 20; in Leonard Martin (ed.) *The Works of Henry Vaughn*, Vol. II (Oxford: Clarendon Press, 1914) p. 419/20. In the original it reads, "Bright *shootes* of everlastingnesse." Available at http://

books.google.com/books/about/The Works of Henry Vaughan.html?id=1_GLcgAACAAJ [5 Oct 2015].

13 Thomas Traherne, *Centuries of Meditation*, III.2; in Alan Bradford (ed.), *Thomas Traherne: Selected Poems and Prose* (New York: Penguin Books, 1991) p. 226.

14 *A Course in Miracles*, p. ix.

15 *A Course in Miracles*, p. ix.

16 A.M. Allchin (ed.), *Daily Readings with St. Isaac of Syria*, (tr.) Sebastian Brock (Springfield, IL: Templegate Publishers, 1990) p. 29; from Dana Miller (tr.), *The Ascetical Homilies of St. Isaac the Syrian*, No. 71 (Brookline, MA: Holy Transfiguration Monastery, 1985) p. 344. [New revised edition published 2011.]

17 Isaac of Syria, *ibid.*

18 Fyodor Dostoevsky, *The Brothers Karamazov* (tr.) Constance Garnett (New York: Lowell Press, 1912) p. 358. Available at http://www.gutenberg.org/files/28054/28054-h/28054-h.html [5 Oct 2015].

19 *Karamazov*, p. 354.

20 Geoffrey Chaucer, *Canterbury Tales*, Prologue, line 72; in Abrams and Greenblatt (eds.), *The Norton Anthology of English Literature*, Seventh Edition, Volume 1 (New York: W.W. Norton & Company, 2000) p. 217.

Discussion Questions

1. Narcissism and paranoia seem to be on the increase in our culture. How does Althea struggle against these personal tendencies? Do you think she is significantly helped by Eckhart Tolle's teachings?

2. Does Lilybanks' prejudice against technology appeal to you? What's at risk when people's noses are glued to their portable screens on public transportation, walks through parks, at family meals? Does the author's emphasis on birdsong, shadows, dust motes and such seem resonant and relevant to the story, or dull?

3. Several characters have intense bonds with their animal companions. Some are intimate with trees and plants. Are such relationships mere stopgaps? Or is it really possible to compare "mysteries of the heart?"

4. In what ways is being "different" portrayed in this novel?

5. Unable to fully accept or publicly reveal a fundamental trait, is Crumrind a victim of his times? Would his affair with Calla play out the same way one hundred years later? Is he a reluctant "people pleaser" with women, or do you sense a sensitive bond between Crum and Calla? Crum and Olive?

6. Micah and Lucy seem genuinely in love at the beginning of the novel. Were there early warning signs that all was not well?

7. Lilybanks "enchants." Can a home, or city, or landscape feel alive and responsive when deeply loved?

8. *By Force of Felicity* is laced with descriptions of Arts and Crafts design and antiques. Most of these are genuine. Did you spot a fictional impostor or two?

9. Tad is a bit exasperated by Marian's parenting skills, thinking she operates Lilybanks "in a well-read, well-intentioned coma." What do you think?

10. Beebe is portrayed as wise beyond her years. Yet at times she seems reckless, even self-destructive; an eating disorder is hinted at; she can be naïve and oblivious to the point of backwardness. She wants to be a saint. Her aunt refers to "hormones and perplexing fixations." What holds these traits together?

11. At lunch with Olive in the Chinese restaurant, Crumrind feels "scalded by a lifetime of longing." What do you think this longing is for? What does Caterina have to do with it?

12. A literary novel in more ways than one, *By Force of Felicity* abounds in references to writers and their work. Professor Crabbe's bailiwick, for instance, was inspired by Bronson Alcott. Althea fears she may be "zero at the bone," like Emily Dickinson's snake. Who else?

13. It's said that people tend to grapple with the same psychological issues all their lives. Did Althea merely trade her dependency on

Casper for dependency on Bakeoven? How do you picture her second marriage?

14. In the book's final chapter Althea says, "One didn't turn one's back on one's friends, animal or mineral." Concern for animal, vegetable and mineral is woven throughout this novel. Does this seem a bit foolish, or can spirituality foster a holy foolishness that the world needs? What's the difference between sentimentality and inspired perception?

15. Is Calla primarily selfish and greedy, or naively romantic? How do you see her?

16. Clothing plays an important minor role in the story as protective plumage, eccentric "uniform," sexual cue, dowdy necessity. What does it tell us about various characters?

17. Althea laments that once she's found safe harbor with Bake she's finally able to feel how terribly she misses Casper. Is this understandable? Do other characters experience delayed, pent-up emotions?

18. Which feline in *The Cats of Lilac Corner* might be Sam Ruffey's portrayal of himself?

About the Author

Suzanne Campbell holds a B.A. in Journalism from the University of Wisconsin at Madison. After a "checkered career" of studies and work in Nova Scotia, Scotland, the San Francisco Bay area, France, and Chicago, she's been settled in Woodstock, Illinois for twenty years. She lives with her husband and cats. Her home, built in 1907, is just around the corner from her grandparents' 1920s' bungalow.

Visit www.bungalowbiblia.wordpress.com.

Acknowledgements

Many thanks to my topnotch readers James Campbell, Nancy Smith and Chris Rice. Their painstaking comments rescued my manuscript from several *faux pas,* many typos, and a wrong turn or two.

My son Christopher Campbell's many years of awesome bagpiping inspired the piobaireachd that closes chapter 10.

Special thanks go to the talented teachers and writers who participate in the University of Wisconsin-Madison's Division of Continuing Studies writing conferences. I staggered out of "Weekend With Your Novel" and "Writers' Institute" laden with so much useful feedback, desperately needed information and a sense of "tribe" to take back to all those solitary rewrites. Thanks also to the friendly, talented members of In Print in Rockford, Illinois, and to the "Wannabes" class at McHenry County College who listened to excerpts from this book.

Heartfelt thanks to Mary Kim for her whirlwind last-minute reading of my manuscript with an eagle eye out for unintentional errors and inconsistencies. Her expertise and delicacy produced a classier text.

Cardamom, thanks for keeping me company in your desk drawer while I typed, and for insisting I take breaks.

Finally, to Eckhart Tolle: thank you beyond words for sharing wisdom with such clarity in *The Power of Now* and *A New Earth.* They inspired this book.

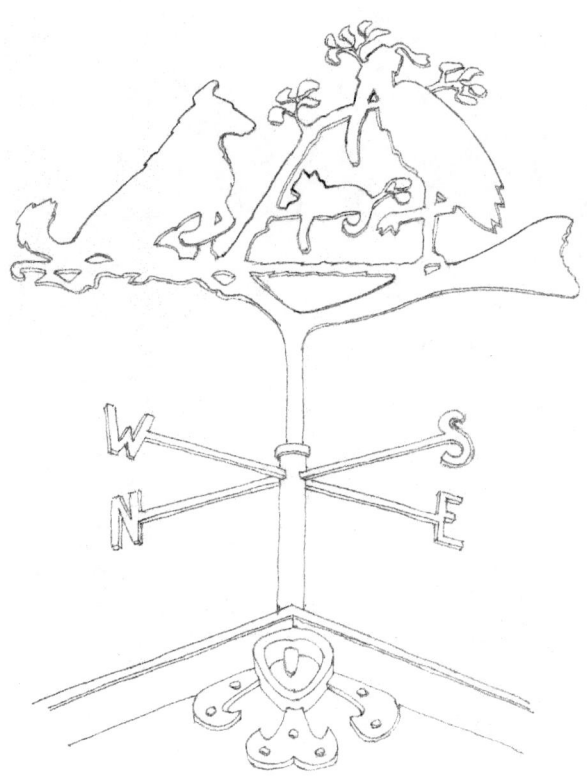